Bequest of a Stranger
A Novel

by

Barrie Edward

DORRANCE PUBLISHING CO., INC.
PITTSBURGH, PENNSYLVANIA 15222

ISBN: 978-1-4349-0784-4
eISBN: 978-1-4349-5322-3
Printed in the United States of America

First Printing

For more information or to order additional books, please contact:
Dorrance Publishing Co., Inc.
701 Smithfield Street
Pittsburgh, Pennsylvania 15222
U.S.A.
1-800-788-7654
www.dorrancebookstore.com

Chapter One

He walked purposefully down the corridor, turned a corner, and continued, his shoes making little sound on the clean floor. He passed by doors, some open with people who looked dispassionately as he passed, some closed with no sound emanating, no clue regarding the presence or lack of life beyond.

He knew, or could guess, what was behind these doors. He had likely administered, or had been responsible, for whatever lay beyond in each numbered room. Each room had a changing, evolving story from a patient with a history, with a secret, with a longing to return to a normal life while trying to remember what a normal life was like and with growing realization that it was not likely to happen.

Turning a corner, two nurses stepped aside as he passed, nodded, and greeted him deferentially, "Doctor."

The doctor had been summoned while in the operating theatre. Here, in a quiet area of Washington D.C., he operated daily on soldiers brought in from Vietnam. Repairing or replacing limbs, he was making decisions on how or if some of these men would walk out of the hospital. Working sixteen-hour days, seven days a week, he had stopped wearing a watch and looked at the calendar on his desk only for the date to put on a report.

His mind quickly went back to the patient he had just left, a lucky one: shrapnel from a grenade had sliced through his upper thigh and broken the bone. It was clean; a comrade had slapped sterile gauze on the wound, and the soldier had held it in place until evacuated. How many times had he seen similar wounds become infected and result in amputation or death? How many times had he told disbelieving teenagers that there was no way to save the limb?

The operating crew was first class. Most, like he, had graduated from medical or nursing school and had been required to serve in the forces, after deferment or as a requirement of a scholarship. When he had received the call, the summons, he was in the operating room inspecting the open incision for infection and taking tissue samples to back his visual observation.

The corporal stuck his head in the operating room and said, "Major Land, the major general orders to report to him immediately!"

"Get out and stay out!" yelled the doctor as the staff watched in stunned silence.

"But, Sir...."

"Get out. You are not sterile, but that could be arranged if you hang about any longer!"

The corporal retreated. The operation continued, though it was clear that the intrusion had caused more than a flurry of interest.

When the examination of bone and muscle had been completed, the doctor said to the chief nurse, "When the samples are labeled, would you please supervise their transport to the lab?"

"Yes, Sir."

The chief assistant was a woman, rare in the military where all of the nurses were women and the doctors, men—nearly all.

"Sir, why does the major general want to see you? Are you being transferred?"

"Doctor," although she was a captain, he always used the hospital titles, "I have no idea. Perhaps, you can finish sewing up this leg and clean up for me so I can find out."

"It will be a pleasure, Sir."

"You are better and more patient than I am at stitching, so I am doing this young man a favor," he said.

It was not strictly true, but she had blushed under the mask at the compliment.

He heard a whisper behind and turned to ask the head nurse, "Is there a problem?"

The problem was leaving a lower rank in charge of the operation while the head nurse, a major, and a person in the military for life were in charge of lesser duties. It was just one of those things he hated about the military and one of the things he was never going to change.

"No, Sir. No problem."

He must remember to thank her for taking care of the room when he was called away. After all, she was going to be working a lot of hours in the same room with him. She was an excellent nurse and an outstanding administrator. There were no slip-ups on her shifts: all the right boys came in, with X-rays and correct charts, and all went to the right hospital ward.

Yes, he thought, *I must be pleasant to her. Flowers?*

No, not flowers. Chocolates? Yes, perfect!

He reached the commandant's office where the corporal had a desk. It was forty minutes since their encounter, and the corporal was relishing the admonishment sure to follow for the major not having immediately obeyed a commanding officer.

"Major Land to see you, Sir," he announced on the intercom.

He got up slowly to open the door but was too late; the doctor was in and closing the door when the corporal heard: "Major, thank you so much for taking the time from your busy schedule to see me."

"But, Sir, I thought there was urgency to your summons," the doctor said.

"Yes, there is," said the general. "Would you like a cup of coffee or tea?"

Completely confused, he found himself saying, "Coffee, milk, one sugar."

He tried to remember when he had last eaten and what time it was, without success.

Major General Rollins was a career army doctor. He had given up surgery on being promoted and given the task of running the biggest and busiest military hospital in the United States. He was about five feet eight inches tall and in great shape from playing handball in the gym below the hospital every day. Mathew Rollins had volunteered, to join the army, while in his final year at medical school on December 8, 1941. Along with the rest of America, he had been shocked by the attack on Pearl Harbor, but not as shocked as his parents in Michigan when they heard he had left medical school. His skills were not wasted as he served in Africa, then in Europe. With the rank of captain, numerous medals, and no practicing certificate, he almost returned to civilian life. However, an intelligence recruiting officer debriefed the still young Mathew and asked if he would consider rejoining the army if the military paid for his degree and smoothed the way.

"Let me get this straight. You do the paperwork, you pay the bills, and I get the degree. Then I consider coming back. What is the catch? And what if I could get into Harvard, not likely, but what then?" asked the cocky Captain Rollins.

"Pick a school—Harvard, Johns Hopkins, Columbia, Michigan...anywhere," said the officer.

"Are you sure you have the authority for this? What is your rank, Sir? Which service are you in? What is your name?"

"I assure you that I have the authority. I have several ranks, but you may call me Mr. Smith. We may also be able to pay you for some work while you are in school."

"Harvard Medical School. When do I start?" said the excited newly demobbed Mathew, forgetting in his present state to ask what the work might be and what his options were when he stood with a degree on Harvard's steps.

Corporal Mazzarese entered with two coffees and a plate of English digestive biscuits. The general offered a shot of brandy.

"No, thanks; I am doing surgery," said the doctor.

"Please eat all the biscuits as I am sure you missed lunch, and I do not need the added weight," said the congenial commanding officer.

"Thank you, Sir. I do not wish to appear impatient, but I still have a few procedures to do today."

"Ah, yes." The general cleared his throat, "I received a call, and it appears that you are due some leave."

"There are so many boys coming back that need my care; I need to be here."

"Well, you will need at least forty-eight hours, let's say, a seventy-two-hour pass," the major general said as though he had not heard a word.

"Corporal, make out a seventy-two-hour pass for Major Land. When? Starting at 1800 hours today, and rail passes."

"But general, who will take my place in the operating room, and why do I need to leave right now?"

"That Captain Price is progressing nicely. Switch some difficult cases over to Brandon; he has the experience. Don't worry. We all managed fine before you got here. I shall keep an eye on Price myself, even get back into my scrubs; be good for me."

"And why today?"

"Oh! Because the funeral is tomorrow. Call your mother; she knows all about it."

"My mother! What funeral?"

Chapter Two

In a reverse walk back through the wards to the operating theatres, the doctor noticed none of the things that had occupied his thoughts thirty minutes earlier.

"My mother," he muttered, "well, at least it is not her funeral." They had no relatives who he knew of who were sick, unless it was Nani Goldman, his babysitter when they had lived in the city. He always called her Nani; his mother always called her Mrs. Goldman. Was there a Mr. Goldman? He did not know. There was a Sara Goldman and a Mark Goldman who would be his mother's age—children who called once a week. They were pronounced the smartest, most generous children to anyone who would listen but denounced once a week for not calling more often, not celebrating some obscure Jewish Holiday or tradition, and, most of all, for not marrying some wealthy Jew to supply her with intelligent "Mensa" grandchildren.

He pulled his thoughts back to his immediate problem—logistically, how to leave and have the patients receive the care that not only were they entitled but had earned fighting an unpopular war.

The hospital intercom was then paging Dr. Land asking for him to call the operator. He did not hear it the first time. When it was repeated with urgency, he picked up a nearby phone and pressed 0.

"Dr. Land," he said when the operator connected.

"I will connect you to the operating theatre," she replied.

"Dr. Land. Trouble?"

"Dr. Price needs to talk to you."

"I shall be there in one minute," he said, hanging up and rushing, without running or panicking, down the clean corridors, past an orderly cleaning imaginary dirt and unseen microbes from the already pristine surface.

Scrubbing automatically, he put on a mask and gloves and stepped into the subdued room with a table set in the center. A bright light illuminated a young face. The light also showed limbs damaged beyond repair—signs of infection and evidence of previous efforts to give the boy back to his family.

"Yes, doctor?"

"The patient is prepped and waiting for you," she hesitated. "We did not expect that you would be so long."

There was no question that she had the feel for this work, nor was there urgency because there was somewhere else she needed to be. *A pretty woman, just out of school somewhere south,* he thought, *Vanderbilt perhaps.*

Emily Price had mortgaged herself to Uncle Sam when her father had said "enough" education for a girl; if she wanted to take care of people, she had to become a nurse, go to night school. "No," she had said. Ever since she had taken her teenage sister to the hospital with a broken arm, she had decided that she had to be a doctor. Her advisors suggested that she be a podiatrist, be a chiropractor, be a....

The doctor who had set pins into her sister's elbow had a magical touch; she had to be a surgeon. There was no money except for the war. Uncle Sam was a means to get an education, to get a medical degree. All she had to do was sign on the line.

She signed.

In 1968, people had just begun to understand that the body bag count was escalating and that the government had no goal beyond "stopping the tide of communism". Optimistically, she believed that four years later, after she graduated, it would be over.

"Well, you will have to manage without me as I have to leave for a few days. You have the capabilities; you are a natural surgeon, if there is such a thing. Sister Fayle can assist; she has witnessed hundreds of these procedures. Listen to her, then go with your instinct. Sister, have one of your best nurses scrub and provide backup. You have the best anesthesiologist in the hospital on the boy so let's save this soldier's life. A double amputation is always dangerous; take your time, and take a small break in between to make sure there is no shock. If in doubt, abort; wait until he is stronger. Okay?"

There was silence, although it was clear that everyone had heard every word.

The sister moved, first going to the phone and asking the operator to page Nurse Weston to the operating room immediately.

The operator was intrigued. What could be going on? A civilian and avid reader of cheap novelettes, she was making up stories and expanding theories with which to enthrall her friends at bingo that night.

In the operating room, the stunned Dr. Price had recovered sufficiently to say, "We had talked about Sergeant Miller with the piece of metal next to his spine...."

Dr. Land interrupted and said, "I shall talk to Dr. Brandon about swapping and taking the sergeant. No offence, but you need a little more experience."

The relief was palpable. "Thank you," she whispered, then, more confidently, "thank you for your confidence, Sir. And now, people, let's begin. Vital signs?" She nodded to the newly installed Nurse Weston who, with a couple of hesitations, gave the information.

"Watch the signs, nurse, and speak up," Dr. Price said with growing confidence.

The realization of what she was doing would not hit her until later, then she should call someone—her father, no, she decided, her sister. So what if she was living in California?

Dr. Land slipped out of the operating theatre and headed for his room. He needed to throw some clothes in a bag, shower, change, and then catch the train. He diverted to his office, actually a spot where all the messages for the doctors were routed and from where they could leave messages, plan meetings, make phone calls to patients' families, patients' family physicians, etc.

It was necessary but time consuming and generally debilitating; he was rarely the giver of good news.

"Hi, Helen, got anything for me?"

The girl at the desk reacted with surprise at his voice but recovered and said, "A bunch! Important stuff! Your mother called! Sergeant Miller's rabbi called! Dr. Brandon wanted to know what on earth is going on in Ops 3 and then a pile of other stuff. Here, a pile of when-can-we-pick-up-our-son messages and your mail. A few of these letters are proposals if my nose reads them right."

"Helen, you will be the first to know if I accept any of them. I have to leave. Can you check on train times and order a taxi for me? Page Dr. Brandon. I need to see him before I leave, and get my mother on the phone while I scan this pile of stuff you have given me."

Two minutes later, Helen announced, "Your mother is not answering. Dr Brandon will come by your quarters between Ops. The train leaves at 6:10, change at Grand Central Station and arrive at Greenwich 11:00 PM. Taxi here at quarter to six; gives you less than one hour."

Helen always spoke in minimalist sentences. She was fifty pounds overweight, yet constantly on a diet. Her current diet consisted of Jell-O in all the different flavors and colors. Perhaps the problem was the half a dozen donuts she picked up and ate on her way to work. She was a wonder, though, and kept all the doctors informed without divulging a word of what might be privileged personal information.

"Thank you, Helen. Keep calling my mother and tell her I should be home by 11:30 so she will not worry."

One hour, he thought; he had to hurry. He was stepping out of the shower when there was a knock, and Martin Brandon walked straight in.

"Heard you were taking off again. Sunny climes, beautiful women, and champagne."

"Martin, as you know, I have not had a day off in four months. I am going to Greenwich in January to see my mother."

Martin laughed. "Your secret is safe with me. What is her name?"

"No secret is safe with you, and a name to you is merely a phone number that you have not yet called. Actually, I have a favor to ask. There is a Sergeant Miller with a piece of metal next to his spine, and within days, hours maybe, it could slip and he will be a quad. Could you take care of it for me? Use Price as backup if you need to."

Martin became Dr. Brandon immediately.

"Of course, old chap. I don't need Price, though; I have my own. You know how touchy they are. Is tomorrow good enough?"

Without further comment, they both knew that although Martin was a hit with the girls, he would not work with a woman doctor.

"You know, next weekend, I may be off skiing, so you could say that payback will be quick," said Martin with a wink. "Have a great weekend."

It was common knowledge that Martin would invite a different nurse away every time he had a pass. They never refused and seemed to hold no resentment when another girl was invited the next time.

Dr. Land, with overnight bag over his shoulder, rushed out just in time to prevent his taxi being taken by a patient's visitor.

Settling in the seat, he was in his own thoughts not looking for conversation.

The driver spoke. "You a doctor then?"

"Yes, I am."

"You a doctor there then?" he repeated

The doctor was instantly on alert. He had forgotten that outside of the hospital was a different world, one in which the view of the military was different. The country was dividing into "us" and "them." Which was he then? Why "us" of course! But then, everybody thought they were "us," didn't they?

"Why? You got a medical question?"

The driver was temporarily nonplussed.

"No, it's just that they are butchers, right? Stands to reason, real doctors are out in the real world making millions. I take families up there all happy, and they come down crying all the way to the bus or the train. They all say that they are not coming back. Butchers, they say."

Dr. Richard Land laid back and closed his eyes. He could no longer hear the driver, and he was so tired. How did he get so tired in just one hour, or was it two since he was summoned, sent away, required to attend a funeral?

Who died?

Chapter Three

The train was late, and the worst part was that no one cared. Richard watched the mother watching her children, watching the garbage blow about their feet. A young man jived to some unheard tune. Fellow workers stood in silence, with nothing to say after spending a day of gossiping and talking about nothing. He was no different, standing quietly within himself, his thoughts outside nothing, with no show of impatience at a circumstance over which he had no power. The anticipation of an earlier age of train travel was missing, replaced with antipathy, acceptance, and silence.

The train arrived noisily amid a flurry of activity, as if the stage manager had ordered the whole clockwork scene to move simultaneously.

People descended: some quickly with briefcases or handbags, others with large suitcases providing an impediment for the anxious travelers to board. Doctor Land helped an older gentleman, probably in his 60s, with a large suitcase who was being instructed without physical help by his large wife. Having carried the case down the step, he wondered if the man would have the sense to find a porter, should one be found, to assist him further. The wife brushed past in a wave of perfume, the man nodded his thanks and struggled after her. Was there an inverse equation, he wondered, on the size of luggage to the ability of the owner to carry it?

He carried his own overnight bag easily. There was no need for excess weight as he had everything necessary for shaving, all his toiletries, and his casual clothes at home. He was only going for the weekend. The bag had his dress uniform, starched shirt, socks, shoes, spare shirt, and a medical bag.

Looking around, he saw the woman with two children, now turned into dervishes, board and turn to the left, he boarded and instinctively turned right.

"All aboard!"

He found a seat, ascertained that it was vacant, and sat next to a soldier who had opened his eyes only to accede that the seat was not taken. They settled into a peaceful coexistence, with the doctor again relaxing into a doze. It was the kind of nap typical of a train ride as its motion and rhythmic sound provided a relaxation that forces the eyes closed, only to have them open as the train lurched over points or the sound changed with the acceleration through small empty stations.

Two events disturbed this peace: first, when the ticket collector checked his pass and, more carefully, the pass of his companion, and second, when four young men of college age, worse for drink, staggered noisily down the aisle.

"Look here," said one, "a nigger soldier."

"Going to die for us, are you?" said another to the amusement of all four.

"Well, answer, boy! The man spoke to you," said the third.

The soldier did not move or speak.

The doctor said, "Go away!"

"Oh, a nigger lover," said the first and biggest of the group. "Is that why you sat together?" This produced more laughter from his three companions.

As Doctor Land stood, his size and weight became obvious, and his civilian top coat opened to reveal his major's uniform.

"As a matter of fact, I owe my life to this man's brother, and when you have finished school and if your glib tongue is unable to keep you from Vietnam, you had better hope that this man is standing next to you. Show some respect for a man serving his country and clean up your language. Now go away before you make a fool of yourselves."

"Let's go! This man's an officer."

"Yeah, let's go. We can be in Canada before the draft board knows that we are gone." There was not the laughter that the speaker had counted on as they left believing that theirs was the last word.

"There was no need to speak up, Sir! They would have moved on," said the soldier.

"If no one speaks, how are we to be heard?"

The soldier was then wide awake. "Sergeant Jimmy Wilson, Sir" he said while extending his hand. "Was it true about saving your life?"

"Major Richard Land, sergeant. Yes, it is true. Actually, I suppose we saved each other's lives, although he might not thank me."

"In 'Nam, Sir?"

"Yes, I was fresh out of medical school. I had a deferment until graduation. Then after some basic training, and I mean basic, I had officer training, which was just an excuse to give some rank to my degree and ROTC background, I was shipped to the hospital in Seoul."

The doctor wondered why he was telling this story to a stranger. It was part of his record, but it was not something of which he was proud. Perhaps he sensed it was a man with his own inner secrets. He was sure that this soldier was not going to talk of his experiences to his family. They did not want to know; nobody did.

"I had been in Seoul a couple of weeks when it was decided that a doctor and nurse should go out to one of the villages and give care to some civilians.

I volunteered, since it was obvious that I was going to be sent. A nurse with a crush on me volunteered also, more to be out with me than from an overwhelming desire to do good. They sent a squad of men with us—cushy patrol—mostly black with a white lieutenant. We drove in three jeeps, and we were met by several old men who directed us to an empty hut. The sergeant, Sergeant James, went in first with two men and inspected the inside, then underneath. The officer stayed with the lead jeep. There were a few patients, very few, too few. So when a boy of about ten came in, the nurse and I turned toward him. The sergeant leapt over the table and knocked me down as the bomb that the boy carried went off. The boy and the nurse died instantly. At the same time, the lieutenant and his men outside were raked by fire from nearby trees. The sergeant was on top of me and had been hit in both legs. We all returned fire, and it stopped as quickly as it had began. We put the dead nurse, dead lieutenant, and the soldier standing next to him who also died in the jeep. I took care of the wounded two who had been standing by their jeeps and Sergeant James. The sergeant was conscious and railed against the officer not securing the perimeter about the Vietcong using small boys, about the heat, the flies, and about the villagers. It was only by my superior rank that I prevented him from burning the village to the ground before he lost consciousness.

"We radioed for additional escort back. While waiting, I managed to fix the sergeant's legs, stopped the bleeding, and found a piece of the bomb next to his spine which would have killed him on the way to the hospital." He paused, overwhelmed by how, in all the trauma, he had managed to keep a hand steady enough to work in the conditions, in a bombed-out hut with a dead bomber just outside.

"They gave us both medals!" the doctor whispered. "Why did I get a medal?" he asked rhetorically, "Because I am white. Sergeant James is black but he acted without asking my political party, without checking my color or even my rank."

He stopped.

They sat in silence, both with their own thoughts, both understanding the other's.

They were coming into the station in New York.

The bustle returned as people recovered their bags and left the train. In the station, there was mayhem as people rushed to find cars, buses, or connecting trains. Into this frenetic mix was another raucous group singing, chanting, shouting antiwar slogans. This group of people was watched closely by a cordon of police. When they saw the two soldiers walking, the chanting was directed at them and a request shouted that they join forces in their crusade.

"What is going on?" asked the doctor.

"A peace rally in Washington tomorrow; this is a send off party," said a nearby police officer.

"Peace rally? With this kind of aggressive spirit, we could use some of them in 'Nam," said the soldier.

"Good luck, Jimmy Wilson. I hope that next time I see you is in peace-time."

"Good-bye, Sir. It was a real pleasure to meet you."

The train to Greenwich was sedate and quiet conversation of the work-week that just ended was interspersed with talk of the peace rally set for the weekend in Washington. The president was out of town, either through incredible good luck or fortuitous planning.

At Greenwich, the taxi driver saw the doctor's uniform and hesitated; the doctor did not. He got in and gave his mother's address.

Mother, Mother! Now, for some answers! he thought.

Chapter Four

The taxi driver's first words after leaving the station were "Three dollars and thirty-five cents." Richard Land gave him four dollars, and they played a waiting game while the driver, hoping for a sixty-five cent tip, fumbled in his change bag and Richard, annoyed at the reception and his treatment, waited quietly. The change finally proffered, and a tip of thirty-five cents accepted, the driver left the doctor standing, watching the tail lights disappear. There was no changing the attitude of people, and there was no way that an explanation, any explanation, was worth the breath.

Richard turned and looked at the house, a three-bedroom split-entry home that they had moved into when he was ten. It was home—the tenement and the life in Yonkers exchanged for the suburbs. He had argued that it was boring, quiet—dull. It was all of those things compared with life in the streets.

It was all those things, but it was also safe, a place where education was in the schools, not learned at the street corners. Not that he had forgotten; he still remembered his gang and some of their pranks. Most were not harmful, but he looked back at some that were aimed at the older people in the neighborhood or those with handicaps and was not proud of the tricks. There were some times when they would backfire, too, and it was as if his father had surveillance on the street as he was interrogated, found guilty, and punished by a man who had not been there, had examined no witnesses, and been presented with no evidence. He could hardly complain, receiving punishment for only a fraction of the infractions of which a ten-year-old was guilty. Where was that gang now? In prison, or were they in the military? Or were they lawyers? He smiled and tried to remember what they had looked like and what they must look like now.

The door opened before he could reach for a key.

"Darling, right on time!" his mother said.

"Did you find a taxi? How was the train? They are so dirty, it is a disgrace," his mother continued as he took off his coat.

"You are so thin. Let me look at you. Are you hungry? Of course, you are. Come into the kitchen; I will fix you an omelet. There is coffee in the pot, fresh made."

"Mother, we need to talk!"

"Yes, dear. But right now, I am fixing you an omelet. When did you last eat? Did you get anything at the station in New York?"

"No, Mother. The food stands smelled of stale fat, and I did not have time to go out of the station with my carry-on," he said, thinking how she had managed to turn the conversation around.

He had been in the house for less than ten minutes, and it was like turning the clock back to the times he had come home from school, home from college. *Thank goodness*, he thought, *nothing changes while everything changes.*

He was hungry. The last time he had eaten was in the office of the major general. When was that? Just eight hours ago, but it seemed like yesterday.

"How is your work?" His mother was still talking, and he was answering the necessary platitudes, the words she wanted to hear. How could he answer in detail? She would understand, but she did not want to understand. He realized that if he tried to explain, then he would become emotional, break down, and become less. His mother understood that emotion was close to the surface and at the root of their relationship. When he had said that he was being sent to Vietnam, she had calmly said, "Take care of yourself," then gone to her bedroom and cried.

She was cooking at the other side of the table at which he sat. Richard watched her and saw her as if for the first time. She was extremely attractive, though she was going to be fifty on her next birthday. Her face had a European peaches and cream complexion. Her hair was a mix of blonde and very light brown, and she had hazel eyes. She still had a good figure with a defined waist which was accentuated by a wide belt holding a multicolored skirt. A woolen v-necked sweater and sensible slippers completed the ensemble. It should not have gone together, but as a girlfriend had said to Richard upon meeting his mother, "She could wear a sugar sack and still look great!"

The ham, mushroom, and Swiss cheese omelet appeared in front of him with two slices of toast, a butter dish, a mug of coffee, knife, and fork.

He ate European style with a knife in his right hand and a fork in his left. Since he had grown up knowing no other way, it was automatic. It was very good, and he ate while his mother, after cleaning the pan and utensils, sat opposite him. She was happy to have him home, happy that he was safe, at least for that night. Then she remembered why he was there.

"Oh, dear, you had a question?" she said quietly.

"Yes, Mother. What brought me out of an operating room and onto a train and home in eight hours?" he asked the question quietly but slowly. They had never shouted at one another, but the shout was clearly heard by both in the cadence of the question.

"Well, there is a funeral tomorrow in Brooklyn, and I could hardly go by myself! And I could hardly ask anyone else to take me."

"But, Mother, I am in the army. They do not stop the war so that I can take you to a social event."

The last remark stung, and he knew, but he did not care. The words were automatic, but they were at the root of his frustration since leaving the hospital. He was tired; he was important to the people who depended upon him.

His mother became defensive.

"I asked Matt if it was possible for you to be away. He said that there were competent people on the staff, and he knew for a fact that it is over ninety days since you were away for a complete day. He thought that it was a good idea for you to take a couple of days and that this 'social event' was an appropriate place for a son to accompany his mother."

"Matt! You know Major General Mathew Rollins? Personally? Why did you never mention that to me before?"

"I didn't say Matt...did I? Oh, damn!"

Richard was shocked as it was the strongest word and the closest to a swear word that he had ever heard from his mother.

"I am sorry, Mother, sorry that I upset you. I am tired, and I have not been taking time away. There is a tremendous staff at the hospital, and I am sure they will get along fine without me for a couple of days."

"What time is the funeral tomorrow? Is it someone you used to work with or a friend?"

Richard realized that his mother had never talked about her work, and her only friends that he knew of were there in Greenwich. The people they knew hardly rated a call to the commandant. A simple message would have sufficed. Nanie Goldman? No. Who?

"The service is at the Holy Name Church in Brooklyn tomorrow at 11:00 A.M. We should leave soon after nine to avoid the traffic. Here is the obituary; his name is—was—Richard Blaine."

"But...," he stammered as he looked through a mist at the piece of newspaper in his hand. "But mother...." He was stunned.

"Yes," said his mother as she left the room so he would not see her tears.

He picked up the paper and stared at the print for a long time. Much later, he went to bed. He thought that he would not sleep, but he was so tired that he slept soundly.

Just as he fell into unconsciousness, he whispered to himself.

"Who is Richard Blaine?"

Chapter Five

Dr. Richard Land woke and, for a moment, could not remember where he was. He had clearly slept soundly and without a dream. There was a familiar sound and a piano playing. But there was something wrong with it. He lay there studying the thought. Well, he was home in his room with a couple of posters and a couple of photos showing him with his teammates in various sports and at different ages. What was wrong, he decided, was that his mother never played in the morning and would never wake anyone.

Well, it was an unusual start to what promised to be an unusual day.

He went through his daily ritual in the bathroom, showered, and shaved. While shaving, he listened to his mother's playing. It was not loud enough to wake or disturb anyone, and the tunes were all familiar to him. However, today, they were somehow slower, melancholic. Humming softly to himself, it became obvious—they were French songs played with the occasional flat note, added to impart sadness. There was also a beat with the left hand in a lower octave that was unexpected. He recognized in that lower beat a march; his boot camp could have paraded to those tunes.

Dressing in his parade uniform, he went quietly downstairs. There was no need for the stealth as his mother sat absorbed with her music. He picked up a clarinet and joined as his mother had changed to a tune popular during the thirties and forties––"As Time Goes By." Having played in a jazz band through high school and college, it was easy for him to pick up the theme and play seamlessly as it had been his mother's request many times. She then turned to him, her face wet with tears with a look of sheer wonder. The tune brightened, and then she suddenly stopped and closed the piano.

"Look at the time! I must look a mess. Can you get your own breakfast? I am not hungry. I put on the coffee," she said without taking a breath and while heading for the stairs.

"Good morning, Mother"

"Oh! Good morning, Richard. I shall be as quick as I can." Richard had found bread, butter, marmalade, and toasted the bread while pouring coffee and putting milk and sugar. He ate quickly, washed his plate, poured more coffee, and studied the obituary that was still on the table. It read:

"Richard Blaine, age sixty-seven of Brooklyn New York. He was born in Brooklyn and studied law before leaving for Spain in 1936 where he volunteered to fight against Franco and the Nazis. He moved to Paris and left as the Germans entered and operated a casino in Casablanca. When the Germans came to Morocco, he volunteered to fight with a guerilla group against them.

A decorated war veteran, he served with the Free French in Africa before joining the American Forces in Africa and into Italy. Upon returning to America, he opened a popular restaurant in Brooklyn. He is survived by a daughter Kate and many friends."

When his mother appeared, she looked stunning in a black suit with dark stockings and black shoes. A black ribbon tied back her hair from her neck. She was wearing a single string of pearls under the suit and a broach.

"You look amazing, new clothes and new broach," he said admiringly.

"New clothes," she said, "old medal."

He looked carefully. It was a cross of Lorraine.

"Dad's!" he said immediately. Then just as quickly, when he saw his mother's face, he said, "Sorry!"

The medal surely had a meaning for that day, and she would not wear a medal to which she was not entitled; she would just not do it.

His mother had turned away heading to the door to the garage.

"You drive," she said.

Richard took the key to the 1969 Chevrolet Bel Air which his mother had recently bought, and he thought how well she managed on the small amount that she must receive from tutoring foreign languages. He knew that she represented a bunch of import/export companies who hired her to teach their staff not only the language but also the etiquette of whatever European country they were representing, but how much could that pay?

They drove in silence to the highway. Finally breaking the tension, he asked, "Do you know where the church is?"

"Yes, sort of; I went to the library yesterday, and they said that it was on Main Street and that I could not miss it." She was relieved that they could talk.

"I did not know," he said; they both knew he was referring to the cross of Lorraine.

"I should take it off. Just a silly thought."

"Mother, who is Richard Blaine, and why is his death so important to you?"

"Richard Blaine was a war hero," she began.

"I know; it is in the obituary," he interrupted.

"There are war heroes and war heroes and those who touch many lives like a pebble thrown into a pond, making waves that go on forever. Richard Blaine was one of those war heroes."

She lapsed into silence, and he thought that either she was crying again or she was finished. He could not turn to look; the road was busy, and he knew that if she were crying, they would both be embarrassed.

"The Germans were looking everywhere for Victor Lazlo. They were not aware that he and I were married, until we arrived in Casablanca. Victor was wanted because of his connections to the underground movement in occupied Europe. We were trapped; there was no way out. I believe that Victor could have disappeared alone into the desert, but then, they would have tortured and executed me. He would not let the Germans do that but wanted me to try to make it to America. I could not, although he did not know—nobody knew—I suspected that I was pregnant. Richard Blaine gave us passes. Two passes he could have sold for a lot of money."

She paused, thinking of how much she knew, what she guessed, and what she would tell her son.

"We were in Lisbon for months waiting for a visa. During that time, there were attempts on Victor's life, including an attack which almost killed me. The Nazis were adamant that we would not make it out alive. Victor would not give up; he met every day with people going to America, learning where they were going, what their technical skills were. Everyone had the same political agenda; this madman was to be stopped. Most had an antipathy to the situation. They had been anesthetized, and they were leaving; they were trying to forget. Victor made them remember."

She stopped speaking, remembering again those terrifying months—hiding, waiting alone for Victor to come back with his compulsive notes, documenting his latest conversations. No, she would not tell her son of the near miss when only her intuition and good luck saved them.

A man identifying himself as from the embassy asked if he could wait for Victor. He showed credentials and carried a letter. When she asked if he wanted a drink of water, he said 'No' and he had kept his coat on in spite of the stifling heat in the room. The Americans that she had met were very informal, always introduced themselves, talked about the States, and would have accepted a drink to be sociable. When Victor had appeared around the corner, she had called out to him in Swedish, "There is a man in here; it may be a trap!"

Victor had waved, seemingly imperturbable. "Thank you. I shall be right back," he said and disappeared.

The man jumped up, "What did you say?"

"I asked if he remembered to pick up bread. Of course, he had forgotten."

Victor returned with two men, all three of them unseen from the single window of their room. The man from the embassy jumped up as they burst into the room, drew a revolver from his pocket, and managed two shots before being overpowered. One of the men with Victor received a flesh wound which she had bandaged. Then they had tied and gagged the man and, in the dark had, carried him away.

"As you know, you were born on the ship and christened by the chaplain. You were automatically American as New York was our first port," Richard's mother stated.

Richard realized that he had been holding his breath, unable to break the spell. There were so many questions. The first was clinical. How had he been able to hold his breath for over half an hour? The other questions would have to wait; they were approaching their destination.

He drove down the street, passed shops selling vegetables, meat, fish, and Italian meats and sausages. There were small bars with men inside. There were triple-decker houses on the side streets with women in black clothing standing on the lower steps. The signs advertising plumbers, electricians, the hardware stores, and shops all had Italian names. "Coviello and Disalvo Funeral Home," he read.

"We must be nearly there!" he said." They always have a funeral home next to the church."

Only slightly surprised, the church appeared at the next intersection and took up the whole block.

"Look at all the cars," said his mother, "and the flowers that they are carrying in."

"Probably more than one funeral, don't you think?"

Richard was directed to a parking space in the rear by a young man in a black suit who asked if they would be going to the graveyard.

"Yes," said his mother before he could consider the implications.

"We are here for Richard Blaine's funeral," Richard added.

"Yes," said the young man "It will be the biggest Brooklyn has seen for a while. It is only twenty to eleven, and we are filling up."

"We must get a seat, Richard," his mother was holding to his arm very tightly and leaning towards him as though she needed help walking.

The church was indeed huge and was more than half full. The early mourners had tended to congregate at the rear so they were forced to walk almost to the front. It was obvious that the purpose of sitting at the back was to observe without being observed. There was a flutter of whispering as they went down toward the front of the church. The ushers were keeping several rows at the front empty and asked a few people to move when the congregation swelled forward, pushed by their tardiness or by the lack of foresight in trying to find a seat. At a minute to eleven, there was a groundswell of whispering, and a party of six men and one woman were ushered to one of the empty rows.

Richard and his mother had been in quiet contemplation, but then, he joined the whispering.

"Is that John Disalvo?" he asked in awe, shocked to be that close to someone so infamous.

There was another groundswell, and the ushers showed Vincent Bonanno, his son, the son's girlfriend, and five heavyset "wiseguys" into a pew just a few rows in front of where they were seated. The girlfriend's stiletto heels made a discordant and irregular rat-a-tat on the floor of the church.

When Vincent was level with John Disalvo, he made an almost imperceptible nod, which was returned.

The coffin then entered the church with the funeral party.

The chief mourner appeared to be a young woman with a black dress and veil. The other mourners did not seem to fit a normal family picture. They were a radically diverse mix of old and young men and women. The one surprise was the chief of police who, far from surprised by the two men who controlled the crime in his city, stopped on his way down to the aisle to greet them both.

What am I doing here? thought the doctor.

Who is Richard Blaine?

Chapter Six

The service began with a welcome and proceeded at a moderate pace, the priest taking time to enjoy having perhaps the largest and definitely the most influential congregation of his tenure.

Richard looked at his mother who had removed the dark glasses she had worn in the car and then looked straight ahead with an inscrutable expression. He was reminded of the Mona Lisa, and then he realized she had transcended pretty and, at that time and place, could truly be called beautiful.

The service droned forward but not without a palpable energy in the air. The silences were occasionally broken by the sound of chewing gum cracking. After the third or fourth time, there was a stage whisper.

"Lose the gum!"

A loud shrill female voice just three rows ahead answered.

"Wha…. at?"

"Lose the f……..gum!" The voice loud enough to be heard for at least ten rows silenced the miscreant, and the offending gum was abandoned to the bottom of the pew.

Richard and his mother listened intently to the words of the priest praising a man as though he was his closest friend and a fellow brother in a fight against all the injustices of Brooklyn, New York. The information was all secondhand, embellished as only a professional could embellish and spoken confidently. Spoken with a surety that there was no possibility of his being refuted by the subject of the praise.

The police chief spoke of having lost a friend. There were many who wondered, perhaps cynically, if he was sorry for the man or some other more personal financial reason. A woman spoke of having known Rick her whole life saying she owed her very life to him. She appeared sincere, but, if the facts were known to many of the congregation, they were not explained and therefore remained a mystery to others.

Finally, there was an introduction of Samuel Wilson who had been his friend for over thirty years.

Instead of heading to the lectern, the old black man stood from the front row and went to a piano in front.

He started riffing as he spoke into a microphone.

"I ain't so good with words, but I will try to tell the story of our friendship with my piano. I first met Rick in Paris."

He began playing "An American in Paris."

The effect on the congregation was nothing compared to the reaction of Richard's mother. She half rose out of her pew, grabbed his arm in a viselike grip, and, half-choking, half amazed, in a quiet tremulous voice said "Sam?"

Samuel Wilson had moved from the classical Gershwin to play a joyful "April in Paris." Then he transitioned to a slow "Marseilles" with a martial bass beat and said, "Those were great the days until the Germans marched in. We left at the last minute and went to Africa."

With a couple of chords, he imitated a train before the transition swifted into a rendition of "We're Off on the Road to Morocco". He began to play the "Horst-Wessel-Lied" with his left hand and a tease background with the right hand, which niggled at the back of their mind. When his mother released his arm to pull out a handkerchief, he knew he was not mistaken; his mother had played the same tune this morning.

"The Germans came to Casablanca, and Rick left just ahead of them to join the French resistance and then the American army."

He was then playing a medley of war tunes—some French, some American. "We returned to Brooklyn in 1945 and opened Rick's Café. I am proud to have been Rick's friend and partner for over thirty years."

Samuel Wilson finished the rendition of music from "On the Town" including a rousing "New York, New York," paused, and then played "Happy Trails" quietly. It was quiet; not a sound escaped the vast nave. No one coughed, no one shuffled, and no one was breathing.

The priest broke the spell with his blessing of the congregation and announced that the funeral procession would be leaving directly for the graveyard, and then Miss Blaine would receive condolences at Rick's Café.

Richard had stood as if in a trance. It was not real; he had levitated, looking at another place, looking down at all those people. Who were they? Who was the woman by his side?

The choir was singing a fired "Ave Maria" as if they, too, had witnessed something they would relate to their children and grandchildren.

There was a moment of comedy when John Disalvo and Vincent Bonanno came out of their opposite pews together. They looked, hesitated, then walked up the aisle together. There was mass confusion among the entourage and a jockeying to provide protection for their paymasters.

"So, John, it takes the death of a friend to bring us to the same room," said an amused Vincent.

"I thought the only time I would be in here with you, you would be in a box," said a less amused John.

"Just wishful thinking," Vincent replied.

The exchange would be replayed for weeks, and each side would add their own twist to the conversation until a declaration of war had been made with threats and counter threats. Before long, there would be three thousand people who had heard the conversation from the congregation of less than two thousand, of which only twenty-five or so could have heard anything at all.

At the door, the two were separated by their guards and taken to their own limousines for the ride to the cemetery.

Along the way, their supporters, or dependants—people who owed them money or owed them favors—tried to make themselves seen. The principals, like royalty or film stars, ignored all the calls and walked in the trough of the wave which parted to the street.

When Richard had reached the top of the steps outside, the sunshine brought him back to earth with a thud. There was a press of people behind, making sure they would not miss any of the drama still unfolding.

"Well," he said, letting out a huge breath.

"Thanks for coming, Ricky," his mother was composed, either she was still in the trance which he had experienced, or the best actress in the world.

The ride to the cemetery was out of a Hollywood movie: there were police cars front and back with sirens and motorcycle cops at every intersection saluting. Saluting who? Richard Blaine, the chief of police, John "Mad Dog" Disalvo, or Vincent Bonnano?

Inside the two latter's limousines, Richard and his mother would have been surprised to know they were the subject of conversation.

Vincent Bonnano asked his entourage, "Who was the admiral sitting a couple of rows behind us?"

"Don't know, boss!" was the almost unanimous reply.

"Then find out."

"How?" asked a very broad former boxer.

"Ask him, knucklehead," said Vincent.

John Disalvo, on the other hand, was more interested in Mrs. Land.

"I wonder how the good-looking broad is connected to Rick?" he asked.

"Who cares, boss?"

"I care!" It was as if there was a command; they all cared then.

At the cemetery, there was another crush of people that parted before the two groups. The ground was soft and would not support stiletto heels, so a mewling ensued from the Bonnano factor.

Vincent senior spoke to his son.

"VIN, lose the f .... broad!"

Vin said to one of his men, "Put her in a cab; give her a C note."

"I'll see you tonight, Vin," she whined as she was helped back to tarmac.

"I'll call," said a slightly disappointed Vin who had been expecting great things but who then knew that he could not call and that in a couple of days, she would be on a bus to Atlantic City.

There was a brief prayer at the gravesite, and then the coffin was slowly lowered to the ground. There was a swell of tears and sobbing from the mourners gathered around the young girl and the piano player.

Samuel Wilson was looking around as if for someone who was not there. The young woman had lifted her veil, and Richard was mesmerized. She was clearly upset, but he could see that she was attractive and possessed a strength that would see her through this difficult day.

He was unable to study her further as they were breaking up, putting dirt on the coffin, and moving away.

Their car was at the end since they had not known the way and, being at the end of the parking lot, were among the last to leave.

Along the way, they were approached in different ways by three men.

The first was Benny Morgan who had been called knucklehead, which he was anxious to correct.

"Hey, Admiral. Boss wants to know who you are."

"Tell your boss that there is a right way and wrong way to introduce one-self."

The second man was nondescript, wearing a dark raincoat over a dark suit. He was of medium height and medium brown hair slightly grey, in his sixties, and was in good shape. "Mrs. Land and Major Land, how good to see you again." He extended a hand to Richard's mother and then Richard.

"You probably do not remember me. It's Charles Munroe. Your mother worked for me. Are you going to the café? Perhaps you could give me a lift. It seems as though someone pinched my taxi."

He spoke with an English accent, or someone affecting an accent. Mr. Munroe was used to acting, playing the part.

The third man heard the exchange and was able to report to John Disalvo that it was Mrs. Land and her son.

Billy Costello said, "I thought they looked familiar. Lived in Yonkers when we were there—tough little kid. They moved away. He never backed down, never cried. I don't think he even cried when his dad, who thought he had picked an old lady's pocket book, beat the snot out of him."

They drove to Rick's Café with Mr. Munroe directing while keeping a running dialog about mundane office-type things which were spoken in a code to which Richard did not have the key.

"So, you are working with Matt Rollins?" Mr. Monroe spoke to him for the first time

"Yes, Sir, I am."

"Fine man, fine man!"

They had reached the restaurant, and his image was shattered again. It was no café in the American sense; it was a café in a European sense, with a small garden in front, seats outside under umbrellas, and bright airy seating inside around a circular bar. There were bright tablecloths and a uniformed staff bustling around.

Just when I believed that the day had no more surprises, thought Richard Land as he stepped over the threshold.

Chapter Seven

It was like stepping into Aladdin's cave and Coney Island. The effect was enhanced by the huge turbaned Arab at the door complete with scimitar. The inside was crowded with people several deep around a large, semicircular bar while most of the tables were occupied. It was much bigger inside than it appeared from outside. To the far left through the smoke, he could see a large round table which was occupied by Vincent Bonnano and his entourage while on the right, occupying a similar table, was John Disalvo.

The Arab gave a start of recognition which was just as quickly replaced by a greeting of a professional, trained to recognize guests.

He clearly had the authority to allow entry and the size to prevent admittance if necessary.

"Good afternoon, Miss. Good afternoon, Sir"

"Good afternoon, Abdullah," said his mother and was rewarded by a flash of teeth, some with gold caps.

Richard looked closely at the man and saw that he was older than at first sight, probably sixty, if older. *He must be six feet six inches*, he thought, *with a sword*. When he turned to remark on this, he realized that Mr. Munroe had disappeared.

The waitresses were busy with appetizers and other finger foods, walking around the tables while there appeared to be four bartenders working hard.

His eyes traveled around to a knot of people near the piano. The pianist was playing quietly, current show tunes but without any enthusiasm. Close by and the cause of attention was the pretty woman with a condolence crowd which appeared to be predominantly male.

Richard studied the crowd and the young woman until she caught him looking, which forced him to look away. His assessment of the male crowd was that they were vendors looking for assurance that their debts would be paid. They were hypocritical in their eating and drinking for free while wondering if there would be sufficient cash to pay for their indulgences. The vendors' wives were nearby, creating their own group and trying to eat sufficiently, not worrying about being paid or the need to prepare supper.

"Mother, shall I find a table?"

"No, dear," she said as she wandered away.

"Would you like a drink?"

"That would be nice, the usual—white wine."

Richard realized that he was thirsty, and he needed a quiet place to think. However, neither appeared possible with the noisy crowd around the bar. He was lucky as a group moved to leave, and he found himself at the front of the bar. A familiar face turned and asked, "Yes, Sir, what can I get for you?"

"Jimmy, what are you doing here?"

"I could ask you the same thing, Sir," said the soldier from the train.

"Well, I would like a good draught beer and white wine please. I brought my mother; she owed Rick from a long time ago."

A voice interrupted from nearby, clearly directed at Jimmy.

"Hey, a V.O. and ginger, and a glass of DOM."

"Yes, Sir, in a moment." Then he turned to Richard and said, "Your mother could join a long line of people who owed favors from Rick. My dad is the piano player, and he said that Miss Kate might need help, so I came along."

"Hey, ragweed, this is a drinking hole, not a debating society."

The young girl on his arm giggled and wriggled while the young man guffawed.

"Is the champagne for the young lady, Sir?" asked Jimmy.

"Sure! Only the best."

"I am sorry, Sir, but she is underage."

"Give me the f .... drink, or I'll tan your black ass."

Richard moved over and said quietly, "I think you should leave."

"You know who I am?" asked the by then red-faced young man.

"I don't care."

The man looked to the table where John Disalvo sat, and two of the men started to stand. However, they were stopped by a whispered command from their paymaster.

The man looked back at the table where John Disalvo gave an almost imperceptible nod to the door. Embarrassed, he looked for a dignified exit, found none, and started for the door, trailing a whining teenager.

"You promised me champagne!"

"Oh, shut up, you silly cow!"

Jimmy said, "You did not need to do that, Sir! That's twice."

Kate Blaine was there. She asked, "What happened, Jimmy?"

"Not Jimmy's fault," said Richard.

"I didn't ask you."

"Girl was underage. I refused to serve her; man asked him to leave," Jimmy replied.

"Thank you," she said to Richard.

"Don't thank me. Thank Mr. Disalvo; he told him to leave."

She nodded, making her own assessment, and was gone again.

Richard went towards the piano with his mother's drink after taking a large drink of Bass ale. *I needed that!* he thought.

The music was livelier, though still quiet, and he was not surprised to see his mother sitting on the piano stool next to Samuel Wilson, the pianist from the church. Actually, he would have been surprised except that, after everything else that had happened, nothing would surprise him.

He doubted that he could ever be surprised again.

"Sam, this is my son, Dr. Richard Land."

"MY, my, my," he paused while assessing the tall military doctor. "My, my."

He stood and said, "Pleased to meet you, son. Your mother and me been rattling on 'bout old times. Good times in Paris, not so good in Casablanca."

John Disalvo parted the crowd, gave Kate Blaine a kiss on the cheek, whispered in her ear, and left the restaurant. Shortly thereafter, Vincent Bonanno repeated the ritual with a final "Remember, anytime."

Vincent Junior tried to give Kate a more than brotherly kiss. When rebuked, he gave a lewd grin and asked "Later then?"

"Much, much later," she said." In fact, not likely to happen in your lifetime!"

When the two limousines were gone, the crowd thinned rapidly, and it appeared that the only people left were employees, Richard, and his mother. As he looked at the bar, Richard almost missed seeing Charles Munroe talking with Jimmy Wilson.

Kate Blaine came to where they were seated.

Sam did the introductions, "Kate, this is Miss Ilsa, an old friend of Rick, and her son, Dr. Richard Land."

"Miss Ilsa, you do not look old." She paused, slightly embarrassed. "I have seen a photograph of you, I think, taken in Paris. You were drinking champagne with Rick and Sam. Sam, I had forgotten that, but you never drink now."

"Yes, those were wonderful days with cheap wine. Rick did enough drinking for both of us after...." He trailed off.

"We must be leaving, but I shall be back to see Sam; he was just going to tell me what happened to Rick after I last saw him in 1942," Ilsa said and rose.

"Why don't we get some food and champagne and all hear the story now?" said Kate. "Rick never spoke of his life before 1945."

She signaled the nearest girl and ordered a bunch of French dishes while Jimmy brought glasses and champagne.

They waited expectantly as Sam spoke in a manner of one telling a story he had been hoarding in his body for years and was finally given the moment, the audience, and the reason to tell it as a testimonial to his friend.

Chapter Eight
Casablanca 1942

Rick walked through the airport and out the front door. There was a strong will in him to run, but common sense told him to act as though he had just waved good-bye to a departing passenger. Well, that was true. He was gripping the gun and knew that his knuckles were white in the raincoat pocket. Why had Reynard not arrested him? Was there such a thing as honor, or was it that there were different levels of dishonor? Whatever the reason, the inspector would be buried for weeks in paperwork.

The plane had left on time, thank goodness. How had Strasser got there so quickly? Would Strasser have shot him? Definitely!

What now? Ilsa was gone. Already, there was a void. The café was sold; he had no home. Well, it was time for a change.

The taxi driver was dozing. How could these people be so out of tune with everything happening around them? Well, he would soon know; he had to become one of them.

He got into the rear seat.

"Where to, Monsieur?"

That was a good question. There were sounds of more police vehicles screaming towards the terminal and more German troops double marching through the terminal. He knew they were Germans because of the precise beat.

"To the café, Monsieur Rick?"

"Yes, yes," Rick replied automatically.

At the café, all was business as usual.

"Good evening, Sir."

"Good evening, Abdullah."

Inside, the crowd was noisier, more exuberant. *Celebrations for the change in ownership*, he thought when he saw a crowd around the bar.

Then he noticed that the mood was louder and less restrained due to the absence of Germans.

He nodded to Ferrari. The new owner was entertaining a mixed group of people—some hopeful of leaving Casablanca and some ready to exploit that need. In fact, it was difficult to conceive a more lucrative market than that for which there was no price list and no price limit. The local community had learned patience, and so, the longer people were forced to wait, the larger the local economy and the higher the price those waiting were willing to pay in order to leave.

Ferrari, seeming to ignore the conversation swirling around him, heard everything and stored away the information like a pawnbroker, willing to sell it back later at a profit. He waved Rick toward him.

"Have a drink, Rick," he chortled, "on me."

"Thanks, but I just came to pick up a few things. Then I am leaving."

"Rick, word is out that Lazlo left town, so I assume that he used the letters of credit," he stopped and tried to gauge Rick's reaction to the information.

"Now, here's the thing, Rick. If he left with Mrs. Lazlo, there were two tickets, which means that you do not have a ticket." He was speaking slowly, his eyes half closed as if he was getting to a point but in his own time.

"Surprise you walking in here. We had a business transition today, and a substantial amount of money was transferred. Now, either you put it in the bank, or you gave it to Mrs. Lazlo, or you are here to retrieve it before skipping town. Number one, you did not go to the bank today."

"You had me followed!" said an indignant-sounding Rick, though he was not surprised.

"Only for your own protection, dear boy.

You would not give it to the Lazlos. I do not believe that even you are so careless as to leave yourself without funds and without a ticket in this oasis. So, you have come back to retrieve the money. Now, if a humble personage such as me has surmised as much, then be careful as you leave."

"Thanks for the warning, in case I need one, but why are you being so nice to me? You got what you wanted at a discount price."

"Well, it would be bad for business to have a robbery-murder right outside my door." Ferrari was chortling again, his belly bouncing like jelly, but his eyes were not amused.

"I just came by to say good-bye to a few people and take some clothes and personal belongings from the office," said a then very wary Rick.

Rick went up to his office. At the top of the stairs, he stopped to survey the room. Ferrari had watched him all the way up and was still watching. The door was opening, and a small Arab was scuttling out. Well, Ferrari was right: he was in danger. Maybe Ferrari was the instigator; maybe not.

He went to his office; it smelled differently already.

It had been searched—no surprise. He packed a few clothes into a small case, changed into casual work clothes, and stuffed socks and underwear into his pockets, thankful that the trench coat had plenty of room. He put his gun into a shoulder holster and picked up a box of shells. Finally, he went to the safe and took out his passport, two money belts, a boxful of cash, and a bag about six inches square with a drawstring. He went over to the desk, took five diamonds from the bag and enough cash to live for a month, and carefully hid those in the clothes he wore.

He put his passport into a money belt which he put on. He then took the rest of the money from the sale of the café, together with the bag of diamonds, and put them into a large manila folder.

Everything completed, he took a final look around his home for more than two years and left.

Rick stood at the top of the stairs, holding the folder obscured by his travel bag. He looked down. Ferrari looked up. The small Arab was back with two other men. *There are more outside*, thought Rick. Sam was playing the piano, and Berger was at the bar.

It was going to take incredible timing.

"Hi, Sam. How's the new boss?" Rick was leaning over the piano, apparently to do what he had said—say good-bye.

"Okay, but when are we leaving?" asked Sam.

Rick lowered his voice so that, with the piano being played, only the two of them would ever know what was said.

"Listen carefully. I am leaving as soon as the police and Germans raid this place. They will raid it because Colonel Strasser is dead. Sam, you have to stay and take care of a few things; they will ask where I am, where I went. You cannot tell them because you do not know. I shall be in touch as soon as I can.

"I am going to leave some money in your piano. Tonight, transfer it into the piano seat." After the scare with the letters of credit and with inquisitive Germans prowling around the place, even a safe was not safe. Rick had built a space below the bottom of the piano stool. It could only be opened by turning the stool upside down and sliding the panel from the side of the stool so that the whole bottom slid out. Only Rick and Sam knew of its existence since the carpenter had left for Lisbon right after its completion.

"Convert the money into diamonds and gold carefully. Everyone will believe that you are working for someone. Stop at the police station, and they will believe that it is the police or the Germans.

"Be careful, Sam. Say nothing, but listen to everything. There are men waiting close by the door for me to leave. They will be suspicious of you; be careful. Say au revoir to everyone for me."

The huge door crashed open. Everyone looked to the sound except Rick who carefully lifted the piano top, put in the package, and walked toward the bar.

All the German soldiers stationed in Casablanca then came marching in.

Rick reached Berger, the Norwegian chief of resistance volunteers.

"Let's go," he said quietly in his ear.

A surprised Paul Berger looked at the speaker then back to the scene unfolding.

"How? Where?"

"Now," said Rick urgently and headed for the kitchen.

A startled Norwegian followed. He could not say then or ever why he had made the decision to follow. They walked without attracting attention through to a small door at the side of the building. Rick slid open the bolts and stepped out into an alley. There was no light, but they could see by light filtering out of the loading dock that there were soldiers, or police, stationed at the loading dock at the front of the building and also at the base of the fire escape. They walked silently and unseen to the front of the building and away into the night

"What was that about, and why did you drag me out?" asked a confused Norwegian.

"Strasser was shot and killed this night. There is a dragnet out for his killer. You would have been arrested, and there is nothing that the French can do for anyone interrogated tonight. It will be Ugatti all over again 'died while trying to escape,' trying to escape with two broken legs."

"Then thank you and good night"

"Paul, let me make myself clear: my help was not altruistic. I need to disappear, and I need you and your friends to make it happen."

Chapter Nine

The next week went by in a cascade of noise and lights.

The German soldiers and French-commanded police force went door to door, bringing in suspects, interrogating them for days, and holding them in jail then in a school which they had taken over. The cars and trucks raced around all day and night, terrifying the innocent together with those with a secret.

Twice, they raided the houses where Rick Blaine and Paul Berger had been kept. Initially, the members of the resistance had been suspicious of Rick, but as the week went by, he impressed them with his quick ideas and his knowledge of the way the Germans used brutality and how their concentration of effort could be used against them. When they took a hundred soldiers and cordoned off an area: they were light on other areas and seldom went back to an area purged of dissidents.

A week after Colonel Strasser's death, a meeting of the leaders of the resistance group was in the upper floor of a building next to the school full of alleged potential assassins.

"We are doomed to join those unfortunates any day," said Johann, a Dutch teacher forced to flee from criticism for insisting on singing his national anthem. He was by the window and nodding across the street.

"I hear that they are using the assassination of the German national hero, Strasser, as an excuse to bring in more troops" said a voice from the shadows. "Maybe we should disband."

"When?" Rick asked.

"Today, as soon as we leave here," said the voice.

"No, when are the reinforcements due?"

"Soon."

"And when is that?"

"Rick, why is this important?" asked Paul. "If we dissolve and return to our pursuits, then perhaps, some of us will be arrested. We know nothing of Strasser's death. It is common knowledge that he was killed by Lazlo. If we tell them, they will free all of these other people."

"Paul, you are a decent man, but very naïve," said Rick. "The Germans have turned Casablanca upside down for a week, so, either they do not believe that Lazlo killed their beloved colonel, or they are using his death as an excuse to find our organization. They do not care who gets hurt or killed along the way. The only way top stop them and free these people you are concerned about is to strike back."

"Strike back!" Johann had left the window. "How?"

"First, go back to the window and watch the street. We attack the train bringing in reinforcements."

"But how? We know nothing about fighting and would certainly not stand up to five German soldiers, let alone a hundred," Myron, the Czechoslovakian Jew who had wanted to disband, said as stepped into the center of the room.

"I don't know yet; but can we get explosives?" It was a question.

It was answered by an Austrian Jew, Stephan. "There are explosives in the yard of Ahmed. He uses it in construction—quarrying rock."

"Okay, who wants to do this?" Rick needed unanimous vote; anyone not doing it would jeopardize anyone agreeing. He got his six "yes" votes, and they agreed not to include members who were not present in order to keep the idea safe.

"Then let us meet tomorrow in the north of the city. Yesterday, the Klein family was all arrested; they were renting a house up there which will now be empty. Paul, confirm that and report to everyone if that is not true.

"Myron, find out when the train is due to arrive with the Germans. That will determine when our attack will be.

"Johann, discreetly rent a pair of camels and a camel driver. Stephan and I will buy sufficient explosives from Ahmed to do the job. If not this job, it will come in handy for a future strike."

Rick lay awake all night, thinking through his stupid idea. How had it happened? How had he assumed command? How were they going to pull it off? How was he going to get everyone back safely?

Stephan and Rick waited until the heat of the day and, dressed as Arabs, slowly walked to the construction office—a small house with a large fence and a padlocked warehouse.

They walked past the sleeping gate keeper. He expected to be awakened by the sound of trucks or the braying of camels and dreamed through the entrance of the light-footed intruders.

They found Ahmed in a room of the house, eating a light meal while being fanned by a nubile, dark-skinned Moroccan girl, not more than fourteen years old.

"What do you want? Can't you see that I am busy? The office is closed, and we are too busy to build anything for you anyway," he spoke dismissively and waved to the door.

"We want some explosives, detonators, and wire," said Stephan quietly.

Ahmed jumped to his feet and said loudly, "Impossible! Get out!"

"Why is it impossible? You have plenty, and we need a little," said the implacable Stephan.

"The Germans, I mean French...the police. They insist I keep perfect records and report all my usage and anyone trying to steal or buy explosives. That is why we have a guard on the gate and dogs at night."

"But you don't report it all, do you, Ahmed?"

"Yes, yes, almost." Ahmed was calculating how much Stephan knew and whether Stephan would report to the authorities his little bookkeeping errors. He was also wondering if he would report this visit.

"We need one hundred pounds of explosives, four caps and junctions, four hundred feet of wire, and one detonator. How much?"

They had decided that Stephan should push to an early decision, "Yes" or "No." If they were rebuffed, they had determined that they would have to steal what they needed.

"How will you pay? The currencies in this town fluctuate and devalue daily," he asked; they had him.

Rick spoke for the first time, keeping his Arab robes around his face. "Diamonds."

"For diamonds, the price is five carats cut."

It was outrageous even by Arab standards, but they needed the stuff—now!

"Two," said Rick. "One now," he said as he showed him a flawless diamond of at least a carat, "and one when we pick up the stuff tonight."

"See how my friend trusts you?" asked Stephan. "Me, I would cut your throat and back up a truck. But we are men of our word and know that you are, too. We should like to take the detonator and caps now just so the world will see that we all keep our words."

"You don't trust me?" asked an aggrieved Ahmed.

"No!" said Stephan. "You ask too much a price; you think that there may be more money in this transaction. But there will not!"

They left quietly, walking slowly and attracting no attention.

Ahmed watched them and thought, *Foreigners up to no good*. If he told the Germans, there would be no reward, and they would take away the diamond he had received. Likely, the foreigners would then return, beat him, and ask for the diamond back or some other retribution. He could tell Signor Ferrari who might then give him a reward and let him complete the transaction with the foreigners.

At 8:30 P.M., Stephan and Rick, together with Suli, a camel driver, and his two camels, were at the contractor's door. The dog and the fence had been a problem, but Suli had been unusually adept at quieting then drugging the dog with a concoction from a bag on one of the camels.

"In the desert, one never knows what animals are about, so I keep the herb with the camels then mix it with camel food and a little spit."

Rick made a mental note not to eat anything prepared by Suli. They had seen Paul and the others at the Klein's. The six had inventoried their arms, with each producing a gun of different size and vintage, some with limited ammunition. There was also a cache of knives. To everyone's surprise, George, a quiet Frenchman, produced four grenades. Rick looked at him questioningly and received a shrug in reply. He took two, tossing one to Stephan, picked up a knife with a holder, and strapped it around his waist.

"We should be back in one hour. If we are not back by 9:30 P.M., disappear."

They all nodded silently, understanding the implications perfectly.

Ahmed stood in surprise.

"You are early," he said.

"Well, we expected Germans to be precise," said Stephen, again the spokesperson.

"You could have called out, and I would have opened the gate."

"It was already open," Stephan lied. A crowbar brought for the purpose had broken the chain.

"Is everything ready?"

"Yes, when I get paid!"

"You told no one?"

"No one, monsieur," said an aggrieved Ahmed. A bead of his sweat fell to the floor, and the sweat on his lips had increased. Was he lying, or was the tense situation really affecting his usual cool demeanor?

"Help the boy load the camels, and then we pay."

Ahmed hesitated, about to argue, but then went out.

"What do you think?" whispered Rick.

"He is a lying bag of shit!" whispered Stephan. "Good idea of yours to come early."

The transaction was completed, and as they prepared to leave, Rick said to Ahmed "Stay in your house tonight; there may be booby traps on your door. Whoever arrives can disable them in the morning."

"Why would you do this to me?"

"Because we don't trust you, remember?" said Stephan.

"What do you think?" asked Stephan as they were outside.

"I think he is sufficiently scared to sit tight until the morning. Why waste a grenade and bring attention to this area? Besides, it is five minutes to nine. Let's go!"

They left with Stephan leading the way, holding the reins of the lead camel.

Suli walked behind the second with a switch, and Rick was twenty yards behind in the shadows.

He was quickly aware that they were being followed. He stepped out with his gun. "Stop there! Where are you going?"

"They go where they please," said a voice behind him that was clearly holding a gun to his back. "Drop the gun!"

He did as he was told and turned to recognize the small Arab from the café a week ago.

"So, Signor Rick, where are you going with this potent merchandise?"

The two large fellows joined them. With a nod, one of them hurried off to continue his trailing of the camels.

"So, Ferrari sent you," said Rick. "Why is he so interested in my comings and goings, and how did you know it was me?"

"Our employer knows all things, and if he does not know, I find out."

Rick fingered the grenade and knife at his belt. They had not searched him so they did not have orders to kill him or to take him with them. Extortion, blackmail—of course, that was more of Ferrari's style. Ferrari knew that Rick had money and did not want to talk to the Germans, so, if he knew where Rick was, then he could blackmail Rick and get his money back.

"Well, go back and tell him that this time, you failed."

"I think I am the one with the gun and will give the orders."

"Not if you want to live," said Stephan very quietly behind him.

They tied the hands of the two Arabs together and to each other. Then Rick rigged a grenade between the two.

"One of you should hold the grenade, and if it drops, you have five seconds to get around a corner. And your friend has a large bump on the back of his large head about fifty yards that way," said Stephan pointing.

Three very chastened Arabs reluctantly reported to Ferrari. They were amazed at the reaction as Ferrari laughed aloud, genuinely amused and just said, "Rick, Rick, what have you got yourself into?" Then he stopped. What was he going to do with the explosives? Perhaps blow up the police station, the Café, or the Blue Parrot.

"Get out and double the security at the Blue Parrot and here at the café!" he snarled.

Meanwhile, Rick was thanking Stephan. "What made you come back?"

"The camel driver said you were no longer there so I dropped back, saw the big Arab, and whacked him on the head. Then I went round back until I heard voices, and the rest, you already know."

"Thank you."

Chapter Ten

A column of seven men and camels left the city before daylight and headed south. There had been arguments after they came back with the explosives.

"This is crazy," someone had said, "We are being watched! What about getting back? What about my wife, my children? We will all be missed if even for a couple of days."

Rick waited until they had all spoken about their fears. He had the same fears the previous night, together with some that he would not mention. He had seen the Germans in Spain and in France; they were machine-like and very, very thorough.

"We voted last night," he finally said. "Today, we bought explosives, hired camels for a trip you do not want to make, asked about train tables, and produced from hiding guns, etc. We voted last night, and we are going before daybreak."

"I must tell my wife," said Myron.

"You will not leave here; there are people now looking for this place. Your wife has handled worse than your being missing for a few days."

It was harsh but necessary. There was a rumble of complaint which was silenced by Stephan.

"Look, we agreed we need to do something. To do nothing or, worse, to be caught planning to do something is not acceptable."

They headed south as if heading to go southwest along the coast. It would appear to be a coastal pickup rendezvous. After three hours, they turned east for an hour and then northeast. At eleven, they stopped, pitched tents, ate, and had a sleep. They were tired. Lack of sleep the previous night, the adrenaline rush of the morning, and the walking for seven hours meant that they were exhausted.

Rick woke everyone at six, and they ate. It was cooling as the sun set brilliantly somewhere over Casablanca. They could not see the city, but each imagined that they could. Everyone was silent at that time, about five minutes, as the sun reached the horizon, seemed to grow bigger, then slipped into sleep.

"We must try to reach the railway line by tomorrow night," said Rick.

"Why?" Myron asked.

"That would be three days before they can assign the troops and send them," said Johann.

"The Germans are always precise, but the Arab railroad may not be. Let us be prepared earlier than late. I do not want to watch the train go by before we set the charges," explained Rick.

There was no reason then not to give them the whole plan, but he held back. They traveled for two nights mostly in silence, each with their own thoughts, their own fears. It was easier walking in the night, following Suli who was reading the stars. The camels' steady cadence made everyone keep up. They saw a campfire once and heard dogs barking which was quickly silenced by a shout carried over the desert. They stopped a couple of times to rest, and all complained of being out of shape. When it was time to move again in spite of the grumbles, they did not want to be left behind. At dawn, they stopped and pitched tents, ate, and lay down. Rick woke with a start. He lay still and thought, *What is wrong?*

He stood, looked around, and realized immediately that a camel and a camel driver were missing.

Damn! Damn! Damn!

He woke the others and pointed to the prints in the sand. "North, probably pick up the railway and follow it to Casablanca, or east to warn them to stop before our ambush," said Rick.

"Then someone should take the other camel and cut him off," suggested Myron.

"He probably took the faster camel. He is an experienced camel rider, and we don't know whether he went east or west."

While they were debating, the remaining camel stood, looked north, and brayed. They stood and could see Suli, turban flying, and the camel galloping to them.

"The railway line is three miles away and in a rocky area with plenty of cover," said Suli, not interpreting the different looks in the faces of the foreigners.

Rick was relieved and surprised. He should have thought it through: the camel driver had not volunteered but was just as culpable and had clearly heard all of their conversations.

"Good work, Suli. As soon as we have eaten, we can go and set up the charges."

"What is the hurry?" asked Johann.

"Let us just do it, and then I can explain the plan," said Rick.

They reached the line and, after a quick survey, saw that even though it would be difficult to dig under the line, the charge would be greater than if it were in sand. Picking points on both tracks to maximize the damage, they went to work in shifts. It was very hot, and the diggers looked constantly towards Rick, hoping he might call a break, but he was working, if anything, harder than they were. The charges were laid, and wires from the caps were spliced and strung to the detonator but not connected behind a rock about one hundred and fifty feet away.

Then, Rick showed each a mark he put on a railroad tie. It was a number "25." He paced twenty-five yards perpendicular to the mark.

"Anything on the train that is worth anything will be buried here. Now, we dig out the sand from this depression."

"Why? Why now? We are tired," more than one grumbled.

"Sit down, all of you, and listen to my thoughts."

They sat around.

"You, too, Suli."

"I need a volunteer to stay with me. We are not going back to Casablanca. The rest will leave after dark with a camel. If you walk, follow the railroad line until you can see the city, but not be seen. Then split up and circle the city before entering. Your story is that you went south on a rumor that a boat was going to Lisbon from the village dock there. If they ask about there being others, say you split and they must have gone further south. Make sure that you are seen in the city, hopefully, before we blow up the tracks."

The men looked at each other and at Rick, each assessing the plan, and each rehearsing his story when he got back to the city. They were just looking at Rick, but he knew what they were thinking; if he had anything to go back to, he would be thinking the same thing.

"Well?" He said finally, "There being no volunteers, we need to draw straws."

"I'll stay!" The voice was strong, determined, and a complete shock.

All heads turned to the speaker.

"I have nothing to go back to. My mother is dead, and my father and brothers beat me. I will stay for the great adventure," said Suli.

"Please take the camel back to the street of the owner and let him loose; he will be fine."

"Thank you, Suli. You do not have to do this," said Rick

"Yes, anyone of us would have stayed," said an obviously relieved Stephan who would have been Rick's first choice.

It made another decision easier.

"Paul, I respect your administration skills, but I am going to give my compass and the reins of the camel to Stephan for the trip back. He will push you all in order to keep you all alive."

They dug with a will and then took a couple of hours sleep before dusk then they left.

Rick and Suli watched them walking into the red orb of the sun, shimmering with the heat rising from their feet. They watched until the sun set and all were engulfed by the desert.

The next morning, before the sun rose, Rick and Suli dug out a smaller depression another twenty-five yards from the first. "Why?" asked Suli.

"Not sure," said Rick. "Just in case there is something that we find that the Germans should not have and neither should the underground, or not yet."

Several times, Suli seemed to disappear, and when Rick asked him about it, he said that it was similar to Rick disappearing in a city into doorways and shadows. He showed Rick how to use the landscape, the sun, the sand, and his cloak to blend and be difficult to see. Rick practiced, and although he improved, Suli always knew where he was and could creep up undetected.

Two days later, they were camped at the track when they felt the vibration and saw smoke in the distance. The train was not going fast due to the risk of sand on the rail or of a rockslide.

Suli shimmied up the telegraph pole and cut the wire. Rick ran to the detonator and connected the wires as Suli joined him.

The train had a machine gun and gunner mounted on top; he was not happy. It was hot, it was windy, and he was thirsty, having drunk all of his water an hour into the journey. Another hour to go, and there was nothing but sand. As he was thinking about being thirsty, that was all he could think about.

The charges went off as planned. As the engine went over the first charges, Rick pushed. There was a hesitation when everything was calm. Then the engine and the third coach lifted straight into the air.

The last thought that the gunner had was that the engine was somehow passing beneath him.

The blast did more damage than Rick thought possible. He saw, just before the blast, rows of soldiers in the third carriage sleeping, playing card, talking. They were doing ordinary and usual things; then they were dead.

He vomited, or he would have if he had eaten anything. There was total destruction in front of him. He had planned it; he had executed. They were soldiers; they were under orders.

Suli had no such emotions. Down in the wreckage, he was scavenging and brought Rick back to the present.

"What do we want from here?" he said, holding a German knife with an eagle's head carving on the top.

"There are probably some armaments, rifles, ammunition, and machine guns that the underground can use. Let us have the camel take them to the hole."

After three hours, the hole was almost full. They spent thirty minutes covering the cache.

Rick wanted to be gone by nightfall.

Rick went back to the other coaches; the second had contained the arms. The first coach had clearly been the officer's coach, so he resolved to spend some time looking for anything useful.

He found some ciphers, orders, and a list of names. The names looked familiar and included his own and four of the five members of the underground.

He would bury it, buy some time, and perhaps save their lives. Having them in his possession would mean an instant bullet. There were two safes. One had been open and the contents—Deutsch Marks—were scattered around. The other was heavy and locked. It was rumored that 50 percent of the safes in Germany used the Fuehrer's birthday. This did not! There was a desk thrown across the carriage broken in pieces. As he looked, he thought, then picked up the drawer and looked on the bottom. Two sets of numbers, two safes—it made sense.

The second set of numbers opened the safe which contained gold coins, obviously destined for the bank which would be receiving currency from all over the world; anyone with any small sense would want a gold base rather than the artificial rates set from Berlin.

They put the bulk of the gold into the second hole and filled it in.

Rick took some of the gold coins and hid them in his robes. He took some and, easing the leather of the saddle on the camel, squeezed them into the gaps.

They left without a backward glance. Vultures were already gathering, viewing the mayhem with relish, while communicating to their feathered brethren by some genetic radio link.

Chapter Eleven

Rick and Suli traveled southeast for the first night and then due east. They had stopped the following morning to eat and rest when Suli said, "Camel and man from the east."

The east was directly into the sun, but by quickly moving his fingers up and down while looking between them, Rick could see the shape of a camel with a rider.

"How did you know?" he asked, but Suli had disappeared.

Strange!

The stranger came to a halt and gave the traditional Arab greeting.

Rick returned it, and although he already had a beard, he realized that he had automatically covered the lower half of his face.

The stranger dismounted.

"Traveling alone?" asked the stranger.

Rick looked back at the tracks they had made. He decided upon a nonanswer.

"Where did you come from?" the stranger persisted.

"West," said Rick finally.

It was a general awareness that existed in the desert where traveling alone was uncommon, that two such men should meet was not necessarily accidental and both were being extremely reticent.

"Yourself?" Rick asked.

"East!"

"Will you eat? Such that I have, I share," said Rick, not altogether sure that he wanted him to stop. In fact, if he refused, he would be delighted and have his fears put to rest, but to not ask would alert the stranger to his concern.

The stranger was pondering the question. *Should he press on, or should he accept the hospitality?"*

"Thank you. If you have tea and bread, that would be most acceptable."

Rick was less accomplished than Suli was in preparing tea. The man went to his bag which was still on the camel and turned with a cup and a pistol. Rick realized his mistake: he was holding two cups.

"Where is your partner? When I saw your camp, there were two people—looks like two tracks coming in—and no one travels alone in the desert," said the gun-holding man.

Rick feigned a casual tone that was at odds with his turmoil. He had done everything wrong. Next time, he would be more careful.

Next time!

There might not be a next time; he was looking down the barrel of a Smith and Wesson.

"Well, you are traveling alone! Or are you?"

The man looked back east for just a second as Suli hit him from behind. Rick picked up the man's gun.

"I guess you are traveling alone. Meet my camel driver." Rick was now in charge. "Please sit down, and we can all have tea. British, that! But you are carrying an American gun. What else would we find in your bag, I wonder?"

"I am going to Casablanca. The train from El Alamein with Germans troops and some currency and gold did not arrive."

"Too bad for the Germans," said Rick. "So, you are German intelligence, and you think that we might know something?"

"Well, do you know anything?"

"Let me see your papers and orders, mister, or is it major?" said Rick.

"They are in my bag," said the stranger, starting to stand up.

"Sit down," said Rick "They are in your boot. The fake ones are in your bag."

The man laughed and slowly took off his right boot. He went to throw it at Rick, but Rick had moved and the boot landed at his feet.

"Thank you! Nice try! Now, sit still while I take a look."

Rick removed the sole and took out three pieces of paper. The first identified a Captain Aubrey Smith, US (United States) army liaison to British General Staff Egypt. Obviously, they still had no confidence that the British could hold any city. Well, that explained the Smith and Wesson and might save him from being shot as a spy even though he was not in uniform. Maybe! The second piece of paper was a map of Casablanca with several landmarks including the Café Americana.

The third letter was in code. Rick stared at it for a long time. He had seen this before, but where?

"Coded orders!" Captain Smith said in a voice that indicated he would not decode the instructions even under pressure.

Rick looked into steel blue eyes and knew it was true. He looked back at the paper and gambled. Looking back at the American officer, he said, "You are to meet a Paul Berger at the Café Americana."

The man was visibly shaken.

Rick had seen the code while being hidden by Paul Berger. He could not read the paper but had obviously guessed correctly.

"Are you Berger?" the soldier asked

"No! Who did you torture for this information?"

"People he helped get to Lisbon. Lazlo…."

"You tortured Victor Lazlo? He would never tell you."

"Obviously, you met Mr. Lazlo, and you are right, he was very reticent. He told us nothing, but he did bring a letter from Paul Berger on a napkin from that café."

"Now, your story, mister…?" asked the major. He nodded at his boot and papers. "You are not German sympathizers, and you are not laden down with gold."

"Mr. Jones," said Rick who believed some of the story but was never going to hear it all.

"Let's eat! Some of your dog chow for our guest, Suli, if you please."

Rick and Suli rode away following the tracks from the east. Captain Smith lay drugged, asleep in his tent. Rick had gone through the camel bags and had left the currency and the gun where they could be found. There had been nothing else of interest but the fake papers indicating another Austrian Jew, a man with a small manufacturing company, a little cash, and a picture of his wife presumed in hiding, waiting for money to spirit her to a new life. The information would have been enough for some zealous Nazi to have become judge and executioner. So what was so important to risk it all?

The more he thought about the question, the more he thought that the question was about himself.

What could be so important to risk it all? What was out there worth winning? Was Inspector Reynaud right? Was he trying to run away?

When he looked down the barrel of the gun, he was not scared. Did he not care?

Captain Smith, if that was his name, thought that there was a benefit worth risking everything for.

What would he risk everything for?

He had! Why had he given the letters of transit to Lazlo?

He could be in Lisbon, or in New York, right now.

Instead, he was following a stupid camel toward the biggest battle ever seen in Africa.

Chapter Twelve

That night, Rick sat looking at a million stars and thought about where they had been, where they were, and where they were going.

He felt responsible for Suli, although, in truth, he was less comfortable in the desert than his sleeping companion. The incident with the stranger was more worrying than he had earlier admitted. The man was evidently not Arab but was in the desert alone. How had he got there? He must have taken the train from Oran, similar to the German troops, and had left the train at Fez, or had avoided the train and joined a caravan which he had left at Fez or Meknes—probably, because no one wanted to take a train that was not going to arrive!

Next question: Were they going back? When and how?

Circuitous route? He drew where he thought they had been and where they might be in the sand. Then he admitted silently that he did not have a very good idea; going west or north, he would eventually reach the sea. South and east was desert and mountains for two thousand miles. So they must be within fifty miles of Fez. To Marrakech was about two hundred miles south. Each had the benefit of a river which went to the sea. First, they needed provisions, then going south, stay clear of Fez, and second, anyone blowing up a train would probably head north or west.

He slept and dreamed of swimming in the ocean, except the water was potable, and he slaked his thirst but still was thirsty.

Suli had already fed the camel and prepared breakfast. Rick was thirsty. He remembered his dream and reached for the water bottle.

"Suli, how far to Fez?" asked Rick

"Two days if Allah is willing."

"How far to Marrakech?"

"Ten, eleven days, if Allah is willing"

"Do you know the way?"

A shrug! Rick did not know if it meant "Yes" or "No," but there was no point in pressing the point since the answer had been given and would not change.

"Where can we get provisions and water?"

Suli pointed southwest, "Three hours," then pointed south, "Two hours."

Since south was the heading, he began instinctively thinking when he thought that the Arab mind was complicated but simple: Suli had pointed southwest first.

"So, that way it is. Why not south?" he said, pointing.

He was rewarded by a big smile. "Bad people kill then steal camel. Maybe steal gold."

It was surprising that the camel was worth more than the gold, but then, they were in the desert, so it made sense.

The camel seemed to understand the conversation and the conclusion as she set off at a brisk pace in the direction decided.

After about two and a half hours, there was a shimmering on the horizon which showed it to be a decent-size town. They circled and then followed a caravan in from the north side

The caravan wound through the town into a market square, harassed by hawkers and small children and watched from doorways and windows by eyes that, without moving, saw everything.

Rick walked as the other men—with a swagger and disdain—his eyes watching eyes watching eyes watching. Suli had moved the camel up from the end, but it still stood out, as unburdened and well cared for, against a slow, undulating struggle of dirty grey hide.

When the camels stopped and the burdens were lifted, a young man detached himself and approached Suli.

"Where are you from, and what are you doing here?"

"North, looking for a load to carry," said Suli.

"We have plans to go back to Oran when we have traded and sold the goods which have come in from across the seas. We are taking dates and raw metals back to Oran. There is gold here and south," the man said.

"I will think about it. Your camels are all old and tired," Suli remarked.

"They are just stupid animals," said the young man walking away. "Good for carrying, beating, then eating."

Leaving the women and children to unload their wares, Rick had walked with the other men into an eating and drinking establishment which they appeared to know and where they were known.

The men separated into groups with the merchants from the town, and a noisy haggling took place.

Rick sat alone with a powerful drink dependent upon camel milk and an indifferent platter of food which tasted much better for the fact that it was hot, not sandy, and tasted of some meat.

A man detached himself and sat opposite Rick.

"What do you have to sell?"

Rick thought with some satisfaction that he had been recognized as an Arab. Without a mirror, he could only imagine that his dirty beard, dirty face, his dusty dirty robe, and the body odor which he was now used to would fool anyone.

"What do you buy? What do you pay with?" Rick said as he continued eating.

"Anything."

"I want to join a camel train south," said Rick.

"Camels leave in two days. You want to buy a camel? You need provisions; ask for me—Mamoud, in the market."

Then he stood and left.

Rick continued eating, watching. The exchange did not seem to have attracted any attention; he had received some information without giving anything, or not much, away.

He saw Suli looking at the door, waved, gave a quick shake, and disappeared. The owner was standing, looking at his empty plate.

"See that, boy?" said Rick "He is probably at your back door; feed him!"

The man shrugged, headed out, then came back.

"Have you a room?" Rick asked.

"A bed," said the big man. "You owe for food and feeding the boy."

They haggled a little, and the man showed him a room with five beds. Rick paid in advance and went to search for Suli.

Suli was still at the back door, eating with the gusto of young people as if it were his last meal and was from a fine dining restaurant. When the owner saw Rick, he put more food onto the plate while Suli showed appreciation and Rick, with supreme effort, kept down his just digested meal.

"Will you stay here, Suli?"

"No, no, I must stay with the camel."

"Then remember to use the saddle as your pillow."

"Yes, Señor Rick. You also be careful."

A very good point, thought Rick, touching the gun under his robes.

"I want to see this Mamoud about provisions for a caravan south. We should take some silk, do you think?"

Suli was clearly not used to being asked for an opinion and shrugged.

"The camels will be happy to be working," he said.

Rick found Mamoud's emporium and saw that he was going to be able to get everything he needed. Then it was a question of price.

The first thing was to start negotiations, with the obligatory tea with dates and figs while asking for less or more of some of the essentials.

"How much is silk? How much for cotton? How much is a load of wine?" Haggling...haggling...more tea.... "Yes, we must meet tomorrow," Rick finally said.

Then the dangerous part—to find out the price he can get for a diamond.

Back at the eating place, the landlord was looking pleased with his business. *He must get a cut of each deal*, thought Rick.

"Mamoud," he said, "is he reliable? Does he give the best price for gold?"

There was a glint which faded in a practiced way from the folds of the landlord's face. "Mamoud is very fair. If you can give me the gold, I can get a price for you from Señor Davide."

"Just asking; I never said that I had any gold," said Rick, leaving.

Rick took a bucket of water to the back and, after putting his gun into the bag he carried, stripped naked, washed his clothes, and, while they dried, washed himself in the cold bucket of dirty water. It was wonderful. He felt clean, well, cleaner.

Rick dressed and went back to the market square, starting to fill again as the sun was setting.

"Señor Davide?" he asked one of the many urchins.

"I will take you," said the eager boy sensing, in a way only beggars could, that there would be a coin for him in that simple task.

The boy took off quickly, turning frequently to make sure that Rick was following then waiting until he caught up.

They were clearly in a more prosperous part of town. Some of the homes had men lounging outside. *Guards*, thought Rick.

"Here," said the boy, stopping in front of a building no different from the rest, except that there, there were two guards.

Rick gave him a coin and said, "Wait. I need a guide back,"

The boy looked at the two guards, a little unsure. "I wait," he said finally.

"I have some business with Señor Davide," said Rick.

"What kind of business?"

"You Davide?" asked Rick as the guard sniggered.

After a long silent stare, Rick turned to the boy. "Let's go," he said and walked away. That time, the boy walked alongside him.

"What do you think, boy, Mamoud or Davide?" Rick asked as he gave him another coin.

"Men who deal with Davide, too many of them get sick and die, or they accidentally cut their own throats."

"Thanks," said Rick and gave him another coin. "Is there another place to stay?" he asked.

"Yes, you can stay with my sister. Come, I will take you."

Rick was taken to a small house with many small rooms. After introductions to a petite young woman, the boy left. There were two small cots in the room which must be folded away during the day as it was also the living room and the kitchen.

It took a great deal of explaining that NO, he only wanted to sleep. She was obviously disappointed until he agreed to pay the same money. Just before he fell asleep, he realized that it was the boy's bed. He slept anyway, knowing he was safe, that the boy was on guard outside.

That his reputation with the neighbors would be acceptably sullied was perhaps a bonus unearned.

The following morning, the boy walked him back, grinning widely. He and his sister were in funds, and his sister had not been crying that morning.

The landlord came running out and said, "Two men were looking for you last night."

"I thought they might, but I found myself a woman," Rick said.

"Ah, there you are," a small man in a white suit with one of his guards had walked in.

"Senor Davide, I presume?" asked Rick, stepping back.

Rick felt a hand grab him and a knife at his throat. The second guard had been behind him.

"Now, let's see what is in the bag," said the guard, stepping forward.

However, before he could reach Rick, the man behind gave a grunt and collapsed. Rick reached into his bag, pulled out a gun, and shot the man in front of him through the kneecap; he fell screaming. Davide stood rooted in fear.

Rick turned around. The guard had a knife in his back; the handle had a swastika on it. He pulled it out, wiped it on the man's robes and gave it back to Suli.

"Thank you! I heard the bird call and moved backwards as you threw, or he would have cut my throat."

"Señor Davide, it looks as though you need new guards, and it is a long walk back to your home. Landlord, I think you had better think up a good story for this mayhem and your part in it before your guests come down. Suli, let's go. You, too, boy, out the back."

Davide was imploring the stricken guard to get up and take him home. The landlord was dragging a very large weight into the kitchen. Someone looked into the front door and quickly withdrew. It was important; there were scores to be settled, debts paid and collected, although it appeared one was settled.

By whom?

Thirty minutes later, sipping tea with Mamoud, a transaction was nearing completion. It had been greatly accelerated by an interruption.

"It appears that there is some excitement in town. The tavern has closed; a guard of Señor Davide crawled into the square where his throat was slit with his own knife. Senor Davide was stripped naked by a mob and is sequestered in his own home. How fortunate that you have been taking tea with me, or you might have been suspected."

Rick spent the night with the boy and his sister, leaving Mamoud with the promise of picking all the necessary silk and provisions in time to leave with the next caravan south. Suli and the boy went around the market buying food. They met back at the house, and the sister cooked for the four of them.

The next morning, Rick and Suli left with the caravan for Marrakech.

Chapter Thirteen

There were several surprises in Marrakech. However, the biggest was before they arrived. Rick and Suli had continued to practice their hiding while on the trek. The benefits of traveling in the caravan were in finding the oasis, being protected from bandits by numbers and from the relationship that the members had forged, not only with each other but with those other travelers they met. A benefit for Rick was that they left him alone.

Rick had asked Suli to teach him pickpocketing since neither of them could hide from the other anymore. It was during one such practice that Rick stopped suddenly, the color drained from his face. The shock was such that he had been surprised in his life but never, never like this.

Suli reacted with the look on Rick's face and, immediately understanding the cause, stepped back and shrank.

They stood silently, facing each other—Rick's face questioning; Suli afraid, apologetic.

"I'm sorry," said Suli quietly.

They were well apart from the rest of the caravan and would not have been heard talking in a normal voice or even shouting.

Rick whispered, "You are a girl!"

"Are you going to beat me, rape me?" said Suli.

"No," Rick said, bewildered. "Sit. Tell me why? Trust me."

The story took most of the night.

Suli's mother had died in giving birth, so mercifully had the baby. Suli was probably nine or ten then. Her father, who had regularly beaten her mother, deprived of sexual attention, turned to Suli. He beat and raped her. Eventually, her brothers had also raped her after she foolishly asked for their understanding. She was tired, doing all the chores expected of a woman during the day and then awake all night fearing the dark.

They belonged to a tribe of nomads. They herded camel from pasture to pasture, guided by the stars or position of the sun, or, sometimes, by the wind and how it blew waves on the desert, or how the trees leaned from the prevailing westerly direction.

Suli planned for weeks to run away. She secreted food a little each day. The catalyst came unexpectedly. Her oldest brother came in the middle of the night from guard duty, watching that the camels were not stolen or wandered away. He smelled. He dropped his clothes and pulled her, roughly tearing the thin muslin undershirt she was wearing. As she rolled, her hands went out, and she felt his knife under her right hand. He jumped on her, oblivious to everything except his current desire. Her hand came over in reaction, stabbing him in the back. The shock stopped him, but he managed to hit her in the face. She hit back, still holding the knife, the handle like a knuckle-duster. She hit and hit him until he was unconscious, or dead.

Without thinking, she put on his clothes, took the knife, then quickly walked to the camels. The smell was reassuring to the herd; she took a camel, putting on the saddle and mounting automatically. She was five miles from the camp when she realized that she had left without her food and without water.

The stars gave her a bearing; she headed west because she knew that the big towns were at the coast. She traveled for two days, and although she had not eaten, she felt a freedom that she had never experienced even when her mother had been alive. She was dozing in the saddle, delirious from lack of water; they had passed just a few miserable plants from which she had sucked some moisture. The camel pulled to the right, and she had not the power to correct him When the camel stopped, she opened her eyes to find a water hole. The camel was drinking. She commanded him to kneel, fell off, and drank until she remembered not to drink too much. She found some dates, dug up some roots, and slept for a whole day. The braying of the camel woke her, and looking out to the northeast, she saw a camel train approaching. It was clearly not her father's, but she was apprehensive since her experience was not to trust anyone. The lead rider was somewhat ahead of the pack of camels.

"Boy, you here alone?" the rider asked.

"Yes, Sir," she replied, relieved that she had been mistaken for a boy; she felt safer.

"My name is Suli," she said, giving her brother's name.

"Where are you headed?" the bearded man asked.

"The coast," said Suli.

"We are headed to Casablanca, leave first thing in the morning, if you would like to follow us."

Suli had been a boy ever since and learned to sit with men and be quiet. Suli had existed picking pockets, carrying questionable loads with the camel, and stealing food when necessary, all without remorse.

The next day, they arrived in Marrakech. There was lots of news about the war. Those who were pro-Vichy said that the Germans and Italians were in

Cairo, that the Vichy garrison in Libya was securing the western desert. Those who were for the Free French said that the Italian army had totally surrendered, that the Allied Forces of Britain, Australia, New Zealand, and India were in Tobruk, and the Free French had the Vichy forces surrounded.

It was very clear to both sides. It was clear to Rick that they could not be both true, but that it was likely that both sides had some element of truth.

The Foreign Legion had claimed credit for blowing up the train and showed, as proof, the guns recovered from where sources had told them to look.

Berger, when questioned on his knowledge of the raid, said that he knew nothing as he had been in Casablanca, which had been confirmed by several reliable witnesses.

The Germans sent a squadron of Stukas and dive-bombed the Free French garrison at Brothersville. Fortunately, most of the garrison was on patrol, and the supplies were all hidden deep underground. It did look good on German film and provided Vichy and Free French propaganda with an excuse for two new conflicting stories.

Rick sold the load of material to a merchant suggested by Mahmoud. He asked the merchant for the name of a reputable goldsmith. Informed that it was an oxymoron, he staked out the three names given to him. He could only approach one, so he had to be sure.

He saw a man approach the storefront, check both ways, and go inside; the man looked familiar. Rick thought hard then remembered that the man had been at the rear of a group of pro-Free French talking about the Foreign Legion raid. As the man went inside, he was about to follow when a movement caught his eye; the man was being followed. Why? Rick remained in the shadows. When the man came out, his follower went inside.

Strange!

Rick followed the man to a nearby café. When he was sure that there was no one following, he sat down next to the man.

"You were followed to the goldsmith."

"Who are you, and why do you care?"

"Rossignol," said Rick. "I have confidential business with a goldsmith. I need to know one I can trust. And you are?"

"Vachon, my Italian butterfly. We have trusted that man, but I need to be as careful as you."

"How much is one ounce of gold worth?" Rick asked.

"Buying or selling? Buying or selling for Francs, or Marks, or Lira?"

"Give me the ranges," said Rick, "it is for the test"

Armed with the information, Rick left.

The address was on a busy street. Rick passed the door before backtracking to a door set into a wall with the basic information of an "international trader." It was clear that either an introduction was necessary, or that business was conducted elsewhere.

He knocked, and a man opened the door a crack, saw a businessman, or at least not an armed bandit, and opened the door fully with the traditional greeting, "Allahu akbar!"

Rick responded, "God is great!'" It was clear that the man was not the "international trader." Rick followed through an elaborate courtyard with fountains and a pool to another door where the man knocked and entered.

Rick was invited into the goldsmith's office, which looked like a film set for Arabian nights, and found a middle-aged, medium-looking man with Arab and European features and a very large Arab guarding the door. The goldsmith was looking through a loop at a diamond which he had just separated from a setting.

"What brings you, a traveler, to my humble home? Where are my manners? Hazma, bring us tea."

The goldsmith had made an intelligent observation, or he knew his customers. He had also, in some strange manner, disarmed his visitor. It was a very clever move and very subtle.

"Allah is great! I need to buy some gold," responded Rick.

"Ah! Very short supply," said the man and quoted a figure at the high end of the range given by "Vachon."

Rick let him see the money they had received from the merchant. "I was expecting that it would be half that amount."

Rick needed to play his hand.

"Do you buy for the same rate?" he asked, showing him the one-ounce German gold coin.

"Where did you get that?" asked the goldsmith, clearly recognizing the coin or its description.

There was a silence finally broken by the goldsmith.

"I can give you the same price," he said without haggling. "Is there more?"

"Let me think about it. I can come back in one hour. Can I trust you to say nothing?"

"With my life!" said an aggrieved goldsmith.

Rick left, but Suli had come into the courtyard and was haggling with the doorman over some silk.

The goldsmith went to the door and watched Rick go before picking up the phone.

The phone rang and rang until finally picked up.

"Herr Braun, if you please."

Suli could only hear the goldsmith.

"A man came in with a coin you described—one ounce with an eagle....No, Arab.... No, he left; he will be back in an hour.... Yes, I am sure. I told him I could buy whatever he had at a very generous price."

Rick, Suli and "Vachon" sat at a table across the street.

"I gave him the new meeting place location this morning. He must have told Heinz. What a fool I was to trust him *with my life*. He must be eliminated or compromised," said a contrite Frenchman known to Rick as Vachon.

"Or both," said Rick.

Rick knocked and entered the goldsmith's thirty minutes after leaving.

"I thought you said an hour," the goldsmith said.

"I thought you said that I could trust you upon your life!" said a very calm Rick. "Herr Braun should be on time, being German. I cannot do business with a man without honor. Good-bye."

The man was clearly sweating; Rick left.

He stepped outside, and Vachon nodded to the left: Herr Braun had just turned the corner.

Vachon thanked them and gave Rick a ring. Inside the ring was a cross of Lorraine, symbol of the Free French. He also provided traveling papers for a boat.

Rick had decided that Marrakech was too hot; they should go back to Casablanca where, at least, he had a better idea who were the good guys and who were the bad.

At the boat, Vachon shook their hands and said, "The goldsmith is dead, also Herr Braun. The swordsman killed both. Apparently, he could not work for a man with no honor, and Herr Braun made the mistake of saying that he would kill the man who killed his source before he took out his gun. Strange sense of justice; sometimes, stuff just happens."

He paused then said, "Rumor has it that an American landing force left the US five days ago headed east. No one knows where they are headed—England, Mediterranean. If the Med, it could be Alexandria or Greece, or a new front in Algiers."

Chapter Fourteen

The return to Casablanca was different and the same as the first time. Rick came by boat instead of by train, scrutinized by an army of watchers. He arrived dressed as an Arab instead of the suit and tie he had favored two years previous. He wore the mahogany skin of a desert dweller, not the pallid insipid color of a Parisian. He smelled—bad!

However, there were other things that had not changed. He still had the memory of the last time he had seen Ilsa. Whether he was happy or sad at the memory depended upon the time of day, the street he walked on, the stage of the moon, or…nothing at all. What a mess! Wanted by the police, not wanted by…. For the first time in his life, he felt lonely. Not unhappy, alone. He laughed aloud at himself. He was alone with a million people around, jostling with the noise only a North African market town can generate.

The passengers all had their papers checked. Rick, separated from Suli, shuffled forward in the resigned manner of his fellow passengers.

"Ahmed Zawfri? What is in the bag?"

Rick grunted as had the previous passenger and opened the bag which contained clothing and a length of fabric which might be used as a gift if one was visiting. There was also the purse from which he had taken his papers with a small amount of local currency. The official expertly pocketed about half of the currency. Rick grunted a protest which both of them knew was merely a gesture. The official had not noticed the money belt nor did he know about the gun Rick had kept in the waistband in the small of his back.

The watchers saw all of this exchange without changes in expression. Rick walked through them unseen; he was invisible, of no interest to any faction. There were, of course, watchers watching the watchers. If a watcher showed interest in someone, anyone, then it was of interest to the second group.

Were there watchers of watcher watchers?

Probably!

After all, it was Casablanca, a crossroad.

Suli joined Rick in a side street with a wide grin "That was good. I noted where he pocketed your money and, in a small altercation, lifted the total contents of his pocket. Quite a haul, too! He must do very well. But how will he explain this to his supervisor expecting a cut of a full boat from the south?"

Suli was laughing while Rick's eyes flicked from side to side to see if there was any interest being shown in them. He could not see any, and they moved away from the waterfront into the streets more familiar to Suli. The camel had been sold in Marrakech.

During the last few weeks, Rick had discussed some of his previous occupation with Suli who had shown a great deal of interest in settling down.

Later that night, actually in the early hours of the morning, the lights were out at the Café Americaine; most of the staff had left. The door opened just enough that a man in the shadows recognized the exiting figure of Sam, the piano player. Sam moved off down the street to the west. There was an almost full moon directly overhead so that it was like daylight. Still, he did not know that he was being followed. The follower noted with satisfaction that he was the only follower.

Then to catch up to Sam and see that they both reached the place Sam called home without being seen.

Sam put the key into the door; something was not quite right.

"Is someone there?" he whispered.

In reply, there was a faint humming, somewhat familiar but out of place. He stopped, frozen. The door not yet open, a chill went through his body in spite of the heat.

"What is that noise? You never could hum worth a damn! Come on in; let's have a drink" Sam spoke without turning, and the follower walked with him through the door which was then double bolted behind them.

"Mr. Rick, I thought…." Sam turned to the dark man in Arab dress.

"Who are you?" he said.

Rick laughed. "Fooled even you, Sam?"

"Almost made me turn white," said a shaken Sam, now laughing. "Now, I need that drink."

Rick explained the outfit and most of what had happened since they had last spoken the night Strasser was killed.

Sam said that the café was not as busy but appeared more profitable. Sam was getting twenty-five percent of the profit shown, but he knew that Ferrari was hiding some. There appeared to be drug sales by Ferrari who was also a user. Monsieur Reynard had been forced to resign and had, it was rumored, gone to fight with the Free French in Brotherville. Sam had converted most of Rick's cash and his own salary and bonuses into gold and diamonds. He had persuaded Ferrari that he should leave the piano on stage to make more room for the tables; the real reason was that he could only move the stool with difficulty.

Berger had been questioned extensively about the train, but since Heinz had seen him at the café the night that the train was derailed, he was released, but followed. Berger and about twenty other detainees were asked about the munitions, some papers, and overdue payroll. The Germans seemed more interested in their pay, according to some accounts.

Then the Free French had claimed responsibility for the train derailment, shot up a Vichy patrol, and suggested that the Germans come and get their stuff back. The Germans had answered with Stukas.

"Sam, have you used different goldsmiths? Who can we trust?"

"Yes," said Sam "Some Vichy, some neutral. I trust NONE of them."

"Well, can you take this," said Rick, producing a coin, "to a neutral or pro-Free French dealer and have him design it into a bracelet? Watch him, make sure that it is done, and let him assume that you got it from the club. Indicate that he is the only one who knows, and therefore, if you are questioned or followed, it will be clear who talked. He will ask you for ten percent; you will offer two or you can go to his competition. Give him five percent; we shall need him."

"Is this...?" asked Sam wide-eyed.

"Yes! Ask no more questions. You know nothing; keep it that way for your safety."

"Then, you were in Brotherville?"

"No!" chuckled Rick. "Ask no more questions!"

"Okay."

Rick continued, "I will send messages using the following: if someone at the club asks you to play "As Time Goes By," ask them when. They will say "now," "sometime tonight," or "anytime." That means as soon as you can get away or when you finish for the night or the next day at nine in the morning. We can meet at the Café Yacoute in the middle of Avenue Lalla Yacoute or at your apartment if it is after the café is closed."

"Okay, Rick. Anything else?"

"Yes. Can you ask Berger to be at the Café Yacoute tomorrow night at ten?"

"Berger has gone—Foreign Legion. Funny, I never thought he was that brave."

"War does funny things to people" said Rick. "Ask Carl to give the message to whoever is now in charge."

"Shall I tell him...," Sam started to say.

"No!" said Rick. "Tell no one that I am in town. Do not explain to Carl. One more thing, can you find a job for a young man at the café?"

"What can he do?" questioned Sam.

"Nothing, but he is very quick and very willing to learn."

"Have him ask for me at the back door at six tomorrow...I mean tonight."

"Yes. Time I was gone." Rick rose and said, "Thank you, Sam."

The next night, Rick stood in the shadow on Avenue Lalle Yacoute watching the café diagonally opposite. At exactly nine, two men in European suits entered and sat at the rear of the café, facing the door. They had both examined the room carefully upon entering. One had done it, Rick noted, in a very professional way. He recognized both; one of them was carrying a Smith and Wesson gun.

He waited. *Where is the watcher? There!*

The moonlight had shown a shadow, not really a shadow but a shape not quite right. He moved away from the café.

The man watching the café heard a noise, turned, and then, just as quickly, turned back to watching the café; it was just another Arab urinating at the side of the building

He was therefore surprised when the Arab spun him around and held a knife at his throat.

"You want money?" he asked.

"Don't move. What are you carrying, a German Glock, or a Smith and Wesson like your new friend?" asked Rick

"What are you talking about?"

"Either is an offense; also associating with known Free French sympathizers, Stephan."

"Who are you?" asked the then bewildered Stephan.

"I am the one with the knife at your throat," said Rick. "Now Berger is gone to the Foreign Legion, so who is the new guy with Mr. Smith, or Herr Schmidt, or Señor Smith, or Field Marshall Smith?"

"Why should I tell you anything?" said a shaken Stephen. Who was this maniac in Arab clothes holding his freedom and life in the balance? There was something vaguely familiar, but the man's beard, clothes, smell were telling him one thing, the Parisian French another.

"Why do you trust the men in there?" asked Rick.

"Hershel Berg is German Jew who recently arrived. Mister...." He stopped. "The other man is an American."

"I want to meet the American alone here tomorrow morning at ten."

"He won't."

"He will! Tell him that we should be more careful of hospitality in the desert and what we eat. Oh, and Stephan, at ten in the morning, he does not need a minder."

The Arab was gone, and Stephan walked along the road in front of the Café Yacoute, a signal that all was clear and to abort the meeting.

The next morning, Rick sat opposite "Mr. Smith," drinking a very good espresso. Rick looked the part of a prosperous Arab businessman.

"Why did you leave my gun, my camel, and my supplies?"

"You were in the desert; it is a very dangerous place. Why are you here in Casablanca, another dangerous place?"

"For Richard Blaine, wanted by the Gestapo in Paris, German Army in Morocco, Vichy police in Casablanca, suspected of aiding the enemy, consorting with known provocateurs, helping enemies of the Third Reich escape, suspected in the vicious murder of one Major Strasser, sabotage, grand theft, wanted for questioning regarding running guns to the armies of the enemies of the Third Reich, and a missing shipment of gold. Did I miss anything?"

"Suspected! Suspicion of guilt means nothing at all!" said a stunned Rick. Recovering, he said, imitating the manner of speech of his fellow coffee drinker, "Suspected in the elimination of a German spy and framing of his spy masters in Marrakech."

"Thank you," said Smith, "we wondered who was responsible. Had we known you were there, we would have put two and two together."

"Your turn," said Rick. "Why are you here?"

"I am here to organize the taking over of certain facilities by the Free French and the Foreign Legion in the event of an invasion by the American Forces"

"This is the week, isn't it? Where?" asked Rick. Smith took a huge breath. This was as strange a circumstance as he could remember, but his gut told him that not only could he trust this man, but that he needed him.

"Because you cannot, with your rap sheet, go to the police or the Gestapo, I can admit that yes, tomorrow at dawn, here at Casablanca. Final meeting tonight, cellar of the house Stephan rents. Stephan will be leading the meeting, of course. Will you be there?"

"Yes, but you will not see me," he sat, thinking. "Maybe I can help. I am a flier. I can take the airport. Give me six very good men, and I will bring them overalls. They should be available to go directly from the meeting since the airport closes at eleven until six in the morning. We can make sure that the runways will be booby-trapped until the marines arrive. Also, since this is their first landing, I need some papers saying to the invaders that I am in a white hat, even if it is a kepi."

They walked out into the brilliant sunshine. It seemed impossible that in twenty-four hours, there would be an event which would shatter the inevitability of German dominations of Africa and the Middle East oilfields and that they would be watching history being made.... No, they would play a part.

Hope everyone is on time, thought Rick.

Chapter Fifteen

It was surreal to be talking and thinking war, shooting, killing, fires, buildings falling, the rumble of heavy artillery, and tanks in the streets while normal life continued in the streets. The day was ordinary while extraordinary events were unfolding.

There was an impulse to grab people, shake them, and make them understand; understand what?

There was an impulse to rush energy, a need to be doing something.

Rick surveyed the chaos; he resisted the impulse to rush. First, he must make contact with Sam, then decide the arms he would need, the cover they would use, and, finally, go over the plan with the men assigned.

The road on which Sam lived was busy, so there was no difficulty in reaching his door unseen. It was even easier to knock and then, with no answer, break in. Sam was gone, and since he had very little outside interests, the next stop would be the café.

The café was not busy, so Rick slipped into the back by the door he had used when he had left six months before. From where he stood in the shadow, he could hear Sam rehearsing songs with a strong European flavor, with a singer he had not heard before. Wondering what to do, he saw Suli passing with a plate of figs.

"Suli!" he whispered. It was enough to stop the fig carrier in his tracks.

"Señor Rick. I did not see you; therefore, you have improved greatly."

"Suli, you look smart in your waiter uniform. Is everything well?"

"I am learning much, and soon, I hope to try bartending and even helping in the casino, although with old habits, it might be a little too much temptation being in the casino," Suli said laughing.

"Suli, I need to speak to Sam. Please go by the piano and ask him to play 'As Time Goes By.' He will ask you when; tell him 'Now!'"

Rick waited long enough to hear the start of the familiar ballad and the new singer's attempt to give a convincing emotional performance then left.

The Rue Valle Yacoute was bustling. On the wide promenade with the trees lining the street; it was just a normal day. Rick sat inside the café making mental lists and plans. He was not surprised to see Sam five minutes into his cerebral circumulations. However, he was surprised that he was not alone. Had Sam been followed, or did he not understand that this was a private code? As they approached, he thought that the reality was something else. He had entrusted the message to the only person who could recognize him, so Suli was also entrusted with the code.

"Sorry, boss. Suli insisted on coming so he could tell you something. He will go as soon as you know," said an apologetic Sam.

"Señor Rick, something is happening. The figs were for Herr Heinz, the German commander, and some other officers. They were talking in German but were agitated and talked of 'Gerien auf Casablanca' and 'heraus.' Where are they going? Will we be unprotected?"

"Well, since you are both here, sit down and listen very carefully. Sam, stay home tonight; call in sick. Suli, I can use you if you are interested in a little adventure. It will be dangerous."

"Another train?" inquired Suli.

"Why, am I no help?" complained Sam.

"Because...," Rick waited until they were served, and everyone had gone about their business, "the Americans are landing at dawn, and we have to help secure the city to prevent the loss of a great number of lives."

Suli left to go back to Café Americana, taking a note from Sam professing an upset stomach to give to the bandleader. Suli was to leave in time to make a rendezvous.

Rick had a revolver and knife. The other men had similar armaments. Suli preferred just to carry his knives, the curved Curia, and a German souvenir. They took some explosives.

The plan was simple. It was made easier by being able to trust Suli to do it right. Rick and Suli cut through the fence and circled back to the guards at the gate as the other five members of the team came walking up to the gate. There were four guards, and they were overpowered by Rick and Suli when they were covered by the others before they could raise the alarm.

The guards were stripped and tied up. Two of Rick's men manned the gate with instructions to let no one in.

It was all bluff. Could they keep up a front for a few hours? Yes, as long as no one panicked.

The two men in guards' uniforms drove a truck from the front gate to the tower. Rick, Suli, and the others were in the back. At the tower, the two in the front seat went into the front door; Suli and Rick went around the back. When they had gone, the fifth person guarded the front entrance against any surprise visitors. It was not necessary since there were no flights after dark; the only people on duty were a radio operator and four other men. The radio operator was listening to the radio, and the guards were playing cards. The men were all Vichy inductees and were not particularly fond of the Germans. They had secured a cushy posting and were a little aggrieved. Their humor was not improving by being stripped and questioned by a disheveled Arab speaking a Parisian French.

Rick found out what he needed to know about the other troops and their locations: There were mechanics working in the hangers and some pilots and navigators in the operations room at the other end of the building.

Rick contacted the front gate and arranged for one man to go back to pick up the prisoners and bring them to the supply store. Leaving a man familiar with the radio in the tower, the other troops were rounded up. The pilots and navigators were next. There was a large padlock on the store room, and even with the stores, no one seemed anxious to break out with these armed men of indefinite numbers outside.

Rick was not inclined to imprison the maintenance workers as they were probably not pro-Vichy, but he could not let them leave either.

There was so much noise in the hangars that they did not know that anything had happened until the lights were switched off to get their attention.

"The airfield has been taken over by anti-Nazi and anti-Vichy forces. The field is completely surrounded!" Rick lied. "You will appreciate that we are going to close and lock this hangar door, so make yourselves comfortable."

There was some grumbling. "I said that I would be home tonight," one said.

"Or," said Rick as though no one had spoken, "you can be locked up in a dark closet until we have completed our mission." The grumbling was diminished and changed to a more enquiring tone, each man asking a neighbor what it meant.

Something was nagging at his brain; there was something he had missed. Rick scratched the back of his neck. *What? What can it be?* Everything was easy. If everyone else at the telegraph office, the radio station, and those watching the main police station were having as quiet a night, then it would be decreed a very successful night.

Suddenly, there was a call from the radio operator in the tower, "German soldiers approaching the front gate. What are the instructions?" That was it! The pilots and navigators were German; no one was making a fuss. They knew that Germans were coming; they all knew there were Germans planning to leave that night.

"How many?" asked Rick.

"Two staff cars and a lorry, probably officers in the cars and a dozen soldiers in the truck"

"Let them in, but try to separate the truck from the cars."

There were some anxious moments, then the two cars came up to the tower. The men should have been recognizable to any of the officers, but that night they were agitated and not giving full attention to their surroundings.

They all gave desultory salutes which were returned by a visibly shaking imposter.

"Is our plane ready?"

"Yes, Sir. We kept it in the hangar out of sight. Fewer people will see you leaving" Hershel Berg said, pointing.

"Quite!" said Heinz, looking a little askance at the Vichy. "Tell the soldiers in the truck to follow."

The staff cars drove to the hangar which opened then closed behind them. It was difficult to know who was more surprised—the maintenance crews or the German officers. The truck came to the tower, unable to see the staff cars, and stopped. The front windshield was broken where the barrier had *accidentally* slipped as they came through it.

"The plane will be ready soon. Step into the operations room; it is more comfortable." There were, in fact, twelve soldiers, and once in the room, they put down their rifles and took out cigarettes. They did not notice, at first, the rifles disappearing. But by then, it was too late. With a few scuffles, they were eventually herded into the storeroom.

As the sun was rising, a crowd gathered at the front gate. It was made up of women looking for husbands to come home and refugees. The refugees were pro-Vichy or German-favored businessmen who had heard on the radio that the Americans had landed. The GIs were fighting toward the city against tenacious, pro-Vichy forces that were badly outgunned and being shelled from the sea.

Fortunately, the soldiers were too occupied in the approaches to the city to bother those at the airport. The Free French troops were then in their own clothes. Smith called with "Congratulations!" and asked if they could hold on for a few more hours.

Rick ordered the release of the maintenance crews, and the officers were transferred to the private office of the chief of airport security. Some of the officers appeared to have bruises. They had expended the ammunition in their revolvers at the corrugated hangar walls

The next morning, a jeep drove to the front gate, accompanied by a contingent of about fifty men.

The gate was opened, but the jeep did not enter. A lieutenant stood in the back of the jeep and said, "Sergeant, go tell these men to surrender their weapons and put their hands in the air." The sergeant came to where Rick stood and relayed the message.

"Sergeant, tell the lieutenant to go f.... himself. We have secured the airfield. We are tired; we have been here for forty hours. He wants my weapons; have him come and take them. We are going home."

It was the officer's first command, and he was rapidly losing face.

"No rag-topped Arab is telling me what to do!" he spluttered.

"But, sir," said the sergeant, too late to warn his commanding officer who was then moving toward Rick, taking out his revolver.

Rick feinted in apparent fear of the lieutenant, then grabbed the lieutenant's gun, hit him in the face, and kicked him in the groin before he hit the ground.

The sergeant stepped forward and said, "Sorry, Sir. He will learn."

Rick gave him the gun and said, "I hope so, Sergeant, for your sake. There are German officers locked in the administrative building and German soldiers, pro-Vichy soldiers, and German pilots in the supply room. The runways are booby-trapped; someone will show you where and how."

"How many prisoners, Sir?" the sergeant asked.

"About fifty! Your lieutenant will get a medal for this!" said Rick.

"How many were there of you?" asked the sergeant.

"Eight!"

"Wow!" Clearly impressed, he came to attention and saluted. "Sergeant Surphlis, Sir. It is a pleasure. If you are ever in Brooklyn, look me up. And you are?"

"Jones," said Rick.

"First name, Sir?"

"Just Jones."

Chapter Sixteen

Several weeks had passed since the Americans had come to Casablanca. It had been an interesting transition for the city. The newcomers were brash, easy-going, and confident, naïve; some were homesick.

They had never seen combat or war, and the ease with which they had taken a foothold gave them a confidence which was difficult to dispel. The officers, with no war experience either, had no incentive to dispel this happy state of affairs.

Other changes were evident, but some were not so evident. The refugees were leaving; most all of them had gone or were going to America. The State Department had a presence in the city, transferring a staff from Portugal. Their first priority had been to help those who had helped secure the city. Some had surprisingly volunteered to stay with the army. Berger was one who made the decision to fight, a decision which was to cost him his life at Anzio. Prostitution followed the army as it had for four thousand years. It led to the usual issues of money, perception of value, religious differences, and those of language and interpretation.

There was money, black market dealings, bartering, and there was drinking, fighting, arguing, theft, and a constant hum of excitement.

Rick was sitting in the Café Americana, pondering the differences and the sameness of life in Casablanca. It was his first visit as a customer since he had sold the place to Ferarri. There were changes in the feel of the place, but it was evidently making a great deal of money. The Americans were spending. They were happy to see signs of home in the form of Sam and a staff which welcomed them, and their money, in English.

A corporal who had worked at the Carousel just outside Boston had sung all the new American songs for Sam who had scored them for the band and included them into his repertoire, so the French songs were at the beginning or end of the evening. "The White Cliffs of Dover" and "We'll Meet Again" were popular, as was the comedy piece "Ma! I Miss Your Apple Pie."

Rick was only slightly surprised when Mr. Smith walked in and came directly to where he was sitting.

"I thought that I might find you here. Mind if I sit?" he asked.

Rick looked totally different from their last meeting, and since it was his first visit to the café, he was contemplating the remark, as he nodded to the seat opposite. Was Smith following him, having him followed? Had someone from the Café called saying he was there, or was it a chance meeting?

Rick did not believe in chance. He waited.

"I want you to work for me," Mr. Smith said.

Before there was a chance for a response or additional information, Ferrari came and, with a gesture, asked if he could sit.

"It's your place," said Rick.

"Ah! But it's your prerogative whether I sit and buy you a drink, or you send me away," said the smiling large man.

"Business must be good."

"Excellent! I do love the Americans and their money."

"Mr. Smith, this is Señor Ferrari, the owner of this gin joint and the Blue Parrot. He is a man to know who knows everything and everyone. He employs a couple of thugs, and if you need a betting or a gambling room, happy to take your money, or he will sell you anything that you cannot find on the black market."

Ferrari did not disagree but looked aggrieved.

Smith was looking on with amusement as he already knew it.

"And he sells illegal drugs at the Blue Parrot," Smith added.

"Ah! You are so kind to believe that I know these things. But one thing I do not know is the location of a certain gold shipment," said Ferrari.

"Perhaps the Germans have it," said Rick, "or the Free French who blew up the train, or some lucky nomad."

"The Germans would not still be looking, the French would be drinking better wine, and I definitely would know if a nomad had found anything."

"But whose money is it?" asked Rick. "The Germans? Free French? Americans? Moroccan government?"

"Oh, Rick, you are so naïve, deflective, and devious. I think that to give it to the Germans is now treason. The French have joined the Allies or the Germans, the Americans do not know about it, and the Moroccan Government is an oxymoron. It is finder's keepers, and I think that you, Ricky, know where it is. Why else would you humiliate some employees I sent to keep an eye on you and then disappear for several months during which a train was looted and then reappear as an Arab?"

"Interesting hypothesis," said Smith "and a great analysis. The Americans are only interested in it not being returned to the Germans."

Ferrari had delivered a message and warning to Rick; he was being watched.

The conversation turned to all of the other happenings in the city, the rumors, speculation, and prognosis. Finally, Ferrari moved away to attend to his business.

"So what is the job?" asked Rick.

"Spy!" said Smith. "Well, actually, intelligence gathering and stuff."

"Big pay?"

"If you live to collect it."

"Life insurance?"

"Who would you leave it to?"

Rick stopped the bantering. He was quiet, reflective. Why had the question affected him so much? Who *would* he leave anything to? It was easier when you had nothing; it was easier when you were blessed with the invincibility of youth. But he had seen too much to ever believe that anyone was invincible. He looked around at the young men and wondered how many of these "invincibles" were not going home.

"Okay! Do I get sworn in, given a badge, a decoder?" He had returned to jocular to hide the fact that he was still shaken.

Smith pretended not to notice.

"Now that you have agreed, we have an immediate assignment. There is to be a secret meeting here in January. It is still secret since our friend did not know about it. Our job is to keep it secret, protect the participants, investigate any rumors, watch known German sympathizers, etc."

"Who are the participants?" asked Rick. "Or am I still on a need-to-know basis?"

"Now that you are on the payroll of the Office of Strategic Service, I can tell you that the participants are Roosevelt and Churchill!"

"Wow! That is big, and I thank you for the trust in me. When do I start?"

"You already started. The information from Ferrari, plus information from all the other people you know, we are collecting and sharing. We shall be meeting to prepare an itinerary and security. With your knowledge of the people, the language, and the geography, we expect that your contribution will be invaluable."

Rick found the task easy. He found plenty of time in the few weeks to plan for the retrieval of the gold. The plan was simple. Suli would go to Fez on the train and buy three camels. Rick would follow two days later. Richard Blaine would get on the train, and "Ahmed Zawfri" would get off and be met with the camels. They would be out of the town before anyone following could pick up their trail.

Christmas in the desert came with all the noise associated with the season. Rick was happy to be working and found it easy to immerse himself in the preparations for the historic visit. It was better than realizing that he had no one to celebrate with since Sam and Suli were working and Smith had returned to the States.

The meeting of the heads of two Allied governments was concluded without incident. Rick was introduced to the president and thanked for his services. Roosevelt seemed to know all about him and his reasons for leaving America. Why else would he say, "Rick I hope that one day soon, we can all return home, resume our ordinary lives, and once again be productive contributors to the American dream"?

Rick thought about it and concluded that Roosevelt must know something. Roosevelt knew things because he asked questions. He was interested in people—all people—and, ultimately, that's what made a great president. It was what made a man great—asking questions, listening to the answers.

He resolved to emulate the president and take more interest in his contacts. He quickly realized why he would never be president; most of his associates were not interesting.

"Rick," said Mr. Smith one day, "we have a spy in Oran."

"Ours or theirs?" asked Rick.

"Why, theirs, of course. It seems they know of our troop movements in advance. Would you care to go find him for us?"

"Or her," said Rick. "Glad to! Contacts?"

"Yes, quite!" Smith had affected the British colloquiums and pace of speech "Ogilvie! Brit. Scottish, actually. Since we are all on the same side, as Monty says."

Rick was quite amused and getting used to the offhand, almost jocular manner used for the more dangerous missions.

It would work out well. He could disappear for weeks, and Smith would have a story for anyone. He arranged a signal to Sam that would be passed to Suli, for Suli to meet him in Fez.

Rick walked the streets of Oran which were in themselves similar to Casablanca but were much closer to the war. The Vichy French had not defected but had fought against the American forces which had landed. They had secured help from the Germans in the form of light tank regiments. There was a formidable force out in the desert, a terrain which the Germans had been fighting on back and forth with the British and Commonwealth forces for over a year.

Sitting in countless bars listening to the conversations, he became aware that the Americans' habits or prejudice follow even into the service and into war zones. Ahmed Zawfri was treated by the American soldiers as though he was invisible, and if they talked to him at all, it was loudly, as if talking louder made their English understandable. The soldiers spoke openly as if no one could understand. They talked and talked and talked; he listened.

The citizens of Oran talked but quietly of where it might be possible to get medicine, or chocolate, and American supplies. They spoke of who was becoming powerful, making profits, buying camels, and marrying daughters.

Rick followed the money.

The Arab who sat for days drinking, eating meager amounts of the cheapest foods was invisible. He watched!

There was a pattern; there was form. He had the scheme. It played out one day. He watched a sergeant meet with an owner of the bar who had not been visible previously. They shared drinks and expensive foods. It was as if orders were being taken for the supply of goods and prices were agreed after some bartering. The sergeant left, and Rick followed the other man to a nearby office building.

Mohammed Rashid was a businessman. When the Vichy was in town, he was pro-Vichy, when they left, pro-Allies. Vichy and the Germans were still customers; he was still a businessman.

When he was asked to provide information for money, he would if he could. When he was asked if he wanted to buy American goods cheap for the black market, he would because he could. When the two businesses coincided, it was like the confluence of planets. All his sons would have camels, all of his daughters dowries, and all of his wives jewelry.

He was blessed. He was careful, but he was unaware that he had been followed and observed using a shortwave radio.

The next day, a delivery by two army trucks took place. The sergeant and a corporal went upstairs and came down smiling and richer, judging by the expression on their faces.

Rick went to the barracks which were in a state of confusion and asked for Ogilvie, to be told that he was away. The next two days repeated the pattern as a story emerged of a major defeat for the Americans at the Kasserini Pass. It emerged that Ogilvie, concerned about the spy rumors, had gone in a jeep to observe. A German tank blasting through the American retreat spotted the jeep on a ridge and put a shell right through it.

The officer in charge of the gate arrested Rick as a spy. They were really paranoid by that time. A large sergeant put handcuffs on him and pushed him repeatedly while propelling him towards a holding cell. When he had gone, Rick unlocked the cuffs with the key he had taken while the sergeant was pushing him, then overpowered the guard and headed for the commanding officer's quarters carrying a jug of water as if he belonged.

"What the hell do you want!" bellowed a formidable officer.

"I want to report a spy! I have information for the commanding officer."

"Well, you look like an Arab, but you sound like one of us, so how do I know which you are?" The man was a caricature—big figure, big voice, big ears, and big ego with pearl-handled revolvers.

"Telegraph three words to Casablanca."

"Three words sound reasonable. What are they, 'Good-bye, Rosie'?" he bellowed with laughter.

"Smith help Jones," said Rick.

Some time later, Rick was ushered into a conference room with nine officers who all looked worried except for the man at the head of the table.

"Okay, son. Smith says you are the real deal. Who is the spy? And who are you?"

"Jones, and the spy is all of you. The excesses you bring and the attitude, the entrepreneurship, and the money." He told of the "loose lips" and of the supply sergeant who would leave the compound with a truck of supplies each time a patrol went out. The sergeant made the arrangements the night before and thereby alerted the enemy twelve hours before a raid. No one checked that an extra truck left, with a big raid two trucks. It was easy for the enemy, made easier by the open nature of the Americans. "Cross checked with other sources; they knew when, how many, and where they were going to be."

There was silence.

"Arrest them! Shoot the bastards!"

The chairman was yelling loud enough for the soldiers on duty at the door to rush in and be told just as loudly to leave.

When he had simmered down, it was obvious that no one was going to speak or countermand any of the orders, and no one was going to take responsibility for the commands.

"If I might suggest," ventured Rick. Eight pair of grateful eyes swiveled in his direction. "General, you are known as blood and guts, that you never retreat. This may perhaps be used to your advantage. Send some sappers secretly, mine the front of the Kasserini Pass, send out an early patrol, no rations and no supplies, around to the heights, then have your regular patrol the next day pull up, as if to retreat. Wait for the Panzers to commit and hit them in your minefield from the high ground and from the front."

Another silence ensued until, finally, a young officer spoke. "General, Sir, how do we know this is not a trap that this Arab dreamed up for us?"

"Because, son, this Arab is an American, and this Arab took the Casablanca airport and held it until our boys had landed. And, son, you need more of his attitude because with an attitude like yours, Hitler is going to die in his sleep of old age and deprive me of the pleasure of putting this revolver in his ear and pulling the trigger. Now, put a plan together and bring it to the mess because I am going to buy this Arab a drink."

Rick left for Fez after sending the message to Sam. He met Suli, and they dug up the gold. They then waited at the watering hole south of Casablanca for a caravan which they joined; they entered the city without incident.

Seated again in the Café Americana, Smith was impressed with the outcome of the mission and never mentioned the missing three weeks. He was obviously basking in a reflected respect from a high-ranking general.

"So where is my pay deposited?" asked Rick.

"In a little bank in the city, a private bank" said Smith.

"Will they invest it?"

"If you instruct them."

"How do I instruct them when they don't know me?"

"Write a letter. I can put it into a diplomatic pouch. Address it to David Skelton, Bowery Bank, New York."

"What about other monies? I sold this bar, invested well. Diplomatic pouch?"

He was pushing his luck a little, but when on top, you can push. The gold that had been bought had been sold by Sam for US dollars. Taking advantage of the change in currency values and selling gold for discounted dollars as they had bought the gold at discount rates had created a 200 percent return.

"Why not?" said Smith." But who is the beneficiary?"

"Sam and myself. We are partners; anything happens, he knows what to do.

How big is the pouch?" asked Rick who was on a roll.

"As big as one man can carry. Why? You want to put in something heavier...like gold?" Smith was not smiling, but the edge of his mouth indicated that he had been thinking about Rick's absence and was putting out a baited line.

"Maybe!"

Chapter Seventeen

Sam paused in his narrative. He was tired. It had been a long day, and although he was energized, when he stopped, he realized just how tiring the journey back to Africa had been.

There was silence.

Around the table at which they were seated, there was a bustle of activity, and it seemed to expand and engulf. Just a few moments ago, it had seemed that they were on an uninhabited island—encapsulated and insulated from the modern world.

They were all with their separate and different thoughts. There was no way to discern exactly what was going on in each head. Ilsa sat with tears slowly coursing her cheeks. Kate was wide-eyed and slightly flushed. Richard was confused. What was he doing here? Who were these people living a lifetime ago? He regretted the thought immediately but wondered why it had surfaced. The girl was obviously moved. *Well, it is her father. She is also beautiful.* Where the heck did that thought come from?

"Sam," Ilsa was the first to speak, "Mr. Smith….."

"Yes, he was here today. He was speaking to Jimmy." The four pairs of eyes swiveled in unison to the bar. There, Jimmy was serving a couple who had just come in. No Mr. Smith.

Kate flagged a waitress. "Have Jimmy come over when he has a break."

That is funny thought, Richard. *I thought he was talking to Mr. Munroe, Mum's old boss.*

He watched Kate. She caught him watching and smiled; she was used to being watched. Jimmy joined the table. He walked to it as if he belonged; it was a comfortable, confident walk.

"Jimmy, what happened to the man in the raincoat at the bar?" His father asked the question.

"He left about ten minutes ago. Why?"

"What were you talking about?"

"Dad, he asked what I did; he was really interested. He was especially interested when I mentioned the military, not like most people these days. He said he might be able to help me with my education and get a job when I get out. I gave him my name. He said that was all he needed. He said his name was Smith, that he knew Rick."

There was an exchange of looks around the table.

"Why, did I do something wrong? He was a really nice man, big tip." Jimmy was smiling.

"No, nothing wrong, son. Mr. Smith seems to have a long reach, but he does take care of his protégés. We can talk about it some more later. I was wondering if you could take over the music tonight; I am beat!"

"Okay, pops! Wow, Saturday night at Rick's Café. Usual rates?"

"No," laughed Kate, "bonus rates. I am also leaving so you are in charge, if you don't mind?"

"Thank you," Jimmy said and blushed.

Richard would later try to remember how he knew Jimmy was blushing. He thought that the dark skin took on a glow.

"Thank you, Miss Kate."

"Thank *you*, Jimmy, and I have asked you a thousand times to drop the 'Miss.'"

"When are we going to hear more of your story, Sam?" asked Ilsa.

"Come back tomorrow for the Sunday Jazz open mike. Bring your 'stick,' Richard," Sam said, addressing the man who looked so much like his best friend.

"Sorry, not this week; we have other commitments" said Ilsa

"And I shall be back in Washington with my patients," said Richard.

"Well, you are both welcome, anytime," said a pair of the greenest eyes Richard had ever looked into—Kate's.

Sam and Kate walked them to the door. "I have your car right here, Miss Ilsa," said Abdullah

"Thank you, Abdulla."

Richard reached into his pocket to tip the large Arab but was stopped by his mother, "Please, do not embarrass him."

She was met by a brilliant smile. "Good night, Miss Ilsa. Please come back soon; it has been too long."

They drove in silence through the busy streets of New York to the parkway. Ilsa was lost in a memory. Good or bad—it was difficult to know as she was crying and smiling. Richard was in his own thoughts—of Mafia, of people out of place, and of discordance yet syncopation. There was a hodgepodge of things: a French restaurant in the middle of America's Italy, a black piano player with stories of war, a black bartender not backing down. He was encouraged; he felt invigorated, reborn.

"Mother, what do you have planned for tomorrow?"

"Planned? Well, we have been invited for brunch at the country club. I thought it would be nice if you met and talked to some old friends."

"I don't suppose Trish will be there, Mother?"

"Well, her mother did say she is probably up from the city for the weekend. You were all such good friends."

"Mother, did you know that Mr. Smith and Mr. Munroe were the same man?"

"Not at the time, no. Now it makes perfect sense. He debriefed us in Lisbon, and we gave him Rick, and he debriefed Rick, and recruited...me."

"What about your little baby—me?"

"You were a perfect child. Nani Goldberg was thrilled to take care of my little angel. We must stop in, and see her soon. I wonder how her legs are."

"Mother!"

He was not to be diverted.

"I did translation work and wrote letters, some were in code, all were to aliases. We recruited candidates for work behind the lines. It was dangerous, I suppose, since there were many German sympathizers in New York. We were constantly in danger of being infiltrated, which was where my languages were invaluable. Also, though I say it myself, my intuition saved us many times. When there was a suspicion, we merely interviewed for an import/export agent for freight forwarding position. Our business book was then for South Africa and South America. A live recruit would be trained and sent into action which was all over Europe. I sometimes met convoys from England, Lisbon, and Middle East where a defector or an incoming German spy might be on board—sometimes to recruit, and other times to see who met them."

"Was it dangerous?"

"It was necessary!"

They drove into the garage. Neither wanted anything more to eat or drink.

Richard thought that he would never sleep but found that when he lay down, he slipped into an emerald green lake; he sank into the eyes of Kate Blaine.

When he woke, the sun was shining brightly; it was past eight o'clock. He went into the kitchen, enjoying the quiet, and poured a glass of orange juice. He then put on a pot of coffee and went to stand in front of a photograph of his mother. He was still standing there when she came up behind him.

"What are you thinking?" she asked.

"How beautiful you were.... are...," he corrected himself.

She laughed. He had forgotten what a beautiful tinkling sound she made when laughing; it had been a long time.

"It is a long time since I was called beautiful," she said as she smiled; she was happy. It was an enigma. They had gone to a funeral sad and come out...happy? Well, maybe not happy, but what?

Richard called the hospital. Dr. Price was doing rounds. Dr. Brandon had called in with a case of "soft powder."

Dr. Price came to the phone and filled him in on the patients. There were no emergencies that day, none yet. She exuded a confidence that had not been there before. Being in charge can have that effect when the only answer is yours and it must be right.

"Major General Rollins came into ops…yesterday," she said. "He said that you had recommended me. Thank you!"

Although Richard had not been quite as forthright, he recognized the mark of leadership which brought the chief down to show that he knew what was happening and then giving credit to another. He picked up the cue and asked, "How did Sister and the new nurse take to their new roles?"

"Very well. Sister, finally, was so busy that she forgot who was in charge of the surgeries and Nurse Weston is a find; we have to find a way to keep her."

"I agree, I shall be back tomorrow at the latest, tonight if you need me."

"No, I should be all right. Everything is quiet, just some follow-up surgeries today."

She never mentioned Brandon—a team player.

The Country Club was busy. Even though it was out of season and the course closed, it was clearly the place to be seen on Sunday. The sun was shining, and members who would never be seen dead playing with one another were making remarks as how great it would be to be out together on that magnificent day.

Richard checked his cashmere top coat and his mother's best winter coat with fur collar. He was dressed in a dark worsted suit, white shirt, and a bright red tie. Ilsa had a modest, knitted grey dress, low heels, and a single strand of pearls. They had taken a great deal of care not to offend and clearly stood out for their conservative dress in this bastion of conservatism

As they walked to the entrance to the dining room, they passed men in blazers and either white or brown slacks wearing the club tie and women in too short skirts with too high heels to be properly enjoying walking or sitting.

The maitre d' showed them to a prominent table. Senator "Bo" (for Beauregard) Wellington rose to greet them, took the chair from the maitre d', and held it for Ilsa. "Welcome! Welcome, Mrs. Land and Richard!" he said, pumping his hand as though Richard might be the casting vote on his election

"Doctor Richard, we should say," he guffawed loudly and was clearly playing to the nearby tables. "You know my wife, Elizabeth and Trish, of course."

"Pleased to see you again, Elizabeth and Trish. What a pleasant surprise," said Ilsa. "Richard just happened to be home, too."

"Mrs. Wellington, it is good to see you, and Trish, you look lovely," Richard remarked.

The Wellingtons had bucked the trend. The Senator's dark suit and white shirt offset the obligatory club tie. Mrs. Wellington was in a spring suit with matched shoes and bag. Trish did indeed look stunning with a designer dress bought in New York and a small diamond necklace.

Well, being a senator did not have to pay well when you marry into a family's metal casting business. The Johnson family was perfectly happy to see Bo off to Washington to protect their defense contracts.

They ordered, with the senator and Mrs. Wellington starting with Bloody Marys and then champagne while their three guests stayed with orange juice and coffee.

There was a jazz trio playing, and it reminded Richard of the first time he had been in the dining room with his jazz group. Then, as now, no attention was being paid to the entertainment. The group responded in like fashion and were uninspired. He wondered if his group had given the same lackluster performance; it certainly had competed with the same indifference from the club members. They had been invited back, and he had been pleased until he found out that it was because they were local and did not get paid for travel. Well, money was money. At that time, it was like manna sent down from heaven.

As if reading his thoughts, Trish said, "They are not as good as your group."

He laughed and asked, "Are you following your father into politics? How is life in New York these days?"

"It is grand. Working on *Wall Street* is really exciting."

"What exactly are you doing?" he asked.

"Analyst. I read reports and find unusual investment opportunities, write a report, and keep looking. There are a lot of young driven people working very hard."

They caught up quickly on their separate lives while enjoying the excellent brunch.

"And you, Richard? You are looking well. I am glad that you are back from that ghastly place. How soon before you can rejoin the human race?"

"Ask your father; he keeps voting to send more men and more metal casting to South Asia."

He regretted immediately not what he had said but the way he had said it. After all, he and his mother were guests of the senator.

The senator looked across, as if he had heard. He had not, but the tone may have sounded discordant.

"Doctor, what is your opinion of those young men who are going to Canada rather than Vietnam, and those hippies with long hair burning their draft cards and American flags in public?" the senator asked.

"Dear, let's not talk politics," his wife intervened.

The senator affected not to hear and kept a quizzical look on his face. In truth, it was a game they frequently played, and she leaned forward, eager for a response.

"Well, Sir, I have been there, and I am engaged in repairing the bodies of those who make it back. I can certainly understand not going into that war zone voluntarily and doing everything legally possible to stay out. I cannot condone the burning of the flag." He paused, thinking of his patients. "I do firmly believe that if the President and members of Congress were to spend a day in my hospital, the war would be over very soon."

"We can't have Johnnie Red running all over Asia, son. He would soon be in America, in Washington, telling you how to run your hospital."

"Sir, your job is politics; mine is being a doctor. You asked for my opinion, and if Congress does not listen to mine and the opinion of all those long-haired hippies, then they will not long be enjoying that comfortable cigar and whisky on the hill. I want to thank you for your hospitality. I need to be getting back to Washington."

Trish ran after Richard and caught him at the cloakroom.

"Will you come visit me in New York?"

"I don't get much time."

"Please. Here is my address and phone number."

"What about Wade?"

"Wade is 3 F."

"Wade is not 3 F, but is that why you broke off your engagement?"

"Wade's father got him a medical exemption, and you just said that men should do what they have to do."

"So why not marry him, infirmity and all?"

"Mummy says it would not look good for daddy's reelection."

"And Mummy said that a decorated doctor would be dandy!"

"Please. Please come and see me. We had a lot of fun at Yale, and I do love you, and I do miss you."

"I miss you, too, Trish. You are beautiful, and you have brains. I will have to think about it, though."

Think about what? Was he nuts? She was the most beautiful girl he had ever met. She had a good job, was very intelligent, and she had money!

Patricia Wellington was any man's dream.

Chapter Eighteen

Trish Wellington.

Richard had, in fact, never recovered from her discarding him. The fact was they had been great together; they had so much in common and so many differences that it was always good to be with her. Trish's friends tended to be a bit snobby, aloof, taking courses in school that were safe, would give them a good degree, and help them find a husband. The degree would then be discarded for the pampered life of the country club, meaningless meetings, charity events, and the obligatory two children.

Trish had been a little like that but was also driven to have a career. It was never clear which mode she might be in. She had been in the husband and procreation mode when they argued that night five years, eight months, and four days ago. Trish was home spending a few weeks looking for a job. He had arranged to take a few days from Johns Hopkins and was looking forward to spending all those hours gazing into a pair of eggshell blues eyes. That lasted about fifteen minutes. He had spent the rest of his time home, gazing at the blue ceiling of his bedroom.

He still remembered every word, every gesture. He remembered the blue dress with a pattern around the bottom and the bracelet he had given to her on her twenty-first birthday. He wondered again whether she had been pleased or had expected a ring.

"After med. school, you can apply at Columbia or some other New York hospital. We can get married, live together, then move back here and open a general practice with privileges at the hospital. We know so many people; it should be easy."

Richard was dumbstruck. He was tired. He had been filled with anticipation; he had not expected the whole of his life to have been planned for him. He was not sure which of the items offended him most. Was it the fact that she was asking him to be married, or she would support him in New

York? Or was it that his direction was as a general practitioner, or that they would live in Greenwich or that her mother, president of the hospital, would clear the way for his career?

He decided that there was still a way to clear the air for the next few days. He asked flippantly, "Who is on the committee to direct my life?"

It was a perfectly neutral question in search of a neutral flip response. But instead, she said, "Well, Mummy, Daddy, Claire...."

"Well, tell the committee that I have changed my mind about Columbia. I will fulfill my obligation to the army and then specialize in surgery at a major teaching hospital."

"No, you are not going into the army. What if you are sent to Vietnam? We can get you a deferment."

"Who, the committee?"

"If you are going to go into the army, I never want to see you again."

"Never?"

"Never!"

Richard stood slowly and very slowly headed to the door. She did not call him back; he did not look back.

"Richard, I am talking to you." He came out of his memories as his mother spoke.

"Yes, Mother? Sorry. I am sorry that I was rude to our host."

"Ah, I am sure that worse has been said to the senator. I was asking what you thought of Patricia. She seems very mature, and she is very pretty. I once thought that by now, I might have a blond, blue-eyed grandchild."

Ilsa was just being a mother. He smiled at her. "You are sometimes so transparent, but sometimes, there is nothing to see. Let us go to the shore and have a walk," said Richard.

"All right," she said. "But not far. It is still cold even if the sun is shining."

They walked in compatible silence, arm in arm. Ilsa loved having her son all to herself, if only for a little while.

"When will you go back?" she asked.

"Tonight!"

"Oh," the disappointment was evident. "I suppose you must?"

"If I get back this evening, then I have all tomorrow in the theatre. Trying to get back to Washington tomorrow could take all day. I shall try to get away more often, Mother, I promise."

They talked of the usual things they found comfortable. It was conversation while they could think their own thoughts. They promised each other that they would drive to see Nani Goldman next time he was home. While Richard packed, Ilsa made a light supper. After supper, she drove him to the station. They said their good-byes, and he walked into the station. Dressed casually in slacks with a sweater under his topcoat, Richard could easily be an executive returning to the city after a day in the suburbs.

He was deep into his own thoughts, trying to make sense of the contradictions of the weekend, his mother, the deceased, the mafia, Kate Blaine, and Trisha Wellington when an object of his thoughts spoke.

"Penny for your thoughts!"

It was like a flash to the past. The lilt was there, the playful tone, and the memories came back—the good memories.

"Hello, Trish. Where are you going?"

She looked beautiful.

"Back to the city. May I join you?" She was sitting as she spoke.

They talked as though their years apart had never happened; it was as though they had never parted. He talked of his work, and she listened. He never mentioned the war; she never asked. He had told her about his pass and a little about the funeral. She talked about her work, her friends. Yes, she still saw Claire; they went to the theatre together whenever Claire and she had the same nights off.

As they pulled into the station, Trisha moved closer. "You do not have to be back until tomorrow. Come and stay at my apartment."

Richard felt a stirring. She was desirable, more desirable than anyone he had ever met. She was available, and she was there. How many times had he fantasized that moment? Even his fantasies had not been as good as that moment. He looked up into blue eyes; they were better, bluer than his memory of them. He was as surprised as she was when he heard himself say, "Thank you, but no, not today."

Her reaction was for tears to well into that liquid pool and slowly overflow.

"I should get back to my patients, and this has been a traumatic weekend. I should like to call you, if I may?"

She nodded without speaking, and as the train stopped, she hurried away down the platform—away from Richard.

The Washington train was quiet.

Why had he done that? He could have been ensconced in a warm chair, with a little champagne and soft music.

The answer, when it finally came, was the comparison of a pair of green eyes. He chuckled and thought, *Timing is everything.* If he had encountered Trisha just forty-eight hours earlier, he would not have hesitated. *Then why hesitate now?* Kate Blaine had shown no interest in him. They had not spoken more than a dozen words to one another. He knew nothing about her; she could be a murderess, a career woman, divorcee, or a foul-mouthed ignorant banshee.

Could be....

The taxi dropped him at the hospital, and he went inside. He was greeted without surprise. Doctors came and went at all times of the day and night.

"Who is D.O.D.?" he asked.

"Doctor of the day is Dr. Price."

"Thank you," he said as he went to the day room where he could retrieve his messages before going to his room.

He saw Dr. Price coming out of a room at the end of the corridor and hurried to catch up to her.

"Doctor," he said quietly since it was almost midnight, "I thought you were on duty all weekend?"

"Yes, well, Dr. Brandon looked like he needed the sleep more than I did."

It was a much more confident doctor than he had left; she was in charge.

"How did the surgeries go? How are they recovering? How were the families this weekend? What have you left for me? Would you like me to take over tonight?"

"Well, a couple of days out of here have revved you up! Patients are all great. Families are on their tearful way home, and no, I can manage. You have a potential double amputee at 7:00 A.M. He is in room 221; his girlfriend is with him."

"Hey, how did you know I would be here?"

"I didn't, but I am going to cross Brandon off and put your name on the sheet in my next pass by the office. The boy, sorry, soldier's vital signs have been deteriorating all day."

He smiled. She was definitely an asset, and she was ready.

Then, becoming serious, he realized that, being ready, she would be going overseas.

She was looking at him with the same thoughts and something else. He had just seen the look on Trish's face. She had a crush on him.

Oh, no! From no interest to three in two days!

He spun and went to room 221.

The soldier was holding his girlfriend's hand. They were quiet; they had cried themselves into silence.

Richard walked in. He had put on a white smock and picked up his stethoscope.

He respected their silence as he checked the chart and looked at the monitor. No question; he was bleeding somewhere. They would need to give him blood before and after the operation. The girl looked up with red-ringed eyes full of questions, questions, and questions.

He didn't know the answers; he was not God.

"They said I could stay," she said as if he was there to ask her to leave.

"Okay. He will be prepped at six for an operation at seven."

"Will he...?" She could not complete the thought. "What can I do?"

"I am going to do my best. He is strong." How many times had he said the same words? The routine examination which was done on automatic reactions did nothing to change the initial assessment but gave the doctor a chance to interact, give some confidence to the patient.

"Are you a blood donor? He is going to need blood. If you want to do something for him, donate. The lab will be open at seven. Ask at the front desk for directions and tell them that Dr. Land sent you."

"Thank you, Doctor. I can. I will. Thank God there is something I can do."

He left and went to bed, asking for a call at 5:30 A.M.

"Another day," he whispered, "was it really only twenty-four hours? So much had happened."

The next twenty-four hours could not be as full of surprises.

Could it?

Chapter Nineteen

Richard Land was tired. He had taken two days off but was more tired than if he had worked a sixteen-hour shift in the operating room. Then, why could he not fall asleep? He tried counting. He tried to imagine a beautiful beach, empty with just the lapping of the waves. He tried breathing in until his lungs were full, then breathing out slowly. He imagined playing soccer. But nothing was working.

Strange how things intruded; they were not even the same things. Sometimes, it was how fate had led his mother and, therefore, him into this place and time. He saw faces—sometimes Trish Wellington, sometimes Kate Blaine, and sometimes the nurse in Vietnam smiling at him and at the little boy moments before she became a fatality, a statistic. *Fate, what was in store for the future?*

He must have fallen asleep because he was dreaming, or was he was imagining? Imagination was so much like dreaming. He was in Morocco, in a harem. There was a large man. He looked and sounded like Senator Bo Wellington, but he was dressed in flowing Arabic robes. The man had a scimitar at his waist and a large hammer which he swung at a larger gong. When the gong sounded, an older Arabian woman—it looked like Mrs. Wellington—opened the huge door. In stepped Trish Wellington in a see through dress and veil.

"You like this one?" asked the Wellingtons.

Before he could answer, there was a swing of the hammer, the sound of the gong, the opening of the door, and in stepped another Trish Wellington.

"You like this one?" asked the duo in unison.

Before he could answer, the process was repeated until the room was full of Trish Wellingtons. They were swaying, dancing in a hypnotic swirling of veils and dresses. The dancing became faster and louder until he could stand it no more. The music stopped, the room was empty, and he was alone, except for a woman at his feet.

She looked up. He gasped. The blue eyes, the blond hair, and the tall lithe figure were gone. This was a trick, this woman had brown hair and green eyes a fuller figure, this was not Trish Wellington, this was Kate Blaine.

The gong sounded again. There was no room, no door, and everyone was running; he was running. Running toward something, or away? Away as fast as he could; something terrible had just happened.

The gong sounded again, and he awoke; it was his wake-up call.

Richard answered his call and lay quietly, trying to remember why he had been running. He gave up and went into the shower. He did his best thinking in the shower and planned his day as well as anyone could with all the emergencies which could, and would, arise.

Dressed and feeling professional, he went to check that his patient was being readied and to show his own confidence to the scared young man.

"Where is the girlfriend?" he asked.

The young man was taken aback since the staff came and asked him the same stupid questions like, "How are you feeling today?" fifty times, and "We'll soon have you out of here," as if that was what he wanted. He knew that when he left, he was going to have to learn to walk again, suffer the stares of people as he sat in his wheelchair watching them watching him. It would be like an art museum where people watched other people on the walls staring back at them.

"She went to give blood," he answered.

"They don't start until seven,"

"Well, she wanted to be first in line"

"You better marry that girl," he told the soldier.

Dr. Land kept up his bedside patter while examining the young soldier's vital signs and checking the condition of the man's legs.

The young man was lost in the patter, too. With a change of pace, he was unable to think of his troubles and the traumas ahead.

"You come to the wedding then?" he asked.

"If invited! I want to dance with the girl who loves you enough to stand in line to give you her blood."

The young GI's face clouded. "Ain't going to be no dancing." His mood had changed.

"Yes, there is, and you are going to lead it. I want you to promise that you will come back here, or go to your nearest Veterans Hospital and get into their prosthesis program. Then I will promise to dance, after you, at your wedding."

The young man was not convinced.

"Let us do our job, and you and that young lady do yours. Okay? See you in a couple of hours. Any questions?"

"You really come down to Louisiana for our wedding?"

"Straight! If invited."

"Wait till I tell Lisa. She thinks you are special."

"She is the special one."

Doctor Land walked away less confident than he had sounded, but a thought was coming into his head. One of the legs was beyond help; the other might be saved. It would leave the patient with a limp and a shorter leg. He smiled. The other leg was going to be made to a custom length so that did not matter. It would be a longer, trickier operation. He must look at the schedule; his extra three hours could be spent saving another soldier. The military surgeon's dilemma: Do we go for quality or quantity?

He bumped into Dr. Brandon in the hall as they both tried to enter their office together.

"You look awful, Richard. You must have had a hell of a weekend," said Dr. Brandon.

"Well, I hope that I look better than you. Actually, I had a quiet weekend with my mother. We went to a funeral, then Sunday brunch with friends."

"Yes! Right," said the skeptical doctor. "Well, a double chop and you could get in a nap before night calls."

"Actually," said Richard "I need to talk to you about leaving Dr. Price in charge of our wing and then not pulling night call."

"She ratted on me and complained to you, probably went to the chief, too."

"No. She did not rat, nor did she complain. I am complaining because I treat this job a lot more seriously than you do, apparently."

"Can we discuss this later, old chap? Busy day, etc."

In truth, that suited Richard. Brandon had got the message; it would not be mentioned, and he would be on his best behavior…at least until next time.

It was good news that the list was short, and everyone was in.

Time to scrub.

Back in his comfortable surroundings, with his team intact, he explained that it was going to be different, a little experimental, and if it did not work then they were in no worse a position. He thanked them for their efforts while he was away, formally welcomed Nurse Weston, and told Sister that he had bought Lindt chocolates from New York for her. She huffed but was pleased at the recognition.

"I shall share them with the girls," she said.

Lucky to get one each, thought Richard.

"Let's do it people!" he said as the unconscious patient was brought into the operating room.

It was after one o'clock when they finally finished. During the operation, he had left for a few minutes to tell Lisa that all was well, not to worry, and thanks for the blood. The relief was obvious.

Richard was happy to see that the lunchroom was quiet. He needed to think, and he was tired.

"What's the soup of the day, Fred?"

"Potato."

"Potato?"

"Cream of potato."

"Sounds revolting. I will have a cup and a roll."

In truth, most of the food was revolting, but what could you expect when they cook for an undetermined number coming in at an uncertain time?

The soup was actually quite good, very good with a little extra pepper.

"Thought I would find you here."

How on earth could anyone expect to find him there? He was thinking as he looked quizzically into the face of Mr. Smith, or Mr. Munroe, or whatever.

"I saw a look like that in Casablanca many years ago. Rick later told me that either I had been following him, or that someone inside had 'shopped' him. In truth, it was neither; it was a happy circumstance and the use of an attention-getting phrase."

"Good afternoon," said Richard "What brings you here? Was I 'shopped' or followed?"

"In truth, a rare commodity in my world. I was here to see Rollie, tell him of the funeral, how well your mother looked, etc. I was walking out when I recognized you through the door. I thought you may have some questions.

Questions! Questions! Damn right, I have questions! thought Richard. *Like where do I begin?*

"Well, I have surgery this afternoon!"

"Not until 3:30, I believe."

How did he know that?

"If truth is a rare commodity in your world, then isn't it like the good white Indians who only tell the truth and the bad cannibal Indians who only tell lies? How do I know whether your answers will be the truth or lies?"

"There is also the 'Truth as I see it Indians'," said Alexander Munroe as he laughed.

"First then. What is your name?"

"My given name was so distant that I forgot it. Your mother knows me as Alexander Munroe. To Rick, I was Aubrey Smith."

"And to Rollie?"

"To agents I ran, I was Mr. Smith—to Rick, Rollie, and," he paused, "others. To agents I recruited on behalf of a government agency, I was Alexander Munroe."

"How did you meet Rollie?"

"Actually, Rick met him first in Italy and was impressed with his fighting ability and his gifts for languages, so we arranged to accidentally meet him and make him an offer he would not refuse."

"Italy? I thought Rick was in North Africa."

"He was until we had a spot of bother north of Rome."

Chapter Twenty

North Africa, 1944

"Rick, it looks as though we are out of work in Africa."

They were sitting in an outside café in Cairo. The main thrust of the armed forces had left for Italy where the fighting was then hot and heavy. The British forces had landed in Sardinia and made very slow progress up the peninsula. The reasoning was difficult to argue against—the army did not want to make the same mistakes made in Africa where the army frequently outran their ability to supply. Also, quick progress made the army vulnerable to an attack from a force circling around. There was also the usual politics. If a general was to be successful with minimal losses, then perhaps he would be promoted to be the leader of the combined forces in the invasion of France. Another argument could be made that the Germans propping up the Italians while they were still committing armies to Russia were leaving themselves open on the French coast. So, a prolonged affair in the 'boot' of Italy stretched the Germans and their supply lines.

The Americans, unable to stand the lack of progress, landed at Salerno and were bogged down on the beachhead by a strong, determined German army. The distress for the Americans was greeted with relief and amusement by the British forces slogging up from the south.

The politicking just grew and grew.

Smith had flown into Cairo from the States via London and Lisbon.

"You could have written to tell me that! How are things at home? Have you cleared my return? Is London as bad as we hear?" asked Rick.

"How astute! But it would have been redundant to write and say that you are redundant. We are still working on your return issues," Smith replied.

The truth was it was not an issue, and he had been far too busy with agents in Europe to give it any immediate attention. Also, he needed Rick in Europe, not the States. "London is quite cheery considering. The US joining the fight in Europe has given everyone a bit of a lift. Plus, Uncle Joe has been throwing men and women at the Nazis like he may never run out. The reason for my trip is actually to ask how your German is, and your Italian?"

"Ah! Worried about my education, are you? Well, since my work in the German prisoner of war camps, it has improved."

"Everyone said nice things about your work there, and we were able to confirm the information we were getting from the cipher group."

"You mean that you knew all that stuff, that I was risking a cut throat for nothing?" Rick was shocked.

"Well, not. nothing. It confirmed. We like confirmation, you know."

"So, what now? You want me to go to Italy and ask the Germans how many bullets they have left?"

"Not exactly!"

Rick, or Jones as he was known, and the man who called himself "Smith" had established a working relationship which used each of their skills. The infiltration of the camps for information were meticulously planned, with fake neck injuries to explain the lack of voice and then to cover the lack of an accent.

Smith thought about how much he needed to tell Rick to have him participate and how much to leave out.

"The ciphers have come up with the information that Allied prisoners of war being held north of Rome are to be *exterminated* by the Germans when they are forced to retreat. It seems that they will be moving too fast to take them, and do not want them back in the fight."

"So, what do you want me to do? Go tell them?" asked Rick.

"No. We thought you might take the camp and hold it until the US army shows up," said Smith without humor.

"By myself?" asked a smiling Rick.

"Well, how many people will you need?"

Rick realized that Smith was serious.

"How long do we have?"

"Not long," said Smith. "We expect the weather to change and be sunny for a spell. There is a push scheduled for tomorrow with a new landing and some air cover. With luck, they will be in Rome in two weeks. Actually, around Rome, since there are orders not to bomb, or shell, anywhere near the Vatican."

They spent the rest of the day planning strategy and determining a team. Rick decided that twenty would be enough, as they were not expected, and all had to speak Italian and/or German passably. Smith arranged for them to have access to American Rangers and British Commandoes. The cover would be that they were delivering additional prisoners, mostly aviators.

The recruiting was done quickly and quietly. The men spirited away without explanation to be vetted by Smith and Rick with linguistic help. All the men chosen were to be fluent in the language required for their role. A British officer speaking German to the men ascertained which were considered fluent enough; the rest were dismissed. Rick observed and asked the officer to join the team even though he was not a combat-ready soldier.

"I need someone really fluent. Where did you learn your German?" he asked.

"Heidelberg University. My father was foreign office attached to Berlin. It was fun. Very few knew that I was not German; we had been in the country for years. I developed a Prussian accent which worked out well. But I have to tell you, if you are covert, I cannot go because of my rank and knowledge, not to mention that my father would raise a fuss with the ministry. I would be forced to stand down."

"We'll see!" said Rick. "Interview a medic?"

"The field hospital had no one, but I did hear a soldier call that young American lieutenant who escorted us in, 'Doc.' Might be something."

"Get him!" said Rick. "We have wasted a week already."

"Lootenant Rollins, Sir!"

"At ease, soldier. You a doctor?"

"No, Sir! Three years medical school, then signed up to kill Japs. Been eating sand, blowing up tanks, and chasing Gerry since. Haven't seen a Jap!"

"How come your rank?"

"Seems the guy standing next to me keeps getting killed, and they make me take his place."

"Doc, you just volunteered for a dangerous mission."

"Yes, Sir. Yes! I better tell the boys."

"Sorry, son, you cannot tell anyone. By the way, how is your German or Italian?"

"I can get laid in either language if that is any good," said the brash young man. "Better in Italian at the moment."

Three days later, after intensive retraining and getting to know each other, they parachuted into the hills northeast of Rome, near a German distribution center. The men were all experienced soldiers and felt comfortable with the language. It was easy for them to steal two trucks, and with all the confusion, it was likely that they would not be missed. The Italians were disaffected with their "guests," and the Italian Army was deserting in ever-increasing numbers. The deserters, if caught, were being shot or hanged by the Germans without a hearing.

The soldiers were all relieved with the ease of their early success but were under no long-term illusions. They were dressed as German soldiers and Italian soldiers and as American or British prisoners of war, which meant that their only friends were each other. The Germans would shoot them; the Italians, the Americans, and the British would all shoot them, if they were not perfect.

To most groups, this would be a problem; to that group, it was a challenge.

The men settled down, hidden in full sight. They set up a loose checkpoint outside a small village and waited for information on the push that the Americans had promised. The plan was to use the confusion to move into and take over the concentration camp. While waiting, the men talked, continued their assimilation, practiced their language skills, and slept. Two of the English sappers argued over their respective local football clubs—Arsenal and Tottenham. Rick, hearing them, told them to change the names to German clubs, in case they could be overheard. Bruce and Kevin spent an hour agreeing with each other on superiority of the English game, then complied with the order.

On May 11, 1944, the Americans launched their attack. With the Poles to the far south of the line and the French units scaling the hills thought to be impregnable, New Zealand tank corps struggled through Cassino and the British troops were forcing their way up the middle; it was too much for the Germans.

The American Rangers and British Commandoes headed southwest as if to join the fight. When they reached the concentration camp, they surrendered the prisoners and indicated that it was believed that the aviators had valuable intelligence.

Colonel Freeman who became a German officer was shown into the commandant's office along with Rick.

"What brings you here?" asked the commandant. There was a man in the civilian dress of the Gestapo also in the room.

The Colonel was wondering about that, too. He had not volunteered. In fact, he was reluctant to be involved, but his arguments had been ignored. So there he was, dressed as a German officer in a room with an agent of the Gestapo and a veteran of the Eastern Front. The latter, he knew from the dossier he had read but was evident from the face of the man behind the desk. It was a tired face with burns down the right side and pain in the eyes.

A black glove on his right hand suggested the reason for the pain.

"I heard that the beaches were wonderful in the spring."

The commandant tried to smile; the Gestapo did not.

"I have brought in some prisoners," Freeman continued.

"We are taking no more prisoners; we are getting rid of them" the commandant said with a glance to the dark man behind him. He was clearly not a fan of the methods used by his associate.

"Well, we can take them with us, but the black American flyers seemed to know something, and the Italians who were sheltering them have knowledge of the resistance headquarters. I thought that a thorough questioning would provide valuable information and a feather in your cap."

"It will take more feathers than that to fly me out of here. Shoot them!" said a weary, pain-ridden commandant.

It had seemed easy in practice. Then what?

Rick sensed the hesitation, snapped his heel together, and made to leave. Freeman turned to seek instruction.

"Wait!" It was the Gestapo agent. He needed feathers to get out of there and to boost his next assignment.

"I should speak with them first. I have never questioned a Black man. They are so weak, subservient. It should be easy to get information out of them. Bring them to the cells under the building."

The commandant nodded a weak acquiescence; it was nothing to him. "Will you take schnapps with an old man?" he asked.

"Yes. Thank you, Sir. My soldiers will eat and then we are to be on our way—drive the Americans back into the sea again," Freeman replied.

"It is not that glamorous, young man." He had produced a bottle and two glasses.

The Gestapo man gave a look of disapproval and left, not having been invited to join in a drink. He would be including the drinking in his weekly report!

Rick left and, putting Rollins in charge of delivering the "prisoners," went to the kitchen, putting a package of herbs, prepared from a recipe he learned from Suli, into the stew prepared for the guards, as the first wave came in for lunch.

Thirty minutes later, Rollins and the five men with him had secured the cells in the basement, and Rollins was treating some of the prisoners down there. The guards in the mess hall and some of the cooks were sleeping and all were disarmed. Rick found a store room, had the stores removed by the cooks, and was having the unconscious Germans carried in; it would be locked. The commandant knew Heidelberg and was reminiscing with Colonel Freeman when Rick returned with Bruce and Kevin.

"Can we escort you to your private quarters, Sir?"

"What is this?"

"This is the taking of your camp by Allied Forces," said Rick, backed by his own gun and rifles of Bruce and Kevin.

"These men will search your room for weapons and then we ask for you not to leave until after we are gone."

"A prisoner in my own prison, eh? May I take my schnapps? The Gestapo will not be happy."

"The Gestapo is dead! He reached for a weapon and was stabbed."

The last part of the plan needed everyone, so they gathered from the basement and from the office. The radio operator had been overpowered and replaced by a Pole who, since his name was unreadable and unpronounceable, was always called Sparkski.

Bruce and Kevin were to blow up the machine gun towers over the front simultaneously, with cover from the main building provided by those not in uniforms. The rest of the group was to take the rear guards and the guardhouse.

The guardhouse was taken by throwing in smoke bombs. The guards exiting mostly dropped their weapons when ordered; others came out firing and were fired upon. There were casualties, mostly German. Two Americans were killed when a German came out of the latrines behind them, and several others were injured by the random firing from the smoke. The two towers collapsed on schedule, and the soldiers falling suffered broken bones.

The next hour was cleanup. Those captured were in the cells; those dead were buried. The Allied soldiers injured were treated in the mess hall; the guards injured were then treated by doc downstairs in the cells.

It was finally time to meet the prisoners of war.

Chapter Twenty-One

It was a little more than twenty-four hours since they had liberated Stalag Roma and almost four days since the American forces had started their push from the beach. How could so much have gone wrong after so much had gone right?

The commanding officer of the prisoners of war was of higher rank than any of the liberators. Brigadier Thompson ordered prisoners released, himself to be armed, and all the German prisoners hanged. Rick, then in charge, denied all three.

"Arrest this man!" the brigadier had shouted. "I intend to bring charges against all of your men."

"When and if you find yourself a court, give us a shout," said Rick on his way out of the door.

There were only sixteen of them, two had bullet holes and one had never fired a gun in anger. He put a guard on the armory, one on the storeroom, and one with the prisoners downstairs.

Consolidation was needed. There were fifteen in the storeroom; he moved them downstairs with only a minor incident as a large guard grabbed the gun of "Titch'Walker," a small Yorkshireman. The guard was immediately sorry as the army judo trainer threw him against the stonewall then, holding only his finger, frog-marched him back into line. Titch broke the finger as he said, "Just a reminder who's boss!"

The prisoners were allowed to elect cooks who were then to provide meals for them and for their captors. Most of the stores were cooked, and the resulting orgy left many sick, having existed for some time on gravy and bread and the stores empty.

The incident also led to the death of another of Rick's team. An Allied prisoner left the kitchen with a knife and went to the armory with a number of his buddies.

"Let us in, get us some guns, and kill us some Germans!" he demanded.

"No! Stand back!" said the guard.

They rushed him. He was stabbed, but not before he fired, injuring one of his assailants. Hearing the shot, Titch Walker and two Rangers rounded the corner and prevented them from getting into the armory.

"Put them downstairs with the German guards!" said an angry Rick when told.

"In the same cell?" asked Titch.

They had been speaking English; Rick reverted to German.

"If there is nowhere else! Get their name, rank, and serial number; I want them up on murder charges."

"Yes, Sir! All right, you lot! You heard; quick march downstairs."

"No, we are sorry," one said.

"Please…it was a mistake," another remarked.

"You can say that again, mate, but you killed my mate!" said Titch, leading them away.

Rick returned to the commandant's office where the brigadier was still alternatively threatening and begging Colonel Freeman to accede to his authority.

A rather nervous and frightened colonel would have done just that if he thought Rick would not kill him. He had been brought up on authority and with a sense of fair play, but the brigadier made sense.

They had heard of the attack on the armory.

"See, we are ready to fight and just need the ammunition!" said the brigadier.

"Brigadier, you can rejoin your men or share quarters with the German commandant, but I need you to leave—now!"

"You mean the commandant is still alive?"

"Perhaps you can regale him with tales of your retreat from Tobruk; bore him to death." Rick knew that was a low blow, but he was tired, and tired of that stupid man. He had been told not to expect much help.

"We need to bring Rico Nardone in here."

A small man appeared fifteen minutes later together with a messenger. He was dressed in the ragged uniform of an American sergeant. The man came to attention.

"Americo Nardone, sergeant 90084274."

Rick realized that he was in the uniform of a German, as were the other men in the room. "Please leave the room," he instructed the men who were waiting for the latest puzzle to unfold.

When the room was cleared, Rick said, You are Napoli, as I am Jones, and you work for Smith."

The man remained guarded. "And I suppose you know that I wear red socks?"

"But only in Fenway Park," replied Rick. "Sit down and tell me what is going on."

"I was working," he hesitated, thinking how much to divulge, "in the hills, when we come across a couple of downed airmen—one was in tough shape and died. When we were surrounded by a German patrol, I changed clothes with the dead sergeant. We were bought here and interrogated. They thought we had some secrets, but thank goodness, they just asked about the plane. We just gave them enough information so they would keep us alive."

"I think you have access to a great number of friends in the hills, and we can help them if we can trust them; always an adventure in Italy knowing who to trust."

Rico interrupted, "There are rumblings in the cell blocks. Why must they stay? Why are they not armed? Where is their next meal? Most are sick from overeating and want to blame someone."

"Do they understand that the Germans were going to kill them?"

"They don't care; they would have died on full stomachs!"

Rick laughed, aware that the soldier was always so. The Roman legions probably complained of having walked so far while enjoying the pillaging of Britain, like the English armies complaining of seasickness after their success in France.

There was a loud knock on the door. Rick commanded that they enter. It was Sparkski. He eyed the prisoner and, after a nod from Rick, said, "I know that you do not need more bad news, but I just intercepted a message. The American forces have changed direction and are heading for Rome. The Germans are delighted; they were under all kinds of pressure. Now, they are retreating and expecting to have time to regroup in the north: time to set up a deferred counterattack. It is German chitchat that they have secret weapons: a plane that goes twice as fast as the Spitfire, rockets that can bomb specific targets, and more big guns on railroad tracks."

Rick was dumbstruck. If the Americans were going to Rome, they were not going to be relieved in days; it was going to be weeks.

"Oh, and the Gestapo are looking for some weekly report."

"Thanks, Sparkski. This is Rico. He will be with us and may be able to identify some prisoners with the abilities we need.

"Please go back to the radio, find a copy of last week's Gestapo report, make up a new one, and send it. Make sure that there is static and interruptions so they cannot guess who is really on the key. Send everyone not on guard duty in, specifically Colonel Freeman and doc. And, send a message to Allied command: 'Smith help Jones.'"

The men arrived within a few minutes and were introduced to "Sergeant" Rico. There were six plus Rick and Rico. It was obvious that they had not heard the news which confirmed the respect that Rick had for Sparkski.

The present situation was laid out, and everyone was given a chance to voice an opinion. The opinions ranges from staying and toughing it out to taking everyone through the German lines to the celebration in Rome.

Colonel Freeman and Rico punched holes in every plan, from feeding the prisoners to arming them, to discipline, even to command, as the brigadier may have his own say.

Rick listened with his eyes closed then said, "We wait six hours to hear what Allied headquarters suggest. Then we decide. Thank you, gentlemen. I need some sleep."

He was awakened six hours later with more bad news: no advice from headquarters, they were not responding to his Smith code, the German activity was increasing toward their position, and the prisoners were hungry and belligerent. It was just before 6:00 P.M.

When everyone gathered, Rick had the brigadier brought to the meeting. "We have a dilemma!" he said. There were some muttering assents as everyone had been thinking of nothing else all day.

"The solution is that we must complete our mission regardless of the situation. Our mission is to save the prisoners from execution by the Germans and return."

It was obvious and too easy; the men were waiting for the plan. "Brigadier, you have asked to lead; here is your chance. Take the prisoners into the hills southwest about fifty, sixty miles, and join the partisans. We can give you some arms and a radio. My men will move through the Germans, south to the coast."

The brigadier looked alarmed. "Why should I not command everyone to the coast? I should not be fighting in the hills with a bunch of peasants!"

"You moron!" Rico shouted as he stood up to punch the brigadier. Rick pulled him down.

"Because, Brigadier, you speak no German, your schoolboy Italian will fool no one, and because we cannot move this number of people with any speed. Now, we have an hour before dark, and we must be gone. The huts will be set on fire so there will be no doubt that we have left."

There were a million things to do in just one hour. Titch was sent with Rico and two other prisoners with fluent German to get uniforms from the guards. The German commandant was told that he was being taken back to Allied command by a group of Allied soldiers dressed as Germans.

He laughed and made a strange request: "Please send a message, and let everyone believe that I have died as a result of resisting the takeover of the camp."

"Why?" asked Colonel Freeman.

"Because, otherwise, there would be retribution on my wife and daughters. They would be killed, and my son would be demoted to private and sent to Russia," he answered seriously.

Bruce and Kevin set the incendiaries round the huts. The prisoners were sent through the open gate with instructions to stay off the roads, stay away from towns, and travel quietly and purposefully all night.

As with any group-given instruction, the further they were from the prison the more they believed that the instructions were for the others, that they, as an individual, were possessed of superior knowledge. So, some five miles or less from the prison, they broke into houses for food, some whose feet hurt sat at the side of the road as if waiting for a bus, a gang broke into a bar and wrecked the place, some were diverted due west, and others were influenced by each obstacle, a stream meant walking alongside instead of across. By morning, they were dead—shot by German or Italian patrols, stabbed by farmers defending their property and daughters, in prison again, or lost. A few with the dedication of boy scouts had finally reached the hill where they were greeted with skepticism, and, oddly, some had their throats slit: such was the paranoia. Some eventually reached Allied lines with such stories of the breakout with their own roles greatly advanced. Interrogation led to strange stories of German soldiers who sometimes spoke English or American versions of English; none of these stories could ever be verified through official channels.

The brigadier had refused to leave and was handcuffed in the back of a truck.

The German commandant sitting unrestrained was the only one amused by the paradox.

Chapter Twenty-Two

The decidedly strange convoy left the camp and traveled slowly south. After a few miles, they could look back and see smoke from the buildings which were burning. Everyone was quiet; each had his own thoughts. They were driving toward the fighting, towards the lines, and everyone knew the penalty of a single misstep.

Rick had explained, as well as he could, that they had to return as soon as possible. The way to base was to go south behind the enemy lines and head for the beachhead, which should be under Allied control. The beaches were exposed and patrolled by Allied planes. Once there, they could risk a radio message to the patrols. That was the plan.

He was sitting next to Colonel Freeman in an open personnel carrier followed by a truck. The more fluent German speakers were in front of the carrier and in front of the truck. Inside the truck were the brigadier in cuffs and the commandant with suitable bandages, being watched by the two in American airmen's uniforms—one black, the other a crack sniper—who, though cuffed, had the keys in their pockets and the balance of the group.

For four hours, they were fortunate since all the roadblocks were checking papers of troops going north while diverting refugees off the roads. They tagged onto the end of other convoys heading south and then backed off when they were back on the road again.

When it was too dark to see and too dangerous to move even slowly, they pulled into a side lane and made camp.

A patrol was sent to reconnoiter and also to ascertain exactly where they were; the maps they had been given could be out of date or have errors, and there was no room for error.

Guards were set, and the rest slept the sleep of the exhausted.

Rick woke with a start at a different sound. Although he was into a deep sleep, he was instantly awake with a Luger in his hand. He had not been dreaming, or not that he could remember. The patrol had returned, and the sound had been the challenged response.

Doc reported that he and Rico had found a cluster of cottages nearby, and a barking dog had awakened a local woman who had provided food, a confirmation of their location, and also information of a German supply dump.

"How did you get so much in so little time?"

"I told you I was good!" said Doc, smiling. "Actually, it was Rico who did most of the talking. The woman asked if we knew anything of the men in the hills, her father and brother specifically. Rico did not but knew of some other men who she knew. We promised to take the food and information to her father. So, a little lie gets the job done, eh?"

"Get some sleep; you have about three hours before we move out. Well done!"

When the convoy moved out at dawn the next day, the brigadier asked why they seemed to be four men short. The commandant smiled. The brigadier was told that he was mistaken; everyone was accounted for. He persisted until he was told that he would be gagged as well as handcuffed if he did not shut up. In order to emphasize the command, the handcuffs were put on tightly by Doc who walked away from the protests.

The commandant, smiling broadly, said, "When I see these men and the ease with which they make personal and professional decisions with no fear of reprisal, I see why the Germans will lose this war. When I look at you, a brigadier, I see that all may not be lost: there could still be German troops in Trafalgar Square."

The brigadier was about to respond when they hit a bump. He fell over and was finally quiet.

About five miles away, two snipers were camouflaged in adjacent trees. In spite of their cultural differences and the colors of their skin, they had a great respect for each other. Both had binoculars and were at a German supply dump. Both periodically swept the surrounding terrain in the predawn light.

Birds had begun their early chatter, but they were sure that they would recognize the call of a whippoorwill which was their signal to attract the other's attention. It was also unlikely that any one else would notice the single call in the early morning chorus.

There was a mist hanging in the valleys and clinging to the trees wraithlike. It was early summer and promised to be hot later; it was peaceful and pleasant. Reb heard the whippoorwill call and turned to look at Amos. Those were not real names, and, although they would both take offence if called by those names back home, there they accepted that it was a sign of belonging, that they could both use the names for the other and accept the code name invented for speed of recognition. Not for the first time, Amos wondered what might happen if he and Reb happened to cross paths as civilians in Memphis or LittleRock.

Then it was business. Amos signaled, using his hands, that he had seen Brian and Kevin down at the edge of the mist coming away from the supply depot. Reb swung his binoculars but could see nothing. He knew that Amos was right and expected that they would be careful. He looked at his watch—quarter to five; they would be a half mile away.

The next sound chilled him, and he knew that he would remember it until he died, whether that was fifty minutes or fifty years. It was the sound of a German Alsatian dog in pursuit. The dog was still in the mist, but it was clearly headed their way. He looked towards Amos who had clearly heard the sound and knew the implications: they had failed. The mission had been discovered, and Brian and Kevin were running and bringing the guards straight toward them.

Brian and Kevin, as if reading their minds, turned north, away from the rendezvous. If Reb and Amos were not to get out, there was no point in leading Germans towards their backup or toward the rest of the group.

A routine patrol had picked up the scent after finding the footprints in the dew leading from the fence.

"The smell of Arsenal supporter set them off."

"Pick up your Spurs size ten shoes and let's find a place to make a stand."

"Maybe Amos and Reb can help."

"They must be half a mile away, and it is foggy."

Brian and Kevin ran in a curving pattern up a rising slope through the lightwoods. Suddenly, they heard a shot. It had been wide, but, obviously, they could be seen. They hit the ground. Kevin pointed to a rock ahead next to a fallen tree. He crawled under the tree and behind the rock, turned, and fired down the slope to cover Brian who's crawling the same way.

"Much ammunition?"

"Naw. You?"

"Full rifle, coupla grenades!"

"Surrender?"

"Yeh, dressed as Germans, having blown up their dump—they should bring us in and give us a cuppa tea, six of the best on the backsides, and send us home."

"Thought so!"

"What time is it?"

In answer to the question, there was a dull thump followed by the roar of a fuel explosion and black smoke that rose from the supply depot.

"Five o'clock cock!" they said and laughed in unison.

"That should tick 'em off."

"Lucky bastards; they were out chasing us. They could have been down there."

It did indeed annoy the Germans who were firing with light machine guns and moving around the slope. Brian and Kevin were doing some damage, but it was clear that there was only one outcome. The machine gunner was picked off by Amos from a long distance. Reb had gone to cover the road and the camp. He shot out the tire of a fire truck going to stop the blaze which also blocked the road out of the depot.

Meanwhile, Brian, who had been wounded, stopped shooting.

"All gone!" he said.

"Me, too," said Kevin. "I have one bullet in my pistol which I had saved for myself, but you have been such a good friend—the best I ever had; you can have it."

Brian had genuine tears in his eyes and said, after a while in which there was quiet and the birds were singing again, "I feel the same way about you, mate. Now, let's see how good you are. Stand up and shoot that officer between the eyes."

"How will we know?" Kevin asked.

"We'll be next in line behind him at the gates of Hell!"

"Do they play football there?"

"Yes, bloody rubbish!"

They shook hands, and both jumped up. There was an immediate cacophony of sound, and Amos, half a mile away in a tree, took advantage of the barrage to shoot the officer between the eyes.

Amos found Reb, and they left, eventually catching the group late in the day. At about seven in the morning, they saw American bombers saturating the depot with bombs, led there by the still billowing black smoke.

A night reconnaissance found that they were three miles from the beach. Watching, they saw a patrol go through and along the beach, marked the route, and returned with a report.

At a little after four, they were through the minefield and on the beach. They had booby-trapped the way in and were concealed under tarpaulin and covered in sand. About a mile down the beach, the truck driver was waiting for the dawn patrol. When he heard the sound of a small plane, he made sure it was British before he set the truck in motion toward the minefield before he stepped out.

The pilot was the same as the one who had seen the hidden depot burning the day before. The exploding mines and a truck turning over made him swoop for a closer look.

Strange happenings were not usual on the dawn patrol. He was flying an unarmed plane over enemy territory as a punishment. He supposed he was lucky in some respects, as he would have been in the brig in other circumstances. The brawl had been a doozy. They had been drinking the local red plonk, but he had not started the fight. It was an Italian who hit him first, saying, "Mi bambino! Mi bambino!" Of course, he had hit him back, and the other guys who were with him and the women in black shawls. How was he to know it was a local custom asking him to marry his daughter who was pregnant? How was he to know that "NO" was not an answer?

The squadron leader knew. He had confined him to barracks and dawn patrol indefinitely.

Strange. What was that man doing, waving? Or was it another strange custom when you ran into a minefield?

Then he heard the message in his headphones. "Jones to Smith. Jones to Smith. Bring us home. Repeat. Bring us home."

He went lower. The message was repeated, and he could see an American flag stretched in the sand.

Strange, very strange, the pilot thought. He told his navigator to make a note to pass on the message; maybe it meant something. The previous day, the bombers had been full of stories regarding their raid after the pilot had reported the smoke from the incident at the supply depot.

He had been ordered to check out the damage at the depot, so he did that and headed back, thinking, *Probably not an urgent message anyway.*

Dawn patrol indefinitely, he thought, *or until the wedding day.* He shuddered, *How long is indefinitely anyway?*

The boat showed up at sunset. It came directly out of the sun; they did not see it until it was close. They sent off a rocket, and a small boat was launched. The members of the crew of the launch were in stark contrast to the group they picked up. The navy men were clean, smartly dressed and, although they were busy with patrols, were rested and well fed. The insurgents were dirty, dressed in Skivvies, as they had finally shed the German clothing, tired, hungry, and unsmiling.

"Permission to come aboard?" asked Colonel Freeman.

"Permission granted. Are you the commanding officer?" a navy officer asked.

"Well, no...yes...I don't know."

"I am the ranking officer," said the brigadier, "and I want all these men put on report."

"There is a Mr. Smith below looking to take a statement from this group. Please speak to him."

"Just the man I am looking for," said Rick stepping around and through the nearest door.

"Rick, how good to see you," Mr. Smith remarked.

The British accent was too much. Rick hit him; Smith made no attempt to get up.

"I take it that the pleasure is not reciprocated."

"Why did you leave us out there, you bastard?"

"Not my decision, Rick. I came as soon as I could."

Rick had not cooled down. "You said you had access to the top—the very top."

"I went to the top, Rick. I was told that your group was expendable."

"And the prisoners of war?"

"Yes, well they were under sentence of death anyway."

"How do you sleep?" asked Rick.

"Who says I sleep?" Smith said as he was slowly rising to his feet.

"It was deemed more important for the American Army to enter Rome than to cut down the German retreat? The Germans are now regrouping in the North. Why?"

"What is in Rome, Rick?"

"Italians, beautiful buildings."

"Who is in Rome, Rick?"

"The Pope! The Vatican!"

"Correct. And the *Pathé News*. The Catholics in America will love it. The Italians in American will love it—the Congress, the Liberals, the Conservatives, Republicans, Democrats. The voters will love it!

"I argued the case for you, the morality. I resigned. It was not accepted. He said if you were that good, you would find a way."

"Well, *I* resign. Give me my papers and my ticket home. I am through with your public good. Now, it is time for *my* good."

Chapter Twenty-Three

"Rick left Italy that week and went back to Casablanca. Together, Sam and Rick embarked for America about a month later with the balance of the money that they had accumulated." Charles Munroe finished his story.

"I did not see him again for about ten years. Doc, of course, I recruited, and we stay in touch. He helps me with his insights, and we steer candidates to him that may be useful," he said.

"So, who do you work for?" asked Richard, which was the first of a hundred questions that had sprung to mind.

"Don't you have surgery?" asked Munroe just as the loudspeaker paged Dr. Land to the operating room.

Richard jumped up. How did he do that? How did he know?

"Can we talk some more sometime?" he asked, walking to the door.

"Yes, I think so."

"About my mother?"

"I think not!"

Richard had very little time for the rest of the day to try to analyze his feelings. He was busy with surgery. Then he reviewed his patients, taking his time, spending time with each. That night, he was the doctor on duty. It was especially busy due to the operating theatres all having been active plus one procedure which had been postponed until the evening with volunteer staff. Because Dr. Land was doing the procedure, there were enough volunteers. Before the patient was prepared, he had a meeting with everyone involved. Dr. Rollins also showed up and stood by the door.

"There is nothing complicated about this procedure. We are going to remove a piece of shrapnel from close to his liver. The reason for the meeting is to make sure that everyone understands the risks and that we do our very best to avoid contamination. The soldier is HIV positive. The name being given to this condition is AIDS."

"Is he homosexual?" the anesthesiologist asked.

"He is a patient! We do not care about anything else. Everyone will wear gloves and mask at all times. Glasses will be worn by surgeons and nurses. The operating room will be sterilized twice after we have finished. Cleanup teams will have all instruments, masks, gloves, boots, and smocks incinerated."

"Is this all necessary?" a young doctor asked.

"I do not know. But I am not willing to find out, and my team will not be at risk if I can prevent it."

"What about the cost, the waste?"

Richard nodded to the back of the room. The commanding officer said, "Authorized! Carry on," and left the room.

"Final word: Safety first!" said Dr. Land.

There were other checks after the operation, and, finally, he went to his office. He found a note on his door: "Your mother called." Below it, a note said, "Again," and "Three times." *Well, too late to call now, and too early*, he thought. The morning shift relieved him at six, and he took another shower. He had insisted that everyone shower after they had finished with the operation.

Then he slept.

The alarm jarred him awake. *It must be 12:30 P.M.*, he thought as he stumbled to the bathroom. He had thirty minutes to get in and out of the bathroom including shaving and having something to eat before he was in the middle of an operation again. *Well, at least it was only ten hours today*, he thought. He was methodical with an efficiency found only in overworked people. Somehow, they were the ones who could do more. If there is a job which needs doing immediately, give it to the most overworked, not to the ones who says they are overworked as they will just talk about not being able to find time for anything.

Dr. Land reviewed his upcoming day while shaving; it helped him find a slot for everything in the next ten hours. He needed a quick review at five over a meal with the day staff supervisor and his own colleagues. He was a bit off track, and he needed to get the routine back together.

The cafeteria was beyond his office, but he had no time to stop. Helen must have recognized his steps because she rushed through the door as he was passing.

"Did you call your mother? She called again this morning; must be important."

"NO. It was too late last night. Call her back for me. Tell her I love her, I am well, and I will call her later in the day."

Well, so much for getting a job done when you are busy. It must mean that includes everything but mothers, Dr. Land thought. It was somehow true: he found time for everything else. But no. It was that, if all was well, she would tell him so for fifteen minutes; if there was a problem, it would create another task which would have to be taken care of.

He ate a fried egg and bacon sandwich and had a cup of coffee. That day, he did not take the usual pleasure in his hurried meal, and he felt guilty.

The day passed as predictable as possible, and after his five o'clock meeting, he found time to go to his office and call home.

"Mum, sorry, I missed you. How are you? Everything well?"

"Richard. I called yesterday five or six times. Helen can be so tiresome. Then she says that she has not spoken to you either. I...."

"Mum, I have five minutes. Is there something?"

"Of course, there is something." She paused. It was clear that it was something she had rehearsed but had forgotten the lines in her exasperation.

"We are instructed to be at the reading of the will, Friday, 10:00 A.M."

Richard was confused. "Whose will? Friday is impossible!"

"I got a letter somewhere.... Ha! Mrs. Ilsa Land and Dr. Richard Blaine Land are requested to attend the reading of the will of Richard H. Blaine. The reading will take place at the offices of Austin Alexander and Roberts at 10:00 A.M. Please advise on your attendance before Thursday in the event that the reading will need to be rescheduled."

"See...'requested,' and you can RSVP that I shall not be there." He was annoyed. Why was his mother making such a fuss?

"I did!" she said. "The partner, Mr. Alexander, called back fifteen minutes later and said he could postpone until we could be there, but, since the business had to have continuity, time was of the essence."

"I don't believe this! How can my life go from fast track to out of control because one person, who I do not know, dies...? The answer is, 'No, I cannot go,' not this Friday, not next Friday, and not the Friday after. Now, I have to go. I will call you tomorrow, Mum. Take care. I love you."

"But, Richard...." She sighed and said, "I love you, son."

He hung up the phone shaking his head and mumbling to himself. "What is it with people directing my life? Unbelievable! Unbelievable!"

Helen put her head tentatively around the door. She had heard the tone of the conversation and was confused as she had never, in spite of great provocation, heard Doctor Land speak so abruptly, and certainly not to his mother.

"I am leaving. Thought to say good night," said Helen. "And a Mr. Alexander is holding the line for you. I told him to leave a message, but he said he has and will wait until you are free to speak to him."

"Helen, tell him...no, I will tell him. Have a good night." Richard stared at the phone and its blinking light. What attorney held the line insistent upon an answer? *Well, this will not take long,* he thought as he picked up the receiver.

"The answer, Mr. Alexander, is 'No! No! No!'"

"What three questions was I asking?" a brisk friendly voice asked.

"Would I be in New York Friday? At your office at 10:00 A.M.? And wasn't I even a little curious as to why?"

"And are you not just a little curious?"

"No!"

"Doctor Land, the instructions given to this office were very specific. There is to be no reading of this will until all of the people on a list that I was given could attend. It is a list of six names. Apart from your mother, it consists of Samuel Wilson, Kate Blaine, Charles Munroe, and David Skelton. The others have all given their word to be here."

"And if were out of the country, in Vietnam, for example?"

"In that event, there was a different set of instructions!"

"Then go to Plan B; I am not interested."

"I would, if I could, but facts are facts. When can you be at our office? Or we can inconvenience everyone and come to Washington. It really is important to the lives of a great many people as there are decisions to be made regarding the business, the allocation of investments, and distribution of personal assets. All of these require appointments, not to mention the filings for liquor license, etc."

Richard needed to think. There were so many "whys" going around in his brain that he could not say which was the first.

"Let me think, and I can call you tomorrow."

"Call anytime. If the secretary says that I am busy, please say that I am to be interrupted or found regardless of who I am with or where I am."

There were immediately things to do, and although he was due to be off duty by 10:00 P.M., it was after midnight when he finally dropped his white doctor's coat into the laundry bin and headed for his quarters.

Usually, a glass of Guinness, a light snack, and a reading of the newspaper would relax his body sufficiently to allow him to sleep.

That night, however, it was not working. His body was tired, and his mind was active—overactive. Twice, he set off to find a snack, only to forget where he was going. Twice, he sat with a newspaper in front of him then put it down without reading a word.

He was discomforted by the fact that he was not in control. Not that he was a control freak, but he did like order in his life. There was also the sense of justice which had cost him his fiancé, had sent him to Vietnam, and had ordained that he be a better than average doctor. *No, that is not justice; that is pigheaded. Stop! New direction. Cannot accept pigheaded. The "sense of right" then!* No. Because he could not be convinced that war was right. Then, was the healing of warriors, right? Did he have the right to fix them and send them back to fight? Only God could decide who went back to fight. Was he, therefore, playing God? Doctors were always accused of playing in the celestial field. *Stop! I am not God. A man can only do what a man can do.*

He was back to the beginning: What was the right thing to do?

He had no idea!

Finally, he fell asleep and dreamed again of Trish Wellington and Kate Blaine.

He awoke knowing what he had to do.

In the cafeteria, Gladys stood by the grill. "Usual, Sir?" she asked.

"No, Gladys. Some bran flakes, milk, and two slice of toast please."

"On a diet, are we?"

"No. But I sense that life is changing."

"For the better, I hope!" said the cook making talk for the sake of talk.

Richard walked away with his tray of food. "I don't know," he said half to himself.

He should talk to his mother right after eating; she would ask if he had eaten, but first, General Rollins.

In answer to that thought, in walked the general, helped himself to a cup of coffee, and sat opposite him.

"I have authorized a forty-eight hour pass but expect you will be back Friday night as you have weekend duty."

"Sir?"

"You could leave Friday morning, early, or if you want, Thursday night in New York. you could be on your away at about three P.M. Thursday"

"I did not apply for a pass, sir."

"No, but Smith said that you might need one, so I took the liberty of being prepared," said the general.

"What has he to do with my business? And is he in charge of the army, too?"

The general seemed to think it over and decided not to answer; he stood up to leave.

"Well, pick it up at the office if you decide to go."

It seemed that everyone was making decisions for him, which almost made him change his mind.

"Mother, telephone Mr. Alexander and tell him we shall both be there by ten Friday morning."

The decision made, and with his new commitment to himself, he found time to call Trish Wellington. She said that, of course, he could stay with her Thursday night; she would be delighted and sounded delighted.

Thursday evening, he took a cab to her apartment. She met him at the door, looking every bit as beautiful as he remembered and even better that his dreams. His dreams included dinner by candlelight and bottle of wine on a patio overlooking the city.

The apartment was two bedrooms and close to the park. The other rooms included a kitchen, but there was no dining table. When he remarked on it, she was aghast. "Nobody cooks at home, darling. There are all these incredible restaurants in New York."

"Well, we can have a nice quiet chat over dinner in a restaurant," he said.

Just then, a small woman came out of one of the bedrooms.

"Oh! I thought it was Wade," she said.

"Nice to see you again, too, Claire."

"Oh, my God. It's Richard Land. Oh my God! I thought you were in the army or something. Oh, my God!"

"You going out with Wade tonight?" asked Richard.

Trish jumped in, "No, we are all going together! A little reunion of sorts."

"But...."

"We all get together every Thursday...." Trish was talking, but Richard was no longer listening. He was taking in the scene—two attractive women dressed in the latest fashion with skirts not much larger than belts, showing a splendid amount of thigh, in high-heeled boots, and wearing colorful blouses opened enough that, occasionally, the top of a frilly bra was exposed; they both looked magnificent.

He was debating a suitable comment and, at the same time, wondering how much he had missed by being away from the modern New York social round of parties and events. He said the first thing he thought. "You are stunning!"

Claire and Trish laughed as though it was the funniest thing anyone had ever spoken.

Richard blushed, which caused another round of laughter broken only when the doorbell rang.

Trish opened the door. Wade stepped in, looked at Trish and Claire over, and said, "Cool! Richard, good to see you. Trish said that you might drop in. How's the great fight?"

"You look well, Wade, for someone sick enough to miss it." There was a look that passed between them, but before either could retort, Trish stepped in.

"Time we were going."

"Where to?" asked Wade, taking her arm and heading for the street.

"The new Italian bistro in the village. Charlie and Alice said they would save a table. I think ten of us."

So much for a quiet evening, thought Richard. But, as it was already 9:00 P.M., how long could a quick Italian meal take?

Had he known, he might have balked. Might, but looking at Trish—how animated she was, how well she fit in, and how gorgeous she looked—he could endure it for a while.

It was clear, as the meal slowly progressed, that the people all worked in the areas of finance, and the gossip of takeovers and the obscene amount of money someone had just made for raising capital, introducing someone, or filing a bid occupied their conversation for almost two hours while they waited for indifferent waiters to serve passable food.

The woman next to Richard finally noticed that he had not spoken and asked him who he worked for.

Wade heard the question and said, "Ms. Alice! Richard is protecting our democratic way of life, our right to be free, to make money, and to spend it. Richard is in the army."

Alice then turned with a look of fear and of curiosity, as one might look at a horror film villain.

"Do you kill gooks or spooks? Do you bomb those poor defenseless people, murder their children, and burn their crops?"

"No. I prefer to look soldiers in the eye and tell them what I am doing before I push a knife into their body or chop off an arm or leg. I get a great deal of satisfaction from it and can go for twelve hours or more without stopping, whenever necessary."

"Well!" said a visibly perturbed Alice. "It's not what I want to know."

"Then why ask?"

Trish leaned over to console Alice and said, "Alice, darling, Richard is a surgeon."

Then she turned to him and asked, "Why did you upset her like that?"

It was a rhetorical question as she was already turning back to a conversation of restaurants.

The bill finally came and the total, out of all proportions to the quality of food added, to which the pathetic waiters were rewarded with 25 percent gratuity.

The bill was split ten ways, and when Richard tried to pay for Trish, she gave him a withering look that asked that he not further embarrass her.

Outside, they piled into taxies, and, although it was midnight, the streets were alive with people; the traffic was heavy and noisy.

Richard was just dozing into reflection of the chaos he was seeing when they stopped in front of a nightclub. The only sign that it was a club was the single door in a long wall. There were people waiting in line to get in while two huge white men with gold chains guarded the entrance. As they walked along in a group, a black man with army pants with no lower legs was asking patrons to spare their change.

Richard slowed and stopped. "What happened, man? What are you doing?"

The man was suspicious; no one cared what had happened to him, not his family, not his friends, not the army, and especially not the rich white folk. The reason he had stopped there to get some sympathy money was that his leg hurt too much to get down to the tourist traps and his leg hurt too much for him to get some sleep.

"Landmine?" Richard asked.

"No. A fucking booby trap in a friendly fucking village in the Delta."

"Why don't you get some help from the VA?"

"Well, smart ass, because the VA is down town, I squat uptown, and I got no legs. The buses got steps, and taxis want to see money before they stop and I ain't got no money."

Richard pulled out his wallet, gave him a $20-bill and an army-issued identification card.

"Go to the VA tomorrow. If they give you any problems, tell them to call me."

The man squinted at the card in the poor light, then almost came upright in a salute. "Yes, Major, Sir! Private Lincoln, Sir!"

Richard was dragged away and into a blast of noise. The room was filled with gyrating bodies as a disc jockey high above was urging more and more sound out of car-sized amplifiers stationed like pillboxes around the room. The floor throbbed, and his head throbbed. He looked for relief towards the bar. It was obviously not a refuge, as there were six deep trying to attract the attention of bartenders in perpetual motion taking orders by gestures and assuming that the bills handed across were the correct change.

Trish came alongside, gyrating; she was glowing. The strobe lights enhanced the flush on her cheeks. He wanted her now, right now! She gestured for him to join the dancing. He gestured that they should leave.

We just got here! she mouthed.

Wade swooshed by, shouted in her ear to dance, and they gyrated away in a maelstrom of heaving bodies.

Richard watched them disappear, then he turned to the door. The cool air and silence that greeted him was sweet. It took him a minute to realize that the air was not particularly sweet, and it was still noisy, but the difference was so extreme that he suddenly thought about the woods in New Hampshire. He must go again soon. Would Trish go, too?

Looking around, he saw the soldier pushing along on an adapted furniture dolly. "Private Lincoln," he called.

"Yes, Sir. It's Abe—Abraham. Get it?" the soldier replied.

"Yes, Abe. Do you know a decent hotel I can stay near here?"

"Follow me. Keep up if you can."

They traveled a couple of blocks and stopped in front of a brownstone in the middle of the street.

"Go hit the knocker and when the man comes, tell Clyde that Abe Lincoln is here."

Having done the bidding, a tall black man answered. The greeting was not particularly friendly, but after the situation was explained, Clyde opened the door and showed him into a furnished apartment.

"The people own the individual units and use them when in town but rent them, usually by the week when they are away. It's some kind of tax deduction, I think," said the then talkative Clyde.

Richard, with the comfortable bed, was instantly asleep.

The next morning, he awoke. In the shower, he was trying to put a lid on the previous day and think forward to the meeting with the lawyers.

Clyde, at first, refused any amount and said that it was a pleasure and privilege to help an officer. He had lost an eye, and that had got him out. He was glad for himself, but he felt guilty for letting his group face the enemy without his help. Later, he accepted the fee and carefully filled the details into a bound ledger using the hospital address.

Richard wondered, as he sat back in a cab, if he should introduce Clyde to Wade. He chuckled at the imagined conversation and arrived at Austin Alexander and Roberts a few minutes after 10:00 A.M.

Chapter Twenty-Four

The conference room was typical of most legal firms in New York or any big city, but what set it apart was the view from the eighteenth floor. The view was to the east, and toy planes could be seen taking off from JFK airport while, below, ants teemed through tunnels of the financial district. On the river were boats, as if in a bathtub, and the impression was that a giant hand could remove the plug and send them spinning out of sight, out of control.

Mr. Alexander rose from one end of the table and introduced himself unnecessarily. "Dr. Land, thank you for taking the time to join us. I am delighted to meet you." He sounded delighted, or was it relief that Richard had shown up?

"Sorry, I am late; the traffic held me up a little," Richard explained but did not add that the reason was that he had spent twenty minutes on a pay phone in the lobby, listening to an hysterical Trish say how they had waited and looked for him, how dangerous New York was, and asking why had he not gone back to her apartment. He said he was fine, got a headache, crashed, and asked if she could put his bag on a Greyhound; the address was on the tag. No, he did not know when he would be in New York, and no, he was not interested in help from her daddy to leave the army.

As Richard entered the room, he saw his mother talking to Charles Munroe who moved away to leave the chair vacant.

Why was he here? Why was Richard surprised?

His mother pressed his hand as he sat.

"You look well," she whispered.

He felt terrible. His thoughts were all over: Trish, Munroe, his mother, and that meeting. Mr. Alexander spoke, introducing his associate first. She was young and bright, apparently recruited for grooming into the partnership. Carol Berger was there to keep track of the proceedings and would be preparing the estate return. There was a list of names passed around and mis-spellings, if any, were to be corrected. She was saying "sorry" in advance.

"I will start to my left and go around the table introducing everyone. Samuel Wilson, Kate Blaine, David Skelton Junior and David Skelton, Charles Munroe, and Dr. Richard Land and Ilsa Land.

"David Skelton has been in charge of Mr. Blaine's investments for about thirty years, and, as I understand, his son is now slowly replacing him in the business."

There was the briefest of nods from a medium-sized, slightly overweight, graying man wearing glasses. There was even less of an acknowledgement from a clone of his father with darker hair.

Richard saw the nod out of the corner of his eye since he was looking at Kate Blaine. He was also aware that everyone was looking at him and wondering what he was doing here; he was wondering about that himself.

"They are here today to have papers signed and to receive instructions from the heirs, although, technically, the executor has control of the funds until finalization of probate and final distribution."

It was probably the quietest will reading that the attorney could remember, but then, they did not know each other. Usually, there were relatives who had lived together for years, or relatives who barely recognized each other, sniping and arguing for rights that they would never receive, disagreeing about the size of their inheritance or about the size of the pot, inflating their closeness of the deceased, and deflating anyone else's claim or participation. It was generally a disagreeable process. The first protest agreed by all would be against the legal fees and the estimate of time necessary to administer. The second would be against the executor's fees. The third protest would be the estimate of time before they saw their money. It was comical how the heirs could take conflicting positions, often in the same sentence. It was hilarious how an antique could be worth much more to the estate but worth so little to the recipient, how it could mean everything as in "It was promised; the only thing I wanted" to "Is this all he left me?"

Yes, it was decidedly quiet. Mr. Alexander wondered if it would change when the distribution of specific assets was revealed. Probably not; his audience appeared to be people comfortable with themselves and with no expectations. He could never remember when he had to beg heirs to attend a reading of the will.

Expectations! That was the root of the dissentions he had witnessed.

The attorney was speaking again. "Everyone here is to receive something of the will, with the exception of my assistant and myself, although, arguably, we are also beneficiaries." He paused, his attempt at levity wasted as everyone was silent within his or her own thoughts.

He cleared his throat, took a drink from the glass of water in front of him, and began to read.

"I, Richard H. Blaine, being of sound mind...."

No one was listening.

Sam was looking across at Ilsa and wondering how it was that she could never age; she would always be twenty-two, about the same age as Kate. He involuntary patted Kate's hand; Kate turned slightly and smiled. She looks a little like Ilsa at that age but with so much more self-assurance. Yes, Kate would be fine. Thinking of self-assurance, there was Richard—Dr. Richard—looking so much like Rick at that age and with a similar aura of self-assurance.

Ilsa was looking at Sam and Kate. She saw the little hand pat and the warmth of response. Sam was older —must be seventy. He looked so much healthier, though. His head completely shaved, he looked like a monk with the quiet intelligence of the ages, one who knew everything but said nothing. The woman next to him was attractive. They had met at the funeral in black. Today she had chosen a dark green suit with a lighter green blouse up to the neck and a gold locket. *Quiet, reserved, in control*, thought Ilsa.

I bet they think I am in control, thought Kate. *They can't be more wrong; this has got to be the worst day of my life, well, the second worst, or third.* She started to smile. *Maybe there have been more bad days than I remember.*

Thank you, Sam, she thought as she smiled at him, misinterpreting the pat on the hand as reassurance. *In control? Sam is. So is that tall man opposite who looks so much like the old photo of Rick. He is either without a care in the world, or he is thinking of work, his patients. What is he doing here anyway?*

What on earth am I doing here? Richard was thinking. *The only good thing is a chance to get a closer look at this woman with the green eyes, except that, today, they are a blue green.* She looked a little like the old photo of his mother. *That must be the attraction*, he thought. No, not attraction—fascination; he could look at her for hours. He looked away as he caught her looking at him. When he looked again at her, she was still looking at him. He was wondering whether it would be more rude to look at the wall or into her eyes when she looked away at the speaker.

"…the first specific bequest is to Charles Munroe, an envelope with Smith written on it." The lawyer paused, looked up from the will, and said, "With the written approval of the executor and in front of these witnesses, I am delivering an envelope retrieved, along with the will from the safe deposit box." He gave a large envelope to Charles Munroe who took it and put it into his pocket without a word and without curiosity. The attorney returned to his task. "I leave to my friend, Sam Wilson, 8.33 percent of the shares in the restaurant so that he will own one third of the shares when added to the 25 percent held in trust for him."

Sam looked embarrassed, shook his head, and whispered, "No, No." He was in tears, silently sobbing, all the emotion of the past week welling out of his body in convulsions of silent emotion.

Kate put one arm around his shoulders and her other hand on top of his hands. Sam was still shaking his head, still was whispering, "Sorry. Sorry. I am so sorry." His embarrassment had silenced the room, not that anyone was feeling badly, but it was more that everyone understood in their own way that Sam had lost a friend. Their quietness then was a common communication with Sam, a quiet testament to their sense that they were witness to an emotion rarely seen, that if expressed at all was behind closed doors.

Sam looked up in silent thanks for the understanding, took the handkerchief offered across the table by Richard, blew loudly, dabbed at his eyes, and turned, now composed to the attorney, Alexander.

"I bequeath to my friend, Ilsa Lund, a box which will be found with my will. With the written approval of the executor and in the presence of those who witness, I hereby deliver to you this box. I am reliably informed that, Mrs. Land, you were known as Ilsa Lund."

"It is Mrs. Land, and yes, I was known to Rick as Ilsa Lund." Ilsa took the small box and turned it around and around as if the outside would reveal the contents.

Should she open it and risk crying in front of these people, or just leave it, as Charles had done with the envelope?

She continued to turn the box as everyone at the table looked as they might at a carnival. What could possibly be in the box? It was a curiosity without envy, a fascination without desire. The box could be good or bad, happy or sad, of great value or greater worth in its history, or of sentimental value.

"The balance of my estate after payment of all taxes and expenses is to be kept together and owned jointly. This, in particular and generally, includes the restaurant, any real estate holdings, any investments remaining at my death, any trusts, trust holdings, partnership interest, or any other assets of any kind, either personal or business, fixed or movable. Disputes or any deviation to my wishes are to be settled by decision of the executor whose decision shall be binding on all parties. The balance of my estate is to be held in this manner jointly by Kate Blaine and Dr. Richard Blaine Land."

"WHAT!"

Both Kate and Richard had spoken simultaneously.

Both Kate and Richard were on their feet, looking at each other. They looked at the attorney, back at each other, then at Sam and Ilsa in turn, expecting that they had not heard correctly, that there was a mistake.

Attorney Alexander, his assistant, Sam, and Charles Munroe looked as if they were not surprised. The David Skeltons looked at each other then back to their papers, preparing documents which needed to be signed.

Ilsa had been playing with the seal on the box in front of her. Feminine curiosity had been gaining strength during the preamble. At the shout from her son and Kate Blaine, she had jumped, so that the box opened. She had a glimpse of the contents, then she slammed the lid closed, and sat with her mouth open—stunned.

Stunned at what? The box contents or the will contents? She did not know; there was too much all at once. It was hard to remember to breathe.

"Samuel Wilson is appointed executor and will take a 7 percent fee. He is encouraged to hire accountants and attorneys to assist him, all to be paid from the estate.

"Signed this thirtieth day of January, in the year one thousand nine hundred and seventy."

The attorney ended, closed his file, passed the original will to Sam who pushed it back and asked if he could have a copy instead. The lawyer's associate left the room to have the document copied.

"Well, that went very well, just over an hour," said the attorney, obviously ignoring the fact that the two principal beneficiaries were still on their feet, unsure of what to do, what to say.

"I have to be going," said Charles Munroe. Kissing Ilsa on the cheek, shaking Sam's hand, and nodding to the attorney, he left.

"Er...," the senior David Skelton approached and, speaking to Sam, said, "we need some signatures, some authorization, and some direction for the investments."

Looking to the attorney for direction, Sam said, "I think I can sign as executor. Do not change direction for now; we shall be needing money for expenses and taxes. Is there enough for that, you think?"

He was already signing the proffered papers.

"Yes, there should be," said the younger man. "Here is a list of investments as of last night. We had been following Rick's advice and had bought some start-up companies, but with the war continuing, we have switched into bonds except for the core blue chip base."

Sam nodded as if he were following the logic and just said, "Thank you. We shall be in touch."

Richard had sat down. Kate was still standing. Turning to Sam, she asked, "What does this mean?"

"What does what mean?" Sam replied.

"This!"

"What?"

"Everything!"

"Is a one-word answer good enough, or shall we go home to discuss it?" asked Sam.

"What is the one-word answer?"

"I don't know."

"That's three words," said Kate.

"Four," said Richard.

"Who are you?" snapped Kate, heading for the door.

Sam shrugged. "You better come along. You too, Miss Ilsa. I am gonna need a lot of support; I be thinking."

The three of them rode in the elevator in silence to the legal firm's parking floor, after having Ilsa's parking ticket validated at the legal firm's front desk. When they got out, a red Camaro screeched to a halt in front of them. Kate was looking straight ahead through the window shield as Sam opened the door.

"This is going to be a long ride home in a very short time," he said.

No sooner was he sat than the eight-cylinder engine pulled the car like a rocket up the exit ramp, Kate changing gears as they went.

"Shall I drive, Mother?"

"Yes, please. This has been a very traumatic day."

They drove out of the now quiet garage into the busy Manhattan streets. It was sunny but cool as they exited and headed, without enthusiasm, to Brooklyn.

"So, Mother, what is in the box?"

"I don't know."

"Another one-word answer," said Richard, laughing.

Of all the questions that there were, why did he ask about the box? Questions!

Richard continued thinking; there were a million questions. Perhaps he did not want to hear the answers to the million questions, and perhaps his mother did not know.

But she did know more than she was saying; he just had to ask the right question.

But what was the right question?

Arriving at the restaurant, Abdullah directed them to a space and opened the door. "Good to see you, Miss Ilsa, and you, Doctor."

"Where can we find Sam, Abdullah?"

"Upstairs, I think. Miss Kate came roaring through here about ten minutes ago." He pointed to a Camaro with one front wheel on the curb. "Sam ran in right behind her."

"Thank you."

They went inside, and when their eyes became accustomed to the light, they were directed to a table at the back where Sam had told the hostess he would meet them. They sat and ordered iced tea. When they were alone, Richard had started to speak, but Sam suddenly hustled in and sat down.

Now, for some answers. Maybe! he thought.

It seemed that the answers were all one word: "I don't know!"

Chapter Twenty-Five

"Miss Kate, she got a headache. Won't be joining us."

"Sorry to hear that," said Ilsa. "I hope she is feeling better soon"

"Sam, you are Mr. Blaine's executor and his friend. Can you tell us what is going on?" asked Richard.

"Same question Miss Kate asked in the car. I'm…was Mr. Rick's friend, but I never always knew what was happening. Then, when I thought I did, I didn't, and then, when I did, I couldn't tell anybody."

"Then you can't, or won't explain?" asked Ilsa.

"Exactly, Miss Ilsa!"

There was a long silence. It was broken by a waitress asking if they wanted anything.

Sam told her to bring some cold appetizers, a jug of iced tea, then to make sure they had some privacy. The waitress left, to be immediately accosted by the rest of the staff asking what happened, where Miss Blaine was, who those people were. The microworld of a restaurant is based on the stories, the truth, and the fiction of people's lives. Bodies enter this exclusive world, become absorbed, become the center of the universe, leave, and are immediately replaced, forgotten like yesterday's newspapers.

"Sam, tell us about the restaurant. How did you decide, get started?" asked Ilsa. Richard had started snacking on the huge plate of fruit, cheese and crackers, nuts, raw vegetables, and cold cuts with breads which had appeared. He looked at his watch and thought about train, overnight bag, and Trish in that order. He hoped to catch the 4:30 P.M. train; it was already after one. He would have to leave 3:30 P.M. at the latest to swing by and pick up his bag, since Trish had vetoed Greyhound. "I need to make a call," he said. "Be right back."

"Use the phone at the bar," called Sam.

Richard hesitated, then the insane thought that he was paying for a third of all expenses anyway came through his head as he changed direction toward the bar.

It did not take long to get through to Trish and, since she fortunately was in a meeting and would not talk to him, arrange for his bag to be left at the desk with the "concierge." The concierge was actually an odd-job person who worked on several buildings changing light bulbs, sweeping the steps, and anything else requested by the management company, but this was New York so he had to have a title.

Richard rejoined his mother and Sam. He took a slice of cheese, an apple, a slice of walnut bread, a pat of butter, and cut them all into bite size pieces.

Sam was talking. "We came back to New York in 1945. We had money, thanks to investing success in Casablanca, and so, we moved into a hotel just down the street. They did not want to take a black man, but Rick says a black man serves his country just like a white, that he bleeds the same red blood, and he dies so that others have the right to make a living. There we stayed, but I had to pay a month in advance." He chuckled at the memory.

Chapter Twenty-Six

New York, 1945.

"Mister Rick, they did not clean my room again. Let's move to Harlem—better music, better people, something to do…."

"Sam, you are right!"

Sam blinked; he was only complaining because he was bored. They were sitting in a diner with indifferent food and nearly nonexistent service. In spite of having eaten there three times that week and having ordered the same thing every time, the same waitress had asked for things to be repeated three times and still brought white bread instead of dark rye.

"We have to move out, and we ought to open a restaurant."

"In Harlem?" asked the astounded Sam.

"No. Brooklyn," said Rick

"But you can't! Can you?"

"Never say 'can't'! Didn't Smith say we…I mean I could come back. Let's test it!"

"Today?" asked Sam. "What about tomorrow?"

"Today. Then we can move out of that crummy hotel."

The first stop was at the police headquarters. Sam sat just inside the door, trying to look inconspicuous, but everyone who came in saw him in the shadows. It was clear that the only black man through these doors had been under arrest. He was becoming more uncomfortable by the minute when a large sergeant rolled out and told him that it was not the bus station.

"I know, Sir," said Sam. "I was waiting for my…." he instantly felt how Peter had felt in the Garden of Gethsemane; he was going to betray his friend and himself. He felt sick, and afraid, and powerless. "…boss, Rick Blaine."

There! He had said it. It was everything they were fighting against; everything they were fighting for in Europe.

The large man turned, made a grunt, and was chuckling on his way back through the door that had swallowed Rick twenty minutes ago. Rick had gone through the door after they had both been left cooling their heels for over thirty minutes in that waiting room. It was one of the longest "hours" of Sam's life.

Meanwhile, Rick, who had asked to see the chief of police, was shown into an office in which a man with a weasel face was seated behind a large desk with a sign, "Deputy Chief of Police Michael Fitzpatrick."

"Rick, what can I do for you?"

"I came to discuss a killing, a murder."

"You're own?" asked the deputy with a smirk.

"Always think that you are funny, don't you?" asked Rick rhetorically. "Where is the chief then? Has he run off to find out what Mad Jack wants to do about my showing up?"

"We don't take orders from Mr. Disalvo, but we do like to keep an ear to the ground. We are not looking for trouble, Rick. We know that a war hero such as you has powerful friends in Washington and places, but this is not Washington; we don't want any trouble."

"Michael, you are a weasel. You always were a weasel. When you were sent to arrest me in '36, it was with 'orders' from Mr. Disalvo that I be shot resisting arrest. So let's cut out the crap, and go find your chief."

It was clear from his color that the deputy was not only guilty of all the charges and the obvious conclusion. There was also anger at having been ordered like a lackey to find his boss and step aside. The rest of the precinct and the population at both sides of the law were giving their apparent next chief a deference he had not earned. He was used to respect, and his eyes narrowed in dislike and spite.

However, the deputy had been briefed and knew better than to voice his feeling. After a silence, he went through an interior door to the office next door. There was a whispered conversation, then Chief O' Connor appeared.

"Rick!" he cried. "They should have told me you were here"

The man was bigger than Rick remembered. But then, ten years had gone by since he last saw the then precinct captain Sean O' Connor. How did all the Irish end up as policemen and all Italians as crooks, and who were bigger villains?

Then he quickly thought how he had fallen for the stereotypical image, and it was probably not fair. Both ethnic groups worked on the docks, and from both groups were taxi drivers, lawyers, and doctors.

"Sorry to bother you Sean, Michael and I were just reminiscing."

"Well, Rick, it's welcome home! Let bygones be bygones. You staying in the area or moving on?" he asked hopefully.

"Thought that we might stay a while. Go back into business, help the economy, and jumpstart the postwar boom."

"You and that nigger." The chief stopped, realizing he had just admitted that he knew Rick was in the building.

Rick did not respond as he already knew that.

"Your license to practice law was revoked when you murdered Alan, and I don't think that they will reinstate," the chief continued.

"Sean, if you and Michael had done your job and arrested Alan Braden for the murder of my wife, then he might still be alive."

"Alleged murder, Rick. Alleged."

"So what is the status of the alleged murder of Alan Braden?" asked Rick.

"The case is officially closed as death by misadventure," said the chief, nodding at his deputy as if for confirmation or challenging him to refute the decision.

"So what kind of business are you starting, Rick? How can we help you?"

"A restaurant. We are going to need a liquor license, music license, and building permits. We just need you to stay out of our way."

"Who is the 'we'? Mr. Disalvo, or someone else we know?"

"NO, the gentleman outside. Mr. Wilson is my partner, and if you call him nigger again, I am going to take your pearl handled gun and stick it up your arse."

Rick stood up and, having received the answer that he came for, left the room. He had been gone ten years, and nothing had changed.

Sam was glad to see him and asked no questions even when they were out in the street. They walked in silence until Rick turned into a cemetery. It was just off the main street which was crowded; the place was empty and quiet. It had been full on the last day that he was there—the day of the funeral. The funeral had cost every penny they had saved. He was owed a little money, but they had no bills. He had taken the evidence of her assault and murder to the police. As a respected, if young, ambitious attorney, they had listened. Sean had listened…but done nothing.

Sam stopped at the gate; Rick went in alone.

It was almost an hour before Rick reappeared and hailed a cab.

"Where to now, Boss?"

"The Blue Lagoon," Rick said to both Sam and the taxi driver.

The taxi driver looked back at Rick, then Sam, then Rick. He shrugged and pulled into the traffic.

"We going for lunch?" asked Sam.

"No! To visit with Mr. Disalvo."

The driver, who was listening, looked in his mirror at Rick, then Sam, then Rick again.

The Blue Lagoon was a neighborhood bar that served food. The sign in front advertised Schlitz and Schaeffer beers; the inside was dark. A bartender was polishing a glass but stopped as the door opened, and his right hand dropped below the level of the bar. On the other side of the room, virtually unseen because he was sitting so still, was another man in dark clothing. There was nothing on the table in front of him, and he did not move as Rick stepped past him to the bar.

"What'll it be?" asked the bartender, looking at Rick, then, with some confusion, at his companion.

"My friend will have a nickel draught, and I will see Mr. Disalvo."

"Mister who?"

Rick ignored his question. "Tell the guy behind me to put down the shotgun and go tell Jack that Rick Blaine wants to see him."

The bartender obviously pressed a buzzer as a door opened at the back and a bulky young man came over. He listened as the bartender whispered then he went back inside.

He pulled a small beer and put it on the bar.

"You want a shot with that?"

"No, Sir," said Sam whose eyes had been wide since they came into the bar. He wanted to turn around to see what Rick had seen, but he did not.

There was silence; all four were quiet. Sam took a sip of beer; the sound was heard all over the room. *How can I be such a noisy drinker?* he was thinking.

"The Rick Blaine who shot Alan Braden in the back?" Rick was spared a riposte when the back door opened again and the bulky head silently gestured him back. When he got there, he was expertly patted down and then steered into a corridor where another young man stood by a dark door. The young man knocked and, at a sound within, opened the door for Rick to enter. They both went in.

John "Mad Jack" Disalvo was smoking a large cigar at a large desk. There were two chairs in front of his desk; he gestured to one.

"Rick, long time no see. How are you?" There was a friendly voice but no friendship in the voice.

"Hear that you want to open a restaurant with a…," he looked down with exaggeration "a Mr. Wilson. What you serving, fried chicken?" He laughed at his own joke.

"I knew that Sean would slither right over here as soon as I left, so I gave him enough time to earn his money. Jack, I came to find out where we are, and find that the story is that I shot someone in the back. That is not a good place to start."

"Sorry about that, Rick, but you know how stories get changed. And call me Mr. Disalvo, you know, a little respect."

"A little respect, Jack, then call me Mr. Blaine. And get rid of Jimmy Cagney over by the door with his hand in his pants."

John Disalvo took the rebuke, saw a determined look in Rick's eyes, then flicked his hand at the young man by the door who quietly left.

"Look, Rick, the thing with Alan…you should have come to me, not the police. I had to protect my own. When he went down, there is a price to pay—for someone. It was either go after you, or wait here for someone to come after me. Alan was wrong; he was mean, vicious. I would have had to do something with him eventually. But he saw your wife, and she slapped his face. He slapped back. Okay, he smashed her head against the wall."

"He tried to rape her, then smashed her head like a pumpkin, came right over here to this bar, and, in front of twenty people, boasted what he had done. I saw her, Jack. Smashed!"

His fist smacked on the table. The door opened, and two young men entered.

"Get out!" yelled Disalvo, clearly emotional along with Rick whose head was in his hands, reliving that terrible time.

They sat, each with his own thoughts until Disalvo spoke. "Had a visit from a friend of yours, a Mr. Smith, he said his name. Funny really. He came right through the front door and the back with three other men. Said that there were a couple more outside keeping the lads company. He said that if anything happened to you, Rick, a certain warehouse of mine would burn. The place would have a gas explosion, and the IRS would be in my office day and night for a year. I told him that my books were here in the desk for him to see. He asked me to call a number which he gave me and speak to my associate. That number, Rick, only I knew. Even the telephone company does not know it. My associate confirmed that the IRS was in fact on the third floor with an armed guard.

"So, Rick, what do I do? I agreed there was no contract, that Richard Blaine could return anytime, and that he could have the keys of the city as far as I was concerned. I will even call you Mr. Blaine."

"That was what I came to hear, Mr. Disalvo. Now, I have got to go before Mr. Wilson has a coronary."

"You have some very powerful friends, Mr. Blaine. They put three of my boys into hospital. We had to go and rough up some of Bonanno's boys in retaliation. Well, it's all about respect and face, isn't it?"

Rick and Sam left as the bar started filling.

"Well?" asked Sam when they were outside.

"Let's find somewhere permanent to live and then build a restaurant."

Chapter Twenty-Seven

Rick asked the driver to drop them at the post office near the hotel so he could make a telephone call and, if necessary, send a telegram to confirm the transfer of funds into his bank account.

Sam read the notices outside advertising for work or items to sell. There were bicycles for a dollar, bedroom suites for twenty-five dollars, "lightly used." There were people willing to do yard work, roof work, house cleaning, and laundry for "cash."

The government just needed to look at the post office notice boards to see how the economy was doing.

He stopped and stared at one notice—house for rent, four bedrooms, kitchen, small yard, make mortgage payment $71.50, and pay all bills. The notice had been there for three months; it was obviously in the neighborhood.

Rick came out, and together, they looked at the notice. Since it was close, they walked over to look at the property. It was tired-looking but clean. They checked the other houses on the street. Clearly, it had once been an upscale part of Brooklyn.

"Well, let's see the reception we might get," said Rick.

They walked up and rang the bell. There was movement behind the door but no response. "It must be my black face," said Sam, nodding to a front window where the curtain had moved. Rick pulled out a piece of paper and wrote his name and where he could be reached. He pushed it through the letter box. There was a noise and a scampering in the hall behind the still closed door.

They waited patiently, though they were feeling like sitting ducks. They could imagine dozens of pairs of eyes watching the drama unfold. Behind the doors and curtains and up and down the street were faces, watching, knowing that Mrs. Hester was home, that she had reasons for not answering. They knew the reasons; they knew everything that happened on the street and in the lives of the occupants.

There was a scrambling, and a little boy opened the door slightly. He looked out and spoke to Rick while staring at Sam.

"My mum says she is not in."

He was about five years old in clean short pants and shirt. The innocent eyes told a story.

"What's your name, little boy?"

"Jimmy."

"What's your mum's name?"

"Mrs. Hester."

"Jimmy Hester, please tell your mum, when she gets home, that a man wanted to rent a house." Rick spoke loud enough to carry to another doorway where he was sure that the missing woman was standing.

"And here is a dime so that you can buy some candy for yourself."

"Thank you, Mister."

The door closed.

It opened immediately. Standing in the doorway was a thin woman in an old dress, wearing a housecoat, carrying a child about two while Jimmy was peering around her legs.

"Here is your dime. You have no right...."

The curtains up and down the street were flapping as people were crowding each other for a better view of the scene unfolding. It was better than the movies, much better.

"Mrs. Hester," Rick could see that she was close to breaking down, "I wondered if you still had a house for rent?"

"Oh, come in!" she said. "The neighbors will have a field day." Then under her breath, "The damage is done anyway." She put down the child she was holding as she backed to let them in.

They sat in the living room. It was cold, and Mrs. Hester unconsciously put on a cardigan. When they were seated, she sent Jimmy off to read a story to Megan.

"I thought you were from the bank."

"Mrs. Hester, do you have a property to rent?"

"Yes, this one until the bank takes it." A tear that appeared was quickly flicked away. "That's not a very good way to do business, is it? But I have to face reality. That's what Mother says. I just can't wait.... I just can't cope."

There was a trembling about the mouth but no tears.

"Sam, can you please find the kitchen and make a cup of tea?" asked Rick.

Mrs. Hester's body was heaving with emotion. There was a silent sob; she was holding on, but only just...no tears.

"The kids miss their dad," she said tonelessly, not saying the obvious—including herself.

"It's his fault. We had to buy the house, and we were going to be all right. Then he gets drafted." She heaved and her lip trembled. "Left the kids…and me. Just left us to cope."

"You are doing fine. The kids look healthy. Where is your husband now?"

"James. In the Pacific. Navy."

"Well, he should be home soon."

"My mother-in-law thinks we should move in with them—in Passaic. If someone rents the house, I will have to move back home. The bank sent a letter; we're behind in payments. I thought you were from the bank."

Sam was back with a tray, three cups, and a bowl with a little sugar in it.

"Jimmy helped," he said as he was trailed by two small children.

"Can we see the house while the tea brews?" asked Rick, standing and moving out the door.

"Yes, not much to see. Downstairs, we have this front room. Then opposite, there is the dining room, and back there is the kitchen. Then a laundry area and washroom with toilet." They moved up the stairs with Megan happy to be carried by Sam.

"On this floor, there are two bedrooms and a bathroom. Then on the third floor, another two bedrooms, although, really, because of the roofline, they are very small."

The house was clean, and there were signs that the updating of the property had been interrupted. Some of the bedrooms were newly painted and wallpapered while others were just cosmetically repaired.

The same train moved back down the stairs, the children uncommonly quiet although it was clear that Sam had won them over.

Seated again, Mrs. Hester poured tea.

"Was there milk?" asked Rick, not seeing in time Sam's look across the coffee table.

"No milk!" said Jimmy solemnly. "Remember, Mum? The milkman said no milk until he gets paid."

"I don't need milk. Thanks," said Rick trying to recover.

"Here's the thing, Mrs. Hester. We need a place for at least six months. We like the location, but we need cleaning, laundry, and cooking."

Mrs. Hester looked confused.

"If we pay the mortgage and expenses, buy the food, would you stay as housekeeper and cook for us?"

"What about the children, what about…. He's black. What will the neighbors say? What will the bank say?"

"Well, if we move you and the children into living room, then Sam and myself, we can take a floor each to make a bedroom with private sitting area. If you are worried about the neighbors, then you will have to leave the house and move to Passaic. If you agree, then we can visit the bank together tomorrow."

"I would rent to the devil himself, sorry, no offence, rather than move to Passaic. And James will kill me if we lost the house and our deposit."

"Fine! We shall return at nine in the morning and go to the bank. That okay with you, Sam?" asked Rick

"That's fine, Boss. These real fine folk. If Mrs. Hester can cook like she cleans, I have no problem."

"Let me give you a deposit. All I have in cash today is twenty dollars," said Rick taking two ten dollar bills from his wallet.

Mrs. Hester took the money, looked at it, and, finally, the tears flooded past the shell that had been set up to protect the children. Jimmy and Megan rushed to her side. Megan also started crying. The tears looked likely to never end as she hugged the children and kissed the top of their heads.

Rick and Sam let themselves out the front door.

Next morning, as they were walking from the hotel to meet with Mrs. Hester, they were discussing the new dimension in their lives.

"You know, there was no milk, no sugar, and no bread in the house. There was some cereal for the kids and some potatoes. Not much else," said Sam.

They were passing a bakery, with the enticing smell of fresh baked bread.

"Well, we need bread," said Sam. "I have money for that. How about some groceries?"

"I'll get the bread," said Rick. "Go next door and pick up some milk, eggs, butter, sugar, flour, and anything else you think of. The butcher is next door; he must have some minced beef and chicken."

"This is the best I felt since...."

Sam stopped; he did not want to reminisce and rake up past memories.

Mrs. Hester was standing in the hall with coat and hat. The children were also wearing outdoor clothes. There were some moments of confusion with all the packages and putting them away. The children looked at the pastries with unabashed longing until they were given permission to have one each.

At the bank, the manager, Mr. Maxwell, kept them waiting for ten minutes. It might have been longer, but the sight of Mrs. Hester, two children, Rick, and Sam all sitting ramrod straight in the waiting room was starting to attract a crowd of curious customers and staff.

"Mrs. Hester, I am sorry to keep you waiting. Please come in." The bonhomie was false; everyone knew it was false. Why did people use colloquialisms? Why were there phrases used with good intent but no sincerity? Why did people accept them? Why not say "I have kept you waiting the maximum amount of time I can to make you feel uncomfortable and therefore give me the upper hand when giving you the bad, bad news instead of 'Sorry to keep you waiting'"?

He looked at the two children as if there was a bad taste in his mouth but made no comment. When he went to close the door behind the woman and two children, he was astonished to see two men following them into his room. More astonishing was that one of them was black and had a confidence in his walk and manner which Mr. Maxwell was not used to seeing.

"Mr. Maxwell, can I introduce Mr. Blaine and Mr. Wilson? My two children, you have met."

"Pleased to meet you," Mr. Maxwell said without enthusiasm and without sincerity.

He cleared his throat and attempted to take control of a situation which he saw rapidly declining.

"Mrs. Hester, the bank has sent repeated notices to you regarding the mortgage on your property, and we have had no option but to put it into foreclosure and to schedule an auction in thirty days. If the presence of these two gentlemen is to intimidate me, then it will not work; the process has begun."

"Mr. Maxwell, I apologize for not having made the payments. As you know, Mr. Hester is in the navy, fighting a war which we thought would be over by now." She dabbed her nose with her handkerchief, then, remembering her resolve, continued. "These gentlemen are renting part of the house, will be paying rent, and will ensure that I can keep the house until James…Mr. Hester gets home."

"It is too late. The process has begun. It is very time consuming to get the paperwork prepared, the notices, the lawyers, and the board of directors. We do not take these steps lightly. These gentlemen may not stay, may fail to make rent payments, then the bank has to begin all over again. No, no, it is too late."

Mrs. Hester visibly shrank; she was the woman they had seen yesterday, not the woman they had met this morning. The children had moved closer to her, standing each side of the chair. They were both touching her, their fear showing even if they did not understand the conversation.

"Mr. Maxwell."

Rick spoke for the first time since entering the room. He was dressed in a grey worsted suit and white shirt with a maroon tie. The cufflinks were French, a fleur-de-lis. He was speaking softly as much to reassure Mrs. Hester and her children as to have to bank manager listen very carefully.

"I have always found that it is never too late. I believe you can find the man in charge of your 'workout' division and that we can work out a solution. We are ready today to bring this mortgage into compliance and to deposit sufficient funds at your bank to make the payments for six months. Unless there is another reason for the foreclosure."

"Like what?"

"Like there is someone willing to bid at auction a very small amount."

"Mr. Blaine!" An indignant Mr. Maxwell was on his feet. "I object!"

"Then let us work together."

"How do I know that what you say is true, that you have the money and will put it into my bank?"

Rick and Sam took out checks and pushed them over the desk toward the bank manager. He looked at the checks with some amazement then back at the two men. He picked up the intercom.

"Mrs. Johnson, have Mr. Millward join us in my office with the Hester file."

In a very short time, they were joined by a middle-aged man with nicotine-stained fingers who entered the room with the smell of cigarettes floating around his clothing. He had a casual smirk as though he knew what was about to happen. He enjoyed throwing women and children into the street.

"Mr. Millward, this is Mrs. Hester, Mr. Blaine, and Mr. Wilson. These gentlemen are going to bring this lady's mortgage current and guarantee payments for six months."

"But...."

"Please prepare the paperwork for signature right after lunch. Then return the file to the mortgage department."

"But...."

"I shall prepare a memorandum for the board with the facts and mention your diligence."

"Thank you, Sir. But...."

"That will be all, Mr. Millward."

That is not all, thought Mr. Millward. He would have his own memorandum to the board, but what would he say to his fellow investors? You win some, you lose some?

"Gentlemen, do I have your permission to check your bank references? I do not believe that I know anybody at the Bowery Bank."

"By all means, call David Skelton. I can write his telephone number for you. We shall be happy to return at 1:30 P.M. to complete our business. There should be no need for Mrs. Hester to return, is there?"

"No, no, we can open the accounts. Will you need checks? Any borrowing, we would need personal financial statements and references."

"Yes, we need checks, but we have no need to borrow at the moment. We should like to see a list of properties which you have going to auction with the date and all the relevant background on each property. We are interested in commercial sites primarily."

"Very good," he said as he ushered them out of the door.

Once on the street, Sam said, "These kids were so good they deserve an ice cream."

"Thank you! Thank you both!" Mrs. Hester had revived to her confident manner from the morning.

Chapter Twenty-Eight

The next few weeks were either fast or slow. Some days, there was not enough time to do all the things that needed doing and other days seemed to drag.

A list of properties and dates of auctions came from the bank and then another list of businesses looking for partners, looking for capital, or just looking for a way out. Rick and Sam studied them all carefully and put them into piles with their comments. Mrs. Hester described the surrounding areas. Then they went to look at the top ten choices. None of them were exactly what they were looking for, even though they could not have described what they wanted.

They were walking back to the house with Jimmy between them when a sign caught their eyes.

"For sale or lease, commercial property 200,000 sq. ft., will subdivide."

The sign had been there for a while, and there was little evidence of occupancy. A panel truck which had seen better days was parked about halfway down, advertising that the owners were expert in the art of installing linoleum on floors. There was another hand painted sign that promised that used furniture, carefully restored, was available at prices that were barely credible.

They walked down the street. The furniture store was dirty and dusty; they were barely able to see through the window. The door was locked; a sign said that they would be back at 9:00 A.M. the next day. In front of the panel truck was an open door. Inside, there were rolls of linoleum. A noisy radio led them to a man at a desk laboriously calculating an invoice.

He jumped up as they entered, turned off the radio, then stepped backwards as if defensive.

"Afternoon, Gents. How can I help you? Need new flooring, do you?"

The man had not introduced himself, so neither did Rick.

"Who owns this property?"

"Well, not me. I just rent, see? I see the bloke who collects, that's all, from the real estate agents on High Street, Watson and Sons."

"Thank you."

"I know where that is. I can read, you know," said Jimmy.

Arnold Watson was just closing the blind when they arrived and was a little peeved when they pointed out it was only five minutes to five.

He pouted, looking at his watch.

"Arnold Watson. I am afraid the staff is about to leave, but perhaps we can set an appointment for tomorrow?"

"We only need four minutes," said Rick, looking at his own watch.

"You have a property on Briar Terrace for sale or lease 2000,000 square feet," he continued.

Arnold Watson repeated the address under his breath as if there were more than a dozen buildings of 200,000 square feet in the portfolio.

"Oh, yes," he finally said. "A fine, commercially-zoned property in good condition. The asking rent is fifty cents a square foot net...net."

"And a selling price of what, one million?" asked Rick.

"Yes, that would be about right."

"What will he take?"

"Well, there are leases in place so to buy them out...."

Rick jumped in, "There are two tenants paying a nickel, and they could be gone tomorrow. The place is a blight on the neighborhood. The owner is paying real estate taxes, insurance, and the place is in desperate need of maintenance. We are willing to take it off his hands for seventy five thousand."

"That's insulting!"

"Then insult him. Here is my name and address. Send someone round with an answer tomorrow."

"Tomorrow?"

"Yes, or we may have found a better location," said Rick, heading for the door.

Next morning, at eight o'clock, a messenger delivered a note asking that Rick attend a meeting at the broker's office at ten. He gave the messenger a tip and a reply that he and Mr. Wilson would be pleased to attend a meeting.

When they entered the office, there was a heightened awareness. The receptionist, a clerk, and the secretary for Arnold Watson were all clearly aware of the story to date and appeared to be anticipating an event that could be the gossip for weeks.

They were shown into Mr. Watson's office by the secretary.

The office was small with pictures of a smiling family. They were gathered around a patriarch, obviously the father of Arnold, and an older, rather plain woman, obviously Arnold's mother. There were other pictures of embarrassed, overweight teenage children around the room.

The room was made smaller by the presence of a very large gentleman in an expensive suit.

"Ah, Mr. Blaine and er," he looked down at a piece of paper, "Mr. Wilson, I am pleased to introduce Mr. Goldstein, the owner of the property that you enquired about, and his attorney, Mr. Austin."

A man appeared around the back of the large Mr. Goldstein, acknowledged his name, and greeted them with the small wave of his hand. It was not that he was small but that he was dwarfed by his client.

"Good of you to come, Mr. Blaine and...Mr. Wilson," said the large Mr. Goldstein in a surprisingly soft voice. He shook hands with them both with surprisingly small hands which were also soft.

"Mr. Watson informs me that you have some interest in my Briar Terrace property. Why?" He spoke as though he had many properties, but it was clear that he knew the disposition of each. It would not have surprised anyone that he knew all his tenants and could recite the terms of their leases and recall the balance on any one of the accounts. He was also obviously a major account of the real estate agent and management firm, Watson and Sons.

"What do you care? If we agree a price, then I could store sugar or explosives or convert it into a supermarket or a brothel," said Rick a little insultingly.

There was a long silence. It appeared at one point that the realtor might break it, but as he looked at the four men in the room, it turned into a nervous cough.

"Mr. Blaine, none of my properties is for sale at any price to a German or anyone trading with or having sympathy with the politics of the National Socialists. In your choice of Mr. Wilson as an associate, I can safely assume that the latter is not the case but I must have an answer to my question before we can begin to negotiate."

"I understand. I can assure you that I have no sympathy with Germans. We have had enough of that. Sam and myself, we are looking to start to rebuild here in New York."

The verbal barrage had taken a toll on the meeting.

Sam stepped in. "Perhaps we should start again by introducing ourselves. I am Sam Wilson, a piano player. I have known Mr. Rick, Richard Blaine, for ten years. Most of the time, we were in Paris and Casablanca. We left both of these places wanted by the Gestapo. Returning to New York, we want to invest and build a business with some monies that we managed to accumulate."

"Thank you, Mr. Wilson. May I call you Sam?" Mr. Goldstein said.

Sam nodded.

"I am Aaron Goldstein. My parents came from Poland just before I was born. The rest of their family's brothers and sisters, nieces, nephews, and cousins have disappeared. My mother and father...hah! You do not need to know." He paused. "My father invested everything he earned into real estate. He bought a three-decker house. We lived on top since he could get more rent for the first two floors. I continued to buy properties in the Depression while working in the clothing market. Now, we are lucky; hard work has paid off. America is a great country. Mr. Austin is my attorney and knows everything about our business. We currently operate a department store on the High Street, which my sons will help me run when they kill every Nazi they see, or run out of bullets."

There was another prolonged silence.

"Your offer was insulting!" Mr. Goldstein started.

"So I was told by your agent. But you are here," stated Rick.

"I need five hundred thousand. I will take three hundred and fifty and stay in as one third partner with a preferred buyout."

"I think you would take three fifty in a heartbeat. It would not take two fifty to not break your heart. I think you are expecting to hold a purchase-money note behind a bank mortgage." Rick was rolling. "You have a property which needs probably a hundred thousand dollars in deferred maintenance to see it through a hard winter, roofs, windows, heating system, and plumbing. It is costing you a great deal of money, and the neighborhood stinks. It may have looked like a great site for a second department store, but your boys went off to fight.

I'll tell you what. We will give you one hundred and twenty five thousand, cash deal, close within the week."

"No way!"

"Okay, I am out of here." Rick rose and left the stunned room.

There was not a sound; no one appeared to be breathing. The broker and the attorney looked anxiously at their client, then cautiously at Sam who was looking dispassionately at the large man behind the desk.

Aaron Goldstein broke the silence. "Does he mean that? Do you have the ability to pass papers within seven days?"

"Yes, he does," said Sam. "We can close in seven days, and he does not need or want partners. I am the only one, and Lord knows why."

"I need to talk to my attorney. Will you excuse us?"

Sam found Rick outside smoking and enjoying the sun on his face. It was still cold out, but the day was bright.

"Well?"

"He spoke first. I kept still and quiet as we discussed. They are now having a conversation. I told the secretary that we were going across the street for a cup of coffee."

It was about forty-five minutes, two cups of coffee, and two newspapers later that Aaron Goldstein darkened the table.

"Did you kill any Germans, Commander?" he asked. Evidently, his time had been spent on the telephone, and he had a lot of contacts.

"That was a long time ago!" snarled Rick, wondering who their contacts could have been.

"We have a deal at $150,000! Mr. Austin will draw up the agreement, and we close here at ten a week from today. No closing, no deal. A copy of the purchase and sale to be signed by tomorrow. Oh! One thing, you pay the broker, Rick. Five thousand dollars should do it, and the lawyer, $2,000."

Rick laughed, was about to argue, then realized that there had to be trade off, and he was getting a good deal. He stuck out his hand.

"Deal!"

Rick had underestimated the work that needed doing. He also quickly realized that he was driving Sam too hard.

They sat one day on a couple of crates with a makeshift table on which there were plans, drawings, and notes. There were men cleaning debris out of the building they had designated as the restaurant. A lot of the walls were damaged or had some rot creating a thin film of white dust everywhere. There was no order to their efforts; they seemed to be going backwards. Looking at the plans, Sam and Rick were contradicting each other and therefore compounding the confusion.

"Let's go get a drink," said Rick.

"I don't drink, and in case you haven't noticed, I am black in a white town." Sam's frustration and anger were close to the surface.

"Well, you can watch me drink and maybe I can send you to the bar for some chips."

Sam was on his feet before he saw that Rick was laughing.

"Let's go!" said Sam. "You need me to get your coat and hat, Massa Rick, Suh?"

They walked down the street laughing for the first time in weeks.

In the tavern, which was quiet, Sam vented his thoughts and his frustrations.

"Rick, I know nothing about building a restaurant, or a bar, or apartments. I have no experience in managing people. I don't know if a 2 x 4 is more money than a 3 x 4 or whether it is longer. I am a piano player, not a pianist, a piano player."

"I know," said Rick. "We have to hire some people who we can trust. It is tough because there are only old men, kids, or disabled people available. It will get easier very soon when the war is about over, a couple of weeks at worst."

"Well, can we wait?"

"We can slow down, change our emphasis, and just do the minimum for now. We bought the property right, hired Aaron's lawyer, and used his realtor; we need some more good people."

While he was talking, there was a small commotion at the bar. A man dressed in a suit which was obviously a "demob" suit given to soldiers leaving the army was asking the bartender for a job, anything, or a lead to a job.

"What can you do?" asked the bartender.

"Anything."

"With only one arm? How are you going to do anything?"

"I have to find a job!" cried the man. "I left the house at six this morning. I told my wife that I would not be home until I had a job. I have knocked on every door; I am five miles from home. Please give me a job!"

A fellow on a bar stool further down said, "What did you do before the army?"

"I was a carpenter."

"A one-armed carpenter." He laughed along with his friends.

The group of men was competing with "a one-armed carpenter" remarks as the young man offered to take them on, which created a bunch of fighting with one-arm-behind-the-back remarks.

The man shouted an obscenity and headed for the door.

"Bring him back, Sam. Let's buy him a drink."

Sam brought back the young man, and they introduced each other. Bruce Harvey was thin, drawn, in his early twenties, and close to collapse: he was a sorry sight.

Rick signaled the bartender for a beer. When the bartender brought it to their table, he mumbled some "Sorry for the other patrons" remarks to the man.

"Have you eaten?" asked Rick

"A slice of bread this morning," Bruce whispered.

"Well, the food here is terrible, but they may have a sandwich. What do you want?"

"I want a job," he said, breaking down.

Rick ordered roast beef with potato chips.

"A carpenter?"

"Yes, fat lot of good with one arm. How do I hold the nails, with my teeth?"

Sam asked, "Can you read plans? Do you know a 2 x 4 from a 3 x 4?"

"Of course! I lost an arm, not my mind!"

"Do you mind working for a black man?"

"I was even willing to work with him," he said nodding across the bar toward the man who challenged him earlier.

"Good. You start tomorrow. Briar Place, just down the road, and here is a buck in advance for your bus fare."

Bruce pushed the money back. "No, thanks; I will walk. Is 7:00 A.M. early enough?"

"You don't know how much the job pays, or the hours?"

"I don't care," said Bruce, stuffing half the sandwich in his pocket. "Thanks. You will never regret it. I will work like a man with three arms for you. Thanks for the sandwich and the beer."

With Bruce in command of the demolition crew and getting quotes from suppliers, both Rick and Sam were able to concentrate on the kitchen, bar appliances, and furniture.

Two months of construction was showing signs of progress, and the kitchen was complete. Word of the happenings was all around the district.

There were constant hassles from the local inspectors and several visits from the police chief. The inspectors were handled by Bruce, the police by Rick.

An elderly man came up to Rick one day and, without preamble, said, "You need a chef!"

Rick could not make up his mind; was it a question or a statement?

"You know somebody?" he asked.

"Yes. Me!"

"And you are?"

"Walter Pritty. Used to own a place before the war. Retired; can't stand it. Wife will drive me to drink."

"Walter, no offence, but you must be 100 years old; kitchen is tough."

"I am only eighty-two, and I don't cook; I'm a chef! Don't pay me. I don't need the money; I need to get out of the house."

"Okay, here's ten dollars. Go buy something and get it cooked for the whole crew. Then the crew can take a vote."

"Serious?"

"Serious!"

"Boy, this is the most fun I have had in ten years. In an hour, you are going to eat the best meal of your life. What kind of food you serve?"

"Mediterranean!"

"Italian?"

"Yes, plus...some Greek some Spanish, some Arabic, you know, Mid-Eastern dishes."

The elderly "chef" had been gone for a half hour when Sam, looking toward the door, said, "Well, good-bye to a ten dollar bill. He either took off for places afar, or had a heart attack at the sight of money."

As if he had been waiting around the corner, the door opened and in trooped Walter followed by two teenage boys carrying boxes of food.

"Had to go to three different stores to get everything I needed. Actually, four, one of them asked about ration coupons. The boys will help. They were standing in the street; I hired them for the afternoon."

The three disappeared into the kitchen. Sam shrugged.

About fifteen minutes passed, and a large antipasto appeared followed by stuffed grape leaves. Paella came and went as did a chickpea dish, meat over rice, and steamed vegetables.

The "chef" appeared, and there was instant applause.

"I get the job, or were you expecting dessert?" Without waiting, he continued his speech, "Dessert is pudding with brandy sauce. I forgot the brandy!"

Brandy was provided, and the dessert was produced with a flaming sauce.

"Well?" the old chef asked.

"You are hired. Start immediately. We need menus that include everything we ate today. That was amazing!" said Sam. "If there is anything left, please have one of the boys take it to Mrs. Hester."

Sam had grown fond of little Jimmy who had to defend his friendship with a black man every day at school. Sam tried to provide treats in a way that would not be misinterpreted by the neighbors.

The restaurant was ready to open a month later, and it looked as though the war would be over before they did. May 8 was scheduled to be an invitation-only dinner, useful as a practice for the kitchen, wait staff, and bar staff. It was also a way to thank providers, tradesmen, neighbors, professionals, and city officials.

There was a table at the back of the room which was a focal point. Rick and Sam had their meetings at this table where there was a view of the door to the kitchen and the front door, as well as a view of the length of the bar.

Rick was doing a final preview of the menu, checking that the proof from the printers contained no errors. He marked a question on an entrée that appeared to have the same price as the same item marked as an appetizer; clearly, one of them was incorrect. He did not see the two men approach, but as he sensed them, he spoke without looking up.

"How can I help you?"

"You need insurance," said the man closest to the table.

"Got insurance! Thank you very much."

"Things happen, might not be covered." The second man picked up a plate and dropped it on the floor.

Rick slowly looked up to see a good-looking man of about thirty and a second man probably ten years older, fifty pounds heavier, with scars making an ugly face more menacing.

There was silence in the building as everyone hearing the plate fall looked expectantly into the corner.

"And you are?" asked Rick, buying time and keeping his temper.

"My name is Vincent Bonanno, and my impatient friend is Frank Collins."

"And the name of the insurer? It's clearly not 'Mad Jack' Disalvo."

"That would be my father, Mr. Bonanno." The young man was smiling, clearly well-educated and used to having people defer to him.

"I should like to meet with Mr. Bonanno tomorrow, if that can be arranged?" asked Rick.

"I am sure it can. Bring cash."

"Here?"

"No. Dad will send a car."

The whole episode had a strange quality; there was a civility and a menace. Frank kicked a chair on the way out, breaking its leg.

The next morning, Sam and Rick were picked up by Vincent Bonanno. The young man from the day before acted as host and guide. They stopped at a meat packing company near the waterfront. Both Rick and Sam had been checked for arms and were ushered into a spacious office which was warm after walking through the cool meat plant. The old man was clearly ill. He sat throughout the conversation. Frank Collins leaned by the door while another man was never introduced.

"Father, Mr. Blaine and his partner, Mr. Wilson, asked if they could speak to you directly about their insurance premium."

"Uh, nice place you built; better to take care of it." The voice was not much more than a whisper.

"Actually I came to personally invite you and your son, together with your wives, to our grand opening next week. We have no intention of paying for something we do not need."

The old man almost came out of his chair and had a breathing gasping attack before the man next to him helped get him a drink. Frank Collins behind was laughing while Vincent Bonanno looked with interest at the calm man that he saw sitting in front of his father. He knew that there was strength there, hidden, and stronger for the hiding.

"You know that I could have Frank wreck the place before you got back there: if you got back there?" the old man whispered.

"Yes, but I think you might talk to the police first; they are having tea at the moment with my staff, or perhaps speak with my friend, Mr. Disalvo."

There was a quiet moment while all were reflecting.

"And by the way, if Frank sets foot in our restaurant, I will kill him. If there is a fire, or any of my staff are hurt going home, I will kill him."

Frank Collins took a step forward but was stopped by Vincent. "Frank, get the chief on the phone and then call Mad Jack. See if he has a hearse available to transport these gentleman."

A few minutes later, the old man was listening to the chief of police while looking across the desk. After a grunted acknowledgement, he put down the phone without good-byes.

Frank was holding the other phone.

"Mr. Disalvo wants to speak to you."

"Vincent, you talk to him; I can't stand him," he muttered.

"Mr. Disalvo, this is Vincent. Yes, my father is well...very well.... Well, your informant was incorrect.... Mr. Blaine and Mr. Wilson...yes, they are here...no, strictly social.... Ha ha.... Yes, I am a funny fellow.... They are friends of yours.... Well, of course, no harm is going to come to any friend of yours.... Yes, yes, let me put Rick on the phone."

"Rick, first, know that someone is recording this conversation. The old man trusts no one. The reason I wanted to talk to you is to say thank you for the invitation. My wife and I would love to come to your restaurant, and please, may I bring an old friend from the West Coast, a film star no less?" Mad Jack asked Rick.

"Of course, Mr. Disalvo. You may bring a guest, and remember to ask the waitress for some of the aged scotch. Just say Rick's scotch whiskey. Yes, Sir. Sam is fine, too. If your friend has a favorite tune, be sure to request it. Thank you. See you next week."

"You have some powerful friends, young man." The whisper was followed by a dismissive nod of the head.

In the car, Vincent was first to speak. "Great performance! Can you deliver?"

"Yes. Is the car bugged too?" asked Sam, looking in all corners.

Rick had whispered to say nothing until they were back at the restaurant.

"Probably," said Vincent, laughing. "My father does not go out at night, but I would be interested to attend your opening since Mr. Disalvo and the chief both think so highly of you both."

"And both will be at our opening," said Sam.

The opening was a tremendous success, as earlier in the day, the Germans had unconditionally surrendered. Everyone was in high spirits. There was dancing in the streets, lights were lit, and drapes and curtains opened, allowing the brightness to spill out into the gardens, sidewalks, and roads.

Mr. Disalvo introduced his wife and his guest and friend to Mr. Smith while the star of film and radio joined Sam and sang for half an hour. Mrs. Hester hugged everyone in the building. Mrs. Harvey was wearing a new dress while Mrs. Pritty told everybody that her husband was the chef. No one wanted the magic to end.

Rick sat at his table with a drink and a cigar. Walter Pritty and Sam joined him.

"Marvelous, wonderful!" said Walter.

"Incredible!" Sam enthused.

"But will they all come back when they have to pay?"

They did.

Chapter Twenty-Nine

"So, the opening was the beginning of a successful business. I am sure there were a lot of things that went wrong along with the things that went right."

Ilsa was making a statement, and Richard recognized that it was a scouting tactic, that there was a question just dying to come out.

"What about the people? Abdulla, Carl, Sasha, and the others?"

"Well," Sam started, "Suli kept in touch. She married the goldsmith, and he taught her to read and write. She enjoyed writing to Rick, sending recipes, and she shared the news with the staff. Sasha disappeared, but Abdulla and Carl eventually reached America. Abdulla, as you can see, lives next door. He is here all the time and provides both security and doorman services; he must be in his sixties, but no one wants to test him. Carl...." He sighed. "He liked little boys, not to harm them; he was too gentle. He would buy things for them, give them money. We warned him that this was not Europe, certainly not Morocco. One night, he was lured by a gang of neighborhood teenagers to a quiet spot, and he was beaten and robbed. He never recovered. I am not sure whether it was his injuries, the injured pride, or whether he found nothing worth living for. Carl never said who had attacked him and said he would have gladly given the money if asked."

"I am sorry," said Ilsa.

Was that it? Richard was wondering when Ilsa, who had been trying to find the words, asked, "Sam, how did you meet...Kate's mother?"

There. That was it—cards on the table, question in the ether, a pulpit challenge!

Ilsa was sitting as though she had just asked about the weather, but she had a slight inclination toward Sam and eagerness in her eye—subtle but recognizable body language to a son who had been waiting for the natural feminine curiosity to show itself. He was congratulating himself on his foresight and then was slightly embarrassed by the thought that he himself was waiting with anticipation for the answer.

"Margaret O Connor worked for us as a waitress on the opening day. She was a looker. Boy, she was gorgeous, just eighteen. She was smart, too. With those good looks, everyone in the room saw her, but she was so innocent, naïve, and oblivious to the attention. Margaret had just come to America from Ireland. Her parents died and her brother married. The new wife moved into the house, and Margaret had to move out. She had a sister in America who sent her money for the fare. Since the U-boat threat was over, it was possible to get a ride on a freighter bound across the Atlantic. So here she walked in one day. She said she needed to pay her sister back and asked how much we pay waitresses, cleaners, etc. When we tell her the base pay, which was pitiful, she said that it was too much and tips on top of that was just 'too grand.' We had to hire her for the pleasure she carried into a room.

"Margaret looked a lot like you Miss Ilsa, just like you were in Paris. I think that may have influenced Mr. Rick to take her under his wing. He smiled whenever she was around. Miss Kate has the same looks but without the naiveté."

As if on cue, the object of the conversation entered the room. All eyes from the table watched her as did half of the patrons in the restaurant. At the bar, a young man Richard recognized but could not place signaled to her. Kate saw him and deliberately walked past. He grabbed her arm. Richard was on his feet, striding forward. Meanwhile, Abdullah left the doorway.

"Let go of the lady," said Richard quietly.

"Kate, introduce me to Sir Galahad," said the man.

"Dr. Land, this lowlife is Vinny Bonanno, and his sidekick, Benny Morgan. And Benny, if that hand comes out of your pocket holding a gun or a knife, then Abdullah will make sure that you open your pants left-handed from today on."

"What is it you want, Vinny?"

"I want you to sell me this restaurant."

"NO!"

"We should at least talk about it. Maybe dinner, or maybe a weekend in Miami, San Juan."

"No!'

"Maybe we should go to Vegas. Get married."

Kate started toward the door.

"Kate, I was serious about getting married, and you know that I always get what I want."

Richard followed Kate towards the door.

"Do you have to keep butting in?" she asked angrily. "Why are you still here?"

"Just leaving," he said, turning to say good-bye to his mother.

"I can get a cab, Mother. I shall be seeing you again soon, Sam."

At the door, Abdullah was starting to signal for a cab when the passenger door of a Camaro opened.

"Get in!" Kate said.

Kate had changed into blue jeans and a white sweater. It was meant to be a casual dress that was not provocative in any way. The result, however, accentuated her long slender legs.

"Where are you going?" Kate asked.

Richard gave her the address.

"Won't it be out of your way?" he asked.

"No. I had decided to go to the cemetery to ask Rick what this was all about, but now, I can ask you."

She was driving very quickly; the V-8 engine was alternatively purring and snarling.

"I don't know," answered Rick. "Do you always drive this fast?"

"No, I usually drive faster."

"And no tickets?"

"I send them to Uncle George."

"Uncle George?"

"Uncle Chief of Police George."

"And the altercation with Vinny Bonanno. Does Uncle George take care of that, too?"

She became serious. "Don't joke about Vinny. He is dangerous, and he does get everything he wants in this city. Right now, he wants me, and your butting in will provoke him to both set you straight and me his wife. Back to my question of why. Why?" she asked. Both of them knew the question of Rick's bequests was the subject.

"Perhaps we should both go to the cemetery and ask the only person who knows?"

"Someone else knows. I bet Sam knows, but if Rick asked him to say nothing about it, then no one will ever know."

"Can I ask a question?" Richard was not smiling as he could see a change in Kate which was unfathomable.

"Were you serious about marrying that jerk?"

"Richard, I am serious about this. I repeat myself: do not take Vinny at face value. Too many have been hurt by him. I can insult him carefully, and he thinks that it is a joke. Also, when Rick was alive, we were somewhat protected. I am not sure I know of all the conversations or relationships Rick had with Vincent, the father, but it may be that soon, we shall be talking with him directly."

"Isn't he a gangster?"

"He is! He is also a successful businessman. The lines seem to be blurred these days," said Kate who was smiling again.

"Not mad at me anymore?" asked Richard.

"I was never mad at you personally," she said. "It's just that my life was so easy, so ordinary. I worked at the restaurant, and I made decisions but always knew that Rick was there. Do you understand? I just started getting used to making decisions and WHAM!" she pounded the steering wheel for emphasis. "I have a new partner— someone I never met before. A doctor for crying out loud! What do I need a doctor for?" she exclaimed.

"You are shouting again!"

"So, what do I need a doctor for?"

"I would say high blood pressure, not enough exercise, and not enough sleep. Do you drink six glasses of water a day?"

"Are you even listening to me?" she asked.

"Yes, and stay away from gangsters."

"A partner who is a doctor and a comedian; this is too much. Here is your address. Fancy section of town. No train station though!"

"No, I have to pick up a bag then call a cab."

"I'll wait," Kate said double parking.

Richard was out quickly. Unable to find anyone, he saw his bag by the front hallstand, ducked in, picked it up, and was back outside. He threw the overnight bag onto the backseat and prepared himself for another charge over to Fifth Avenue.

"I went out with Vinny and his friends a few times. They are a wild group; they have a lot of fun and know all the places where there is live entertainment. No waiting in line, the best table in the house. I could enjoy that for a while. But…."

"But what?"

"They have no respect for people, for places, or for anything. They could say the most terrible things to girlfriends, to waiters, taxi drivers. They would take the best table even if someone were sitting there and talk and laugh throughout the show. They have no moral fiber, no basis for the real world."

"Then why allow them into Rick's?"

"They are different there. Rick never put up with it. He would ask them to leave, and they would. There are some who Abdullah will not allow back in, that jerk of Disalvo's at the funeral for example."

"I think that you do a wonderful job, and since I am only a doctor… and a comedian, I hope that you will continue to do whatever you are doing. I would hope that you overpay yourself and Sam, and if there is anything left, a corned beef sandwich on dark rye with a pickle would be nice. I have no intention of operating a restaurant, even one as classy as Rick's."

"Ah! Wait until you see the books; you might change your mind. Here is the station. When are we likely to see you again?"

This simple question was to occupy Richard all the way to Washington, entering his consciousness at any moment during the following week. He replayed his answer, changing it every time.

"I don't know. Thanks for the ride."

Chapter Thirty

Richard was back into the routine immediately. He worked as hard and as long as he had since joining the army, but there was calmness. Everything was in slow motion. When he made an incision, he could see the scalpel working its way across the leg, the arm, the abdomen, and it stopped within a millimeter of the optimum place. He had been able to do this before, but now, everything had slowed down. When he sat and thought about what was happening, he realized what great athletes had always contended—that the fastball seemed to take longer to get to the plate, that the jump above the hoop defied gravity for seconds, and the wide receiver was in the clear for minutes after the ball left the quarterback's hand. These were the great athletes: Roger Maris in '61, Carl Yastrzemski in '67, Wilt Chamberlain, and, of course, Joe Namath in the Super Bowl.

Did this happen in other fields then? Did the accountant see the problem as it unfolded, did a lawyer like Perry Mason see the courtroom in slow motion, and did the car worker put parts together as the assembly line slowed to his efficient hands?

"You look content today!" Major General Mathew Rollins had entered the sitting area where medical records were being reviewed by the doctor.

"Yes, I have come to some decisions. Do you have time to hear them?"

"Sure, I was looking for you anyway."

"Well, Sir, I have decided that in May, when I leave the army, I am going to practice in New York. I hope I can ask that you will give me a reference if called upon?"

"No, Colonel. I will do better than that. I will personally call the medical director and tell him to make you head of the surgical team. I observe regularly and speak to my doctors on a regular basis and they are never, never in agreement with each other on anything, except that they, to a man and woman, would work with you anywhere, anytime on any procedure."

"Thank you, Sir. That is kind. And thank you for the accidental promotion."

"Oh, the colonel. That's right. That's what I came to tell you. Promotion to colonel effective immediately. Had to find you; word is spreading fast," he smiled. "Congratulations!"

"But, Sir, didn't you hear? I am leaving."

"Yes. Too bad for us, but you never know when it might be handy. New York, eh? A young woman, I wager. Well, good luck and let me know when you are interviewed." The major general rose and saluted, and Richard stood and gave his best salute, which would have been unacceptable from a third-day recruit.

A young woman? Was that the reason he had come to a decision? The decision had in fact been easy when he had stopped thinking about it. There must have been something in his subconscious thought and he was searching for it now.

The facts were that he had done his time for his country and had paid back a sense of indebtedness for his good fortune and happy sense of belonging. Did the second, third generations think that way? Some did, just as some recent immigrants or first generation Americans came with a sense of entitlement. Who was right? Both probably, since it was America and you could be what you are. He smiled to himself.

There was an inheritance for him in New York and a mystery. He did not like mysteries; he liked facts. Religion had been beyond him with its mysteries until he accepted faith as the belief in what might have been, and the stories as embellished fact based on a possible scientific notion.

He would solve the mystery, and the answer was in New York. So was Trish Wellington, possibly the most beautiful girl in the world.

New York was also home to Kate Blaine, his new partner who needed his practical advice. *No, she did not!* Richard thought. She needed nothing, or nothing from him: she did not even like him.

In New York, he would be close to his mother—his mother! He realized that he had not called to tell her of his decision.

The call would have to wait as he realized that he was being paged for the operating room: "Would Colonel Land please report to the OR. Colonel Land."

Well, if people did not know before, they certainly knew now, he said to himself, thinking about his promotion. He put a file on top of others and quickly walked out, passing the doctor's desk to ask Helen to put the file away for him except for the top one which should go on his desk.

"Yes, Colonel," she answered. "Your mother called," she said to a receding back. "I said that you would call back tonight." Richard waved a "Thank you" as he turned a corner.

Back into the work of the day, he immersed himself into some of the harder operations on his schedule. He allowed himself the luxury of remembering how efficiently they were working. The whole team was proud of the job they were performing. It was surprisingly late when they finished, and he was further surprised that no one had made a complaint that they were working late. It was never voiced as a complaint but more like, "I told my boyfriend that we might make it to the movies tonight" or "Rats! My mother is making pizza. I like pizza hot, don't you?"

That night, there was nothing. In fact, the opposite was evident as there was disappointment when they had finished.

Richard smiled; they were a good team.

"Good night, Colonel." They all made a point of letting him know that they knew of his promotion. There was no envy, just a genuine respect.

Dr. Brandon was heading out as he arrived at his quarters. "Colonel, a couple of us is going out for a steak and beer. Want to join us?"

"Thank you, Martin. I think I will. Who is on duty? Not me, I hope."

"Well, there are a couple of 'firsts.' The first time you have spontaneously agreed to go out—it usually takes a week's notice—the first time you have not known who was on duty and, and the first time you did not volunteer to do night duty. The promotion suits you, Richard." He was laughing as he headed for the door.

Richard laughed himself. He was still smiling when his mother answered the phone.

"Well, you are happy!" she said.

"How can you tell from five hundred miles away?"

"Richard, I have known you all your life." She started laughing herself, that tinkling sound missing for so long in her life.

"What has made you so happy, Mother?"

"Seeing Sam again, reliving old times, happy memories of my youth, and looking at you, a grown man, with a life before you. I hope that you make the right choices and are happy."

"Well, I chose to accept Martin's invitation to join him for a steak and beer."

"Silly!"

"I was promoted to colonel today."

"I know; Helen told me. Congratulations, dear."

Right then he knew that everybody knew!

"Mother, I have made a decision. I am going to leave the army at the end of this tour and practice at a New York hospital."

"That is wonderful. No more tours abroad, thank goodness. I assume that the decision was because of a young woman. I can only hope that grandchildren are in my future, my not too distant future." Then a tinkling laugh came.

Richard was about to explain but thought that if his mother was happy thinking that he was moving to New York to begin seriously chasing Trish, where was the harm?

"Perhaps. You will be the first to know."

Richard put the phone carefully on the cradle, looking at the instrument as if it could answer the question of "What was that all about?" Another mystery! Why had his mother called? What was she not telling him?

Ilsa put down the receiver, looked across at the bequest from Rick Blaine. She had been going to tell Richard all about it that morning but since then had come to the conclusion that she would not.

The group in the steak house was noisy. It was easily recognizable as a tense-driven group of young people being able to unwind with their peers. The comradeship was there, and so was the familiarity. There was also professionalism in the conversation as people working with each other divulged personal facts and listened carefully to concerns, problems, and fears.

Richard was greeted warmly by all. He ordered Bass ale with the admonishment that the glass not be frozen. Many had already had appetizers and salads. He asked for a sirloin steak, medium rare, and baked potato. Declining dessert, he had a cup of coffee and surveyed his fellow doctors. *The army is a leveler*, he thought. *These professionals are from all over the country with all different backgrounds.* He was going to miss them.

The bill came, and he left more than his share. Some were going to stay and have more drinks. Martin was in earnest conversation with a nurse who Richard did not recognize; she must be new. She was evidently asking about Richard, by the glances they were both making, while Martin was bringing the conversation back to Dr. Martin Brandon.

Richard walked back to the hospital with a lively trio of doctors and nurses coming up for a tour of Vietnam. Would they all come back? That night, they were invincible. He hoped that soon, the war would be over and they would not need to worry their mothers, their girlfriends, or their boyfriends.

At the hospital, he updated the file on his desk and signed the notice of discharge. Another success but how would the patient fare in South Boston? Checking with doctor of the day, all was well. He stopped by to tell the young man that he was discharging him home. They chatted about some of the challenges. The boy had a large loving Irish family; he would be okay.

The next day, at a break, he called a New York hospital and asked if there were any surgical staff vacancies. He was quickly transferred up to the head of personnel who said that they could put together an interview panel for the following week, if that was convenient. The early train could be in by 11:00 A.M.

Richard checked with Corporal Mattareze who, after conferring with the major general, issued the orders. He called back, confirmed with the hospital, and then called Trish.

"Richard, how marvelous to hear from you."

"Trish, I have a lot of things to tell you about. Can we get together next week?"

"Sure. Where?"

"In New York. I have arranged an interview for next week, Wednesday."

"How wonderful. I will let Mummy know."

"Trish, I am doing this on my own. I will explain when I see you. There have been so many things happening lately."

"I would say so. Did you see the riots on campus this weekend? Please don't wear your uniform."

"Trish, I have to go. Do you know a place in Brooklyn called Rick's?"

"Yes, of course. Very good. But I heard that the owner died, so no one goes there now."

"Well, meet me there at seven."

"Okay, Richard. See you then."

It is going to be a selling job. It should be easier actually at the restaurant. What would her Mummy and Daddy think of a doctor who owned a restaurant? And is a comedian! Why should it be an issue what Mummy and Daddy thought? But everyone had to endure the 'my parents want to meet you' ordeal.

The interview board consisted of three men, one of whom came in late, mumbling an apology which no one heard. The youngest was about fifty and the oldest looked past seventy. They all looked tired and were not exactly a good advertisement for a position at the hospital.

The younger man, Dr. Cooper asked all of the questions. Most were based on the very sparse resume provided by Richard—growing up in Connecticut, school, ROTC, and military service.

Dr. Cooper described the work, the pay, the hours, the staff, and facilities. He glossed over the staff shortage, which was resulting in the doctors having to work excessive hours.

The older man, Dr. Paul Levy, stirred himself as if from a snooze. The other man, Dr. Davies, who had come in late, may have been sleeping for all the contribution he made to the proceedings.

"Young man, why do you want to work here?"

"I have an interest in surgery, and I should gain a lot of experience here."

"Bullshit!"

Richard was shocked, and so was Dr Cooper. Dozing Dr. Davies came upright.

"You failed to mention that you are a highly decorated colonel in the United Sates Army, that you served two tours in Vietnam, and that you have practiced more advanced procedures than anyone in this room."

"The citations were grossly exaggerated," said Richard, wondering where and how he had learned this while apparently not paying attention.

"We are grossly understaffed, underfunded, and working in poor conditions with a turnover of staff that means we have more recruiters and personnel staff than orderlies at this very moment. The reality is that 'Coop' would hire anyone upright and breathing, but it is also reality that they will be gone in a week, maybe a month."

"Why are you dissuading me from this position, Sir?"

"Because Doc Rollins said that you can head any surgical unit in the country. Because Doc said that he thought you were going to Columbia where you can immediately earn twice what our budget allows and have every perk presently known to our profession."

"I want to make a difference. It is not about money, and I hope that it never is," said Richard as the pieces fell into place.

"I taught Doc Rollins and had the privilege of having his job before I retired from the army and came home to New York. I asked him if he thought that you were as good as I was in my prime. He laughed at me and said that you were even better than HE was. I have my pension and don't need the money either. Mind you, it's nice to be independent and have an income."

"Thank you for your honesty. I should still like to take the position, and I promise Dr. Cooper that I will still be here after a year."

"Paging Dr. Davies. Please report to the emergency entrance."

"Fuck!"

Dr. Davies, having made his one contribution to the proceedings, left.

"I am still a servant of the US for a few more weeks. I will start immediately after my discharge," Richard said with finality.

"Take your time, young man. Take some time off, start slowly; I am sure that we can hold the fort for a few more days. Maybe when I am in Washington next, begging for funds, we can have dinner together, take Mathew with us."

Shaking hand all round, they hurried out. He had toured the hospital before. Walking out, he noticed the obviously deferred maintenance. *Well, this is where I wanted to be. A little money and some paint can work wonders,* he thought.

Calling a cab, he realized that he was early but gave the address of the restaurant. Riding through New York, the streets dark with rain, he was thinking of his decision and felt comfortable with his thoughts. Doc Rollins thought he was at Columbia. He chuckled and thought, *Surprise, surprise*. The only person who was not going to be surprised would be his mother.

His mother. Why was she so happy lately?

Ever since the funeral!

That was bizarre!

Chapter Thirty-One

Dr. Richard Land arrived at Rick's at mid afternoon. He intended to say "Hello" then find a place to stay. The place where he had stayed before, the private hotel, he had forgotten the name but someone would surely know and recommend a place nearby.

There was another question there which he was refusing to answer: "Why not stay with Trish?" After all, he was going to give her all of his news which was all good as far as their relationship was concerned. Wasn't it?

I will think about that later.

The restaurant was brightly lit with the lights on full. Sam was at the piano, playing unconsciously as his thoughts were a million miles away from his fingers. He jumped when Richard came up alongside and said "Hi."

"Sorry if I surprised you," Richard said.

"I was just thinking. I do my best thinking at the piano."

"Then, I am sorry that I disturbed you."

"No, it's all right. I was thinking about you, about Kate, about Rick, about Margaret, Alice, about all kinds of folk. I was thinking about relationship, friendship, and such and whether they endure...how they endure."

Richard said, "Kate and I had a discussion last week on a similar subject. She wondered whether the protection from the Bonanno family would continue; that some time, we should check it out."

"Well, that was one of those strange strong relationships. I believe it should endure with Vin. But the son, he is something else. Vinny is nothing like his father. Doesn't even look like him. Handsome enough, Italian enough, but he is self-centered, among other things."

Sam paused, thought, and changed direction. "So what brings you to the city again? A girl, I warrant?"

"Well, no.... Well, yes.... Not really, but in a way," Richard stammered.

"Don't tell me; I don't need to know."

"Actually, I came in for an interview, need to stay the night, and yes, I am meeting a young lady here at seven o'clock. Which reminds me: I need a place to change."

Why had he said change, not stay? Was he expecting, hoping, to be invited back by Trish? *Well, why not hope because....* He immediately added, "And perhaps some place to stay." There! He had covered all bases. That was more like the Dr. Land he knew when he looked in the mirror.

Sam smiled and said, "You can change here, stay here! Rick's apartment is empty and since you are entitled to at least a portion, you can use it. It is on the third floor. Miss Kate, she lives on the third floor in our old apartment. We—Jimmy and me—we live on the fourth floor. We used to live on the third floor, but after Miss Margaret died, we moved up so we could have three bedrooms as my wife was taking care of Miss Kate and then little Jimmy was born."

Sam was back into a short reverie, remembering those good and bad days—Kate being born, Margaret killed, his marriage to Alice, their taking care of Kate, and finding out that they were going to have a child of their own.

"Let me show you," he told Rick.

Sam led the way to a door just before the kitchen. He unlocked it and hit the button for the elevator inside. The door opened immediately, and he put another key into the number three button, turned it, and the elevator rose. The door opened into a short passage with a door on either end. He turned right and opened the door on it.

The room was surprisingly large after the short corridor. It was clean and neat with a comfortable sofa and a large leather chair facing a television. There was a large oak desk with a leather swivel chair and by the window was a dining table. To the left was a kitchen. At the back of the kitchen and the entrance wall were two bedrooms and a bathroom.

The furnishings were masculine, the room was masculine, and nowhere was there a sign of a woman's touch. *Not surprising*, thought Richard, *after twenty years.*

Sam wandered around with him as they went from room to room. "Pretty much as Rick had it. The cleaning woman comes in once a week. There should be fresh towels. Anything missing, make a list; we will have it here for next time."

"Next time." The words were involuntary.

"Well, you did say interview, you did say girl, so I...."

Richard was embarrassed. "I am sorry. It seems like that is all I keep saying to you. Thank you, Sam! How do I get out of here after a shower? Which shower do I use?"

"Richard, I am pleased to see you again. Rick's ways were strange but.... Use either shower, either room. They are yours to use when you are here. Keys, I will have Mrs. Hester bring up a set for you. Oh, and a check."

"Mrs. Hester? A check?"

"Yes. Accounting is on the second floor, and Mrs. Hester is in charge. Not a trained accountant, but we trust her with everything."

Well, this was very nice, and a couple of hundred dollars a month will offset the salary I have just accepted a bit. A bit? The hit was more like 50 percent of what I could have negotiated at a major teaching hospital! Richard thought.

Richard took a long shower and did his thinking while in there. He shaved but could not remember as he was still thinking. Mostly, he was planning his speech for the evening. However, every time he got to the response, it was different, and so, every answer he could anticipate was different—from wonderful "It will be perfect," to "Let's see what happens," and "We can work it out."

Dressing, he found some aftershave lotion. There were only full bottles; someone—the cleaner—had taken all the partially-used toothpaste and toiletries away.

Richard walked through the living room while putting on his tie and switched on the television. The news was all of Vietnam with clips of Nixon and Kissinger promising an early end and withdrawal. Was this real, or a president only saying what the voters wanted to hear?

The front door opened with a bang.

"What the hell are you doing here?" Kate exclaimed.

"Whatever happened to knocking first?" Richard asked.

She stood in the doorway, feet apart in a fighting stance. If Richard had thought that the anger had subsided since he last saw Kate, he was no longer in doubt. Was this new anger, or was she still angry from the reading of the will?

"Well?"

He was looking at an attractive woman in a fashionable green dress with a green matching coat. She was in heels with panty hose that might also have a green tint. The pearl necklace and pearl bracelet said someone was going out, not working at a restaurant.

"Sam let me in to change."

"Sam! I will kill him. This is Rick's apartment."

Kate had advanced into the room.

"You are even wearing his aftershave!"

That was a mistake, thought Richard. *Ah, well, nobody is perfect.* Actually if Kate was correct, he could be the most imperfect person on the planet.

"Kate, nice to see you again! Have you a nice night out planned?"

"This is…. was Rick's apartment and seeing you here…." She burst into tears.

They were interrupted by a polite knock on the door. Mrs. Hester, who now bore no resemblance to the thin overwrought woman Rick and Sam had first met, entered. She was a matronly, quietly pleasant woman.

"Evening, Miss Blaine. You must be Dr. Land."

"Pleased to meet you, Mrs. Hester."

"Mr. Wilson asked that I give you a set of keys and a check." Mrs. Hester handed Richard an envelope and a key ring with four keys and a medallion with the restaurant logo.

"I put into the envelope all the extension numbers so if you wanted to call the bar, or the restaurant, Mr. Wilson, Miss. Blaine, or myself, for example, just pick up the phone and dial. Press the button for an outside line. If I can help in any way, please let me know."

With that, she turned and left.

"See, wasn't that a lot more civilized?" Richard asked Kate.

"I am not civilized," said Kate "You can go to hell! I have to meet Vinny."

"Kate," Richard called after her. He wanted to say "Be careful," but instead he said, "Fix your makeup." She slammed the door as hard as she could. As the door closed, he saw her eyes flashing green—green with anger!

"Well, that went well I think," he said aloud to himself.

Although it was early, he decided to go downstairs and watch the operation of a restaurant.

He still could not get used to the idea that he owned part of it; it was just a fantasy.

Leaving the elevator, he turned into the restaurant and bar area. It was pretty quiet. A few people were sitting at the bar and a couple had appetizers in front of them. At the back of the restaurant was a table of employees. A man was standing in front of them as they were eating small portions of food. The cook was explaining the specials of the evening as the wait staff were sampling the prepared food. As Richard approached, there was silence. "Marie will seat you, Sir." The cook turned to meet the interruption.

"That's okay," said Richard, "Sorry to disturb you."

He walked away embarrassed. He did not belong. He was not part of the fraternity—an intruder.

Mrs. Hester rescued him as she was leaving.

"Dr. Land, sit at the table back there. Someone will get you a drink. Mr. Wilson will be down; he usually eats at this time."

Richard sat and after explaining to the waitress who approached that he was waiting for Mr. Wilson, he was left with his own thoughts.

The envelope! He remembered that Mrs. Hester had given him keys and an envelope.

It was a number ten envelope with the preprinted address of the restaurant on the front. He opened it and removed a check worth $3,333.33. He looked at it. It was made out to Richard B. Land, dated that day. He put it on the table. It was a windfall, a mistake, a going-away stipend!

He was still looking at the check, stupefied, when Sam sat down.

"Hello, Sam. Mrs. Hester gave me a check. There must be a mistake."

"Well, Mrs. Hester does not make mistakes. But if you want to look at the books, that can be arranged." Sam was a little defensive. "Let me see."

He picked up the check, looked at the date and amount, and said, "That's about right: the restaurant has been very profitable. We have no debt, and, being able to pay our bills timely, we take all the discounts available. Kate has very little turnover in staff so we are really efficient. She should be around somewhere, I think."

"Oh, I was not criticizing the operation. In fact, I had told Kate that she and you should take extraordinary salaries, that I would be happy with the odd ham sandwich. By the way, she went out."

Sam was pensive as though absorbing something. "Well, she is entitled to some time off. The staff is well trained. I hope she is careful."

Richard was surprised, a little shocked at Sam's reaction and of the information. He wished that he had time to think about it and absorb it, but they were interrupted by a waitress.

"The usual, Mr. Wilson?"

"Yes, Noni. Caesar salad with tuna and a glass of white Chablis." Noni looked at Richard expectantly. She was a large woman, dark-skinned, no longer young, but she moved with a particular grace. In spite of her size, she moved with elegance and efficiency of motion.

"No, thank you. I am eating later with a guest. Well, perhaps a draught Bass ale. Please ask them not to frost the glass."

"Yes, Sir, a real beer drinker. I will ask the hostess to come over and make arrangements for your guest."

"Thank you!" Richard said.

When she had left, Sam asked, "Did Kate say where she was going?"

"No. Somewhere with Vinny, I believe."

They were again interrupted by an attractive young woman in a smart dress carrying a clipboard.

"Good evening, Mr. Wilson, Sir. I understand that you would like a reservation for dinner for two. Would that be for this evening? We are very busy, but I can try to fit you in."

Richard was a little nonplussed. He had assumed from the comments that midweek would not be a problem. Sam saved him embarrassment. "He can have this table this evening; Noni will take care of them. Seven o'clock, did you say?"

Receiving a nod, Sam continued, "And Megan, charge the bill to the same food and beverage account as Miss Blaine and myself, under Dr. Land." Sam stopped talking and ignored the questions that Megan was nonverbally asking; she could get her answers from Kate.

"Yes, Sir."

"Sam, thank you. Kate made some mention of a special relationship that Rick had with Vincent Bonnano and was saying that the continuation of that relationship may now be jeopardized. Is that why she is seeing Vinny, or is it something else, or am I sensing a concern on your part that is unrelated?"

"Too many questions, Dr. Richard," said Sam, smiling. "Yes, they had a special relationship. It started, I suppose, when Vinny's grandfather died shortly after we opened the restaurant. Vincent, the son, was a regular visitor.

He sat at the same table most nights, and he signed the bill which was settled weekly without fail." He paused, reminiscing.

"Then his father died."

Chapter Thirty-Two

"I am sorry to hear that your father died," said Rick. "I only met him the one time, but he must have been a very strong man. I never knew my old man, died in an accident at work when I was eleven. He was a strong man. I miss not having him as I grew up."

"Rick, you must be the only person in New York not at the funeral and the only one to express concern for my feelings. I think half of the people showed up just to be sure that the bastard was actually dead and buried and the other half to eyeball the crowd to see who is going to be their next meal ticket, who will fill the void."

Vincent Bonanno lit a cigarette, blew the smoke pensively upwards, and watched as it spiraled and disappeared into the ceiling. Rick also watched it and thought that he was going to have to close soon to repaint, as the ceiling, in spite of the extractor fans, was showing the effect of rising cigarette smoke.

"The families all decide on the territories, as you know. I hope that they do not expect me to carry on the family tradition."

Rick gestured to the waitress. "Same again, Margaret, and some of those cheese nibbles."

"Yes, Rick," she said as she made her way to the bar watched by both men.

"What would you like to do?" asked Rick.

"Probably teach. I got a degree, as I am sure you know. Missed the war. I guess I had already served in the 'trenches.' Studied history, studied women, and played football. I was terrible." He did not elaborate on which of the studies were a failure. "Teach, I could do that! Out west where no one knows me or my family."

They both watched as Margaret returned with their drinks. No one spoke as she placed clean napkins and a dish with nuts and cheese crackers within easy reach before them. She was aware of their eyes but did not acknowledge either of them. Every move was smooth; she had a natural gait developed from walking everywhere while growing up in Ireland with a total lack of public or private transportation. She still enjoyed the walk down to the market.

"Will they let you?" Vincent was caught off guard by Rick's question.

"Let me what?"

"Teach!"

Vincent's answer was to send another smoke ring upwards.

"There will be blood!" Rick had heard rumors of trouble. Greed fueled the unrest as did old feuds. Opportunities to address perceived wrongs; slights exaggerated by time and fanned by others with different personal agendas had created an atmosphere that was like a firework waiting for a match.

"But if I am teaching in Oregon, it will not be mine. Nor will I have spilled it." Vincent smiled sardonically.

"Rick, I feel comfortable talking to you. There was never time to talk to my father, and if I talked to my mother, she would ask 'What does your father say?' I had no brothers, and my older sister was too preoccupied. At school, everyone knew who I was and stayed away because of my father. I could talk to whoever my minder was but the conversation was going back to my father. Always my father, and I could not talk to him. Why would I live that life?"

"Because," Rick said, "many of those things are taken out of our hands. Events take over our lives. We think that everything is perfect, and it will never change. Then it does. We can do one of two things: sit and drink our way into the next life or go out and see what is around the next corner. Some will call it fate, some say that it is preordained, but the fact is that one just puts one foot after the other."

"Rick, you are getting too serious. Let us drink to a happy ever after."

"No!" Rick realized that he had spoken louder than he had intended. He recovered, "To whatever life brings!"

They raised their glasses to each other, but before they could drink, there was a loud noise—a gunshot outside. Rick moved quickly toward the bar.

"David! And kill the outside light."

The bartender, David, reached and flipped a revolver to Rick who kept walking to the front door followed by Vincent and trailed by Hank Giovanni, Vincent's guard who had been sitting at the corner of the bar near the back door.

"Watch the back door, Hank!" Vincent said and caught up to Rick.

Outside, all was quiet. The street appeared empty. There was the sound of a car driving off at speed. Rick and Vincent looked in the direction of the sound and then turned back toward the front door.

Abdullah stood holding a scimitar in one hand and a sawn-off shotgun in the other.

"Are you all right?" asked Rick.

"Yes, suh, Mr. Rick."

"What happened?"

"Man came. I told him that he was not allowed in. He said he was here to see a man. I asked if he had an invitation. He said this was his invitation, pulled this."

Abdullah was waving the shotgun by the barrel. "As I took it from him, it went off. Then another man with him pulled out a pistol. I pulled out my weapon, and they both ran away."

"Did you know them? Can you identify them?" asked Vincent.

"Yes, suh. The man was asked to leave by Mr. Rick for breaking a chair. The other man is now missing a finger."

"Well," said Rick, "it looks like events take away certain options. The first guy was Frankie Collins and the second should be easy to recognize. They were clearly looking for you."

"Thanks, Rick." It was said without irony. "I cannot think of anyone else who would have gone through that door with me. I will not forget."

They sat, and Hank was asked to join them.

"Hank, that was Frank Collins and someone else! Any ideas?" Vincent asked him.

"Frank talks a lot. I saw him talking to the chief at the wake pretty seriously."

Rick stood up. "Gents, your job may be politics, but mine is running a saloon. Include me out of your conversation."

When Rick reached the bar, he was greeted by George Surphlis.

"George, some detective you are. Didn't you hear the shot?"

"Of course, but it was a shotgun. Why would I go outside where someone is wielding a shotgun against my 38? So!"

"I think someone is looking to eliminate any competition in the insurance business. If you want more details, go ask Vincent. You may want to be careful what you say to your boss, the chief."

"Thanks, Rick! Loud and clear! It may not hurt for Vincent to know that I am around and watching. Not that I care one way or the other if they kill each other, except for the paperwork that it will create."

Vincent took his case to the family council. The chair was John Disalvo. The meeting was in the Catskills late one night. The road to the cabin was one way in, same way out, down a mile long dirt road. Every quarter mile, there was a car parked which allowed the Lincoln Town Car to pass but could easily be used to cut off a retreat or to box in uninvited guests.

The council listened politely. It was clear that they knew everything Vincent had found: Frank Collins and Gus Ionello had concluded that Vincent Bonanno was the front-runner for his father's position even though he had said that he was not interested. They had also concluded that there would always be division as long as Vincent was alive. The council also knew that Frank and Gus had disappeared.

"Vincent, what do you want?"

"I had thought that I could leave the business, raise a family, coach a little league, you know, the American family thing: two kids, two cars, and a dog."

"Nothing stopping you! But think carefully. Frank Collins would take over the business by default but there would be a small war to make that happen. Some of my colleagues may see pieces of lucrative business in Brooklyn and old timers loyal to your father may be moved aside for the new inner circle. You understand, Vincent, that we will have no responsibility to protect you if protection is needed," Mad Jack said as he nodded to his fellow council members who nodded back in approbation.

"Your father was a valuable member of the council. Your mother was protected; she is cousin to Aldo, a good alliance! You are not married, yet?" It was a rhetorical question.

"Well, go with God!" There was a pause as Vincent reached the door. "I had heard that Frank Collins was down the shore."

"Thank you, gentlemen, for your time," Vincent said as he walked out.

Vincent already knew where Frank and Gus were. The bigger questions were the messages hidden in the meeting. It was clear that his mother was protected; the message was that he was not. He was being instructed to marry within the community. The message was also that he had to deal with Frank Collins, but there would be no interference.

Best man wins; losers gone!

Three days later, in an early evening, Bill Surphlis sat at the bar and asked if Rick was around.

"Important?" asked David.

"Sort of! A couple of friends of his turned up stiff."

Dave called the apartment and passed on the message. Fifteen minutes later, Rick appeared in his signature charcoal grey worsted suit with white shirt and gold simple cuff links. He was wearing a dark blue tie.

Sitting next to Bill, he ordered a club soda.

"I am intrigued, Bill, since I have only one friend, Sam. So, who were the unlucky guys?"

"Frank Collins and Gus Ianello! The chances are it was not natural causes."

"A lucky guess, or is that a result of your great detective work?'

"What do you think?"

"Why are you here? Think I had something to do with their early exit? It doesn't grieve me, but I didn't do it."

Bill laughed and ordered another beer with a chaser.

"No, actually I know who did it."

"Then you are a great detective."

"I got a call at home five thirty this morning; nobody has my home phone number. A man says there were two guys in a shoot-out back of Blue Lagoon. Says they're both dead, like killed each other so they're out by the dumpsters. Good excuse to raid Disalvo."

"What did you say?"

"I said, 'Thanks. Who is this?' He says, 'No friend of your, chief.'"

"Strange! So, what did you do?"

"Well, I thought about it and decided not to do the cowboy thing, so I called for a car to meet me at the site, uniforms and no sirens.

"It was just as advertised. I called it in and ordered a door-to-door starting at the Blue Lagoon. Funny as all hell! When the chief gets into work at about nine thirty, he has a fit, asking why he was not called and who gave the order to go door-to-door. All the uniforms are having a ball. They frisk the Disalvo boys—seems they were all carrying except for Mad Jack who was laughing so loud and hard there were tears streaming down his face."

"That I would have paid to see," said Rick "But how does that tell you who killed Frank and Gus?"

"It is obvious, Rick. They either shot each other, or it was a murder/suicide. That is my report, though how Gus pulled the trigger with no fingers, I am not sure, and Frank got a bullet in the knee before the one in the back of his head killed him."

"Great work, detective. Justice does seem to work in mysterious ways. I always wondered why the statue of justice is blindfolded; now I know. How is Chief O'Connor taking the news?"

"No one knows. He got a headache and went home after apologizing to Mad Jack for some reason that started Jack laughing again."

"Strange. Thanks for sharing the news. Drinks' on me. You should try to get home."

"Thanks, Rick. You are right, strange day. I will try and sort out what it all means," he said then laughed. "But not too hard!"

Chapter Thirty-Three

"I had better go to work."

Sam stood and moved away. "This is your table, just sign the charge, and it will go on your account."

"Thanks, Sam."

"No problem. Noni will take good care of you."

Richard sat back and felt much more comfortable. He realized that he could see everything that was happening without being observed himself. The restaurant filled quickly, and there was a quiet efficiency in the movements of the staff. They worked together and seemed to genuinely enjoy their work. It was also clear from the number of people who nodded to or greeted Sam that it was a crowd of repeat customers.

At about ten minutes past seven, when Richard was starting to wonder whether it was clear that Trish was to meet him at the restaurant, she entered. She did not enter in the conventional way; she caused a commotion. The conversation quieted as people at the bar swiveled and there was a ripple of curiosity which traveled outward.

Sam had been playing variations on "Summertime" when he looked up and wound into his variation, "See the girl with the red dress on...." Red dress on! Trish, with her long blond hair, was wearing a mini dress of a vibrant red. It was expensive; it looked like a million-dollar dress. The women in the room were speculating on the cost, envious of the legs which showed the latest fashion as it was meant to be shown. The men in the room were looking for the man lucky enough to be buying dinner for her. Trish looked regal. The look was one of not appearing to notice the attention while having the satisfaction of having achieved the desired effect.

Richard stood up to move toward this vision and knocked into an empty chair. Attention switched to the noise; there were a few titters then conversation started again as the "who" question was answered.

Passing the piano, Richard glanced toward Sam who gave him a look of admiration and of mock disbelief.

"You look fabulous," Richard remarked.

"Glad to see you, too, Richard." She kissed him lightly "Busy. Did you get a table?"

"Well, yes!"

He guided her to the table under jealous looks of the patrons seated at the bar.

Noni appeared and gave them a preview of the evening's specials. As she spoke, it was possible to taste the dishes described.

"For appetizers, we have smoked salmon citrus salad, hand cut imported salmon mixed with a spring salad soaked in citrus juices, blood orange slices, lime, lemon and grapefruit.

We also have dates filled with goat's cheese and a fruit cup of seasonal Mediterranean fruits. The soup special is a seafood cappuccino, seafood broth topped with whipped fresh cream. Our featured entreés are smoked duck with mango and baked lamb with couscous. Would you like a cocktail or perhaps some wine?"

"Champagne, Noni! We are celebrating," said Rick.

"Richard, champagne. It must be very good news although I called Mummy and she called all of the hospitals in the city to make sure they would know you were...."

Richard interrupted, "Acceptable!"

"No, no, that she and daddy would personally give you a recommendation."

"I wasn't aware that they had seen me operate."

"Of course not, silly. A personal reference."

The conversation stopped as the bottle of champagne arrived. Richard knew very little about wines and was comfortable enough to say so and to give an affirmative wave after tasting the sample given to him.

Trish and Richard silently watched the bubbles. Their thoughts were similar: *Why are we arguing?* Trish had no idea. Richard was conscious of an irritation which stemmed from imagining Mrs. Wellington calling every hospital in New York to ask about an applicant, Dr. Land. He knew why it bothered him, but why did he care? It was not about Bo and his reelection, was it?

"Trish, I was interviewed today and accepted a position at the Veterans Hospital."

"The...Veterans Hospital up town?"

"Yes."

"Richard, I am sure that Mummy could have helped with a position at Columbia."

"Except that I did not apply at Columbia. I do not want to practice at Columbia. I thought that you would be pleased that I would be living in New York."

"I am, but they are all poor people on welfare, mostly black. Richard, how can you do that to us?"

"Is 'us' you and your parents Trish, or you and me? The fact that his son-in-law is a doctor is good, but the kind of patients he treats, since they do not vote Republican, is bad."

"I am sorry, Richard. This is a celebration; it is what you want. Good luck," she raised her glass to his, and they drank.

The mood lightened, and they returned to the menu. "I think I will have the citrus salad and perhaps some fruit for a main course," said Trish. "The other items seem to be full of calories and a girl must be careful."

"The soup special and a steak with baked potato have been on my mind all day. They have a steak aged in Bourbon, but maybe a steak au poivre. What do you think?" Richard asked.

"I think they are high in cholesterol and could be fattening."

"So, remember, I am the doctor."

"Well, I will remember for tonight."

They were both smiling.

"I have another surprise for you," said Richard.

"Hey!" Trish was looking toward the entrance. "Isn't that Wade?"

"This surprise is also a surprise to me." Richard was continuing his conversation.

"I'll say it's a surprise he is with Claire." Trish was standing and looking toward the front of the café.

Claire was looking around to see which celebrities might be dining at Rick's Café when she saw Trish standing at the rear. With mouth open, she waved.

Wade was arguing with Megan at the front.

"What do you mean an hour's wait? It is Wednesday. I didn't think that we would need a reservation."

Wade took out a twenty-dollar bill. "Will this get us a table sooner?"

"No," said Megan. "We may not be able to seat you at all."

Claire had advanced to where Trish and Richard were then both standing.

"How did you get in? Did you have a reservation? Wade was so uptight; he said we should come and see how empty the place is," she tittered. "Now he is annoyed because there are no tables, and here you are with the owners' private table: he will be completely inconsolable."

She barely stopped for a breath as her thoughts and words tumbled out. She was dressed in a very expensive gold hot pants suit which looked badly on her. The bottoms of the shorts were stretched against heavy upper legs while the lower calf of her leg was muscular, giving the impression of a lamb chop. The upper garment was tight and squeezed her bust upwards into a view which was not intended by the designer. The boots were black in contrast to the gold lame of the suit.

"I just bought a pant suit like that!" said Trish.

"Yes, I know. This is it. I knew you wouldn't mind if I borrowed it. Doesn't it look great?"

Before an answer, either affirmative or truthful, could be given, Wade came up to the table. "I told the girl that we were joining friends. She said that Dr. Land had not told them he had more than one guest. Not interrupting, are we?" he asked, pulling out a chair for Claire.

"Yes," said Richard.

"Not at all," said Trish. "We are celebrating Richard accepting a job in New York when he leaves the army. We should be seeing a lot more of him." She squeezed Richard's arm in a suggestive manner.

"Where?"

"Where what?" asked Trish.

"Where is the new job?" asked Wade.

"At the Veterans Hospital," said Richard when Trish seemed unable to repeat the name.

"The freaking Veterans! You are joking, right? All those black junkies."

"All the patients there did your fighting for you, Wade." There was an edge to Richard's voice.

Noni came with two place settings while giving a sideways glance at Richard.

"Are you ready to order?"

"Yes, I think so."

The order was taken by Noni without notepad in spite of Claire changing her mind twice then settling on the special duck which she had seen being delivered to a nearby table. Wade wanted the French onion soup, the largest steak, rare, with a Mediterranean salad. He also ordered from the wine list a Merlot and an Italian Soave.

"The war will be over soon," said Claire.

"Says who?" asked Wade.

"Well, we are bombing them to their knees according to the news."

"We'll see," retorted Wade. "I think that it is too good for business to ever end. Your family must be putting their golden eggs away, Trish."

"I have no idea what you are talking about. Daddy is a public servant."

Wade's loud laughter turned a few heads.

The wine arrived, and Wade vetted it before pronouncing that it was "drinkable." Richard looked at his glass while the others drank.

What was happening? He was used to having a plan, a schedule. It usually took a particular course, and although there was crisis, he was able to anticipate, adapt. Why had Wade and Claire shown up at Rick's? Why had they chosen this place from the thousands of equally good choices? If he were to be uncharitable, he could rationalize a setup. Or it could be as simple as Claire overhearing the plans and unconsciously triggering a response to the question of where to eat. Another thought was jealousy. Was Wade jealous of Richard's relationship to Trish? Was there something between Wade and Trish? There had always been something. Wade's looks and little disguised ambitions to make a lot of money were attractive to a family even with the money that the Wellingtons had accumulated. Wade's desire to be part of the family was transparent. Was love involved? It was too hard to tell, but all the other ingredients made it likely that it was somewhere in the mix.

Wade rated the first course "edible." Where did he get these cliques from? He left nothing of the soup and asked for more rolls while Trish ate about half of her salad and no bread. The seafood soup was outstanding and Richard said so, unashamed that he might be biased.   .

"So why did the other hospitals turn you down, Richard?"

Wade was playing the table, but for him, it was more checkers than chess. It was about winning face, earning more, and receiving the accolades.

"Because I did not apply!"

"I don't understand. Couldn't Mrs. W. get you in?"

"More than likely, but using Mrs. Wellington never occurred to me, and besides, I wanted to do some good. It's not always all about money, Wade."

"Well, rich or poor, it's nice to have money." Wade got the laugh he had played for.

"You can only eat one loaf of bread a day," said Richard.

"But I like caviar with mine!" Another laugh-producing comment! The main courses arrived, and Trish tried to change the subject as it was clear that Wade was baiting Richard.

"Richard had another surprise he was just going to reveal when you joined us. What is it, darling?"

"Well," Richard was already annoyed and embarrassed. What had started as a celebration and a chance to rebuild his relationship with Trish was in shambles. "It doesn't matter."

"What is it, Richard?" Claire was full of curiosity. There was nothing she liked better than a secret, and a secret received was a secret to share and therefore no longer a secret. Richard had no intention of letting the world know that he had inherited—inherited monies and a part interest in a restaurant. He could hear Wade braying loud enough for the room to know that Richard was not only practicing medicine in the third world but also a saloon keeper.

"Tell us, Richard. You are among friends," Claire was referring to the table, but Richard smiled as he thought the remark may be truer than was intended.

"I was going to tell Trish privately that I was promoted to colonel."

"Well, your secret is safe," said Wade. "Why on earth would we tell anyone that a colonel in the US of A army is a friend of ours?"

"Is that a suggestion that I am not a friend, or that a colonel is not fit to breathe in the same room?"

Richard promised himself that he would not rise to the bait, and he had. He promised himself that he would not allow Wade to make him angry, and he had.

There was silence at the table as the sound of Sam playing "Moon River," a request, as it was a tune he would not have chosen, changed to "Kiss Me,

Kate." Richard turned and was rewarded with Kate, making the movie character seem charitable, in a clear fury walking straight to the bar and ordering a gin and tonic.

It was obvious that it was the first time that that behavior from Kate had been witnessed. She then went over to Sam, told him to stop playing that stupid song then stomped to the door, to the elevator, and to her apartment. In passing the table with Richard, Trish, Claire, and Wade, she gave them a look—a look of evaluation. It was cursory and full of curiosity. To each, the look was different and memorable. The amusement almost took the edge off the fury—almost.

The conversation returned to the dining table along with the dessert menu.

"Was that the new owner?" asked Claire.

"I believe that it is," said Wade. "I believe that I would like to meet her, perhaps not tonight."

It generated the most natural laugh of the evening since the speculation was that Wade would jump into a woodpile if he thought that a snake in heat might be there.

Trish opted for herbal tea, no dessert, while Wade ordered a chocolate bomb. Claire took coffee as did Richard who was persuaded by Noni to have the tiramisu. When the desserts came, Claire ate half of the bomb and most of the tiramisu. The tiramisu had a flavor of brandy, was well suited to the coffee, and was an excellent choice.

Wade looked up quickly and the rest of the table turned to see Kate emerge from the door near the kitchen. She had changed and apparently cleaned up as she had a different image from the one that had disappeared through that same door twenty minutes earlier. She was wearing a knitted dress up to the neck with short sleeves and a simple gold chain. It was an outfit that was made for a person who was running a restaurant. The dress was not flattering but appeared to be perfect and quite sensual. Richard thought, not for the first time. *Kate Blaine can probably wear a sugar sack and look at ease and exotic.*

Kate Blaine was bearing down on their table.

What now? Richard thought.

"Hello, Richard. How was your meal?" She was smiling.

"Excellent, thank you. Kate Blaine, may I introduce Trish Wellington, Claire Powell, and Wade Phillips, friends of mine from school."

"The food was outstanding and the wine superb," Wade gushed, clearly captivated by Kate and turning his considerable charm in her direction.

"Thank you, Mr. Phillips."

"Call me Wade, Kate."

"Call me Miss Blaine, Wade!"

Wade laughed.

"Your celebration was a success?" Kate had turned to Richard.

"Thank you. Noni is a great waitress and the ambiance just right."

"I must go and apologize to Sam. I think I yelled at him on my way through earlier. Pleased to have met you, Wade, Claire, and Tracy."

"It's Trish!" Trish corrected.

"Have a good night."

"Good night," the table replied in an uneven quartet.

"You did not say that you knew her." Trish's voice had an edge.

"I was not asked."

"I think that she knows you very well," Wade jumped in.

"Butt out, Wade!" Trish was now steaming. "Was that why we met at this restaurant? Is this another of your secrets?"

Richard answered in perfect honesty, "Well, yes it is."

There was no hesitation. Trish jumped up and headed for the door with Richard trying to keep up. As she was waiting for her coat, Richard tried to remonstrate, to explain.

"Trish, will you wait? Can we talk? In private, please."

They were joined at the door by Wade and Claire.

Claire seemed a little embarrassed, but Wade was clearly enjoying the showdown as was the patrons closest to the door.

"Wade, take me home." Trish was crying. "I can't believe that I expected a wonderful evening and then the Veterans. Mummy will be so disappointed. Daddy always said you were not good enough for me. He was right." She left in a swoosh of cold air.

Claire said, "Good night, Richard. Good luck!" She kissed his cheek.

Wade shook his hand. "Women!"

He was smiling. Richard could almost read his mind. "Good night, Richard. The bill came. I left cash for half on the table, excluding the champagne."

His grin said it all. He had been baiting Richard all evening.

Richard needed air but could not go outside. He needed quiet—in the middle of a restaurant and bar. Sensing rather than feeling, moving without recognition of motion, he found himself seated back at the table.

Noni appeared. "Fresh coffee, Sir?"

"Yes, please. That would be nice."

When she returned with the coffee, he waved absently toward the bill.

"I do not know what to do with that, Noni. I am sorry."

A hand picked up the money and the check.

"I will take care of this for you." The voice was soft.

It was a new Kate Blaine. He tried to smile.

"I am sorry. That was my fault; I should never have called her Tracy."

"No," said Richard, "I should thank you. I was never going to be good enough for her father or rich enough for her mother. She and Wade are welcome to each other."

"She is very beautiful."

"Yes, she is."

Chapter Thirty-Four

Sam waved from the piano for them to join him.

"Go sit with Sam. I shall join you when I have taken care of the check and Noni," Kate said.

"I am not good company tonight."

"And I am?" She gave a rueful look and went to the cashier.

Sam was playing the opening bars of "American in Paris." The Gershwin classic sounded different outside of a symphony hall.

"Great, great man, Gershwin. Could change himself, know what I mean?" Sam stated.

The question was going to be answered by Sam himself since Richard did not know what he meant.

"This little tune classical music—jazz—waiting for words, what is it? A great songwriter writes a symphony and everybody looks for the words. Then finding none, they go back to the songs and look for the symphony. Man changes, or was he both those people—? Know what I mean?"

That time, Richard knew what he meant.

"You two people had a bad night. Put everything into perspective. Music got to have rhythm, got to have purpose. Know what I mean?"

Richard was lost again, but he was sure that he was headed in the right direction.

Sam was playing "I Got Rhythm" in double time as Kate sat at the drums and started driving. Richard took a reed from his pocket and a clarinet from a box beneath the piano stool. He made no attempt to join in the frenetic scene but was contented with adding the odd note or scale until they had finished. As they stopped, he began the New Orleans tune, "Just a Closer Walk with Thee" as slow and low as he could. Kate joined with the brushes and one of the employees showed up with a trombone. They played through a series of duets and solos with Sam doing a thirty-second trill at the top of the piano keyboard before the trombone and clarinet picked up the pace and the volume into a full marching rendition. There was a transition into "When the Saints Go Marching In," which ended with laughter and cheers from the customers, staff, and from the participants.

"This is not good for business," said Kate "No one buys drinks while we are making this kind of racket."

"No," said Sam. "But they will be back. And look at the change in mood. Know what I mean?"

Richard knew what he meant.

The three of them sat at their table as the restaurant emptied. Sam was drinking coffee with just a little whiskey, Richard had a glass of Spanish port, and Kate was eating a dish of vanilla ice cream with crème de menthe poured over it.

"Well, shall we play 'who had the worst day?'" asked Sam.

"I'll go first," he continued. "This would have been Alice's birthday; I miss her. It has been nine years; I miss her. I miss them all, and today, I remembered them—Alice, Miss Margaret, and Mr. Rick. I am getting old. You young kids got to take charge—Miss Kate, Dr. Richard, my Jimmy, our Jimmy."

"I miss her, too," whispered Kate. "I had forgotten her birthday. We never forgot her birthday—Jimmy and me. We would make birthday cards."

"What was she like? How did you meet her?" asked Richard.

"She was an angel." Sam was looking into the space of remembrances. The memories were in danger of overwhelming his ability to speak. "She walked in one day, fall of 1949, and said she needed a job. One look, you could tell she was starving. Come up from Memphis following a man, except he had already moved on. I asked her what she could do. She was like every twenty year old and said 'Anything.' Then she blushed and said 'No, not anything.' I had to laugh and give her some food and a job as waitress. While she was eating, I was watching her and tinkling on the piano. She was watching me watching her. Then she started singing, 'Well, no matter my man is; I am his forever.' Said that she had auditioned for *Show Boat* and knew a few songs. In 1949, Alice was no singer, but she had a voice, and I offered to teach her during her off hours if she was around. Now, I have got to admit that it was not an altogether altruistic offer. I was smitten. We were married within the year and then she took care of Kate, and later, Jimmy came along. Good times, those...some."

He stopped and looked into space. The silence was broken by someone dropping a pan in the kitchen. It was enough to break the spell.

"Now, who is next?" asked Sam.

"Well," said Richard "I suppose I should fill in what you have not worked out for yourselves. Today, I accepted a position at the Veterans Hospital. The woman I thought might someday be my wife was decidedly unhappy with that decision, as were her friends, and she was of the opinion that her parents would not approve. I don't care for her parents' approval. Her father is a senator by the way. Nor do I respect the opinion of friends who found the war inconvenient and any association with servicemen just not their 'scene.' In a nutshell, she is not going to be walking down the aisle with me, but I strongly suspect that she will find many ready substitutes." He stopped and looked into their faces.

"Does that sound pathetic or what?"

"Yes!" Kate exclaimed.

"Yes, it does!" Sam said.

"Well, you didn't both have to agree!"

They were all laughing in a companiable way.

"Well, I guess it is late," said Kate, standing.

"Not that late, honey," said Sam with concern.

"Nothing to tell!"

"Then tell us plenty of nothing."

"Perhaps, I should leave," said Richard.

"No, you might as well hear along with Sam. I went out with Vinny. He is very charming, very persuasive. Dinner, perhaps a show. Home, not too late. I had refused several times, but this time, I agreed. So off we went to the Top of the Sixes with Benny riding shotgun. They had both had a couple of drinks. When we get to the restaurant, he tells the maitre d' that, no, he does not have a reservation but he wants a window seat. Benny gives the guy fifty bucks. The maitre d' showed us to a window seat for four which already has a re-served sign on it. Vinny looks out and says, 'If I wanted a fucking view of a building site, I could have stayed in Brooklyn.' He turned to see another table at the other side of the room and said, 'Give us that table!'

"It was set for a party of six. The maitre d' remonstrated but Vinny threatened to have all the kitchen staff call in sick the next day if he did not get the table. The poor man acquiesced, and I saw him later trying to accommodate the unlucky six, actually a young couple who were meeting each other's parents for the first time. I was too sick to eat. Vinny had a couple of martinis and half a bottle of red wine. He was getting louder, and I was getting more embarrassed.

"When we left, he expected that I would be impressed. He laughed and said I should get used to it. When we were leaving, he suggested that instead of a show, we should go back to his place and watch a little TV. I said that I needed to go to the lady's room and make myself beautiful for him. I walked straight through the emergency exit, called a cab, and came here."

Before any comment could be made, Kate continued, "I win! I had the worst night because tomorrow, Vinny is going to come here and kill me."

"Isn't that a little melodramatic. He may be upset, but he will get over it," said Richard.

"You think! He is a nasty person who bullies his way into what he wants." Kate fired back then whispered, "He wants me!"

"He is not a nice person," agreed Sam. "Let's sleep on it and then decide what we can do in the morning. Now, I am tired, and an old man like me needs his sleep."

He looked tired; they all did.

They went through the door to the elevator, put in the floor keys, and said a very quiet "Good night" to each other. There had been a bond created. What had created that bond? It was destiny. They had been brought together by a will. Why? Did the writer believe in destiny, or had he seen a need for these very different persons, individuals at the very definition of the word, to be together, to work together?

No, it was too easy to characterize that bond as chance. In fact, there was a link through friendship and family.

Richard did not believe that he would sleep and, in fact, tossed and turned for a long time. When he awoke, it was with a start. Where was he? What had woken him? He sat up, looked toward a door of a room which he did not immediately recognize. However, at the door was a sight that he did recognize.

"Don't you ever knock?"

"Good morning, Richard. I would have knocked, I could have shouted, but with the noise from the snoring, it was the only clue that there was life in here. I am making breakfast. See you in fifteen minutes," Kate said.

It was a statement; not a question, but a command.

Then he knew where he was, and it was all coming back to him. In the shower, he reflected on the previous day—his pleasure at the new direction in his career then the evening disaster. It was not better that morning. Kate, however, had appeared bright and optimistic, or was it a façade? He would know in a few minutes. He shaved for the second time in just over twelve hours— the problem with a dark beard! That time, he remembered to use his own after-shave, Old Spice. He did not have a great selection of clothes and momentarily considered opening the closet to check on clothes which might be around, but he dismissed the idea for a couple of million reasons.

Finally, he decided upon a clean dress shirt, slacks, no tie, and no jacket. He glanced at himself in the mirror by the door. Check hair: in place. Shirt collar down, one or two buttons open, one. Check shoes: fastened. Check zipper. Why did he think of that! He walked through the door, smiling, and knocked at the opposite door.

There was a loud shout from within, and, although the words were indistinguishable, the meaning was obvious.

He entered.

Immediately, he was aware of the difference in that apartment from the one he had left. Where one was masculine, this one was all feminine. The dining table had a white tablecloth and was set with three places. He was disappointed in a way that he would have had a hard time explaining. There were frilly sheers at the windows with floral prints, oversized in brilliant reds and yellow, drapes, and cornices. The chairs were covered in neutral tones as was a rug in the center of the room. The floor was plain wood in the original flooring, sanded and polished. The planks were of slightly different widths of probably a foot or more. Flower power was instantly in his head and almost out of his mouth. He checked to remind himself to think before speaking. The wall above a fireplace had a portrait, beautiful, smiling, and relaxed. *Mother*, he thought.

"You thought that was your mother, didn't you?"

How did she do that? How did she know what he was thinking?

"No!" he lied.

"It is my mother, Margaret. Beautiful, wasn't she?"

"Yes, she was!" he answered truthfully.

He stepped forward for a closer look. Closer, there were differences. The young woman was relaxed in a way his mother had never been. He sometimes thought that his mother had never been young, although that was obviously not true.

"Remarkable."

"Eggs, easy over. Bacon, sausage, black pudding, mushrooms, toast, and marmalade. Did I forget anything?"

"Yes! Coffee. I am dying for a cup of coffee."

"Of course! Sorry. Milk and sugar is on the table"

"We are expecting someone else?"

"Well, I thought Sam might join us, but he has gone off somewhere. Cleaning crew said he left early and has not yet returned. Strange. We shall have to have to eat without him."

She disappeared into the kitchen and returned with two steaming mugs of coffee.

"Mugs okay?"

"Perfect!"

He continued to walk around the room. It seemed that he was not embarrassed or self-conscious as he wandered up to a desk. It was more of a writing table with drawers down the side and center drawer beneath the writing surface. The top of the desk was where his attention was drawn, drawn like a magnet to the photographs arranged in frames of various materials and of different sizes holding black and white photographs.

There were obvious photographs of Kate dressed for the prom with a tall, spotty adolescent who had clearly outgrown his strength and, from the look on his face, his intellect. How many of these pictures adorned how many shelves? Parents could point to their daughter and the "dork." Richard suspected that whatever the number of existing prom photographs, not one adorned the shelf of the young man in each of the frames as it marked their passage into manhood for eternity.

He picked up a frame with Kate and a man he assumed was Rick—assumed because of the obvious pride and because of a strange feeling that he knew that man. They had never met; he was sure. It was a graduation picture from college and must have been taken the previous year. The man, Rick, looked to his doctor's eyes, to be tired and ill.

Another picture had Rick and Sam in front of the restaurant at about the time of the opening, the picture taken from so far back that features were impossible to distinguish. The photograph that had taken his eye from across the room which he had deliberately not looked at he now picked up with hands that he noticed were trembling. *Not good, doctor*, he told himself, *trembling hands!*

"They look good, don't you think?" Kate was carrying two plates from the kitchen.

Richard put down the photograph using both hands as he did not trust either one alone. He did not need to look at the picture anyway as the image was burned into his brain. "Very! That smells good. More coffee?"

"Mum and Dad. Her twenty-first birthday, I believe."

"He...." Richard stopped.

"Yes, he looks like you, and she looks like your mother. It has been strange and confusing and frightening and spooky. When I first saw you at the funeral, I thought that Dad had returned. Then I thought...never mind. Eat your breakfast; it will get cold."

They both lapsed into silence and their own thoughts while helping themselves to the breakfast. When they spoke of the food, neither could remember the polite small talk as they were both responding by remote control; they could have dialed in without being present. "Good bacon!" "Local butcher!" "Black pudding. Fresh?" "Yes, same butcher." "Mushrooms too?" "Don't know, just picked up some from the kitchen" "More coffee?" "No thanks."

Kate's eyes drifted to the writing table.

Richard stood and began to collect the plates. "Let me wash up," he offered.

"And let you see my dirty kitchen. No!"

"I am sure that your kitchen is as spotless as the rest of your apartment."

"Have you been looking at the rest of my apartment?"

"No, sorry I didn't mean.... Damn." He was blushing.

Why was he blushing? Almost thirty years old and still blushing?

Kate was laughing. "Someone comes in and cleans when they do Rick's apartment. Otherwise, I would be a slob."

"I will wash up for you then and clean your dirty kitchen."

"So, it's a dirty kitchen I have now?" Kate said with a fake Irish brogue.

They were both laughing as they went through the door to a very neat, clean kitchen which had a small eating area at one side with a large refrigerator, and, opposite, a sink with an adjacent stove. There was a frying pan soaking in the sink and a pan filled with water on the stove.

Richard efficiently washed the pans then put in clean, hot water with liquid soap and carefully washed the plates which Kate dried and put away.

"A man unafraid of the kitchen? That is the first time a man has done that for me. Actually may be the first time a man has been through the door. Most expect that I will bring them a fresh beer or ice in the living room."

She was smiling and looking young, vulnerable, and beautiful. Previously, there had been tension. Richard had found her attractive. Relaxed, she looked more like his mother at the same age.

The smile left, and she said in return to the mock brogue. "Now, what kind of way is this to act on the day you are about to die?"

"I can't believe you are serious," said Richard calmly.

"Then you know nothing! Go back to Washington. Go!"

"No, I want to help. What can I do? Come with me to Washington."

"You think that will help?"

"I will go and reason with him. Go to the police. Something! What about Uncle George?"

"Reason? There is no reasoning. Go to the police? They will hold you while he hits you. I will, however, call Uncle George. He may not be able to help, but he should know anyway what is going on."

"Well, at least it's doing something. We should talk to Sam again this morning."

Kate thought and said, "No, he is getting too old for this nonsense. He must be kept out of it."

Kate went to the writing desk, found a phone book, and dialed.

A distant voice said, "Chief's office."

"Can I speak to the chief? Please."

"Sorry, he is not in. Can I take a message?"

"Yes, Eric. This is Kate Blaine. Tell him to put down the newspaper and pick up the phone."

"Kate, how did you know it was me?"

"I look at your picture everyday, Eric. We went to the high school prom together, didn't we?"

"Kate, I am a married man now with a baby, you know."

"Yes, I know Eric; woe is me! The chief please."

"Yes, Kate. Okay, Kate. See you!"

"Chief Surphlis," a new voice said.

"Uncle George, it's Kate."

"I know. That idiot Eric thinks that you have the hots for him. I won't get a thing out of him all day. What can I do for you, Kate?"

"I think that Vinny Bonanno may have put out a contract to correct a perceived slight similar to the one Eric has invented."

"Think? Well, as I heard it this morning, there are things that he would have someone do to you but he wants to do them personally."

"Uncle George...chief, do something! Or, tell me what I can do."

"I think you have done one thing that might work."

"I have? What is that?"

"Sent Sam to talk to his father."

"I didn't know. Is that where he is, that crazy beautiful man?"

"I will talk to Vincent, Kate. I heard a story once about a man who could help, maybe. The fable is that he can scare Mr. Bonanno and also Mr. Disalvo."

"Maybe Mr. Disalvo will help me," she said sarcastically "Who is the man? James Bond?"

"Something like that. Do you know a Mr. Smith?'

"Yes. No. Everyone who wanted to take me out called himself Smith. I don't know anybody whose real name is Smith, and if I did, I would not be able to get hold of him in time to save my skin."

Richard interrupted, "I know Smith!"

"Who is that?" asked the Chief.

"It's okay, Uncle George. It's Dr. Land. He says he knows a Mr. Smith. Thanks for your help."

"You are welcome, darling. I will talk to Vincent now and let you know how I make out. Make a call to Washington."

"You know Mr. Smith?" said Richard. "He received an envelope from Rick's estate."

"His name was Smith? I thought it was Monroe."

"Munroe, not Monroe, and Smith sometimes. His number must be in Rick's room."

"What do you think that crazy old man, Sam, is doing over there?" Kate was worried. "And what can a crazy old man like Mr. Smith do?"

Kate was seated at the desk in Rick's old apartment. She opened the front drawer and was looking through an orderly stack of papers, mostly blank writing paper or memo pads. Richard opened the top drawer of a nearby cabinet and was looking at a stack of photographs.

"I think there is a thin book of names and numbers. I saw them when we were tidying up." Kate was talking as she was looking.

Richard was silent, struck dumb for the third or fourth time that day. He had promised himself that he would not be surprised by anything again, and there he was unable to move, unable to breathe, and unable to think.

Kate took the photograph from his hand.

"Odd picture, this. Nobody has any idea why it is here. You look like you know!" Kate stated.

"No, I don't but, but it is a picture of me playing soccer in high school, about 1959 I think."

"So what is it doing here? Where did it come from?"

"I don't know," he said slowly.

"Well, I have found the book" Kate said triumphantly. "What are the chances that we will find him in town, or that the number still exists, or ever existed?"

"These are not real names. Look—Victory, Doc, Reb, General, Tyke, Vincent—that's a real name. And look—Ilsa, Suli, Rico, and here colonel with parenthesis MP.UK. Here is Smith with two numbers: one Washington and one in New York. There are more numbers and names. No addresses and nowhere is there a full name."

"Let me see." Richard took the book. "Ilsa. That is our home phone number, and Doc, that is in the hospital. Some of these numbers are overseas. Well, your Uncle George said call Washington, so try that number first."

"You call! I feel silly asking a stranger to prevent someone killing me!"

"Okay, though I fail to see why you would not call the devil himself to save that extremely pretty neck of yours."

"That was a little sexist," said Kate to hide her blushing.

"You are right; you could call the devil himself or herself."

The phone was ringing in Washington and was answered by a woman. "International exports."

"Mr. Smith please. Dr. Land calling."

"I am sorry, Sir. You must have the wrong number." She hung up.

"You were right, Kate—wrong number. Now what? Try the New York number?"

"I guess so," said a defeated Kate. Even though she had not expected any help, it was still a let down not to be even afforded the right to have her low expectations unrealized.

The phone rang.

Richard picked it up gingerly, thinking, *Who will call?*

"Hello," Richard said,

"Smith here! Obviously, you found my number while sitting at Mr. Blaine's desk. The number came up on our identification system. How can International Exports help you?"

"Well, maybe you can, or maybe not. I am here with Kate Blaine, and she has had a traumatic experience."

"I am not sure that a traumatic experience is really in the nature of the business that we perform; importing and exporting is our business," said a very upbeat salesman's voice. "And Miss Blaine is not an employee or a customer of ours. Perhaps you had better explain."

Richard gave an explanation in a nonemotional way. When he was finished, Smith asked to speak with Kate. "Didn't anyone tell you that playing with matches is dangerous?" Smith asked.

"No, actually, my mother died, and Rick, well, Rick shielded me from a lot of harsh realities."

"Well, now you have a taste of reality. These things sometimes have a way of working out. Good luck!"

"That's it? Good luck? Uncle George said that you once scared both Mr. Disalvo and Mr. Bonanno, but he suspected it was a fable. He was right! Good-bye and good luck to you, too!" She slammed down the receiver.

After a moment, Richard said facetiously, "That seems to have gone well!"

"Nobody seems to give a damn that there is a problem here!"

"If you mean nobody, you exclude me, Sam, and Uncle George."

"Men! You are all alike. You make fun of me; you make fun of my predicament." She was crying as she left the room.

Well, things are getting a little better, thought Richard. *She did not slam the door*. He put the photograph into his pocket as he left the room. His overnight bag was on the bed, ready, and he picked it up and went down to the restaurant.

Kate was right. She was on a predicament, and nobody seemed to have a plan. It was not necessarily true, but Dr. Richard Blaine Land had not got a plan—not even a clue.

Chapter Thirty-Five

In the bar was a pleasant surprise.

"Good morning, Sam. Out early?" Richard asked.

"Morning, Richard. Yes, just picked up a newspaper."

"Mm, must have walked to the printers. Kate know you are back?"

"No. I rang her apartment when I came in; there was no one there."

"Try again. We were actually in Rick's. I mean the other apartment, calling Smith," said Richard, giving Sam a quick synopsis of the morning's happenings.

Before Sam could make a call, the object of their discussion propelled her way into the room.

"I heard that you were back. Someone called as I was checking the morgues."

"Good morning, Kate. Yes, I should not be surprised that you and your legions of spies know of my every move. Okay. I could not sleep, so at seven thirty, I decided to go right to the lions' den and speak to the ringmaster. At least we would know the lie of the land as I had decided it was time to check our status.

"Good news all around, I think. He says nothing will happen to Kate, and he would like to believe that his friendship with Rick will continue with Rick's partners. He asked for a table for four tonight at eight. All in all, not a bad morning's work for an old man."

"You are a wonderful, crazy, lovable old man," Kate said.

Across town, a different conversation was underway. The chief of police was just leaving Vincent Bonanno. Vincent did not want trouble with the police; it was bad for business. The visit from Sam had disturbed him, too. He was an elderly black man who waited two hours to see him.

That man's loyalty to a dead friend was awesome, powerful, and, in some way, scary.

Vincent left a message for Vinny to be found and for him to come to the office. Meanwhile, he played back the conversation with the Chief.

"Remember, Mr. Bonanno, Rick Blaine and five men took an airport from the Germans and held it for weeks."

"Chief, the story gets a little wilder every time you tell it. The airport was taken from the Vichy French, some Germans were rounded up, and the cavalry, your unit, showed up within a few days. And chief, as I recall, Rick Blaine is now deceased."

"Yes, Mr. Bonanno, but what about the other five?"

"Yes, indeed. If they exhibited the loyalty of a Sam Wilson, that could be formidable."

"Hey, Dad! What's happening?" Vinny said as he appeared.

"Vinny, come in. Sit down."

"I don't have long; my weekly sparring match is at one with Julio."

"Should not take long. I want you to stay away from Kate Blaine."

"Dad, I think I should marry her!"

"Out of the question! Find a nice Italian girl and settle down. Have a dozen kids."

"I am twenty years old; I am not settling down. I know she is Irish and her mother never married that father. It doesn't matter these days. She is feisty. I will tame her, show her who is boss around here."

"You may choose to remember, Vinny, that I am still boss around here. Mr. Wilson and Mr. Surphlis were both here today to say that your behavior is unacceptable. I agree!"

"Unacceptable! Tell Mr. Wilson to go back to the jungle, and the chief can kiss my ass!"

"Vinny, you are a good-looking kid. You can take your pick of girls. I am asking you to stay away from this one. There are things that you do not understand."

"I understand, Dad. You would side with the Chief Dick in town and some nigger over your son. Those rumors and myth of some bogeyman protecting Rick Blaine and his precious daughter will be put to rest. So rest easy, old man I am going to kick some serious butt over at the gym, then maybe play a little pool or go see the delectable Kate."

"That would be a huge mistake."

Vinny stood up. There was a palpable tension in the room. Vinny broke it with "Boo!" He laughed as his father sat back in the chair more in surprise than in fear.

"Let's go, Benny!"

They left the meat plant and headed out in a Cadillac Eldorado convertible. The electric roof was stowed as they headed to the gym about a mile away. Vinny replayed the conversation with his father with exaggeration for effect and with frequent interruptions of laughter.

Driving into the parking lot, he nodded to the attendant and parked half blocking the exit. There was no "turf war" at that moment, but it was still prudent to park close to the attendant's booth. Vinny nodded, and Benny gave the attendant a twenty-dollar bill. It was also important to show who owned the premises.

The gym was clean and the locker room empty. Vinny went through his routine—changing into silk shorts and a tee shirt with white socks and the latest sneakers. Benny watched as Vinny warmed up, picked up a towel, and headed for the door. As they entered the main room, the public address system announced that there was a phone call for Benny.

"Get that, Benny. If it is my father, tell him that I am busy." Vinny smacked one clenched fist into the palm of his other hand. "Julio is late; he is going to regret that!"

They had entered a large room with weights and lifts at one end. In the near corner, there was a punching bag and a lighter punching drill ball, skipping ropes, and other paraphernalia of a boxing gym.

Vinny reached for gloves and then for a sparing helmet when he was stopped in mid reach.

"Hi, Julio had an emergency, and since I was to work out later, he asked if I would train with you. Vinny, right?" a woman asked.

She was good-looking, a little thin, maybe one hundred and twenty pounds with light brown hair, freckles, and in her early twenties. Vinny was thinking that he could go a few rounds but it would not be in the ring which took up about half the space of the room.

"Yes, I am Vinny. Sorry about Julio. Usually, we spar for about half an hour. I am sorry, but I am probably forty pounds heavier and with three inches longer reach; it would hardly be fair."

Actually, Vinny never worried about fair, which was why he sparred with Julio who was twenty pounds lighter and a couple of inches shorter.

"Well, we can take it easy. No helmets, just a few practice reps. Perhaps you can teach me something."

The call had come in after ten.

"Black? Smith!" Smith said.

"Yes, Sir," Black replied.

"How is your assignment at the UN?"

"On track. All assets accounted for and operating as expected."

Even though the line was secure and rooms were "swept" daily, there was no extra information. Black team was in New York watching for a transfer of secret documents. The missile design was to be passed to a South American diplomat, but there was no doubt that it was going to China. The diplomat's hotel room was already bugged. He was due to arrive back in New York that night.

"Up for a little R and R?"

There was rarely rest and never relaxation when Smith was involved. There was little point in arguing either, or questioning.

"We're just going to get some, Sir, then a bite to eat then a little sleep; it could be a long night."

"Gloves is there, right?"

"Yes, Sir."

"It might appeal to her."

Smith had laid out a basic plan for the people in the field in that case. Black (a name chosen for being the youngest black belt in the US), Gloves (who had sparred with her brother before he went to the US Olympic boxing trials) Byte, and Shocks, who were technical professionals.

It was pure coincidence that they were in New York and free, although Smith would have found a team or person somewhere in the vicinity able to make the intercept.

Vinny was smiling. "Oh, I can teach you something."

"Good, let's get started." She turned after lacing his gloves and pulled on her own, which she was carrying and already laced.

"Aren't they loose?"

"Well, it won't matter if we are just doing a little sparing and jabbing, will it?"

In truth, they were snug as she wrapped her hands around the rolls of quarters she had put there and the elasticated gap was closed.

They danced around, loosening up, and met in the center of the ring. He was watching her breasts and hips; she was looking at his posture and footwork. He obviously had boxed before and looked as though he liked to throw punches high for maximum bleeding.

She came in closer and put a left jab on his forehead. It was dangerous because of the height differential, but she was counting on surprise. He completely missed the opening that she had presented. Staggering, he recovered and jabbed, missing by an inch; it could have been a mile, but she wanted him confident. He jabbed, setting up a combination, but she let the jab go over her shoulder and jabbed under his arm. It hurt him as it was just over his heart. Vinny came in high. She ducked and hit him low in the ribs six times before pulling away from his desperate uppercut. He was panting a little from the strength of the body punches and the frustration of someone who was never where he punched. Seeing him with a low guard, she hit him under the eye hard. Roaring like a bull, he spat out the mouthguard and charged, swinging high. Backpedaling, she waited for a swing which took him slightly off balance. Then she put one hundred and twenty pounds and ten dollars of quarters into his lower rib cage and had the satisfaction of hearing it crack. The look of shock was nothing compared to the onslaught as he dropped his arm too late to save his rib and too soon to save his face. His mouth, unprotected, lost teeth, and his other eye closed.

"I will kill you!" he gurgled from the mat.

"You don't get it, do you? Stop beating up women!" She turned to walk away.

Vinny, in a fury, tried to sweep her off her feet. Gloves neatly jumped in the air and came down on his leg, breaking it just above the ankle.

The door, which had been mysteriously locked, opened. Black, Byte, Shocks, and Benny came in.

"What happened?" Benny asked, looking at the crumpled bloody face crying in the center of the ring.

"He just tried to beat up his last girl. If he ever lays a hand on one again, we will be back." said Black. "Got your stuff, boys?"

"In a minute, Boss." No names were mentioned, not even aliases. A ladder was retrieved, and Shocks climbed up and retrieved the camera which had been recording the whole event.

"And if your boss goes within one hundred yards of Katy Blaine, or sends anyone, this film will be sent...." Black started to say.

"What good would that do her?" asked a cowed but defiant Benny.

"Sent to Disalvo's boys. They will die laughing... and so will your boss!"

Vincent Bonanno arrived alone and was shown to the owners' table at the back of the restaurant. A few heads turned, but he generally escaped scrutiny. On the way, he nodded an acknowledgement to Sam. The hostess was Kate; she gave him a menu and laid three more on the table.

"I think you will be comfortable back here not waiting at the door for your guests," she said.

"Have you a minute, or are you busy?" he asked quietly.

"We are generally busy, but I will find a few minutes."

"Please sit down." After she was seated, he studied her very carefully and smiled. "You are very beautiful."

"Thank you. Is that all?" She started to stand.

"No, I am sorry. It's just that an attractive intelligent young woman, who my son describes as feisty, is rare."

"If you are here to plead the case for Vinny, please save your breath. He could be the last man on earth, and I would not spare a glance."

"Well, he was right about feisty! I was actually going to tell you that I have told him to stay away from you. He may have got his looks from me, but he got his mother's brains and his grandfather's disposition." He chortled a little although she thought that the ad lib had been used before. "You, on the other hand, inherited your mother's looks and your father's brains."

She blushed. "I had forgotten that you knew my mother from way back. Thank you for the compliments and for the support with Vinny. I think your guests have arrived. Shall I charge the bill and send it round?"

"Thank you for remembering Rick's accommodation. It avoids the scrambling of people trying to impress me and please add twenty percent tip. My in-laws are celebrating an anniversary, and we have not been here in a while, so when I saw Sam this morning, he reminded me. It used to be my favorite restaurant...but...." It was clear that he was not going to finish the thought, so Kate went to greet Mrs. Bonanno and her parents.

"Vincent, how can you sit here with our son nearly dead in the hospital? We just came from there; he looks terrible."

Maria Marciano Bonanno was a small woman. She had been petite and cute, but that was a long time ago. Now she was wearing a lot of make up to cover the touch up surgery. The long skirt could not hide the thickening of thighs and weight around her hips.

Vincent ignored the comment and greeted his in-laws. "Hi, Ma!" He kissed her cheek; she pursed her lips about three inches from his face.

"Rocky!" He shook the hand of a big man who looked like his namesake and from where he took the nickname. Nobody could remember his given name. Rocky looked like an enforcer. He had been with Mad Jack Disalvo in their early years and was somehow related, but no one bothered to figure how.

"How can you sit here while those four men who beat up your son are out there preying on other people just going about their business?" Mrs. Bonanno paused just long enough to order a martini.

"The doctor says that he may always have a limp. They cannot believe that someone with those injuries fought off four assailants and made it to the hospital."

"Incredible!" said Vincent." Could I have a Scotch on ice and if there is any of Rick's Scotch back there, I would appreciate your asking."

"The story I heard was there were three assailants, and where was Benny?" asked Rocky who had learned, in life, to question his wife and daughter but never in a direct manner.

"He was tied up," reported Maria. "Vinny untied him and then they went to the emergency room."

"Incredible," repeated Vincent. "Maybe after dinner, I will check in at the hospital."

"You are a little blasé. Your son and heir could be dying."

"Well, I thought that this was a special night for your parents."

"So it is, but tell me that you have people scouring the city for perpetrators."

"The city has been scoured, and they are gone. Must have been from out of town!"

"Who would want to hurt my little boy? He has done no harm."

"Maybe an irate husband," suggested Vincent with a glance at Rocky.

Vincent liked Rocky because he was always sure of what he was: there was no pretense. There could be no pretense. There could be no pretense because Rocky's face was like an open book. Now, Vincent saw clearly that Vinny was not his favorite grandchild. Maria was his daughter though, and the father would not like her to see his dislike for a full-grown man she treated as a boy.

"Not my baby. Don't say things like that, Vincent, even if you are joking. I am hungry. Let's order. Another drink first, I think."

The meal passed in tolerable conversation. Vincent watched Kate slide between customers with the grace and experience her mother had shown. When she passed, Maria waved her down and asked her to tell Sam to play "Moon River," her favorite. Kate promised to ask him; the emphasis on the politeness was lost on Maria who was back into a conversation about veal marsala with her mother.

When they had finished the meal and Maria had finally eaten the last of the tiramisu, Vincent ordered a brandy and cigar for himself and Rocky. The mother and daughter had Kahlua and cream.

Rocky leaned back a little and said, "Vincent, where are your people?"

"There is no one here. Hank drove me, and he is outside with the car."

"Aren't you worried that you may be next after Vinny was attacked today?" asked Rocky.

"Yes, Vincent, aren't you worried?" asked Maria, looking around.

"No. They have all left town."

"Well, I am going home and locking all the doors."

"I think I will go along to the hospital. Was Benny still there?"

"Yes," said Rocky. "You want me to come along?"

"No, thanks, Rocky. See the girls home, will you?"

"Sure, Vincent," said Rocky with a look of relief. He was almost seventy and looked a little tired.

Vincent sat back as they left and blew a smoke ring up toward the ceiling. "Thank you for the tip, Mr. Bonanno. Is there any thing else I can get for you?"

"No, thank you, Noni. Please thank Miss Kate and Sam for their hospitality."

"I will Mr. Bonanno. Good night."

At the hospital, they parked near the front door as visiting hours were officially over and the area was quiet. A uniformed security man came toward them to ask that they move the car. When he was close enough to recognize them, he instead touched his cap.

Hank and Vincent went unchallenged into the elevator, and Hank, without asking, punched the floor number. The doors opened to a quiet corridor. Near the nurse's station, Benny was asleep in a chair, leaning back against the wall. Vincent was tempted to kick out the legs but instead shook his shoulder.

"Oh, Mr. Bonanno. I am sorry; I should not have been asleep. Vinny is in there. Shall I get a nurse or the doctor?"

"Let's take a walk." Hank sat down in the chair vacated by the now completely awake Benny.

"Okay, take it from the top. What happened today?"

"We left your office and drove to the gym. As we came out the changing door, we were jumped. I was knocked down and tied up. Then they were beating on Vinny with baseball bats and a sock full of lead. He was fighting and knocked down two of them, but they got up one at a time. Vinny took the bat and I think broke one of the guy's arm while another definitely had a gash in his head. Then they ran out. Vinny crawled to where I was, untied me, and I drove to the emergency room. There was blood everywhere."

"Okay, Benny. Now tell me the truth. No one had been treated for a gash and nobody has had a broken arm fixed. Vinny's knuckles are not bruised and, hold out your arms, there are no rope burns on your wrists."

"Vinny, he said…."

"I know. He told you to stick to the story no matter who asked."

"Yes, Mr. Bonanno."

"But he is not capo, is he?"

"No, Mr. Bonanno. I didn't see anything. I was called to the phone as we came into the gym. Vinny thought it might be you. There was no one on the phone, but when I came to the office, there was a man I never saw before holding a very big gun. After about ten minutes, we went to the gym. He opened the door, and when we went in, Vinny was wrecked and crying and threatening, but mostly crying."

"Who else was there?"

"A girl and three men, the hard one and a couple of college kids."

"They did not try to disguise? Did you know any of them? See them before? What did he say?"

"No. They were regular people. Difficult to describe—no scars, not big; never saw them before."

"And what did they say?" Vincent was persistent.

"Not much, not very talkative. The guy with the big gun asked if they had their gear together. The two kids were in the ceiling taking something down."

"And?" Benny was shuffling and, clearly under penalty that Vincent could only guess, not to finish this tale. He lowered his head and mumbled, "I was to tell Vinny to stay away from Kate Blaine."

"Thank you, Benny. I am going to assume that you would rather not be around Vinny for a bit so I will have Tony P. relieve you and see you in my office at ten. Two things. You said there was a girl and the people know Kate Blaine. Could she have sent them?"

"Thank you, boss. The girl was an attendant, I think. She was in shorts and a tee shirt and was carrying boxing gloves. I don't think they knew Kate Blaine because the guy called her Katy."

"Okay. Go call Tony P. while I see Vinny."

Vincent walked straight past Hank and into a dimly lit room. The only bed in the room had Vinny with bandages covering his eyes and an elevated cast; he did look like a wreck.

"Vinny."

"Dad, is that you? Did you get them?'

"No, Vinny. I think they left town."

"A good job they did. I will be out of here tomorrow or the next day. Who do you think they were? Who sent them?"

"I have a strong suspicion, son, that you met a myth, a figment of imagination. I think that it would be a good idea for you to leave town, Atlantic City, I think. We do not want a repeat performance, do we?"

"I do not want to go away; I will be ready next time."

"And dead in thirty seconds. These are pros, like we are amateurs; this is a different league. I think that girl you were sweet on is still down the shore."

"Yes, okay. Benny and I can go and take a little sun and relaxation while I rehabilitate."

"Hank will go down with you for a couple of weeks. You are staying there!"

"But Hank is no fun. He reports everything back to you."

"Exactly!"

"But Dad! These guys weren't that scary!"

"Just your ignorance is scary. You think I am capo without knowing what happens? The women you beat up and pay off to not report you to the authorities?"

Vincent was thinking back to just before he left the office. A slight woman in motorcycle gear came into his office unannounced and gave him an envelope.

"Vinny, stay away from Kate Blaine, or I will personally kill you!" he told his son.

Vincent was whispering very close to Vinny's ear.

"I have a movie of everything that happened in that gym. The girl in the movie, she walked right though our security to deliver it."

Chapter Thirty-Six

For Dr. Richard Land, life was as complicated as he could have imagined. He thought about where the past few months, or was it weeks, had taken him—taken him and brought him back, more or less. He was the same, but different. Every time he thought that there were no more surprises, nothing new, that's when something happened. What if he just sat there? Would nothing new happen? Would be there be no surprises, shock, and upheavals?

He laughed aloud and then looked around the cafeteria to see who had noticed this erratic, irrational behavior. No one had, so the blush that had started slowly receded. Looking back...where should he start? Well, how about six months ago, sitting in that very seat? It was not really the same seat as he had probably sat in all the seats in the room. Now, that was already interesting observation. It was in the same room but not the same seat. He took out a pen and, turning over the paper—a tray serviette—he wrote his observation down. Then he made two columns: then and now.

The paper was covered with writing within ten minutes, and he had also eaten an indifferent, quite fatty, corned beef sandwich and finished his mug of coffee.

His review of the page showed that six months before, he had no idea of what he was going to do with his life.

He was surprised to see that staying in the service as a doctor had appealed to him as had applying to one of Boston's teaching hospitals. The fact that he had no attachments, Boston would be closer to his mother. It was the only item to make it on both sides of "Then and now"—closer to mother.

There was something missing from his "now" list. Was it accidental, or had it been subconsciously suppressed? Kate Blaine. Wasn't she part of his "now"? Was she? Had he been thinking of her when he applied to a New York hospital? No, he had not! Or had he? His life was certainly changed after he saw her at the funeral.

He turned the page ninety degrees and wrote down the middle: Kate Blaine, funeral. It was the focal point; that is when the "then" became "now."

"I understand that you have a girl in New York." Dr Martin Brandon could not keep the curiosity out of his voice or the smile from his face.

"What makes you think that?" Richard knew it was probably a losing battle, but he could perhaps get some new information.

"Well, your weekly visits. The fact that you have been scribbling—probably wedding invitations," he said and laughed.

"Hardly!" said Richard, holding up the paper for scrutiny but pulling it away before anything could be read.

"Kate Blaine!" said a triumphant Dr. Brandon. "Yes, she is the one Helen just took a message from. She asked me to pass it along if I saw you. Written all over your paper?"

"Thanks for the message, Martin."

"That's it! Just "thank you." No explanation after all the stories I have shared these past few years."

"Most of your stories were either sordid, untrue, or both."

Richard stood up and reflected that he had never shared any of the details of his weekends with Martin. Martin, however, had never "not" shared a story of any of his weekends away.

Well, too late to change now. Martin would have to use his not inconsiderable imagination, Richard thought.

As it happened, Kate was not available when he called and afternoon surgery could not wait until she was back from the market.

Richard lost a patient during the afternoon. The soldier had told stories of an orange defoliant, and, although his injuries were serious, they had seen worse in this hospital. Nonetheless, the shrapnel had nicked his lungs, and it just would not heal.

The loss of a patient was always hard. Added to the pain were the family notification and the paperwork. Richard added a memo to the major general requesting information on an orange chemical.

The stickers on the wall were mostly from Kate, though he picked up one from his mother and several from his dead patients' family, squad commander, and a minister. His mother, he was happy to know, would be out that evening; the other calls he sorted and walked to his desk.

He called Kate, or rather, the restaurant. It was noisy. "She says she will call you back immediately from her apartment," the voice from the other end said.

He hung up and waited, imagining her going through the door, to the elevator, unlocking her door, and walking through to her sitting area, throwing herself down and picking up the phone.

It rang.

"That was quick!"

"I ran. I promised to let you know what was happening. Vincent Bonanno came to dinner; he was very nice and seemed to know what had happened, told me not to worry. Then I heard that Vinny was in the hospital. Beaten up by four masked hit men! Then....." She paused for emphasis. "The rumor is that Vinny is leaving town in case they come back for him."

"That does not sound like the Vinny we know—to leave town." Richard was still concerned.

"No," said Kate, frowning. "But it is a start. I might know more tomorrow; Vincent Bonanno made a dinner reservation. Fifteen years, he never came near. Now, twice in a week. Is our food that much better?"

There was no question that Kate was feeling better. The old tone was back in her voice, and so was the slight tease in everything she said.

"The food is much better," agreed Richard.

"Bull. You only ate here twice, both lately, the last time on the house." She laughed. "How was your day?"

"Dreadful!" he said. "Lost a patient and hate to do that. I will spend the next hour or so explaining why to his family."

"Oh, I am sorry!" She sounded genuinely interested.

"Can I call tomorrow, after speaking with Vincent, if he has anything to say?"

"Yes, I would like that. Good night."

"Good night"

He hung up and realized that he was already looking forward to speaking with her again. Slowly, he picked up the other messages and started dialing.

Chapter Thirty-Seven

The next evening, Kate had dinner with Sam and ordered the dinner special. She was strangely excited and could not put a finger on the reason. Was it, she wondered, that Vincent Bonanno had made a reservation for that evening? Was it that she would then have a reason to call the cool, handsome Dr. Land? Or that it was clear that Vinny Bonanno had left town?

Sam sat watching her face. How many times had he done that? Of course, when she was a baby, and then as Alice took care of Kate and then he was watching as Kate and Jimmy grew, played, argued, and fought and their friendship grew in spite of their age difference.

He did not ask; she did not offer any explanation.

The meal was delivered. Sam had his usual meal.

"What is this?"

"The special, Miss Kate," said a bewildered new waitress.

Kate picked up the menu and quoted, "An eight-ounce serving of pork shoulder stuffed with Mediterranean cheeses and herbs with vegetables and long-grained rice.'"

"That's right, miss!"

"If you think that is what you have brought to me, then we have two problems. Take this back to the kitchen and weigh the serving of pork."

Sam raised his eyebrows as the plate was taken away.

"Well, you are in good form tonight."

"Yes, actually," said Kate, smiling. "I am in very good form. That serving was twelve ounces. At eight ounces, we have forty meals. At twelve ounces, only twenty-six. Since this is an extremely profitable main course, we could lose up to one hundred dollars in profits."

Sam was about to challenge her but realized that in her present state of total awareness, she could be right, and it was also a lesson for the kitchen and wait staff.

There was a flurry of activity around the kitchen door. A red-faced chef came scurrying across the room.

"Miss Kate, I knew the dish was for you, and I got carried away. There was a little more than eight ounces."

"Three things, Albert: one, it should not matter who is being served; two, the staff should be busy with customers and not gossiping about who they are serving; and three, when is twelve ounces a little more than eight?"

"It was not twelve ounces!"

Kate looked up at the abject face looking down, looking for redemption, and looking for absolution.

After twenty seconds, he whispered, "It was almost twelve ounces."

"Albert, tighten up your staff and watch the controls. That means quantity and quality."

He turned and left.

"Which part of the Mediterranean does stuffed pork?" Sam asked.

"I found the recipe from Suli; it was for goat. I could not find goat, so I cooked it myself with pork and with chicken. It works with both, so the next time chicken is cheap, it will be featured. Here, taste it, it is very good."

"That was good," said Sam "Maybe crab apple jelly, or a date jelly for a relish? Now, I had better go to work before someone yells at me."

Kate gave him a hug of affection as he headed towards the piano.

Kate headed back to her thoughts and mechanically declined dessert and had a cup of coffee. She signed the slip, noted that Sam had left enough of a tip for both of their meals, and headed toward the front to check on reservations, allocations, and telephone inquiries.

Vincent Bonanno entered at exactly eight thirty. The room went a little quieter, but he did not seem to care as Kate showed him and Benny to the table she had recently vacated.

Benny ordered the pork special while Vincent had a fresh fish salad. He was watching the room, watching Kate.

Sam was watching and playing in an unusual desultory manner.

Kate, aware of being watched, came over.

"Everything to your satisfaction, Mr. Bonanno?"

"Yes! Have you a minute?"

"Of course, I was curious...." Kate was interrupted.

"Benny, go eat at the bar. Stay alert."

Benny rose and reached for his plate.

"Wait, sit!" Kate spoke quietly and looked for a waitress. "Penny, take this gentleman and his plate to the seat at the end of the bar."

Penny looked with undisguised interest at Benny who was doing the same, though with possibly different intentions, or maybe not.

Kate and Vincent also watched them walk away with similar conclusions but with entirely different thoughts.

"Thank you!" said Vincent. "He could do with some good manners taught to him."

"I was thinking of her training in good public relations. Given the nature of the man and his business, it is not a relationship I would encourage." She suddenly stopped and flushed scarlet. "I am sorry. I didn't mean that, and, given the question I was going to ask, is totally inexcusable."

"You are excused; you are forgiven. You are so much like your mother. It is like having the clock turned back twenty years."

"You knew her? What was she like? Nobody ever talked about her. Rick would just say 'Wonderful, just like you, darling,' and then go into one of his silent moods and drink bourbon. Sam says that it was such a long time ago that he forgets; he never forgets anything!"

Vincent listened and ignored his food. He was studying the beautiful young woman in front of him who was desperately seeking answers.

"She was wonderful. Margaret had the same looks but with an Irish brogue and a naiveté that was charming and disarming."

"You were in love with her?" It was a question and a statement.

"Everybody loved her."

"Except Aunt Bridget!"

"Except Aunt Bridget," he chuckled. "She loved her, too, but the Catholic religion is very hard if you are a believer. Aunt Bridget believes that every papal edict is directly from God and, as such, must be obeyed. She believes that Margaret's death and her descending into Hell was a sign. She missed the fact that Margaret went to Heaven, and we who loved her were sentenced to live here in Hell!"

He stopped and was silent. Vincent Bonanno had said more than he had intended, revealed more than he had ever shown of his inner emotions. But then, she was easy to talk to, in the same way Margaret had been. Bringing himself back to the young lady in front of him, he asked, "You have a question?"

"Yes, though, I am unsure how to ask."

"You want to know if Vinny, my son, has gone away for how long and should you be concerned, particularly since one of the rumors circulating is that you were responsible for hiring armies of thugs to attack him?"

"Yes! How did you know?"

"I did not get to be where I am by not knowing, by not being ahead of my enemies and my friends."

"Well?"

"Vinny has gone away. He will not come back as long as I am alive in spite of his mother's entreaties, and if I tried to quell the rumors, it would merely give credence to them.

"They will go away. You, Sam, and the restaurant will continue to be protected. Not protected, but have nothing to fear from me or my...my business associates."

"Thank you. Is it true that Vinny was badly beaten by four masked thugs?"

"Well, I wasn't there."

"Of course! But you know everything!" she mocked him with a sideways glance.

"Yes, well, he was badly beaten."

There was the truth. Why was he worrying about the truth? It had never occurred to him to worry about it in the past. The truth was what he decided. If it was not, he made it true. Veracity was never necessary. *Why now?* he thought.

Again, he saw the image of a young Margaret.

"Mr. Bonanno, since you knew my mother, what happened and why won't anyone talk to me about her?"

"It was a long time ago. I don't remember. We have to go!"

He stood, and Benny, who had kept an eye open for that signal, stood, swept the room with his eyes, and led the way to the door.

Kate caught up with Vincent. "I am sorry. Please come again. I promise to try not to upset you," she blurted.

Vincent moved to the door without speaking. He turned as he reached the door handle. "I should like to come again. I need to come again. I miss…the evenings I spent here with Rick."

"Then why…?" Kate started to ask, but he was gone.

Sam watched carefully, looking for body language that might tell him what was being discussed and how the tenure of the conversation might give him insight into the progress. Why did he think of it as progress? The more honest reflection would be of his own concern for Kate. She had been in a strange mood earlier. Was it contemplative of the dinner guest, or was there some other catalyst, a man in her life perhaps?

As Kate came toward the piano from the door, a smartly-dressed older woman came forward from the dining room. The woman was headed straight for Sam. Kate recognized that the woman was on a mission, so she veered away and slowed in order to hear the exchange.

"You call that music? Sounds like a dirge to me!"

"Excuse me?" Sam turned and gave a quizzical look at Alvin who was leaning on his double bass.

"Lady got a point, Sam."

"What?" asked Sam who had been looking for support from Alvin and instead got Benedict Arnold.

The woman was then up close.

"You been playing some awful tunes and with no enthusiasm. My friend and I came up from Harlem, for her birthday, and I told her, Pauline, some fine food some fine music here, and what do we get?"

Alvin saved Sam from answering, "That handsome woman is called Porcine?"

"No, fool. Porcine is pork, and she may be a little wide with plenty of cover, but her name is Pauline."

Alvin, who was close to three hundred pounds, said, "She looks a real handsome lady to me."

"I am sorry, miss; got things on my mind."

"Then straighten out, boy, and it is Mrs. Mr. went to his reward so you can call me Bess."

"Bess, Alvin and me are going to play in your honor. And we would be pleased to buy you dessert and after dinners drinks if you join us at the piano when you have finished eating."

"Well, Sam.... May I call you Sam?" After a nod, she continued, "That is real gentlemanly, and I will ask my friend. Maybe we will and maybe we won't."

As she walked away, Alvin said, "Yes, they will!"

Sam was then smiling; the mood had been broken. He realized that music was like the view into a soul. He reached for the microphone and announced, "For my new friends, we are going to play a medley from Porky and Bess."

He looked over to Bess and her friend who was saying, "He means Porgy and Bess. That's for us!"

"Yes," spluttered Bess who was doubled over with laughter.

"What's so funny?"

"We are going out drinking with those two gentlemen. The one on the bass, he fancies you."

"Isn't he a little heavy?" asked Pauline.

Bess laughed aloud. "Handsome though!"

After a spirited medley, Sam wound up singing, "Bess, you are my woman now."

Kate appeared and said, "Well, you have certainly perked up."

"Uh uh!" Sam agreed.

"Well, I was just going up; getting quieter down here. I thought I would call and leave a message for Richard. Vincent says that Vinny had gone away and will not be back, that we have nothing to fear. You believe that?"

"Uh uh. I do."

"Sam, Vincent knew my mother, right? But he does not want to talk about her death."

"Uh uh!"

"Well, you are not very talkative tonight either. I will see you tomorrow."

Sam watched her with a frown then turned with a smile as Bess and Pauline came and sat at a table in the bar close to the piano. He signaled to the waitress and ordered fried banana dessert with a flaming rum sauce, fresh whipped cream on top, together with a tiramisu.

"Just a thank you for putting me straight tonight," Sam said and nodded.

Nodding to Alvin, they played, "Somewhere Over the Rainbow," and as the left hand continued to play, Sam's right hand was playing, "Happy Birthday to you."

Kate was surprised and pleased when Richard answered the phone.

"You sound tired," Kate remarked.

"I am. I hope you had a better day than I did."

"Yes, I think so." She told him details about her evening.

It was strange. She did not normally like talking on the phone, and several times, she had to ask if he was still there.

He was, and he could feel the weight of his day lifting as he listened to her. It was unlikely that he could have remembered a fraction of what was said. He chuckled at the verbal induced vision of Sam being confronted.

When she had finished, Richard said, "Sam believes that Vincent is on the level. Then I feel satisfied. I know there is a strange code within the gangster fraternity."

"He does not act or look likes a gangster."

"What does a gangster look like?"

"Vinny!"

"His son."

"Okay, Richard. I get the point!"

They closed with "Good night" and would have been surprised to see that each of them sat looking at the phone dead in its cradle.

Richard was surprised at the phone ringing. He picked it up hopefully then visibly sagged.

"Yes, Congressman. I was the doctor for the young man who died, and yes, there is a connection to an American defoliant."

It was not going away.

Chapter Thirty-Eight

For Richard, the remaining time in a military hospital passed as before—with a frantic continuing stream of problems and faces both of staff and patients. One of the highlights of his remaining time, however, was the return of Doctor Emily Price. There was a gathering which he attended and was introduced to her fiancé, someone she had met in medical school and with whom she had been corresponding from Vietnam.

Richard was genuinely happy for her.

The war was going away. There was no end, but the feeling was that the political will had gone. The people's revolution against war had made it impossible for any politician to be reelected who was willing to support the benefit of fighting a war lost. It was difficult to explain soldiers dying for a people from a country halfway around the world, locked in a civil war. The military establishment in the USA had fostered the idea of invincibility out of entering two world wars already in progress and the combatants and methods of fighting already defined. Then the US was drawn into the battlefields of Korea in an era which saw communism as the source of all evil. The infiltration of the US, as defined by Senator McCarthy, was proof of their goals—the total and complete control of the USA.

The force of arms, and the vast amount of money into Vietnam had to prevail. This ignored the facts that British forces had backed a royalty movement for years before deciding it was cheaper to house the royal family in the UK, turning the royalist forces over to the French, and back the Nationalist movement. The French had soldiered on until, convinced that the US would push the communists back into China, they had themselves returned to France.

Richard was leaving the military world, but would still be part of it, as he would be treating many of these young men and women for years at the Veterans Hospital. He had also returned to the routine of spending whatever days off he had on covering the absence of other doctors. There was no particular reason, he told himself, to visit New York or his mother in Connecticut. On those quiet days, he did write to his mother and to Sam and Kate. He always wrote to the two of them and frequently thanked them for his growing bank account. Kate wrote back and always signed "Kate and Sam." He also continued a lively correspondence with the congressman from Massachusetts.

The day finally arrived, and he packed his bags and, with many promises to see them soon, said his final good-byes to people who had been his life and who he would never see again.

During the ride to New York, he felt exhilarated. There had been challenges everyday, but there was a new one, the same one—treating patients, but different.

There was a surprise at the station as Kate met him from the train. He was speechless.

She was attractively dressed and had carefully chosen greens and yellows, giving an air of joy. The slacks she was wearing were perfectly tailored and the roll top sweater with no sleeves was conservative but, in some way, provocative.

"Welcome home, soldier," she said doing a poor imitation of either Marilyn Monroe or Mae West. Her ponytail swung as she spoke.

"How did you know? How did you find me?"

She changed into an Irish brogue. "And what other train might you be on? And you, a tall handsome fella!"

He was forced to laugh. "That is the worst Irish accent I ever heard. Thank you for coming. Where did you park?" He had both hands full with obviously heavy bags in spite of having mailed most of his books ahead.

She took one of the bags after a brief hassle.

"I am right outside."

"You will have been towed."

"Only if they have arrested Uncle George."

"Chief George is minding your car?"

"Yes, he stopped me, asked me where I was going so fast. When I told him, he insisted on making sure that we had no trouble with the law."

Outside the station was the red Camaro with the chief of police cruiser behind, blue lights flashing with a grinning deputy at the wheel. Uncle George got out of the back seat to greet them, and a patrol officer wandered over to complete the foursome on the sidewalk.

"Sergeant Williams has never been to Rick's, Kate. Can you imagine that?" Chief Surphlis winked at her.

"Sergeant, you must come. Bring your wife and ask for me." Kate produced a business card from her purse and wrote "comp" on the back.

"Why, thank you, Miss. Anytime, I can do you or Chief Surphlis a favor, please let me know."

He ambled off, satisfied.

"Uncle George, it would be cheaper to pay for parking."

"But not nearly as much fun. He will send more business. Besides, there was nowhere to park within two blocks. Now, get along and try not to speed."

"I can see that I am going to have a vastly different life from now on."

They were in the car, driving back to Brooklyn, and either Kate was driving more conservatively, or Richard was already accustomed to the speed of the New York streets. He suspected both were true.

"Vincent Bonnano is coming to the restaurant tonight. You should meet him. I need support!"

"Kate Blaine needs support from a spalpeen such as myself?" Richard said, feigning a brogue.

"Your Irish accent is worse than mine." She laughed. "No. Yes, I should like the support. I want to press on what happened to my mother. He knows and won't tell me."

"Perhaps he has good reason, and you should not press."

"Not you, too! Fine, you won't support me. I can do it myself." There was the fiery nature and maybe the reason that she met him at the train station.

"Kate, I will have dinner with you and Vincent and support and protect you."

"Thank you!"

They both lapsed into silence for the rest of the way.

"Thanks for the ride!" Richard said when they reached the café.

"Abdullah can get the bags. See you at six. Sam is looking forward to seeing you again. Can't think why!" Kate's mischievous grin was back.

Richard went upstairs, still a little hesitant. It was hard to think of that place as home. He wandered around, opening doors and drawers before unpacking. *Food*, he thought, *I am going to need food.* Opening the refrigerator, he stepped back. "Wow!" escaped his lips as he surveyed the full shelves, including six bottles of Bass ale. *I can get used to this*, he thought as he reached for a bottle and found a glass and, in the third drawer he opened, a bottle opener.

Taking the glass through to the bedroom, he sorted and put away his clothes, making a mental note that his underwear and several shirts needed replacing, as well as his socks and shoes.

Richard sat and put on the television—news of the war, protests, Congressional "flip flops." He kept changing the channel until he found sports. He considered getting another beer but decided that he needed a clear head.

With the realization that he was not on call, that there was no duty until the next day, and nobody would die that day on his watch, he fell asleep.

"Are you going to dinner like that?"

Startled, he opened his eyes. "Don't you ever knock?"

"Why?" Kate asked.

"Maybe I was in here with someone."

"No, I would have seen it on the monitor."

"What monitor? Do you have a closed-circuit television?"

"Of course, for security. That's why I never...." She blushed.

"Never mind! It is five thirty, and I came to check that you had everything. I did knock; no answer so I opened the door which was unlocked."

"Right! Sorry! I will be ready and downstairs by six."

"Okay. Look, I am sorry. It is strange. Rick was always here...then gone. Now you. It is like having a long lost brother move in. Know what I mean?"

"Yes," he lied. First of all, he did not feel like a brother but he did realize that he should examine that conversation from Kate's side. She had certainly laid out her position, and a lot of it made sense. He, Richard, was the interloper, the one for whom they had made accommodations.

"By the way," he said "You look terrific tonight. Are those the pearls in your mother's portrait?"

"Yes," she said, touching them. "I never wear them, but tonight, they seem to go with the dress. I shall have to remember how observant you are," she said, smiling as she left the room.

It was a little after six when Richard entered the restaurant. Sam rose to meet him and neither he nor Kate mentioned his tardiness.

They sat talking of the restaurant and business: the profits had not been affected, nor had the gross receipts year to year. The consensus was that people would eat out where there was good food and convivial ambiance. New carpeting was discussed and whether a complete makeover of the bar was in order. Richard sat through most of the conversation but was interested to note that when Kate referred to some chairs being dated and chipped, he could see the restaurant business in an entirely different light. It was decided that Kate would draw some plans, talk to designers, and prepare a budget. The restaurant would be closed either on the week of July 4 or the first week of August, depending upon the timing and the extent of any proposed makeover.

Sam said, "I need to know as soon as possible so I can decide on the date for closing. I am thinking of taking a vacation."

"A vacation? You have never taken a vacation. In fact, you have to be pushed to take a day away. How long do you plan to go for?" Kate was wide-eyed.

"A week, I thought. Up to the Catskills, catch a couple of shows."

"A week...the Catskills. You are not going alone, are you?"

Kate was on the scent; a bloodhound could not have set off at the pace that her mind was working.

"Bess!" She was triumphant, exultant. "Have you told Jimmy?"

"I haven't told you! You are guessing."

"Right though, aren't I?"

"Maybe you are, maybe you ain't." Sam rose to leave, then said, "Not mad, are you?"

"Nothing to be mad about; makes you happy, makes me happy!"

The show of affection embarrassed Sam; he left.

"Gotta go play the piano," he said.

They watched him leave.

"How did you know?" Richard asked.

"Oh, we seem to be hearing a lot of the Show Boat tunes."

As if cued, Sam started playing and singing, "Fish gotta swim, birds gotta fly...."

Richard and Kate turned towards each other and laughed a warm-shared experience. It was like nothing they had known before, like knowing and understanding without speaking.

They continued their earlier conversation, with Kate expanding on some up-to-date ideas. She was thinking less Morocco and more Italy. How would the patrons accept the changes? She saw it not as a gamble, but the opportunity to put her own signature on the décor.

"How about a change of name?" asked Richard.

He almost wished that he had kept his mouth shut when he saw her face. There was a flash of emotion, anger, terror, and sadness.

Richard quickly recovered. "I was just thinking of dropping the 'Café.' Everyone calls it 'Rick's' so make that the name on the door and on the menu."

Kate was immediately sorry for showing anger. "Good idea, but I think that a change of name must pass the 'Sam' test."

"Maybe he will want to call it 'Bess.'" Richard was joking and clearly broke the ice.

"Speaking of which, here comes Bess headed to the piano, and Mr. Bonnano being shown this way while Benny heads to the end of the bar."

"Good evening, Kate," Vincent Bonnano greeted.

"Good evening, Mr. Bonnano. May I introduce Dr. Richard Land?"

"Pleased to meet you, Doctor. I was told that you shared remarkably similar physical attributes to my late friend. If you have the same temperament, perhaps we, too, can be friends."

"No disrespect, Sir, but I think that our two chosen professions would preclude friendship."

"Ha, ha. I think Rick said exactly the same thing."

"I thought that Richard...Dr. Land, since he is a partner, might join us for dinner," Kate interjected.

"Good idea. I will enjoy the conversation with a man who is clearly not looking for favors from me, nor is subservient or in awe. And I always enjoy my conversations with you, dear Kate."

Kate ordered meals, and they were delivered while Vincent and Richard talked of his military service. Vincent was remarkably well-informed and had some insights into the workings of the politicians in New York and in Washington. It did not take a lot of imagination to determine how he came by that knowledge.

They all declined dessert. As coffee was served and the waitress left, Kate started on her agenda.

"Mr. Bonnano, if you and Rick were such good friends, why did you stop coming to the restaurant?"

"It was a long time ago; I forget."

"It was to do with my mother, wasn't it?"

"Margaret...." Vincent was lost in reminiscence. The memories were as vivid as if they had been lived just yesterday.

"Yes. It was an accident," he finally whispered.

"You killed my mother?"

"No, there was an accident. Rick asked me not to come here again as it was a reminder of the good times we had. Margaret and Rick and me, we spent many evenings such as this talking."

"Then talk. Tell me what happened. Why will no one tell me why there is no record of her death, just a tombstone?"

"Okay, I suppose it will be better to come from me and be factual rather than from rumor and urban myth." Vincent paused; pain and anguish was etched onto his face. He looked his age. Whereas he had always had the physique, the looks, and step of a man ten years younger, his face suddenly showed lines that had not been there, and his body slumped.

"Margaret came to me one afternoon. You, Kate, were sleeping; Sam's wife, Alice, was babysitting. We argued. Twenty years ago, everything was so black and white. I was used to getting my way, but then, so was your mother. Boy, she had a temper.

"Anyway, she ran out of the room. I told her I would drive her back. She told me to 'Sod off!' I went out and jumped into my new English sports car, a Jaguar, and set off. As I rounded the corner, she stepped off the sidewalk. I couldn't stop. She...she died in my arms. The police came; George Surphlis was the detective. I confessed, but the confession disappeared. The coroner said accidental, and I have lived twenty years with.... The car was driven into the river, and I have never driven a car since that day."

"Thank you. I did ask for the truth," Kate said, her faced streaked with tears but her voice was steady. "But now, you have to go!"

Vincent started to say something but changed his mind and stood up. She stood and watched Vincent walk through the restaurant and through the door. Walking slowly, she moved toward the corridor to the elevator. As soon as she was out of sight, a great sigh of anguish came from the bottom of her torso and her heels beat a staccato as she escaped the curiosity of those who had seen her leave.

Richard had listened in silence. Then he went to Sam and gave him a quick version. Sam was shaking his head.

"Some things need never be said!" Sam was shaking his head.

"Come on, Bess. Let's go get drunk."

"But you don't drink!" Bess protested.

"Not hardly ever."

Richard went upstairs; he could clearly hear crying through the door. After hesitating several times, he knocked on the door with. no response, so he walked away. When he reached his own door, he thought he would see if the door to Kate's apartment was open.

To his surprise, it was. Then he remembered the cameras. *Oh well, too late to worry about that now*, he thought.

She was a mess. Shoes had been flung across the room, her dress was on the floor, and she was in a fetal position in the middle of the room.

Richard turned and thought to leave, but instead went to her. She looked up then sobbed in his arms. Eventually, she went to sleep, and he carried her into her bedroom and placed her on the bed. He stood, looking at her for several minutes. She looked so small—a little girl again. She whimpered in her sleep.

Richard left, locking the door and temptation behind.

Chapter Thirty-Nine

The night seemed long; the bed which had been so welcoming was suddenly lumpy. He was hot. He was cold. Twice he went to the refrigerator for a drink. The second time, he stood with the door open, trying to remember why he was there and how he had got there.

The fact was that his mind was full of images—images of Margaret being struck down, of the daughter's reaction after almost twenty years. The question was whether the knowledge of what happened was worse than not knowing. Well, she had known but just not how; there were newspaper articles, there were rumors, and speculation.

Now she knows, or did she? There seemed to be more missing pieces, more questions. Would they be asked, and if so, would they be answered?

The image most confusing was that of holding the hysterical young woman then carrying her into her bed. Of course, he had seen hundreds of people in bed; after all, he was a doctor. But this time was different. This young woman was what? He broke it down clinically. She weighed about one hundred and twenty pounds, five-foot-seven, and of average body mass. Compared with Trish, she was shorter, heavier, and better endowed, probably not as beautiful but beautiful in a different way. Kate had a bone structure like his mothers, was it the reason for the attraction?

My mother! He jumped and realized that he must have fallen asleep. What was it? He looked at his watch—after six; there was no point in trying to sleep. *Mother, yes, I must see her today as I shall be starting work tomorrow*, he thought.

Richard showered, shaved, made himself instant coffee, and resolved to stop by the kitchen where there seemed to be fresh coffee twenty-four hours a day.

Dressing casually, he looked at his pitiful old wardrobe and mentally reminded himself to shop. *Perhaps today with my mother.... Perhaps not!*

On the way out, he stopped at Kate's door and knocked; no answer. He tried the handle—locked. Putting his ear to the door, he could hear music—slow, sentimental jazz. *Well, she is alive and apparently looking for privacy*, Richard thought.

Ilsa was excited that her son was planning a whole day with her. She took two steaks from the freezer and prepared potatoes and vegetables before taking a shower and dressing. When Richard came out of the station, she had been waiting half an hour.

"What would you like to do?" she asked.

"Can we have a talk, Mother? There are questions which have been building for the last six months."

"Of course, dear. Though I am not sure I know any answers." A frown passed over her face. "Let's go down to the shore park, and then walk."

During the ride, they chitchatted about the weather, the war, old friends, and old neighbors. It was warm, and the lots were busy, mostly young families with children heading for the beach. Ilsa took Richard's arm as they walked, wondering, not for the first time, how he had grown so tall.

"Mother, why did we receive a piece of the estate of Richard Blaine?"

"We discussed this before. I do not know. He was a friend a long time ago, and we owed our lives to him."

"That might be a reason for your leaving a bequest to him, not he to me! You never did say what was in the box you received."

"No. I didn't."

There was a considerable silence. Ilsa was remembering the contents of the box—jewelry, a gold coin and a letter. She knew the words of the letter by heart and wondered again why she had not destroyed it.

Richard strolled along and thought that his mother was probably never going to answer the questions.

They walked with a strained silence. Whoever spoke first would lose.

"Would you like an ice cream?" Richard spoke first but it was a truce, a white flag, something they could both shelter under.

"Yes, please, dear. Do they have the swirled chocolate and vanilla?"

"If not, we can walk on to the next ice cream vendor."

"We shouldn't really; it will spoil our meal. I took out a steak for you."

"I never knew a time when I couldn't eat steak after ice cream."

They sat on a bench with ice cream cones, watching the children on the beach running with no effort in perpetual motion. It was very calming—the warm sun, the happy laughter of children, and the sheen from the water—and although they were too far to hear as they watched the waves hit the beach, they could imagine the slap on the sand and the swish as it receded.

"Mother." Ilsa stiffened in anticipation of their return to the previous question. "Do you think Trish is beautiful and smart?"

"Trish Wellington?" she asked, buying time while she thought of the implications of the question and of the answer she would give.

"Of course. Trish Wellington," Richard confirmed.

"She is beautiful and smart. Did I tell you I saw her last weekend in town? She has a new Cadillac convertible, red. She was with three friends. I think they were heading to the club to play tennis by the look of it."

"Those Cadillac's have a V-8 engine and cost a lot to run," Richard remarked.

"Well, I suppose I should have said that it is probably her mother's car. Have you heard from her?"

"Not since I told her I was going to work at the Veterans Hospital. I don't think that went down very well with the country club crowd. What about Kate—Kate Blaine? Do you think she is attractive?"

Ilsa needed more time to think of the response, and, as Richard had taken away the obvious delaying question, she asked, "Why did you describe her as attractive and Trish beautiful?"

Then it was Richards's time to buy time.

"I don't know. Certainly, men turn to watch Kate go by, but it is because she is exuding confidence; she's comfortable with herself. Or that is the image that she portrays. She smiles at people—everybody. Trish, well, she is supremely confident but she smiles to herself; she knows people are looking and she looks good."

"Well, Kate Blaine is attractive. She is.... Let's go make lunch. I still have potatoes to bake, and you need to light the coals on the grill if we are to eat today." Ilsa stood and immediately started walking away.

Richard ran to catch up with her.

"What were you going to say, Mother?"

"Nothing, just an observation. I can see Kate in the Veterans Hospital or the Country Club and be equally comfortable."

Richard realized that there was considerably more to be said but he would not hear it that day, if ever.

"I need some new clothes. I think I have stayed the same weight, but the places for the pounds have changed."

They were both on safe ground.

"Well, don't buy any fad clothes. A nice suit, grey slacks, and blazer are always going to be in fashion."

Richard smiled. He recognized the conservative nature but also the frugality. Mixing and matching slacks with blazers was easier if they were the same color. He smiled at his mother and then to himself; he had been looking at what men were wearing on the train. The Nehru jacket was never going to be suitable for the hospital, and a blue blazer would give him status without pretension. He might even be able to buy them ready-made; that would really please his mother.

The rest of the afternoon passed quickly and quietly. Richard cooked the steaks while enjoying a beer. Ilsa stayed in the kitchen, fussing over the rest of the meal. They enjoyed a bottle of wine and talked of Ilsa taking a day in the city when he knew his schedule and they could meet and go to a show.

Richard walked into the restaurant which was operating with quiet efficiency. Sam was just announcing that he would be taking a break. Richard sat at the bar, refusing a drink, and waited until Sam finished the song. Sam joined him.

"Seen Kate?" Richard asked.

"Not since last night. Must have been some bad surprise!"

"But you were not surprised, were you, Sam?"

"No, Sir. I am never surprised by anything. Not anything in this crazy world. I have seen it all."

"That's not what I meant."

They were interrupted by the entrance of Kate, smiling and carrying a bunch of papers.

Sam and Richard looked at each other to gauge each other's reaction before turning again to face the oncoming apparition. Their joint reaction must have been similar to Alice when first spying the white rabbit.

With a flick of the head to indicate that they should follow down the rabbit hole, she changed direction to the empty table at the back of the restaurant.

"I have been thinking. I have been working all day. We can close for just one week to repaint and recarpet. The furniture and traffic flow can be changed, and we can make the other side of the bar bigger, just by knocking down this wall."

She had pulled out a sketch showing a modest expansion.

"What is behind there now?" Sam queried.

"Storage. We can put some of it in the basement—the old records—and some in the attic."

"Purpose?"

"Sam, you always want the purpose first. Well, more seating. This will mean going to the city council and a different traffic flow. I like the idea of a name change to Rick's." She pulled out another page with a drawing of a new sign. "I also want to call the other side, 'Rick's Café,' with a simple menu and decorated with a flavor of the left bank or Venice." She was pulling pages like a magician pulling handkerchiefs.

"What do you think?" she finally asked.

"Menu?" asked Sam

"Menus!" said the magician. "Keeping some of the southern Mediterranean specialties, I should like to make the new items those from the South of France, Italy, and Greece." She smiled slyly. "I think we can then sell more wine."

"I think it looks terrific, Kate. Leave them handy, and I will look in more detail tomorrow. I have to return to the piano."

Richard had nodded his assent and was looking through the papers, feigning a knowledge that he did not possess.

"Kate. Last night...."

"I know. Thank you!"

"But...."

"I asked Vincent for the truth; I got it. Was it what I wanted to hear? I plotted and planned to know what really happened. I was successful! Vincent was between a rock and a hard place. If he did not tell me, and I found out anyway, he would look like he was guilty of who knows what. If he tells me, he risks the reaction he evidently received from Rick." Kate was looking down at the table as she spoke.

"I was distraught. I cannot even remember getting into bed, but I slept. When I woke, I thought it through. I did a lot of thinking. What is past is gone, so I started planning for changes to the restaurant. I realized we can take some of the old restaurant and ideas and add some of the things that the new generation wants today. Did you stop by last night? I vaguely remember."

"Yes, you were distraught. I did not stay long."

Richard returned his attention to the drawings.

What had his mother said? What did she mean? It was clear that there were many sides to Kate Blaine.

Did she really not remember his being in her room?

There was no way of knowing from her demeanor. She did seem to be alert and excited while he was tired and...excited?

Excited? Why? New job, new life, and new relationship?

What was the relationship?

Still many more questions—just too many questions. He must go back to his mother for answers, but how? When?

Chapter Forty

In Washington, a man was looking at the envelope in his hand. There was no need to open it since he had memorized every word. In fact, some of the words, he would remember forever. He sat, thinking of all the phrases he had remembered going back fifty years: "It was the best of times; it was the worst of times," then the book ended. "It's a far, far better thing that I do than I have ever done. It is a far, far better rest than I go to than I have ever known." Dickens had it right; *A Tale of Two Cities* could be his life story. "Oftentimes, the instruments of darkness lead you on to win you with honest trifles to betray you in deepest consequence." Yes, yes, his life was Macbeth's.

There was certain irony that these two masterpieces should reflect his life as he saw it. There was an ambition to do great things then ultimately accept that we return to dust sometimes having fulfilled those ambitions, sometimes not—but still dust.

"The moving finger writes, and having writ, moves on."

The envelope gave no clue to the contents, and, in many ways, the contents, he mused, could be a summation of his life, of others' lives. Macbeth's was here, and Sydney Carton, but, maybe it was Omar Khayam who had the final word in it: "Not all your piety or wit can call it back to cancel half a line nor all your tears erase a word of it."

Though there was no need, he opened the envelope addressed simply "Smith" and read.

"There is no question that you recall walking into Rick's Café, November 5, 1956. You were the last person on earth I expected to see and the last person on earth I wanted to see...."

"Hi, Rick. Remember me?" Smith asked.

"Smith, and the last I time I saw you was flat on your back in a launch off the coast of Italy. I would offer you a seat and a drink, but I can see that you are leaving."

"Rick, that was over ten years ago, and I admit that the punch I took was deserved. But let's try and look at the good times as well as those we should forget. I allowed you to smuggle enough money out of Casablanca to set yourself up for life."

"You allowed? Remember: that was all American currency."

"Not all, but why quibble?"

"I am sure that you did not crawl all the way from wherever you reside and take the time to find me to pass the time of day. Are you looking for a share, a shakedown? Is that it? Forget it as I have a free pass if you recall."

"Yes, Rick, I recall. And I recall having a chat with Mr. Disalvo about that very, very safe passage."

"Touché."

Rick really had no complaints about how he had been treated. The order to abandon his group in Italy had clearly come from above. But this was not an intrusion he was looking for. Everything was already going well: his investments were growing, the restaurant was profitable, he had plenty of friends, and there was Kate. Kate, then eight, was everything to him. Already in school, he walked her there and home everyday. When he worked or was busy on weekends, she was always around Sam and Alice, learning music, reading aloud, or helping in the kitchen.

"Rick, I need Mr. Jones for a job only he can do."

"No. Never. Now leave."

"Rick, I have an agent in a communist country severely injured or sick, and he is paranoid; will not trust anyone. He disappeared on one of my agents and shot at a Brit who we sent in."

"So what? I don't care. I don't care if he shoots up all of MI5 and the C.I.A. I don't care if he shoots himself. I have not been behind enemy lines since you left me there, and I have no intention of doing so again. I am almost fifty and am very comfortable. Thank you very much."

"Don't you want to know who the agent is?"

"NO!"

"Victor Lazlo."

"Victor Lazlo is still playing boy scout, and I am supposed to care. But I don't care. Send someone else."

"I can't. You, he would recognize and trust."

"Why? Why would he trust me?"

"You saved his life once, I remember." Smith knew the story, as well as anyone. Ilsa Lund, now Land, was his secretary.

Ilsa was not aware of Victor's problem. In fact, she was unaware that Victor was an agent. It was difficult to maintain, but the file was in his locked drawer. Ilsa believed that Victor was working for an International Relief Organization.

"Yes, I did and had to sell a profitable business and leave town in a hurry. That is what I remember. Goodbye and don't bother letting me know how it ends."

"Okay, Rick. Just so you will recognize him, I brought a photograph taken last Christmas. My direct line is on the back, in case you change your mind. I am sending Doc in next Tuesday; it would be good if he had company."

"Goodbye and tell Doc 'Good luck!'"

Rick watched him leave a grey figure indistinguishable from a thousand other grey people. He idly blew a smoke ring up to the ceiling.

"Who was that man?" young Kate asked.

Rick looked down and smiled at Kate. He always found himself smiling when she was in the room.

"Nobody!"

"Of course, he was somebody, silly Daddy. Who are these people?" She was holding the photograph Smith had left.

"I don't know." Rick did not look.

"It says Vi...," she was sounding out a new word, "...ctor, Ilsa, and Richard. Look, it's your name."

"Let me see." Rick found his hand trembling as he reached for the photograph.

Kate moved around to share the view. "Look, the boy has a ball. Did he get the ball for his birthday? I got a doll for my birthday."

Rick did not hear; he was staring at the image of a man who had aged considerably since they had last met in 1942, a woman who had not changed, and a teenage boy almost as tall as his mother.

"Damn!"

"Daddy, Auntie Alice says we should not use swear words, and that is a swear word."

"I am sorry, sweetheart. I will try not to let it happen again."

It was two days later that Rick dialed the number on the back of the picture. A voice answered with the name of an import company. Rick asked for Mr. Smith and was asked his name and number. "Jones, and he knows the number," he said, hanging up the phone.

The phone rang in less than fifteen minutes.

"You are a bastard, Smith."

"Why, Rick? And I thought you didn't care," Smith replied.

"Straight in and out."

"That's the way. Doc leaves tomorrow for Rome carrying the details, contacts, visas, medical kit, and cover documents. You will leave tonight, fly to London—British Air—one day, then rendezvous in Rome. Doc expects you on Al Italia the day after tomorrow. Wednesday at ten. He has your cover papers, too."

"You were expecting that I would go."

"Of course, Rick! There is a British Air rep expecting you." Rick hung up the phone and sat looking at it. Although there was little time to pack, he decided he would make time for a few calls, a few arrangements, and some backup; he would not be left behind again.

At Heathrow Airport, as he exited carrying a garment bag and a briefcase, he saw a sign held by a young man. It simply said, "Jones." He walked over to him and asked, "You a New Yorker?"

"Yankees fan all my life!" the man replied.

They drove into the city in companiable quiet. It had been a long time since Rick had been in England—before the war—and things had changed. Although there was the occasional sign of the bombing, everywhere he looked, there was construction, a positive attitude overcoming the demoralizing realities that war had brought to the people's doorsteps every night.

They stopped at a side street not far from the river—a small private hotel. Given a key, he went to his room and, though early in the morning, lay down and slept for two hours.

Rick woke, washed up, and changed into a worsted suit, clean white shirt, and tie. He looked at the phone in the room and decided that any calls would be from a telephone booth. He had picked up a London Street map at the airport and walked past the desk with his briefcase. Once he reached the main road, he easily mingled with the other businessmen in grey suits and white shirts, many of them starched. He lost the man assigned to follow him without difficulty. There was an instinct, and he thought that he might have lost a little over time, so he was pleased to have the exercise. He walked into a larger hotel, found a bank of telephones, and pulled out a handful of coins.

The caller reached by Rick arranged a meeting at the Savoy. In plain sight, they mingled and briefly discussed old times then, in depth, the reason for the requested rendezvous. The briefcase was exchanged for the twin, which had been brought by the titled man opposite, enjoying afternoon tea.

Rick reappeared at a corner close to where his watcher had "lost" him, to the man's considerable relief. Once back at the hotel, the new contents of the briefcase were committed to memory then destroyed. The money given would purchase and transport his shopping list.

In Rome, there was another sign, "Richard Alexander"—his new passport name.

"You from New York?"

"DiMaggio, only one worth spit! Good to see you again, Mr. Jones," the man replied.

"Rico, what are you doing here?"

"Making a few liras, catching up with old friends. I am a war hero, have a taxi company, so!" He shrugged and said, "And lots of children." He laughed.

He had told his whole life story in one sentence. Rico was much heavier than when he had been found in the German prison camp.

When they were on the road, he said, "Remember, Maria asked me to go find her father and brother? Well, they turned up okay, and she thanked me. She thanked me so hard that we had to get married." He laughed again, although it was clear that he had been telling the story for years.

They arrived at a comfortable villa sat on the side of a hill which was hidden from the road. Since the driveway was uphill, when they were inside the house, the view from the patio was of vineyard and a clear view of the road from the village. It was obvious that they had been seen as there was a raucous welcome by five children and two dogs.

Rico introduced them all including the dogs. The names all sounded the same since they all included Mary or Maria, and Rick was instantly confused.

"No matter. Come and meet Maria," Rico said.

Maria was pleasantly plump and might have been pregnant. There was an affectionate greeting, and it appeared that it was not a surprise; he was expected. The reason, as they went out onto the patio, was in the recumbent form of Doc.

Doc greeted the new arrivals with a raised glass.

"Try the red, a Montepulciano, from over there," he said, pointing vaguely out over the valley.

The children, though curious, had been taught not to question the strangers their father brought home. The conversation, by silent mutual agreement, was generalities, the weather, local sports, and local politics. It turned out that Rico was also the mayor, owned several pieces of property, and frequently bartered with the owners of local vineyards which accounted for an exceptional cellar. They sat and ate olives and excellent cheeses with freshly-baked bread.

When the children had retired, Maria served pasta with homemade sauces, local sausages, ham, and chicken, then cannoli. Rick had to have the recipe but knew he could not have it mailed and he could not write it down. He resorted to asking what the secret ingredient might be. Maria rewarded him with the whole recipe which included a cup of local brandy. Rico immediately jumped up from the table and came back with a brandy bottle, three glasses, and three cigars. It was the signal that the three men were going outside to conduct business.

"We will leave before dawn, then no one will see us go. The children and Maria will know nothing; they would never talk.... But.... We will go north about 400 miles then wait until night. Night crossings are easier," briefed Rico.

After the wine and food, it was easy to fall asleep. Too soon, it was time to leave. The three men were in the front of a truck loaded with wine. The manifest said that it was bound for Budapest via Zagreb. Rico had provided local peasant hats and coats. Having settled into the front, Doc promptly fell asleep. Rick and Rico shared the driving in two-hour shifts. When they stopped for nature breaks, they also snacked on the packed food baskets so it was not necessary to use any facilities where they might be noticed. The border crossing north of Trieste was relatively easy with Rick hidden under the front seat in a specially-constructed hideaway.

The colonel in charge recognized the truck and, at first, was disappointed in the contents until Rico assured him that the "Frascati" case with a red "B" actually was a case of brandy for which the village was famous. Doc transferred the case into the colonel's car, already half-full of confiscated or donated goods, and their visas were stamped.

There was a moment of anxiety when another guard with a dog stopped at the cab door. Rico looked in and saw Rick's American cigarettes on the seat.

"Here, my friend, for you. I picked them up off the table of an American tourist in Venice."

The grateful guard pulled away the dog. When they were through and back on the road, they did another check of each other for silly mistakes like carrying American cigarettes. Rick thought for the thousandth time, *Why am I here? I am too old for this stuff.*

In Zagreb, Rico picked up someone to go back over the border with Doc's stamped visa. The wine was dropped at a shipping agent. Rick and Doc made their way to the railway station separately but were watching each other to make sure they were not being followed. It seemed that getting in was easy; it was not helpful to think about the obstacles when getting out.

They had been together for almost three days, and Rick realized that he and Doc had never spoken of the mission. When Rico had been there, it had not been appropriate, but then they were traveling separately, minding each other's backs. Did Doc have a plan? Was there a plan?

The train rattled along, across a countryside which was exciting but bleak—exciting that it was new, different; bleak in the color of the people wearing drab grey clothes, living drab grey lives.

Rick dozed, shaken by the curves in the tracks, and awakened by the arrival of stations which seemed to pull up alongside full of drab grey commuters and the bright splash of clean uniformed police and railway officials. There was also the clean grey trench coats which screamed, "Look at me! I am an undercover policeman." Those men were dangerous since their ego and pretension could only be sustained by a justification of their undercover status.

The tough part was going to be the border crossing. The access to Budapest was bound to be monitored closely. There was a rumored mass exodus of Hungarians from Budapest, and a couple of Russian-speaking Hungarians returning home from Yugoslavia where they had been for several weeks were not deemed important. At the border, a train in the opposite direction emphasized the exit problem as it was being closely searched by dogs. The occupants of the train meanwhile were standing on the cold platform with their luggage to be reexamined before being allowed to continue. A young man came out of the train with his arms in the air. As he stepped off the train, he was shot in the back of the head.

"A fascist instigator wanted in Budapest trying to escape justice," a man in grey trench coat announced, already composing his report of a struggle and running fight in his mind.

The dark grey line shrugged, accepted the lie they had seen, and shuffled forward. There were few people leaving the inbound train and heading out of the railroad stations past the Russian troops. Tanks had been strategically placed overlooking the squares in Budapest, and, although the fighting had been effectively over for a week, there was a palpable tension in the air. Walkers studiously ignored the tanks while walking around them.

Rick needed to make a telephone call. How much to tell Doc was the problem. Since they were watching each other as they headed toward the dock area, there was no way to be surreptitious. The next telephone box he saw on the street, he went in and pulled a torn piece of paper from the depths of his pocket where it had become covered in lint and dust. He looked at the writing and dialed.

The ringing telephone was answered, but no one spoke.

"Smith, Hotel Central."

"Twenty minutes." A man's voice and disconnected. When he came out, Doc was standing as if waiting to use the phone.

"What was that then?" he whispered.

"A shipment! We have to wait for it." Rick replied.

Doc grunted, not happy with the unexpected delay. Being a professional though, he entered the box dialed and watched Rick. Acting as if the number was busy, he retrieved his coins and stood out of the way of the foot traffic. He watched Rick enter the Hotel Central lobby then appeared at a window with a view of the street.

Twenty minutes later, Rick emerged as Doc terminated his one-way conversation to a dead phone.

"Shipment intact?" Doc asked as he walked a step behind. He had not seen anyone, as, in fact, the British agent had shown exceptional skill in finding Rick by coming in the rear entrance from a bar.

"Yes," whispered Rick. "A Luger, untraceable, taken from a Nazi collaborator."

When they reached the dock areas, they were both feeling more comfortable. The eclectic dress allowed then to move without being noticeable, and any secret policeman was not going to linger in that area of the city.

Doc led them unerringly to the square designated for their contact. There were four bars in the square, all busy, though it was early evening, and all looking seedy. Having identified the rendezvous, Doc went in; Rick stayed outside to see if there were any interested parties. Seeing none, he went in the back door.

"Beer," Doc ordered. "What time do you close?"

"Smart guy. We never close." The bartender was suspicious as the "Hungarian" had a Russian accent. Hungarians were being educated in Russia, but normally, they spoke Russian with the Hungarian accent.

"Johan working tonight?"

"No Johan here, just me." The bartender was huge but with biceps from moving kegs of beer, pulling beers, and breaking up brawls. However, his biceps gave him away as the tattoo wavered and flexed as he reached down.

Rick, behind the bartender, whispered, "Leave it; answer the man."

The bartender glanced around, saw the Luger, and put down the ax handle.

"Guy in the kitchen might be called Johan; just started working here,".

"He is taking the night off," said Doc, heading in the direction indicated.

Rick replaced Doc in front of the bartender. He tasted the beer and pushed it across the bar. "Pour this away and refill it from the pumps that the regulars drink."

The man scowled, confused, but did as he was asked. Rick drank it and left through the front door. He met Doc and a thin young man who was obviously a student. "Thank God you arrived. I worked there four days, waiting; it was four days too long. It is getting dark. The Russians have a curfew but it is still easier to move around; there are fewer people and more shadows."

"How is the man?" Rick asked.

"Broken leg. We got it set last night, finally. A dentist in the group got the stuff and did it."

"Far from here?"

"No. We should get some food to take. I took some leftovers last night. Awful!"

Rick gave him some local currency. "Are dollars useful?"

"Black market, yes!"

Rick tore a seam in the bottom of his trouser pocket and reached in, bringing out several used notes of different currencies. Sorting out the dollars, he handed them to the astounded Johan.

After buying bread, meat, and cheese at different shops as they were closing, they walked, Johan and Rick ahead and on the other side of the street from Doc.

They walked steadily and quietly, staying in the shadows, aware of every sound. A sudden sound, and the next step was slower. Turning down an alley and then into the back of what would have been described as brownstone in England and three-storey row of houses in America, they turned into a gate which creaked loudly from lack of grease. They froze then went through to a door which led down into the basement.

"The man you are looking for is on the third floor," Johan announced.

Doc was plainly anxious; Rick shrugged.

"Let's see what we see!" he said as Johan watched the back street. The lock was picked, and they went quietly upward, carrying the food.

At the third floor, there were two doors. One unit faced the back, the other the main street. John nodded, and Rick knocked.

"Victory, we bring food and a ride home."

"Who is there?"

"A friend!"

"The last friend brought the Russians."

"Well, you have to be more careful. We met in Casablanca."

There was a long pause. "Rick?"

"In the flesh. Ask me a question."

"Why did you give me the passes in Casablanca? I always wondered."

"Ask your wife!"

"Only you could know that answer."

The bolts opened, and there stood Victor Lazlo with a gun. Rick, Doc, and Johan filed in with the food into an empty apartment. There were two chairs, a table, and a mattress which seemed to be everything. A large sink was on one wall, and a small cupboard which should have been a pantry was bare.

Victor Lazlo limped to one of the chairs by the table and clumsily sat down. Victor Lazlo, but not Victor Lazlo. The man was gaunt, pale, and old. The pains of his broken leg was etched into his face, and his prematurely grey hair had not been cut in a while, or washed. His eyes went to the food.

"I don't remember calling for takeout."

They talked as they ate. Doc cut his hair while he continued to eat. Then Doc put Victor on the table, gave him a shot of morphine, and examined his leg and other bruises.

Apparently, the Russian troops had broken up a meeting of students and middle class Hungarians. Victor had a list of their names and also a personal account detailing the duplicity of certain Hungarians and a list of contacts in other countries.

"Well, Doc, what do you think?" Victor asked.

"I think it will be a week before you can move freely on the leg. By then, slowly with a pronounced limp. We should try to get transport out of the city, or wait."

"Wait? Smith said this was in and out," Rick remarked.

"Sorry, Rick," said Victor. "I will manage."

"No, we came to bring you home," Rick said.

"Not everything works out, you know. Sometimes, fate just takes a hand."

"Defeatist Victor. Not like you!" said Rick

"The Russians are different from the Nazis. Everybody is for everybody. We are all equal. Therefore, you do not notify the authorities about fugitives for gain or revenge but for a common good—the right to continue the good life as it has been given to you and nurtured by Father Stalin."

"Bravo!" mocked Doc. "Now can we talk about getting out of here."

The noise of several vehicles was heard, and Johan, by the window, announced a Russian truck with troops piling out at the front of the building.

"Well, it seems fate and I have a different journey," said Victor. "Did you bring them?"

"NO!" There was a universal reply, but they each looked at each other and then quietly considered their own fate.

"Quickly gather up your junk." Victor was the first to react. He moved a chair to the middle of the room and pointed to a trapdoor into the eaves. "They want me. They will burn the building if needed." Johan jumped up and pushed the door aside and pulled himself through. Next, Doc threw up the medicine kit, the left over wrapping from the food, and the overnight bag he shared with Rick.

Victor gave Rick the list of names from his shoe and a gun. Boots started crashing up the stairs, caving in the doors of the hapless tenants on the first and second floor who were herded petrified and shivering into the street.

Rick pulled himself up and closed the door.

"Rick!" Victor called.

"Yes?" Rick moved the trapdoor slightly and looked down at a face which showed no fear—a man who knew what was likely in store.

"Take care of the boy!"

Victor moved the chair back to the table and sat.

Rick moved toward a light—a small window in the end of the attic. They could see the truck below—a Russian-made vehicle with a noose hanging from the rear as a mobile scaffold for summary executions.

It was not to be Victor's fate, however, as he was bundled inside. Johan touched Rick's arm and pointed down the street. There was a light, very small on the second floor; someone was looking through the drapes.

The three of them went through the skylight, expecting that the Russians had left a guard to arrest anyone showing up at the apartment. Going through a skylight further down the row, they eventually emerged in an alley.

"What was the light?" asked Doc.

"The dentist's office," said Johan.

The three men made their way very carefully to where Johan lived. Johan was nervous the whole time and was clearly uncomfortable with them using his room.

Johan made a cup of tea while they speculated on the troops arriving at Victor's bolt-hole so soon after they had walked in. Doc and Johan were doing the talking; they had not seen the list handed to Rick, nor had they heard the final exchange.

"Take care of the boy." Rick analyzed each work and each omission. *No, please, no name, no instruction, not a question*, he thought. It was, however, in context, a deathbed wish. But why him? Why not a relative, a friend, Smith (well, maybe not Smith)?

"...don't you think, Rick?"

He was brought back into the present by a question from Doc.

"Don't I think what?"

"That the dentist must have turned in Victor," said Doc who was a little exasperated that Rick had not been listening. He assumed, therefore, that Rick did not care.

"Johan wants to question him then have a trial but the members are so scattered that it may take a while to get organized."

"We shall organize and take care of it tomorrow," said Rick. There was a side of Rick that Doc had seen in Italy; it was decisive, and he saw it then.

"Our job is to get out safely," Doc said as he was aware of Rick's initial reluctance to be behind the lines again, and for him, the mission was a failure and therefore over.

"Our job was to bring Victor out! If you are out, then I can take care of it myself tomorrow. Let's try to sleep."

Doc had heard the tone of voice before and knew there would be no arguing. Even though they espoused democracy, when a hard decision was necessary, sometimes, it was easier for men to follow the visionary. Rick had a hard time sleeping, thinking of Victor and what was surely happening, thinking of how they had been so close to being there, thinking if the dentist was the traitor, or someone closer, or just bad luck.

"Are we together, or am I to talk to the dentist alone?" he asked.

"Rick, I want to help, but we must be out of the city today. Victor might have talked; people are bound to notice somebody new in the neighborhood, and we can't stay here long."

Johan was looking very pale. "I am going to help. I must: did you see the way he looked at me? He thought I brought the Russians."

"You did not bring the Russians, or we would have been caught, too. We should plan on leaving the city tonight with the evening commute," Rick replied.

Just before noon, Johan entered the dentist's office. There was a nurse receptionist at the desk. The dentist did his dental work on the ground floor which was up three steps from the street.

Since he lived above his office, the dentist was always available. Business had been very slow since the Russian tanks had entered the city; people were just venturing into the streets, some picking up necessities then scurrying back to the safe confines of their homes.

"Dentist in?" Johan asked.

"Yes, can I help?"

"No. I have a question for him. My uncle is having problems after having his teeth out."

"Ah!" She picked up an intercom. "Doctor, a young man has a question about his uncle."

"Yes," she said, then to Johan, "go in."

When he had closed the door, the doctor who was watching warily, said, "Highly irregular."

"Well, there is a small crisis. A meeting tonight at 'The Sun.'" The bar was across the street from where he had worked and was usually full of very hard men, mostly sailors and stevedores.

"Very well. What crisis?" the dentist asked.

"They took the American last night, the one with the broken leg, and almost got the other American."

"There was another American?"

"Yes, so we have to help him. We shall discuss how at the meeting tonight."

"I will be there."

Johan turned to leave. "Doctor, this American has a toothache." He chuckled then said, "He also has dollars. Is it possible that you could see him? I could have him here in half an hour."

"Well...my nurse...."

"Send her out for an hour. It would be better that she is not here."

"Quite right. Bring the American; I shall be waiting."

Johan, followed by the doctor, went to the door.

"Nurse, it is very quiet. I have some things to do upstairs. Why don't you take off for an hour? Be back by 1:30."

"Thank you, Doctor."

The nurse was surprised but happy to be able to go out during the day since the curfew had severely restricted her shopping.

The doctor returned to his office after making sure that the door was locked. He picked up the phone and opened his drawer for a number which he dialed.

"Moscow," he said then, "Cavity," and then hung up the phone.

He sat, drumming his fingers on the desk, it being the only sound in the room.

The phone rang.

"Cavity, this must be important. You have taken me away from talking to our American connection."

"Yes, important. There is a meeting tonight seven at 'The Sun' to discuss the other American."

"Which other American?"

"The one you just missed last night and who will be here in my office in twenty minutes' time."

"I will be there as soon as I can. Keep him there."

The dentist sat back with a smile. Forcing his goatee beard to rise slowly, the smile spread.

The goatee slowly subsided as he realized that he was not alone.

"So, you are a friend of the Americans?" Rick reached over, took a cigarette from the desk, and lighted it. His Russian was with a distinctive American accent.

"You are early. How did you get in?" the dentist asked.

"I was real early. Actually, I have been next door in your laboratory cum supply room since before the boy came with that totally fabricated story."

"Now what?"

"Now, the Hungarians will know of your duplicity and will never forget, so goodbye dental practice, and the Russians will show up in ten minutes and may want to discuss why you let me go and why you wasted their time. They may even put you in the same cell as the American."

The doctor was white but had reached into the drawer. Before he could withdraw the gun there, Rick had taken out the Luger and shot him between the eyes.

As the Czech-made revolver dropped on the desk, Rick exchanged it for the Luger.

"Thanks. That made it easier," he said.

Rick was outside on the sidewalk when the Russian car came into view at an urgent speed. It stopped fifty yards short of its destination and three men moved into position on the street within sight of the building. Rick moved toward the leader who was looking at the building that housed the dentist's office. Rick shuffled and dragged a leg, watching timing.

The row houses were three steps up to the front door but underneath, six steps down, were basements. From one of the basements came a red-eyed drunk, staggering and shouting Hungarian abuse at an unseen female companion. He staggered and healed over toward the Russian who instinctively took his hand from his pocket to fend him off and accidentally bumped an old man shuffling along.

The Russian hurled abuse at the two fools who were in the way of his ticket back to Moscow. Two Americans arrested, and he was sure of promotion.

Down the street, Johan called the local police and reported a gunshot.

By the time the police arrived, Rick, Johan, and Doc were on their way to the Central Station, together with the contents of the Russian's pockets. A Russian spy catcher was trying to explain why he had no gun or identification in the presence of a corpse. The only gun was a murder weapon with his prints—the gun that he had been holding. The dead man—a dentist, a respected citizen—was clearly unarmed. Investigations later showed that the basement flat from which the drunk had emerged was empty.

Rick stopped to make a phone call. At the station, he bought a very large, grey hold-all then followed a traveler with a blue hold-all into a men's room. There was a brief moment when they met and the blue hold-all went into the gray one. The man came out without his hat and coat and disappeared. Rick went into a stall, transferred the contents, and left the blue hold-all.

If anyone had followed the agent, then they would have seen many similar hold-alls and bags and would have missed the transfer. With so many people traveling, it was impossible to say who met and where they were going.

Johan persuaded two different young women to buy him a round-trip ticket to Bratislava. The tickets, he gave to Rick and Doc.

"The girls were asked why they were going to the border. They both said to see their mothers. Since they went to different sellers at different times and because they were pretty and their student passes were valid and checked out, there was no problem. The security is clearly more efficient with the Russians watching."

A man emerged from the men's room with a blue hold-all. He gave an imperceptible signal that he had the contents that had been left behind—an envelope addressed to "Smith."

The exit from Hungary was less eventful than imagination would have allowed. In truth, the planning and execution were the reasons, along with good fortune and a population not sure what it wanted but sure that it was not Russian.

They left the train two stops from Bratislava and proceeded to Sopron on separate barges along the canal. The two agents were already watching each other on reflex, and the slightest interest shown in either one occasioned a change in direction or in appearance.

At Sopron, it was three days before they found someone who could discretely take them over the Alps and point them towards Graz.

The bag they had received in Budapest contained the necessary winter gear as it was early December.

The good luck was that, although there was snow, there were no visitors. It made them conspicuous, but to a rural population, they were welcome guests with welcome money.

"Rick, we were to meet Rico in Zagreb. Our plans were to reverse our course. Why are we in Austria? Why are we splitting up? Where did the clothes and plans and money come from?"

"Doc, didn't your mother teach you to never trust anyone? Here, you are trusting me; you were ready to trust Smith."

"But we work for him."

"I worked for him in Italy."

"I was there, Rick, and you did a great job getting us out."

"Another failed mission! Failed because there were different priorities. What if some politician is asked to give us up so that the military establishment can sell more armaments to the eastern bloc? How long will they take to debate the fate of two over-the-hill operators?"

"You are a terrible cynic."

"No, I decided to make my own way out this time."

"So, my questions, you are not going to answer?"

"The money is mine. We are outside the iron curtain. That is all for you to know."

Rick came back through London and, having called into the restaurant, did a good deal of Christmas shopping for Kate and Jimmy, as well as for Sam and Alice.

Smith found him in London, said that he had debriefed Doc, received the document from the diplomatic bag, and looked forward to chatting when he got back.

Yes, I bet you do, thought Rick.

Chapter Forty-One

Smith knew most of the information in the letter. He knew that Rick had made a deal with the British through Duke who had been in Italy, a second son who had inherited the title after his older brother died in a car accident on his way home from a hunt ball.

The fact that Duke was in a similar position to Smith was known to him, but he had been unaware that Rick knew that piece of information; he must be losing his touch.

British Intelligence had provided a gun, clothing, and passes in exchange for a first look at any intelligence. They confided to Rick and Smith that they believed that the Americans were selective in what they shared.

Rico had been stopped at the border and the truck taken apart. They found the caviar and vodka in the secret compartment but were apparently looking for something or someone else. How did Rick know? How did the Russians know? There was clearly a mole. Where? In the American embassy? In his own office? In the State Department? He had searched and never found out; he or she must still be out there. Rico had eventually been released and had promptly resigned.

The last part of the letter had taken Smith by surprise.

Victor Lazlo was tortured in Budapest. His Russian capturer was discredited for a botched raid on a pub following the disclosure of his identity in a murder investigation. He was recalled to Moscow but not to the promotion he had envisaged. Victor was ignored for months. The problem became what to do with him. No useful information had been gathered. The Americans had not acknowledged he was missing. Ilsa had been told that he was missing, presumed dead, but there was no funeral.

Victor Lazlo was transferred to Lubyanka in Moscow. Unable to release him without saying why he was there, he was sent to a gulag. He had a terrible limp. A number of requests for information had been made; they had come back with information on people with differently spelled names, re-questing further clarification of the requests, with "no such person exists," or ignored totally.

A British agent was told by someone who knew an engineer who had returned to Leningrad that they met an American who spoke seven or eight languages fluently. The man had a leg shorter than the other and survived by beating the engineers and other imported experts at chess and playing for cigarettes which he traded for food. The man could not recall the exact name but when asked who he was and why he was there, he had said, "A man made famous by the Nazis," then laughed.

"Victor Lazlo lives! This, my dear Mr. Smith, is the legacy I leave to you" ended Rick's letter.

There were two phrases which were to be with him everyday for the rest of his life.

"Take care of the boy!"—it explained everything.

"Victor Lazlo lives!"—it explained the rest.

Mr. Smith—Charles Munroe—was doomed to a living hell; a burden carried for all the years by Rick Blaine was passed to him.

Smith knew what he must do. This day had been coming for some time.

Reaching for a lighter in his desk drawer, he watched the flame for a while before putting it to the envelope. When everything was burned, he took the files from his drawer. There were two—Victory and Jones—and put them through the shredder.

Opening a safe, he took out several passports and put back all but one. Inside another envelope was a driver's license, expired, and a code list—his getaway kit! Reaching back into the safe, he removed all the cash and bearer bonds that he had accumulated.

Sitting down again, he reached for paper.

Mr. President,

The day has arrived. I am leaving after serving this office for thirty years. There will be people looking for me. That will be futile as I have no intention of setting up a shooting gallery for those who would prefer permanent silence.

I have seen a great deal, and I have missed a great deal.

Good luck to you.

Charles Munroe

He left the envelope with the letter on his desk addressed simply to the president.

He went home, showered, changed, and left with only an overnight pack. The plan was to backtrack, giving indications that he was headed for the Bahamas. The real destination was through Oregon into Canada, back to the

East Coast then down to Maine where he owned a house in his mother's name on an island in Penobscot Bay.

Who would be looking for a lobsterman?

Chapter Forty-Two

"Rick's" was resplendent. There were balloons and streamers around the bar and fresh flowers on every table.

There was to be a grand reopening with the new décor on view for the first time.

All day, the staff had been chasing around with deliveries of fresh seafood, fruit, and vegetables, as well as flowers while setting out linens and cutlery. Kate had insisted that every piece of glassware, every plate, and platter, all the cutlery, and china be washed. There were groans but not loud enough for Kate to hear; she was already off on another crusade anyway. Passing a piece of fish in the kitchen, she called over the chef and insisted that the smell was not fresh—not fresh enough. He had to return it and replace it before five.

Over two hundred invitations had been sent for the celebration. It had been worded as a thank you to loyal customers, and, although it was mid-week, the honor of having been recognized, together with the curiosity of who else had made the list, guaranteed that there would be few no shows. Richard had cynically asked if they were all coming for the free food and drink. Sam had smiled; Kate had scowled at him.

At four, a silence descended on the restaurant with everyone sent home to change. The kitchen was still active but now, with the bustle of people coming in and out having stopped, there was a quieter, more measured professional atmosphere.

Richard had been at work in the hospital throughout the tumult. He had tried to make his day easy, but, as always, he was running late. The surgeons and a couple of long-term nurses had been invited so they were also trying to leave early. The group practice already had stability, and, after Richard had insisted that some of the discharged medics be given intern positions and help with medical school costs, there had been an increase in black assistants.

The surgeons felt much more comfortable in their "on call" beds. False alarms were greatly reduced, and even minor emergencies were being stabilized until the morning.

When Richard pulled up to the restaurant in Kate's red Camaro that he had borrowed, he was instantly aware of an increase in the valets. Three young men descended on the driver's door. Abdullah stepped forward and pointed imperiously to the garage down the street where it was kept.

There was a police car parked at the end of the street already and an armed officer at the door. It was an acknowledgement that important civic people would be there that night.

Abdullah nodded to Richard as he held the door open. The quick flick of his eyes showed his disgust at having a pistol-carrying babysitter. Richard smiled sympathetically to show that, indeed, he had confidence that Abdullah was more then a match for any problem.

Inside, Kate rushed over.

"Where have you been?" But before he could speak, she continued, "Never mind. Go and change. Your mother arrived around three, is talking to Bess over there. People have started arriving. Food will start going out in fifteen to twenty minutes."

Before she could open her mouth, again Richard interrupted.

"Hello, Kate. Sorry to be late. It looks absolutely sensational, and you look radiant, stunning."

Those were the right words obviously.

"You don't think that the flower was a bit much?" she asked.

There was a white rose attached to the red dress she was wearing.

"No. I think it perfectly sets off your mother's pearls."

She beamed radiantly. They were standing, beaming at each other as the door behind them opened and more guests arrived. The moment passed.

Richard, after greeting his mother, Bess, and her friend, Pauline, went upstairs to shower, shave, and dress. He came out to find a white rose boutonniere on the table. Smiling, he carried it down; his mother would help put it onto his suit lapel.

When Richard entered the restaurant, the sound level had increased; there must have been a hundred and fifty people with drinks and food. Some were sitting at tables in the dining room, some in the bar area, and more standing in groups.

Over by the piano, Sam and Al were playing show tunes while another familiar face, Jimmy, was playing drums.

Richard, white rose attached, found Kate and whispered a thank you in her ear.

"I met some of the people you work with. They are over there," Kate said, pointing.

Richard went over to one of the tables in the restaurant area and was introduced to the wives. There was Elizabeth "Call me Beth," Levy who walked around the table and gave him a hug. Richard was slightly embarrassed as she announced loudly, "Thanks for joining the group and sending my husband home to bed where he belongs."

Mrs. Cooper agreed, looking at her husband who turned bright red.

Dr. Davies had his eyes closed with a drink in his hand. He was leaning back.

Mrs. Davies looked, then, standing, said, "Sounds like a good idea; I am going to take him home before he is comatose."

The group was laughing as she shook her husband and headed for the door. It was clear that they were all feeling much less strain with the spreading of the workload.

Dr. Cooper said, "Richard, that use of medics for non-life threatening...."

"Not for tonight, dear," his wife said.

Rick excused himself and went to join his mother. Sam was also sitting there, and when he followed their eyes, he saw that Jimmy was playing the piano and encouraging a small black woman to sing. When she did, it was hesitantly. Jimmy moved the microphone in front of him and joined in a duet while his eyes never left the ebony face of the beautiful young woman.

Sam was enthralled. He was seeing a rerun of his own, suddenly recognizing that his son was grown up and would be starting a new life soon. Glancing to his side, Bess sat comfortable and happy for Sam

There was a small commotion, and Vincent Bonnano entered with his wife. She looked like there were other places she would rather be.

Mad Jack Disalvo had arrived with a large entourage some time earlier. Vincent's eyes scanned the room, saw Jack, and nodded. It seemed that it was neutral ground.

Kate moved over to welcome the new arrivals as she had all night. On the way, she grabbed Richard's arm as he was trying to get a drink. Together, they stood with Victor and his wife.

"Good evening, Mrs. Bonnano, Mr. Bonnano," Kate said.

"Good evening, Kate, Dr Land. I don't think you met my wife, Doctor?"

"No. Good evening, Mrs. Bonnano," Richard said.

"Good evening, Doctor. Are you and Kate...?" She left the question in the air.

The other three people in the conversation were left with their own various interpretations of the balance of the question.

Lovers, friends business partners....

"Yes," said Richard realizing it did nothing to answer the question—a question that had been rude to ask.

Vincent Bonnano smiled.

"Vinny always asks about you, Kate. He is seeing Theresa a lot, but I am sure he will stop in when he is back in the city."

"Vinny is going to Vegas," Vincent looked meaningfully at Kate, "with or without Theresa."

"When was that decided?" his wife cried.

"Just now," said Vincent.

"That's so unfair; it's so far!" She turned her mousy face to Kate. "Shall I give him a message from you, dear?"

"Yes. Tell him to drop dead!" she said and turned.

"Nice to have met you," mumbled Richard as he followed Kate.

"Vincent!" she shrieked, but Vincent was sampling a date filled with goat cheese from a generous sampler platter Penny had given to Benny.

"Well, it looks as though you might have grandchildren before I do," Ilsa said as she was watching Sam watching Jimmy. "Trish Wellington and Wade are getting married at Christmas. I wish...."

"He is a good-looking boy, and I have seen all the young ladies give him a second and third look. He will be fine. Even Miss Kate gives him a look."

"Sam?" She paused; she had to ask the question carefully as she knew Sam would not say a word if he had promised not to.

"Yes, Miss Ilsa?"

"Sam, I just saw Vincent Bonnano. Margaret was killed...accident, right? But why? What was she doing over by the docks?'

"Long time ago, Miss Ilsa. Long time."

"But you know?"

"Yes'm, I know."

She thought for a moment that he would not speak of it and knew she could never ask again.

"Long time...Miss Kate just a tot then. Vincent had not come by for a couple of weeks, and Margaret went to find out why."

"He was that close a friend?"

Sam continued as though Ilsa had not spoken.

"After the funeral—no wake, no food—Rick, he was sitting over there watching Kate play when Vincent came in. 'I have to explain,' he says. Rick says nothing, face as black as thunder.

'Margaret came over to ask that I marry her, and I told her I was to marry Maria Marciano. She was furious. I told her it was necessary, that, otherwise, the family—the family business—would fall apart, that Mad Jack was Maria's godfather that he insisted, Margaret pleaded we could go far away. She doesn't understand, Rick; there is nowhere far enough. When I told her the wedding is in two weeks, she asked what was the rush is she pregnant? I nodded, and she started throwing things. She was yelling again and again, "And you fucked her! What about our daughter?" She ran out slamming every door. I ran after her, jumped in the car. She was running. Then she turned and ran right at the car. I couldn't stop.... I couldn't stop!'

Rick sat looking at Kate all the time Vincent was talking. He looked up at Vincent and said, 'Get out! If I ever see you again, I will kill you.'

Sad day, Miss Ilsa. Them all being such good friends."

"So...I thought.... Why is Rick's name on the birth certificate?"

"Well, Miss Margaret being Catholic, when the hospital asked the name of the father, she said Rick, because if it were known that it was Vincent, it would be dangerous. Rick, he didn't know till after she died. Then he didn't change it. Loved that little girl. Boy, how he loved that girl."

The crowd had thinned considerably. Jimmy, at the piano, was enjoying a mutual admiration society.

Kate and Richard were sitting, looking like Cheshire cats sipping imported brandy. They were looking deep into each other's eyes when Richard's clouded.

"One minute. I have to speak to my mother."

"Good idea. I think I have the same question."

"Mother, Kate and I have developed a strong friendship."

"Yes, dear. I am very glad," his mother said.

"But, Mother, is there any reason that it should not go further?"

"What do you mean, dear?"

"Is there any biological reason for us not to…?"

He stopped. She was his mother. Kate put her hand in his.

"Oh, no, dear, none at all." Ilsa was trying to hold her face from splitting.

Kate squeezed his hand; Richard squeezed it back.

"Okay. Then good night. Good night, Sam."

Richard and Kate turned hand in hand, and as they walked out of sight, they could hear Ilsa laughing and then Sam started laughing, sounding like the baying of a basset hound.

"Older folks are strange," said Richard.

They walked on through the restaurant unaware that they were still holding hands. A look on each of their faces was of a restful smile. *Contentment must be like this, a realization that at this moment, in this space, everything is perfect.*

There were things to say though neither spoke, and questions, though neither could voice them. There were plans for the next day, next week, and next year, but they were irrelevant at that moment, in that space. So they walked in silence toward the elevator.

A pan dropped in the kitchen and broke into the mood.

"A penny for your thoughts," Kate said.

Richard thought quickly and said, "I was thinking that we might take a trip."

"I wasn't thinking that either!" Kate retorted. She smiled at a secret thought then teased "Where to?"

"Well, I thought it might be nice for you to get some new recipes in Italy"

"Maybe we should go visit Suli, see Casablanca."